Corporal Hitler's Pistol

Also by Tom Keneally

Corporal
Hitler's
Pistol

TOM KENEALLY

VINTAGE BOOKS
Australia

VINTAGE

UK | USA | Canada | Ireland | Australia
India | New Zealand | South Africa | China

Vintage is part of the Penguin Random House group of companies
whose addresses can be found at global.penguinrandomhouse.com

Penguin
Random House
Australia

First published by Vintage in 2021

Cover photography: Smith Street, Kempsey, NSW,
NRS-12932-1-[X2450]-10-102, courtesy NSW State Archives and Records
Cover design by James Rendall © Penguin Random House Australia Pty Ltd
Internal design by Midland Typesetters, Australia
Typeset in 13/17pt Bembo by Midland Typesetters
Printed and bound in Australia by Griffin Press, part of Ovato, an accredited
ISO AS/NZS 14001 Environmental Management Systems printer

A catalogue record for this
book is available from the
National Library of Australia

ISBN 978 1 76089 322 4

penguin.com.au

MIX
Paper from
responsible sources
FSC® C009448

*To the memory of my mother, Elsie Coyle of River Street,
and of my father, Tom Keneally of The Harp of Erin store,
later Chaddy's, East Kempsey. Some of the stories told are theirs.
The rest are entirely the author's fault.*

On the Sydney pier, a Presbyterian minister addressed the arrivals on the *Midlothian* in 1837 and told them in Scots Gaelic that they would raise 'the altar of God' in the areas they occupied – in their cases the charming valleys of the Manning and the Macleay rivers in northern New South Wales. The Thunguddi of the region did not yet know what blessings were on their way.

Thomas Keneally, *Australians, Origins to Eureka*

They found that . . . the Bavarians had provided, in an alley ten yards back, a number of roomy, sunken dugouts, covered with four feet of earth. Ten yards further still were deep, comfortable chambers approached by stairways . . . Some of them contained wounded or sheltering men.

C. E. W. Bean, *Official History of Australia in the War of 1914–18*, vol. III

1

Kempsey, New South Wales, 1933

On Friday afternoons Flo Honeywood, wife of the eminent master builder Burley Honeywood, was required to go forth, her body bathed, her face powdered and rouged, her figure, which was not that of an old lady, enhanced by a corset ordered from Sydney, a secret not shared with the women who sold such things in Barsby's store in Smith Street. She wore, too, a best umber cloche hat bought at Anthony Hordern's in Sydney, and she went out in her innocence as a woman ordained to meet and talk with the august of the river, the big people from the big acres from Toorooka northwards – the wife of Dr McVicar, the wife of the solicitor Sherry, the aged spouse of the other lawyer, Cattleford, the wife and eldest daughter of Collopy, the Shire president.

It was essential that Flo be on Smith and Belgrave streets pausing to speak, to discuss the Sydney schools to which they would send and had sent their children, the forthcoming tennis weekends at the homesteads up along the river, how

1

their husbands were, and whether the frock salons along Belgrave Street had anything worth buying before each of them made their twice-yearly raid on Sydney.

Mrs Dunster had a daughter in Paris learning to be an artist! If she had a daughter on the moon it could not be more astonishing. Mrs Dunster must be heard from. There was much talking to do with that. Mrs Dunster admitted she did not understand what her daughter was learning – it was all described in letters, but in terms which evaded the limits of a town like this. 'Half the time I don't know what she's telling me,' Mrs Dunster very happily admitted.

But what a thing for a girl from here! A Macleay girl! Paris. Men had been sent, of course, to France in the Great War. But for someone to experience it with an artist's eye – that was exceptional and, indeed, without precedent.

Kempsey had suited Flo – till she saw the boy. She had had a sense until then that it was her appointed place in the dispensations and empires of man.

The blot on Friday afternoons these days was the number of travelling men in old fragments of suits who had been able to pick up food ration tickets at the police station as long as the previous stamp in their ration books showed they had travelled more than fifty miles since the last week. They looked battered, dispirited, and carried a swag wrapped up in a blanket. But Friday was a day they could rest before moving on to the next town, to be replaced next week by another tribe of the poor who lacked jobs.

Flo had no malice against them, and in fact felt for them, but they were unsightly in their misery and detracted from the spirit of shopping day. Today, though, her progress possessed a torment that exceeded theirs, as she looked for, and feared seeing, the boy's face.

Did *they* know, she wondered. Had the townspeople even noticed the boy wearing Burley's features? Did they know, from that boy's face, seen in passing, what Burley had been up to? Some years back, but when he was already married to her! Was what Burley had been up to noteworthy to some, or condemned as sin, or barely spoken of, or long forgiven as a venial matter? Did some of the other women ever see half-caste boys whose faces came from their husbands? Or did they all have some easy power, as she had had till now, not to notice in the first place? She had noticed only last Friday. How many other Fridays had she seen the boy without knowing she had? But what if they *had* seen, as she had just seen now? Could their power to deny seeing their husband's features *undeniably* in a kid from the blacks' camp remain intact? If it could, what a gift that would be!

If you went on appointed rounds, though, as regular as the moon visiting the oceans, it made you feel as if you were fixed and permanent and necessary to the world. Well, now, after seeing the boy, she felt fixed to Belgrave Street by a thread, and she feared the thread would break very soon and commit her into a chaos of clouds. All solidity within the valley and the town was gone now. She felt she was a mere whisper. She dressed her bathed body well; she used the hatpin, better designed for a heart, perhaps her husband's, than for a cloche hat, to tether hers in place.

After her encounter last week with what had to be her husband's Aboriginal son, she had continued on up Belgrave, smiled and smiled to the point of aching, let her eyes glitter and glitter again, like a woman happy but, most importantly, safe from shame, and she knew herself that her laughter was strangely ardent and belonged to someone else. The wives of poorer people, the labourers, the carpenters, the timber-getters, slid by her with deference, and the sort of implicit envy she had until now enjoyed being the quiet object of.

After a conversation with some ladies on the corner of Belgrave and Verge streets, she progressed as far as the Commercial Hotel, at the back of which Mrs McIntyre kept reserved for the ladies of the town a lavatory, attached to the hotel by a covered way. There Flo went, after her perambulation of the town, and voided her bladder and then the contents of her stomach into the creosoted smell of the lavatory hole, and howled and swallowed again and again, and wiped her mouth.

The anguish of what had happened and a sense of the unexpected, vague demands it made on her had not gone away, nor been reduced to size by the passage of a week. She could not forget what had been seen. She could not fall back on any other men who looked like Burley and ascribe the kid to one of them. Time magnified the matter, in fact, the longer she stayed silent. She knew that she must now come out into the bitter and relentless light of the afternoon, to force herself back onto the street, and that she was ready to break her silence in ways Burley would certainly not like.

In Smith Street she ran into pretty Mrs Anna Webber – wife of Bert Webber, owner of a number of dairy farms and a hero of the Great War – and her daughter. They had to be spoken to for normality's sake; it was not that *she* thought times normal, but *they* did. The Webbers were prosperous and owned dairy and cattle farms, as well as timber leases up and down the valley. The daughter had finished at the Presbyterian Ladies' College in Sydney, and her complexion and eyes had a wonderful clarity, but today there seemed to be a few grave secrets clouding pretty Mrs Webber's eyes, this child of German farmers, that were somehow and sadly comforting to Flo Honeywood to see, that made her feel less lonely – and all the more so since, as Flo and Mrs Webber and the clever daughter named Gertie walked up Smith Street, Anna Webber proposed tea at Tsiros's Refreshment Rooms.

The effeminate and stylish Chicken Dalton, the straw-boater-ed pianist at the Victoria Cinema, passed by and bowed too theatrically to them. He might be as young as thirty-five or so, but she thought he had that look lilies get of going off, of crimpling and browning at the immaculate edges. The fact his cheeks were rouged – he did rouge his cheeks and, when he was performing, used lipstick – seemed designed to give him the look of someone suffering from TB, which he was not. Everyone knew he liked to see the new clothes from Sydney on the mannequins in the window of the dress salon owned by the Quinlan sisters, who had somewhat more fashionable clothing than that purveyed in Barsby's department store.

Chicken was a town favourite in his way. Boys whistled at him and mocked him, but his answers were always so determinedly cheerful and unresenting, and he raised his boater in the manner of a vaudeville artist. Even Mrs Webber and Flo automatically smiled at each other as he passed, and Gertie sang, 'Chicken Dalton!' The town's musician and licensed pansy – and you had to admit he could play the piano. On top of that, a number of men had testified that he had done great service in the war as a hospital orderly in Sydney.

To Flo, he seemed blithe. That might be why they called his type *fairies*, she surmised. Despite her dead feeling, she called, 'We'll be visiting you tomorrow evening, Mr Dalton.'

'So are we,' cried Anna, rejoicing in the minor coincidence.

Gertie addressed Flo: 'My father, if you can believe it, Mrs Honeywood, is going to the pictures for the first time since he left the army. That's fourteen years!'

Flo made the appropriate noises and found herself rewarded with the proximity of the great timber bridge over the Macleay, at the corner of Smith and Belgrave. She had got this far and not seen the boy.

She had, since she first noticed the boy, done nothing to break the routine of the household. She answered Burley functionally. Her elder son, Jerry, was holidaying on the south coast with a school friend's family and was chary of spending too much time at home because Burley wanted him on one of the worksites about town, and currently that meant a new timber mill (and very welcome it was, said Burley, since there was not a lot else on the horizon) on the Crescent Head Road. Jerry had no ambition to learn the craft of hewing wood, and Burley did not have much time for a son who did not.

Jerry had been sullen with Flo and Burley during his time at home before Christmas, but had given Christian Webber, a young university student, driving lessons, and said he would do the same for Gertie if she ever got her head out of the film magazines. Flo's two younger children went to school in Kempsey for now, and were minded by a girl named Bonnie, daughter of a large clan, happy for the work and very affable, and employed as an indulgence of Burley's towards Flo.

So who was she as yet to say she would not parade the

6

streets as his wife, and though a contrary intention was forming in her, there was no reason to resist the Saturday night routine of the pictures. Reserved seats at the Victoria. There, Chicken Dalton, wearing his tails, played the piano and musical contraption in the well beneath the stage.

2

Kempsey, New South Wales, 1933

The greatest imaginable luxury on earth for Gertie Webber was reserved seats at the Victoria. The main picture was *42nd Street*, a silent before that and an interval. And all the various joys of newsreel, short feature, serial and so on. Sharing a Scorched Peanut Bar with her mother in the interval. This was the height of life to her.

Christian Webber went along with Gertie since he saw her enthusiasms as the realms of light, whereas his could not be spoken. He desired Chicken Dalton, the ageless pianist. Tell the worthies in the reserved seats about that!

He looked at Gertie's right side and saw, in the light of his own oddity of desire, unspeakable in the son of a war hero, how her enjoyment diminished her beauty, her jaw hanging a bit, in a way he did not exactly like, as if she were gasping from the effort to get them all here like this, in her place of treasures. She had promised them so much, and so confidently, from this outing, her mother and father and him, that now, once they were in their seats in the stalls, she hoped they too would identify the overwhelming sense of occasion.

Christian hoped his father would pretend to, for Gertie's sake. He hoped that Bert would vocally bemoan all the years that had elapsed since his last experience of the flicks. Yet he knew his father could not normally manage that sort of demonstration. From going on weekends at boarding school to visit families in the city he knew that many of the fathers were different, louder, more exclamatory than his own. Christian saw that Bert was very careful with word and gesture, like someone keeping a secret. But not the same secret he himself was keeping.

Gertie's best chance of parental enthusiasm was Anna – pretty, frowning Anna. She would pretend to get blown over, at least, for Gertie's sake. As for Dick Powell and the other stupid actors whose names he had seen on the posters in the lobby of the Victoria, and Mae West, for God's sake, a stupid cow if he ever saw one, and Toshia Mori, some Japanese woman – they didn't have Buckleys of hitting the sides of the hole he sensed in his father. That was why it was so pitiful to see good old Gertie persist in sitting with that grinning, open-gobbed stare of hers. Christian examined his mother too, as she sat with her lips pursed. She didn't look like a cow that doesn't know it's arrived at the abattoirs, the way Gertie did.

All Quiet on the Western Front – now that was okay with Christian, and with his friend, the ironic and worldly third-year law student Walter Jupp, who believed the film to be the *dernier mot* in passivism and the exploitation of males in war. Lew Ayres, the German soldier who is killed when reaching to touch a butterfly, was an exemplar, the way he rather liked Chicken for his more worldly ones. Whereas Christian believed he would have willingly shot wise-cracking bloody Dick Powell if ever the bugger came to town.

Christian, now hemmed between his father and his sister, enjoyed best the tobacco-y smell of the old man. Pa had an air about him and didn't look too bad for a fellow who must be getting close to forty. Let's see, twenty when the Great War started, twenty-four when it ended, plus fifteen. Yes, staring at forty. Pretty well preserved, the old bloke.

Christian hung on Bert's infrequent words. When he was away at school or university he imagined conversations he would have with the old man about ancient history or property law, but when he came home none ever developed. It was as if they were scared of finding out too much about each other, but worse, as if they did not share the same vocabulary. He would tell his father the school term had been pretty good, and his father would say the farms were pretty good, and so everything was pretty good. The missingness between them, the big vacuum. That wasn't pretty good. That was a mongrel. He inhaled the rum-flavoured tobacco smell – Bert smoked a pipe – but no words developed even now, before the lights went down. Neither was contented just to sit together, Christian suspected. Both wanted to fill the gap up with words. He certainly did. They just couldn't do it.

At the front of the theatre, beyond the Aboriginal seats in the front stalls, angular Chicken Dalton appeared in his tails and bow tie, bowed and was whistled, and sat down at the piano to play some Chopin. In Sydney in the picture theatres they had Wurlitzer organs that came up through the floor, and organists in dinner suits who spent all their time playing blind while grinning at the audience. The Victoria just had the piano and Chicken Dalton. But he was a pretty good pianist, you couldn't take that from him.

While Christian and his father sat listening to Chicken glissade from Chopin to 'The Tramp's Waltz', there wasn't any lack of words between Gertie and her mother. Chicken Dalton's piano music didn't stop them. They pointed people out, commented on hats. They seemed particularly interested when Flo and Burley Honeywood came in without any of their kids. Their son Jerry was someone Anna knew Gertie 'liked', a potential beau, though Gertie herself had sworn never to settle for anyone contented with Kempsey. Flo had on a white straw hat and a beautiful brown frock and looked pale. His mother and Gertie decided that, yes, she must have bought that in Sydney. No, they wouldn't carry it in town. Not even the Quinlans.

Burley looked sleek, and his hair was parted and slicked just like a character in the pictures. Everyone curtsied to the Honeywoods — they were right in with the big cow-cockies up the river — the *Argus* was full of news every week about whose property near Willawarrin or Bellbrook the Honeywoods had stayed at. Some said Flo was stand-off-ish, others that she was genuinely shy. Burley was a prince in terms of that river town. He and Flo seemed to Christian as if they would walk through a hail of Tommy gun bullets fired by James Cagney — that was a good picture too, *Public Enemy* — and not have a hair knocked out of place.

Gertie and Anna really began talking a streak when the Reverend Andrew Westbury, the Anglican curate, came down the aisle. He nearly tripped over a boy from the convent school who got mixed up in his head about whether he was in church or at the pictures, and genuflected before getting into his seat. The damn tykes always did that – one of them would anyhow. They probably genuflected before they got on the lav, Christian wanted to say as a joke to his father, but could not manage to. Gertie and her mother muttered and laughed about the Reverend Westbury for five minutes – or that's how it seemed to Christian. Gertie heard her mother say, 'But he never brings his wife.'

Gertie pretended to know why. 'She thinks the pictures are sinful,' said Gertie.

'Some of them are,' Mrs Webber half-chided her daughter.

Chicken was the master of these particular revels. Sometimes semi-drunk yokels wandered down past the Aboriginal seats to throw zacks and trays and pennies at him, some of them tossed jovially with no attempt to hit him, others aimed. But Chicken never objected since he came from a poor family and was in fact tough.

That was how he got his name – it was believed he practised chicken hypnosis and brought the immobile and mesmerised birds he stunned by this method home to his mother. And thus the family survived.

A black woman who knew Chicken by some means, one Alice Kelly, had yelled out one night, 'Hey, Chicken! In your suit!' For Chicken wore tails when he played the piano. 'You a real pox doctor's clerk!' This was a sort of compliment. It was idiom for 'dandy'. People came to call him that too. The pox doctor's clerk. His real name was doubly lost.

As light dimmed in the cinema, Chicken, the pox doctor's clerk, who had been playing a melodic rag with soft pedal, hit the sustain and played his own informal overture, signal that the Monarch of the British Empire was about to appear on screen. There was a scuffling sound as men and women rose to await Chicken's 'God Save'. Some of the Irish, notably Breslin the train driver, would not stand, and were hissed. The maiden Quinlan sisters, who had Irish parents, and both of whose fiancés had been killed in the Great War, certainly stood, for the apparatus that had consumed their potential husbands commanded awe, and in any case their customers were above all loyal women of the Empire.

Light finally vanished, except for a dust-filled beacon that sprang from the projection room, and the audience, some with a very slovenly civic piety, rose. The head of George V appeared and the music of 'God Save the King'. Christian saw his mother whisper to his sister. He knew what she always said at this moment.

'He's really one of us,' she always said. The King, she meant, was ancestrally a German, as they were, though that could not be said out loud.

The heroic music surged. Once, on Salisbury Plain, when the world was young, Webber had seen the King ride by, taking time to inspect the Australian Imperial Force, or the bit of it to which he belonged. Christian Webber looked at his father's profile and saw no hint there either of devotion or resentment. What would happen, Christian wondered, what would happen if I just sat one day, like the crazy old Irishmen in the audience whom people hissed but who remained, with set faces, on their rebellious arses?

The image faded and the anthem ended. The big screen revealed itself, white-grey cloth backed with black, a dead rectangle. How could it carry the population of a moving picture and make their yearnings memorable? In the darkness people rumbled as they found their seats again. The title of a short feature presented itself. *The Humble Husband*. Men in the audience whistled. They knew that they were about to be shown up as witless victims, and women as potent sources of mystification.

The courting couples grabbed hands now in excited anticipation, wondering in their mutual delight with each other why married people complained so much. The unreliable boys didn't worry one way or another. There were times Christian wouldn't mind being an unreliable boy himself, sitting down in a picture show not with one's destiny but with random opportunity. Neither was available to him. Neither destiny nor the reverse.

The action started. So stupid, Christian thought. Since he had heard Mahler, since Mr Stivens had played it for him at school, nothing would match it. It reduced everything to triviality, and especially the triviality, which this idiot film with its vacuous-faced couple was, even compared to other films. Bring on the main feature, this new craze, *42nd Street*. It was believed to be a marvel of its kind, and Christian had lusted for its director, whose picture he had seen in Gertie's film magazines. Busby Berkeley was his name. He was young and he had an artist's face.

Imagine anyone in the Macleay calling a kid by such a get-up-and-make-mayhem name as Busby.

———

Flo was the other person in the cinema definitely not liking the short feature on marriage. She heard Burley laughing beside her as if she had much in common with the brassy wife in the short film. Behind the idiocy of the little marital tale, there existed the proposition 'and forsaking all others'. Forsaking all others . . . it made sense to Flo because not forsaking was a mess, and mess was against her nature.

Not forsaking was all grief and blood. But it hadn't been grief and blood for Burley. He had not seemed to pause in his gravity as a town father. Yet here was that boy.

Was that boy down the front tonight? She had the desire to go down the front and look for his face. Angry as she was, she was not angry enough to do it at the moment.

She hoped the people around her, in the good seats, did not notice the rebellion in her, but she also didn't give a damn if they did. She wanted with part of her to retain what she was even as she felt herself beginning to fly apart, as if someone had put one of those rods they made milk-shakes with right at the centre of her soul and flayed her with it from within. The town which had been so habit-able for more than fifteen years of her marriage . . . well, it wasn't habitable anymore. But here she was, pretending to be entertained, pretending to be looking forward to *42nd Street*, pretending to be a fond wife.

Her motherhood too was falling apart, she felt, since she had seen the boy. As if Jerry and Betty and young George came from one womb, kangaroo-wise, and the boy from a second one. Mad magnets had descended from nowhere, and a love had swung like a compass needle, from them, her true children, to the boy. How did this happen? Yes, it was Burley's crime, but it was bigger than a mere crime. Her momentum towards the boy had a force much bigger than Burley.

Now, how they laughed at the marital comedy on the screen, Burley with them. She was relieved when an anima-tion came on – first, that sort of thing was a great novelty, and secondly, it was honestly stupid.

The newsreel started. This one silent and titled. Chicken moved into Fingal's Cave-style of music. A surf carnival in Sydney, boys who looked like Greek gods wearing surf caps and swimming togs with their club symbols on the chest. Carrying rescue reel equipment, marching up the long sand with such precision. Surf boats pitched and swamped or streaming in on waves, all oars lifted except that of the sweep in the stern. Flo had seen such carnivals – Burley had endowed the surf boat at Crescent Head, and the name of Honeywood was on the vessel's flank.

Then an intensification of tempo for an English motor race with collisions and engine flames and the drivers literally hot-footing it away from their machines. Now, in Germany, elections, and old Hindenburg who had fought in World War I and still wore that funny hat with a spike, and a new man with a clipped moustache, severely clipped, in fact. Up in the stalls, as the man gave Hindenburg, who had just apparently appointed him, a series of curt nods, Flo idly wondered what was the sense of having a moustache at all if you cut it so narrow?

As the man with the stupidly economic moustache stopped moving and gazed at the camera lens, there came from somewhere within the Victoria Cinema an unearthly wail. Flo had never heard anything like this, so profound a thing, something too close to the bone compared with the easy range of feeling the motion pictures and, above all, the newsreels should provoke. It contained in it a sense of loss and an angry protest as well. It had not been rage, particularly, or even chiefly terror. It was the strangest cry, a howl of regret perhaps, but other things in it too.

On Saturday nights the citizens of the Macleay Valley took the moving pictures with some of the same religious seriousness that applied to church the following morning. Even when they laughed it didn't seem to go too far. The secret courting of the young in the back rows, the possible improper straying of hands, was something the soberer members of the community chose not to think about, and it ended in any case with the lights-up and the changing of the reels and Chicken's resort to light, chirpy music. They left the disorderly laughter and the occasional yell or mock-scream to the blackfellas at the front of the cinema and the town louts in the cheaper seats upstairs. But this cry was out of order. It was an unwarranted shriek. Above all, it came from someone as affronted as her.

Ushers' torches began to play over the crowd, seeking the source of such extreme anguish. They caught a man, aghast in the torchlight, who had stood up in distress. Yes, that was the thing too. It was a man's shriek. But men did not shriek that way in this town.

Flo saw now the cry had come from the war hero, Bert Webber, owner of dairy farms and pastoral acreage, feeder of the British Empire with butter and meat, who had, beyond all reasonable belief, made the noise. Bert was a neat man of average height and, Flo knew, not a man to scream. As a soldier he had won the Military Medal, as an officer he had won the Military Cross. Shire President Collopy said of this double feat, 'Beat *that* as a quinella!' And no one else could. Old August Weber, Bert's rather elderly father, had like Anna's own parents been Lutheran in a valley full of Catholics from Bavaria, but in a town that lacked enough Lutherans for a church of their own, they had taken up Anglicanism in the years before 1914, and adopted an extra 'b' in their name, as a further proof of loyalty.

Suddenly, the Quinlan brothers, who worked together as projectionists, cut off the film and the cinema lights went on and the screen went blank. People's voices were raised in speculation, and tall Chicken stood by his old grand piano as if wondering whether to play something to soothe the hubbub. What had set Bert Webber off? Flo Honeywood could tell just by the quality of the sound that Bert had gone through some gate of the kind she herself had gone through. She wished she could find a gesture equivalent to his to make her misery manifest. 'Such a quiet fellow!' everyone was saying around her and in amazement at Bert. Burley himself turned to her and looked a little flushed. 'He's not anyone who *wants* to scream in public.' 'Nor am I,' she wanted to tell him. Flo Honeywood thought Bert Webber might have screamed for her, standing instead of her, making the brave noise she was too cowardly to utter.

Ushers and Mrs Anna Webber and Christian and Gertie surrounded and assessed Bert. The hero was trembling, and had stark and unseeing eyes. Anna muttered something commanding to her children, since she did not want to expose this version of her husband to the town for fear that somehow they would take advantage of him. Christian leaned forward and said something to his father but Bert looked bewildered and now in a panic, displaying naked anxiety to the Saturday night crowd and perhaps fearing their passion for gossip. Anna Webber rose and could be seen saying, 'Come on then, Gertie,' as she steered mute, unprotesting Bert down the glaring aisle. Christian was behind, hand on his father's shoulder, an unexpected intimacy between father and son. 'On top of all that just happened,' Christian could have told them, 'he has me for a son.'

————

Outside, in the quiet street, Gertie felt lacerated by that wail, unheralded and unapologetic – it was so close, it so scored her daughterly soul. Christian Webber, law student and son of Bert, could not believe it either, but his concern suddenly was that his father had had a revelation about him, Christian, and that Bert was uttering some form of protesting shame in front of the town, in front of these hayseeds who would talk about the noise forever, this noise of noises his father had emitted.

As the Webbers gathered themselves, Bert still looked dazed and made modest choking noises. From inside, Chicken Dalton's piano could be indistinctly heard, launching into 'Maple Leaf Rag', 'Tico Tico No Fuba' and 'The Entertainer' until the Quinlan boys got the reels all sorted out again and magic was restored. Their father from Cork had opened a store named The Harp of Erin, and all the Quinlans were nicknamed Harper, the equivalent of 'Harp of' in the Australian tongue.

Anna felt grateful when Dr McVicar, neatly suited, some years older than Bert, emerged from the Victoria. He had been in the audience but did not seem as surprised as they had been.

'I'll give the poor fellow something to help him sleep,' he said. 'I could admit him to my little hospital in East if you like.'

But ultimately, he and Anna decided it was best if Bert slept at home for tonight. Bert, his hair awry, seemed dazed, but he had suddenly enough presence to ask McVicar, 'Did I just make some sort of fool of myself, doc?'

At home, Christian helped get his father into pyjamas. A slight man, an inch or two taller than the norm, brown-haired, a boyish face given the caste of masculinity chiefly by prominent jawbone nodes. The face of a certified hero. But he was not talking and he emitted a low moan of complaint, and pain. Christian was aware of his own resemblance but knew there was no Military Cross or Medal in his future and hoped not ever to have the opportunity to win one.

His father, having spoken to Dr McVicar, was silent now, did not answer any question. He was thinking about something too big for conversation. It was very frightening and out of character.

Aren't we all out of character since Bert's yell? Christian wanted in his anguish to ask.

———

From the next day onwards Bert Webber was a patient at the East Sanatorium on the same side of the river as the house where Anna and the children normally lived, as did Bert when not travelling in the bush. Bert had, until this night of his sudden affliction, stayed on his cattle farm for most of the week, and normally visited his house in town for Friday afternoons, Saturdays and Sundays, driving over those rough roads from Comara in his meticulously kept Ford Cabriolet which, arriving amongst the town's Moons and Tin Lizzies, gleamed through the layer of dust it had picked up from the powdery surface of the Armidale road.

While Dr McVicar kept Bert asleep with bromides and opiates at the sanatorium in East, the Reverend Andrew Westbury, the awkward and dreamy curate at St Luke's, went to visit the patient, but Bert could not talk, except for occasional incoherent fragments of utterance. The Reverend Westbury was reputed to be good with people in distress and took the trouble of visiting Anna Webber and telling her that Bert was sleeping peacefully, as Anna knew.

'Your husband is a hero of the Great War, I hear?' asked the Reverend.

'Yes, he is.'

'I was too late,' the curate apologised. 'I enlisted as a soldier. Padres' spots went to the more senior men of the cloth.'

'Yes, Bert had a friend who was a Lutheran minister, and an ordinary soldier.'

'Our troopship was off Southampton when the war ended.'

Anna would have said, 'I think you were lucky,' but that might have sounded disloyal. She could tell they both shared an instinct, though, that it was some mental bomb left in Bert's brain from the war that had gone off at the Victoria that Saturday night.

Dr McVicar had also consulted Anna and confided that Bert would have to go to Sydney – if Christian and Anna could take him down, an ambulance would meet him when the Northern Mail came into Central and take him to an excellent sanatorium with a soothing name, Derwent, which Dr McVicar himself knew and had sent patients suffering from intractable mental states to. They had all the most advanced treatments there. McVicar himself had once visited it and spoke highly of it.

The drugs were keeping Bert tranquil, said McVicar, but there was something underlying that needed to be attended to as soon as could be reasonably done.

'You're aware of electric therapy?' he asked. 'That might be needed. I know from the war that the human mind is complex and our medical means are primitive, but electro-shock therapy works.'

There were a number of men from the war, McVicar said, more than she would believe, who had had these seizures. It didn't mean they weren't brave. It often meant they were the bravest. He'd sent some of them to Sydney for the sake of discretion, and they came back in top-notch form.

That's the thing, Anna thought. Bert's scream in the pictures on a Saturday night had not been discreet. She walked bravely in the street, but people who talked to her were different – a wariness in them as if she might suddenly scream too. And the women, oversweet as they asked, 'And how is your *dear* family?'

No one said *dear* family unless they already considered you tainted or rendered odd. She knew they found Christian a strange boy, not a man's man. And Gertie adopted over-dramatic poses and behaved as if she were in a film. And now the scream. That cemented it all together to make them a *dear* family. From now on she would forever be the wife of Bert Webber who went crazy on a Saturday night in front of all the town who could fit in the Victoria.

And yet she felt defiant of them. She wanted her own space in the town's mind. She was *not* Bert and was just as mystified as they were by Bert's howl. But then perhaps she should scream in public too, so they could have their way and get it over and write off the whole family. And she would have done it except for Christian and Gertie, whose futures – with any luck – would be in the city. Yet for all she knew they too might have to live here in the valley, where they deserved to be seen as more than the children of raving parents.

3

Macleay Valley, New South Wales, 1933

In the meantime, Johnny Costigan, an Irishman who had worked with dairy cattle west of Sydney, had been keeping the Webber dairy farm on Nulla Creek going. He had taken the job two years ago, since Bert had wanted to concentrate on the beef cattle business. Nulla had a sentimental value for Bert Webber – it was the first Australian farm of old August Weber, his father. Costigan lived there now, managing it with his Australian-born wife, Dulcie, and his four sons, aged six to nine – Andy, Paddy, Kevin and Oliver – all four of them at least half-literate from attending the school at Mungay Creek after morning milking, and leaving class early for the afternoon session.

Anna Webber had been against her husband employing Costigan, since the man had a rhythmic Irish sullenness in his voice and a strange over-smart wariness, combined with an occasionally submissive manner of the kind she believed covered a well of jealousy and resentment and unguessable other unpleasant things. Anna never liked the Irish because of their double souls, and she thought of Costigan as typical. Yet his wife Dulcie seemed to keep him in check, and it was a lucky thing they had four boys to do the milking and mind the stock. And though Anna retained something hard and Germanic against him, she did not deny the place was being well run. She was sure when he was alone or in a pub, though, Costigan cursed Bert Webber for his good fortune. How well, too, she could imagine Costigan bad-mouthing Bert to the refrigerated truck carter, who moved up and down the river collecting the dairy churns – another Papist named Rossa, driving four days a week, and then Billy Hayden the remaining three.

On Nulla, the Costigans lived in the old blackbutt house down on a knoll near the lower paddocks. On Anna's rare visits, she found the Costigan house smelled of a humid and unaired mix of soured lard and boys' musk, and of bitter and unhappy proximity, which suffused the place. And of course the kids were bush kids, half-wild and yet devoted to their mother, and taking moody Costigan as he came. Bert was perhaps a little cheap with the wages he paid Costigan – that was the old August Weber in him. But there were hundreds who would take Costigan's lot, given the Depression, and she suspected if he paid Costigan double the place would still smell the same. The truth was she'd come herself from a house like this – her parents had struggled on a forty-acre dairy farm down the river until she married Bert on the war's eve.

She actually quite liked what she had seen of Dulcie Costigan. She got the idea Dulcie was struggling with that smell, trying to get on top of it. That she was a matriarch to the boys and implanted them with her disappointed wisdom. She had married a fellow who would not rise.

Anna Webber was very pleased to live in town these days and leave to a number of employees the managing of the three dairy farms and the cattle run by shrewd old August. Bert's austere father had bought and put them together at the end of a drought in 1928, and in bad times for small farmers in 1931, before dying unexpectedly at the end of that year and leaving them to Bert, who proved a good steward and a competent owner of fat dairy and beef cattle.

But now Bert was in the sanatorium, Anna felt she must visit the Webber properties in a dusty loop between Comara via Nulla to Hickeys Creek and Toorooka, to let Costigan and the other managers know that even if Bert might be ill, they were not entitled to consider themselves unsupervised. She visited the rouseabout Sullivan and his son on Bemurrah, the cattle farm, and the manager at Hickeys Creek, a decent, shy fellow named Carlaw, whose main sentiment seemed to be he was lucky to have a job in these times, and to be far enough up the valley away from the tramps, the swagmen and travellers – the *really* hard-up who came through the town of Kempsey, given the railway.

———

Anna was wrong to think Costigan envied people their farms. He could see her thinking it and the silly woman was wrong. He envied people their souls. He had lost his own in the old British barracks at Ballymullen, within a decent walk from his home in childhood. He was a dupe

25

and a gull, and his worst enemies paid for his steamer ticket to Australia, ten years before Bert disgraced himself in the Victoria. Johnny had travelled to Australia in an eight-bunk cabin with Cockneys and Yorkshiremen. They had souls, but ones only a few inches deep. They talked as if it were all the height of life, their brute pawings with the servant girls and governesses, or with the sisters going to join *their* sisters and brothers already in Australia. His fellow travellers' conviction that they were in charge of the rough and tumble of it all, depressed him. For his own relief, he had sought out a waiter the day before, a Mauritian. He intended to find a church when the ship put into Galle and confess these groping sins committed aboard, and get his absolution and promise never to grope again.

It was in Galle he found the war was over. His war, that is. When, the ship having docked, he put on a suit, his feverish and hungover cabin companions accused him of preparing himself for a Sinhalese whorehouse to which two offered to accompany him.

'I'm going to Mass,' he told them. The priests advertised Christ as the Outcast of the Earth. Gulls and traducers welcome.

'Ceylon is famous for its Catholics,' he told them, and they groaned and cursed the Pope, but left him to disembark on his own into that gravid air.

Even on Nulla he remembered Galle, since it was where, in one of the old Dutch-style hotels with its deep veranda, he ordered a whisky like a gent, and read papers that had come on the faster steamers than his.

On page 8 of *The Times* he read a report of the surrender by the Kerry rebels to the Irish Free State troops. A small corps of the never-surrender men, who would still not accept an Irish state without Ulster, was making its last stand out at the Clashmealcon Caves on the coast and was holding out, since General O'Daly of the Free State could not get artillery into that rough locality. Even so . . . the Kerry rebel brigades had thrown in the towel. And then the report closed with the mention that rebels who had surrendered were speaking of Free State summary killings throughout Cork and Kerry. Oh Jesus, look on my father, a dairy hand, our house burned down by the British Auxiliaries in the days we were all fighting for Ireland before the terrible Treaty, when there was still an Ireland to fight for.

Well, he saw when reading *The Times* that morning years past in Ceylon that all the strut and vanity and efforts, all the treachery and blood, had counted for nothing. The news drove him by instinct to a church where, before Mass, a Dutch or German priest with a first-rate command of English heard his confession. That confession in Galle wasn't the first confession since he had lost his soul. He had gone in Dublin and told the priest how, if Christ was forever hammered to the Cross, so Paudeen O'Casey, Frank Mangan and Seamus Quoyne were forever chained to that satanic mechanism General O'Daly used. The priest had cheerily told him his duty was to live and do well, to live for those men. To be a good man and honour them.

That day in Ceylon, though, it was time to say something to a priest about his weakness, his improper relations with other men. 'But,' asked the European priest that day, 'do you not find sufficient attraction in the broad sphere of Catholic womanhood?'

Broad sphere? He liked that. It gave him a passing sense of promise.

The priest said, 'You are a sincere young man. You must pray to the Virgin Mary most energetically to send you a wife.'

On the way back to the ship he went for another whisky at a sailors' bar, a place of transit where the reek was as strong as mercy. There was however a Sinhalese waiter there with eyes like lakes . . .

And now, ten years gone.

A family made by applying himself to the good Catholic wife who did eventuate and present herself. He was half-saved here, and could depend for solace on the daily stupefaction of milking cattle.

———

Dulcie Costigan was pleased with the house Bert Webber gave them at Nulla Creek, high on the banks above flood level and amongst some blackbutts Bert had saved for eventual culling, and which their three-bedroom house was built from after an earlier culling. On creosoted foundations, it had a boarded floor. There were cobwebs of the spiders which Dulcie called wobbegongs, but she made pretty brisk work of them. 'The whole farm,' warned Bert Webber, 'is bad for snakes. Just watch out for them. Not bad enough to kill a man, but poisonous enough to finish a child.'

Dulcie said, 'Don't worry, Mr Webber, I grew up with snakes in Mulgoa.'

Why did Johnny's soul crimp up like paper in a flame when he heard sentences like that, and her harmless, unhappy boasts? Why did he grow annoyed – though annoyed was a pretty pale word for what he felt? He felt an abomination which bounced forward to her like a missile, and deflected back and lodged under his breastbone. You silly woman to have married a silly man!

O'Keefe's wife from further down Nulla Creek helped deliver the first child, which Dulcie insisted on naming Andy to honour her father. Now Andy, Paddy, Kevin and Oliver filled the blackbutt house, Oliver just old enough to help with the milking. All the Webber dairy cattle were tended to by this labour force of Costigans. Just occasionally Johnny Costigan would ride to the pub at Bellbrook and not be seen for a day or two, and then it was Dulcie and the four boys. An old blackfella named George Munter helped out, too, with his wife. A reliable man. Between whoever Dulcie marshalled, they milked more than eighty cows each day. By hand, of course, no electricity for one of those Laval milkers. Everyone had hard, creased and cracked milker's hands. Even the kids.

And kerosene lanterns were still the main illumination in the great yawning nights of Nulla Creek.

———

Anna had been aware for years of Bert Webber's night cries and sweats, but they did not seem excessive to her. She had heard wives of less notable veterans of the war mention the visitation the war still made to their husbands' worst nights. Once woken, or awaking on his own bat, he needed no calming, he knew where he was and had no delusions. Nor was he like some of the men who had become souses, hanging around the Railway Hotel, drinking with each other as if they were part of the same jealous secret never to be disclosed. He was soft on them a little, would give a man drinking money if he was an old soldier, and he helped support Mrs Spooner's son in West. Her boy's mind, said Mrs Spooner, when encouraged to talk about it, had been affected by the explosion of shells that released something called monoxide, which apparently deranged him. Some did not believe Mrs Spooner's monoxide poisoning idea and just thought young Spooner had been soft in the head anyhow. Yet he did not move or speak, a sure sign of monoxide poisoning as far as Mrs Spooner, and the unobtrusively generous Bert, were concerned.

Anna had congratulated herself until now that she had not had to make up a saving lie about Bert or explain away his behaviour. But now he had shamed himself in front of the town – and she could not help thinking of it as shame. It was not the kind of shame that drove her away from him, but it drove the town away from her. It was, she knew, mostly the recurrent dream about the Reverend Corporal Lembke of Woolgoolga, the ghost she shared Bert's attentions with.

4

Kempsey, New South Wales, 1933

One afternoon, Chicken Dalton sat at his kitchen table in Clyde Street, Kempsey, a towel on his lap, beside Alice Kelly, one of the Aboriginal women from Burnt Bridge who sometimes went to Sydney, working a few weeks on the street and bringing back temporary riches for her ailing, shattered husband.

Chicken loved this chance to do beauty work on a woman's features, especially since Alice's were so ample. He held her broad, good-looking face with a single finger under her chin, lifting her visage to the light from the window. He had bought his rouges and powders from Barsby's, and the contemptuous country girls behind the counter thought that he was buying all this for himself. They did not understand he was buying it for the sake of owning it. It was only a small amount of rouge and a modest amount of eyeshadow and lipstick he applied to his

31

own face before taking to the piano at the Victoria – no more than any stage performer might use.

Meanwhile, he had a dresser and indeed a cupboard stocked with unopened jars, and tubes and bottles, which he bought on payday, every two weeks. He had an impulse to acquire these things – foundations, powders, rouges, for their own inherent beauty and because they offered him promises in which he chose to believe.

One day when he came out of the store, Alice stepped up. 'Are you gonna make a pretty girl out of me, Chicken? Or yourself?'

Chicken looked at her. From the Victoria, she knew he was good-natured, and now he considered this a happy coincidence. His smile was because he saw this as a great chance, sudden and magnificent. He had lacked a living body other than himself on whom to test and dab these wonderful substances which, like the moving pictures themselves, came from far away and a better, kinder place.

So that day he took Alice home to his little weatherboard cottage in Clyde Street, and sent her forth splendid. She did not care, and Chicken knew she didn't, whether the whites laughed at her – they were likely to laugh whatever you did. She was pleased to be transfigured.

It was curious that black women going to Sydney on any business at all, or faced with a marriage, wanted to be made up by Chicken. Sometimes they were shy, virginal girls, and sometimes raucous, irrepressible women like Alice and her late sister. They seemed to believe that what Chicken applied would last them a week or more, would be their armour against the glare of events or of the city at the end of the Northern Line.

Alice was so pleased by his craft that a number of other

Burnt Bridge women presented themselves, though you never quite knew when it would happen. Some were going to visit relatives in Nambucca or Macksville or Taree and wanted, as women did, to look flash. Marriages of Aboriginal people brought the brides to his gate. It was his missionary vocation to apply makeup to these women. It was his joy. They thought him a wizard. He knew and they knew together that they suffered an exile within their own country, and if he made their faces shine for a day it was an assertion, a refusal to be the under-creatures the world had made of him and of them.

He had not studied specifically how to make up Aboriginal women. He had read in magazines only of how to make up Carole Lombard, Marlene Dietrich and Greta Garbo. He did his best with Alice's generous and nearly unblemished features. He applied a foundation which was said to suit a darker skin tone. He applied this matte foundation with a brush, evening out some of the variations of pigment in her face across her brow, down the cheeks and around the lips.

'Black Madonna,' he whispered, and felt reverent.

Alice said, 'Chicken, you really talk flash.'

'You are so beautiful,' he told her, 'that it makes me want to talk flash.'

'What a pity you don't have a sheila. Your mouth could be sweetness to a girl.'

'You make me wish I wanted one,' he breathed. He had to wait with his brush until her face stopped juddering with merriment.

He finished with the foundation, named Black Opal, and probably designed for the Commonwealth of Australia's small population of Southern Mediterranean women, for he knew there were no cosmetics made or imported for

Aboriginal women. He then moved on to the powder, using a different one for the eye sockets to give them definition, and a matte powder for the bulk of the face.

'The Queen of Sheba,' he breathed again, and when she creased her cheeks to laugh, he said, 'Don't move!'

Her face somehow now shone evenly under the powder – the perfect form of transparency.

The skin of the black women fascinated him, and if he yearned for whites to present themselves to him, which would never happen, it was only that he might learn to expand his craft.

He picked up the white brow cosmetic pencil he had happened to buy when the ivory look was in fashion, and underlined her eyes, trying to exaggerate the arches of the eyebrows. Then he used a small brush to put a copper powder on the eyelids themselves and applied a copper oil named Copper Magic to the apples – and what apples! – of the cheeks with a further brush. Then a plum, non-tarty lipstick he had bought from the contemptuous girl at Barsby's with Alice in mind.

He said, as he always did, 'You know, Alice, this won't last you for all the time you're down there. You're sure you want to go, all that way? I know what you intend, you naughty girl. You intend to sell yourself.'

'Come on, Mr Chicken,' she said, but she turned her eyes down.

He sighed. What else was there for Alice? Being a laundrywoman, or minding a white child now and then, though half the white women in town didn't like to have black women doing that.

'You be careful,' he advised her. 'Don't have anything to do with men with razors.'

34

'There ain't any men with razors anymore. Police cleaned them up.'

'Well, whatever,' said Chicken. 'What do they use now? Acid?'

He told her to close her eyes and then worked on the mascara.

She said, while obeying him, 'You're such a hayseed, Mr Chicken. You don't know anything about Sydney.' Indeed, Chicken's small-town concerns seemed to amuse Alice, who was going down to the Big Smoke for defined and confident purposes.

He told her she could open her eyes again. He considered her and decided himself not quite finished yet. He picked up an opened cardboard container with pastel pink blush, and began to apply it to her cheeks, and when there was enough there, sponged it to evenness. Then he worked on her lush lips with lip liner, thinning them out a bit by the way he applied it, giving them a slightly puckered appearance.

He said, 'I think if I was a boy I'd give you money just to be my girlfriend, Alice.' He was in fact half-enchanted with her.

'Come on, Mr Chicken,' said Alice. 'We all know you're a sissy.'

'Yes,' said Chicken, grinning at her. 'I'm a sissy. But that means I don't go home and beat a wife.'

She said to him, 'You's a magician, Chicken.'

And he said, mysteriously and fully satisfied, 'And you're the pox doctor's clerk's sister.'

———

It was half past two the next Friday that Flo saw the boy again. He was staring into the window of Kennedy's general store. She had thought so much about him that now she thought it nothing to approach him, and ask, 'Why aren't you in school?' He stepped back from the vision beyond the glass, the boiled lollies he'd been contemplating.

'Went to the nuns', missus,' he told her with lowered eyes. Then he looked up and gave her Burley's grin.

Oh my boy, my boy, she thought. 'You don't go to the nuns anymore?'

'Didn't have the uniform, missus.'

'Would you go back to school again if you had the uniform?' He puffed his long cheeks out to consider this and shrugged.

'Wouldn't mind it, missus,' he told her.

'All right.' She thought a moment. The boy didn't smile. Neither did she. No easy smiles would serve.

'Do you see anything you like in there?' she asked, pointing into Kennedy's window.

'No thanks, missus,' he claimed. 'There's nothing, missus.'

'Come on,' she told him, 'I saw you ogling something.'

'I like them humbugs, missus,' he admitted, his eyes still lowered to the ground but then looking up with a calm speculation at the sky, a pose she had seen Burley adopt in discussions with other men. 'But you know, the red ones, not the black ones.'

'The colours of St George,' she told him. 'Red and white.'

He looked at her in mystification.

'Hold hard,' she told him. 'Don't run away.' She could not understand why she should love this boy, when she ought instead to abominate him as evidence of Burley's fall.

36

She went into Kennedy's. The shopgirls raced to serve her. They did not know of her disgrace.

'Quarter of a pound of the red bullseyes, please,' she said. She looked around and the boy outside was gazing in the window now with the honest appetite she had seen earlier. It confirmed her in her purpose. The girl who was serving her measured them out, on the generous side, she was pleased to see.

Flo thanked her, turned around, walked out the door and could be seen placing the bag into the Aboriginal boy's hand. To the girls behind the counter, this was nearly as amazing as Bert Webber's howl the other night. As if it had tilted the town off its axis. Anyway, as she handed the boy the bullseyes, she didn't know whether she hated him or loved him – it must have been both, but love above all, since he was so chirpy, a bit of a larrikin.

'Thanks, missus,' he told her. His eyes got as broad as any mocker and scorner of the blackfellas could have wanted to see, so it would confirm their idea of Aboriginal simple-mindedness. But they were Burley's wide eyes. She could have wept.

'Do you want to go to school?' she asked him.

'Yeah, missus.'

'Do you really want to go to school? Every day?'

'Yeah, missus. Every day.'

But she did not know whether he was saying, every day if it were his choice, or every single assiduous day like a model student.

'You know the primary final exams?'

He said he did.

'If you could get a uniform, would you pass the primary final?'

He nodded. 'Yeah,' he said. 'I reckon I could.'

Did he agree too easily? she wondered. Upriver there were old white men and women who remembered the wars with these people. Did he think the price of the humbugs was to turn his entire soul to her? If he was human, he would know the stories of shooting and poisoning upriver. And he was certainly human, half of him in the mode of Burley.

She could see from the edges of her eye that the shop-girls in Kennedy's were talking to each other behind raised hands. As if she could hear! She felt like looking in the door and telling them to talk openly, that they needn't go to that precaution.

Now she asked the question she had not dared ask earlier. There was some barrier in her against asking it. It was as if the whole weight of the time and the place would bear down on her when she knew the boy's name. So she asked the question. She asked the unimaginable question which passed the boundary thoroughly.

'Eddie Kelly,' he told her.

He would have got the name from the Kellys far upriver. After one killing session in the last century, it was known, the Kellys had adopted a surviving child whom they named Edward Kelly, and this Eddie was probably his grandson or great-grandson. But the centre of the issue had not been reached yet.

'And your mother?'

'Can't say the name, missus. She's gone on.'

He had a bullseye in his mouth but his eyes were full of genuine disquiet.

'Gone on?'

He looked at her full on. 'She's all fall down. She's gone, missus.'

38

'But her name?' Flo Honeywood insisted.

'Don't say her name, missus,' he told her in a lowered voice. 'She hears it, she gets real unhappy.'

She remembered. They didn't use the names of dead people. She was pleased her rival was dead. Her rival for a night. Or how many nights. Though, who was she to ask that, given that Burley turned to her now and held her only once a month, perhaps not then. She had once enjoyed it but, despite good intentions, now bore it. She had had desire. Where had it gone?

'So you were going to the Sisters of Mercy?'

'My oath, missus.'

'And what grade?'

He swallowed the juice he'd sucked from the red and white confectionary and said, 'The fourth grade, missus.'

'Do you know Rudder Street?' she asked him. 'Do you know 58 Rudder Street? A big house, right on the corner. Up from Quinlan's store. You know it? Number 58?'

'It's got pointed out to me, Mrs Honeywood,' he told her. So he knew her name. Had his mother, the one who couldn't be named, pointed it out to him on the way to town when he was little? Had she even gone as far as saying, 'See that house there? That's where your father lives.'

Or maybe she didn't even remember Burley. Perhaps he and one of his mates thought it sport to be at her one after the other. These things were muttered in town.

'Will you come there tomorrow morning? I want to measure you.'

'Measure me, missus?'

'Measure you up for a uniform,' she said. 'So that you can get the primary final.' What am I doing, she had time

39

to ask herself. 'Will you come up there? Number 58. There's a frangipani in front. You know the frangipani?'

He nodded and sucked, almost as if to show her he was a child, and not an actor in this grown-up drama or tragedy.

'Now you must come,' she insisted, because everyone said Aboriginal people didn't have a sense of time – their best footballers didn't turn up for matches sometimes.

'I'll tell my Uncle Mallee,' he assured her. 'Uncle Mallee'll get me there. So, see you then, missus.'

She said goodbye to him, watched him a while as he made his way, and she felt love. Love for the Aboriginal Burley. Even as she despised the white, large-framed Burley Honeywood. It could not be explained, she decided.

She marched west towards the railway line. She knew the Sisters of Mercy over by the Sea Street swamp because Betty had piano lessons there. For the Protestants of the town, the nuns' chief purpose was piano lessons delivered with a Byzantine discipline. The intersection between the town's Catholics and Protestants was the piano, and the science of the piano was apparently owned by nuns.

She turned right beyond the railway gates, and if people saw her crossing there as a humble pedestrian, she didn't give a hoot. Then left at the Railway Hotel and over towards the Catholic Church and school. In normal times, all this could have been postponed until Eddie Kelly had turned up to be measured, but in her mind now it could not be postponed, and she knocked strongly enough to be heard on the front door of the dun-brick two-storey convent.

A young nun opened the door. One of the Hennessy daughters from up the river, consecrated to Christ and now come home to teach in her own valley.

'Sister,' she said with all the assurance of one of the town's nobility, and indeed of her own urgency. 'Could I see the Mother Superior?'

The young nun knew her. She said, 'You had best come in, Mrs Honeywood.'

The hallway smelt of polish and virginity, and Flo thought it not a bad smell. The young nun led her into a parlour where, amidst a number of chairs well upholstered, and across a polished table more for meetings than for meals, Pius XI looked down on her, his hand raised in a blessing which purported to reach into all the crevices of the earth – yea, even unto the crevice known as the Macleay Valley in New South Wales.

The young nun left and Flo sat on a settee against the wall under a painting of the Last Supper and breathed in the child-free neutrality of the room. But my living room is as cold as this, she thought. A room from which all the misery slinks away to be on its own, shivering. We all end up like nuns. Even when people came round for a drink or to play cards, Flo did not like her own front room, though its furniture was as august as, though more modern than, the stuff in this room.

An old nun Flo knew through Betty's piano lessons, Mother Ignatius, thick in the hip and a little triangular, entered, her beads, hung from a leather belt, jiggling. Flo watched as the slightly stooped but forceful woman advanced, the celluloid-backed sharpness of her hood cutting the air.

'Mrs Honeywood it is,' said the nun in an Irish accent. 'How is your young Betty then?'

'She is very well,' said Flo, standing. The monastic ensemble of a woman accustomed to command, and the

41

alien yet commanding habit, caused her to explain, 'I have given her a rest from piano this term, Mother, since I find her other studies are tiring her a little. But she's generally well.'

'Praise-be-to-Jesus!' murmured the nun, as if the pious phrase were one word.

Mother Ignatius signalled her to sit down again. Then scoured her with her eyes from within the square fortress of her hood and the redoubt of her wimple. But Flo would not take a seat.

'You have a student named Eddie Kelly. He's from Burnt Bridge.'

'Yes, we did. He's been a truant, however, on and off, and for the past week. A charming blackguard of a boy.'

Did the nuns notice his state and wonder where he came from?

'But you'd take him back, wouldn't you?' asked Flo. 'Because he says he hasn't a uniform.'

Mother Ignatius shook her head. 'We gave him a uniform,' she said. 'We are, after all, the Sisters of Mercy. But somehow it's vanished. Sold to the rag and bone man.'

'Then I will have him fitted for another,' said Flo.

'It will go the same way as the first, I fear.'

'I will have it done anyhow. You will take him back, Mother?' Flo smiled tightly as a stratagem. 'You are, after all, the Sisters of Mercy!'

Mother Ignatius shook her head and smiled. 'You have us there, Mrs Honeywood. We'll take him back for as long as he comes to us. We have other black children, you know. Some with better records.'

The two of them looked at each other. Flo wondered if she was being urged to a wider beneficence of a donation. I must not frighten her or mislead her too much with my motives, she decided. 'It's because he's an orphan,' said Flo to explain her individual ardour. It was true, as she realised later, that she had forgotten her own children at that moment in which Eddie Kelly was the central concern.

'These people are God's children right enough,' said Mother Ignatius. 'But they are not in any way designed for scholarship.'

'We'll see what happens,' said Flo.

'Please do sit down, Mrs Honeywood,' Mother Ignatius urged her, pleasantly now. 'You look as if you're hot, and on my old pins . . .'

Mother Ignatius, who looked agelessly cool even with her black cloth, indicated a chair and took one herself at the head of the table.

In defence, the seated Flo decided to elaborate. 'I . . . met him in the street. I bought him a bag of bullseyes. I asked him why he was not in school.'

'There are many such children on the streets on Friday afternoons. Even some of the whites. We have a lot of wild boys here. The youngest Quinlan from over East . . . you wouldn't believe it. Uncontrollable, I fear to report.'

'Does Eddie Kelly take well to discipline?' Flo asked. For the nuns were said to be heroic caners.

'No one can deny he needs it,' said Mother Ignatius. 'But he is amiable about it.'

No, Flo wanted to argue, don't punish him. He was conceived in treachery and born in innocence. And is now an orphan. The idea of his being caned pained her in a special way.

'But caning has not improved him?' Flo asked.

'Indeed,' Mother Ignatius admitted dolorously, 'as in so many cases, we might have saved ourselves the trouble.'

'So you'll take him back and perhaps take a different tack with him?'

'Oh yes. We'll take him back. But these people choose to have nothing to pay.'

'I'll pay his fees,' said Flo Honeywood. 'His mother is dead.'

Ignatius was genuinely puzzled. 'Are you sure on this, Mrs Honeywood? You are not a Catholic, but you want him raised in the Holy Catholic and Apostolic Church?'

'Well,' said Flo, 'it's what he's used to. Yes. It's where he's been before, after all. You will treat him with patience though, won't you?'

'I will put him in Sister Barbara's class. She is a saint. Her children love her and exercise themselves not to disappoint her.' She smiled. 'Saint Barbara is the patron saint of artillery, but this Sister Barbara is the gentlest soul.'

Indeed, Flo, child of Anglicans and Freemasons, felt a surge of sorority towards this Barbara she had never met.

Flo told Mother Ignatius, 'Then you *are* a Sister of Mercy and I must thank you.'

She stood up. She was glad it was over. When Mother Ignatius rang a bell on the sideboard, she was relieved to be shown out by the young nun from up the river. Beyond the gate, in the clear air of the town that considered itself Protestant but in which the Catholics were more pious, she was nonetheless happy to draw the secular air into her lungs.

5

Sydney, New South Wales, 1933

Anna Webber had a widowed sister, Eunice, living a mile or so from the Derwent sanatorium. Here, she could sit at a table without the knowledge of being spied out and discussed on the streets in between the two locations. For this was the city. Cities offered the guarantee of anonymity, and her sister Eunice offered a guarantee of sympathy.

At the Randwick sanatorium they seemed to use on poor Bert the same method as Dr McVicar – a deep, drugged state was the order of the day, but then, as well, he was given the prescribed electro-shock treatment, of which he occasionally woke to complain in broken sentences. But he would not or could not continue the conversation with her. It seemed that the more conscious he became, the less he could or would speak, and that he had uttered more in stupor than when conscious.

Anna always entered the gate of the hospital into a well-tended garden – tended by someone who was, no doubt, pleased to have a job in these hard times. The double front door was closed and there was an air about the place of locked-uped-ness. She hammered with the knocker.

A well-starched nurse answered the door. Her manner was for some reason a comfort to Anna. Anna explained she was to see Dr Bulstrode and was taken to a waiting room where a harried-looking middle-aged woman was softly weeping. Anna averted her eyes, for a person did not interfere. Another woman, bleak-eyed and put-upon, kept her miserable counsel. This one looked like the sort of woman who if she survived, it was on cleaning other people's housing, ironing other people's clothes. Wife of another hero. They reckon sixty thousand died between 1919 and 1931. She had read it in *Smith's Weekly*. Another sixty thousand casualties in the age of peace, falling to gas and hidden injuries and madness. The heroes Billy Hughes said would never be forgotten. The unforgotten were this woman's husband and hers, but now both of them were off in the corner of their misery. The other two did glimpse at her, sharing momentarily the news that the world made men mad one way or another.

Anna sat. She was pleased it was her turn first. The silent, enduring woman didn't even look up when Dr Bulstrode, a small man with a moustache, thin, a scholar's face, opened a door and called Anna's name. As she went inside, he closed the door and took his seat behind a desk. Behind him was a photograph from the war, orderlies and medical men all smiling, ready to help the valiant men returning from the front line.

He sat down and signalled Anna, with easy and accus-tomed power, to a chair, and asked her solicitously about her health as if that was why she had come. 'How are you this afternoon, Mrs Webber?'

When she answered him conventionally, he pursed his lips and looked serious. 'Your husband was very, very sick with war neurosis. I think he has been depressed a long time. And with symptoms of mania. Did you notice any signs, Mrs Webber?'

Notice it? Notice his lack of appetite for my body, his distractedness? 'He seemed a bit abstracted,' she went so far as to venture. 'And of course he spent a number of days a week up the valley. But he talked a lot about business . . . Sometimes at night he would cry out.'

'Yes,' said Dr Bulstrode, making a note. 'Has he spoken to you much since he came here?'

'A few cries . . . Bits of sentences.'

'But not a proper conversation?'

'Nothing like that.'

'And does he seem angry?'

'No.'

'Then it's a protest? Or a pleading. Please don't be offended. In treatment men tend to speak to us if to anyone. They don't trust themselves to speak to wives and children. Because they love them. It's a kind of self-restraint. They don't want their loved ones to be burdened.'

'He says in his sleep he should have shot the runner.'

'The runner?'

'A German runner.'

He mused on this and then decisively tapped his desk. 'This electro-convulsive therapy – we pass a small shock through the brain. No one knows why it works but it has had rapid results with depression, and a failure to eat, react

47

and speak. I didn't ask you before, but how had his appetite been until . . . until the crisis arose?'

'He's been eating like a bird. His work should make him very hungry, but it doesn't.'

Bulstrode wrote notes again. He was not a bad fellow, she thought, as she studied the crown of his chestnut-haired skull, and not as pompous as some medical men.

But, 'What sort of thing is my husband saying to you?' she asked a little brusquely. For she was offended despite herself that Bert spoke to a man who passed electricity through his brain, and yet not to his own wife.

'Corporal Lembke . . . Has he mentioned him to you?'

'Now and then.'

'You knew Corporal Lembke was killed?'

'Yes, and he was a parson. As well as an ordinary soldier.'

'Yes, not a chaplain. But your husband considers him something of a . . . I suppose, a guru. His death shocked your husband.'

'Yes, I think it did.'

'Now this other thing. He says . . . your husband says, "I saw his eyes." He's convinced he shared a bunker with the man who is now the German Chancellor. The new one. The one with the little moustache. He's convinced of this.'

'He got upset,' she said, 'when he saw the man in a newsreel. That's when he cried out.'

'I don't know,' said Dr Bulstrode. 'But it seems at first sight unlikely, doesn't it? Was the German Chancellor in World War I? An officer? I don't know. I'm a doctor. I have written to the Minister of Repatriation to see if he can help me – perhaps your husband's battalion faced the Chancellor's. But that seems to have brought it all on, doesn't it? Seeing that face. I mean, the newsreel face could

48

have served as a trigger for some standard Germanic face the German Chancellor shares with a million other men, and your husband met one of those million others. But something in the newsreel brought back a memory to your husband, and it was something that had been too much for him to contain. The dam burst, as it were. I think, in time, with the electro-convulsive therapy, he'll make a full recovery.'

Would Bert walk down the street on Friday afternoons again? Would people avert their eyes? It wasn't a town for screams.

'Pardon me,' asked Anna, 'but what happens next?' The way Bert was now did not bespeak 'full recovery' to her.

'It's a matter of continuing the treatment,' said Dr Bulstrode. 'Your husband speaks often before and after the shock therapy. It's a sign it's doing him good.'

'Or that it frightens him,' she dared to suggest.

'I suppose he is frightened,' Bulstrode admitted. 'But not profoundly. Not at the deepest level. Not like he was in the battles. It is not said, but even heroes were frightened in the battles. It was only normal to be.'

The thing was, Bert thought the Chancellor had killed Lembke with the pistol now at home in her bedroom in Kempsey. The Chancellor, or a German like him, had killed the saint. It was all something to do with that.

She complained to Dr Bulstrode, 'He just doesn't seem to recognise me. He thinks I'm someone Scottish. A nurse.'

'Don't be distressed, dear Mrs Webber,' said Dr Bulstrode. He tapped a pencil on the table. *Tap*, to give him an idea, *tap*, to make him frame it. *Tap*, to utter it. 'He talks to me after shock treatment. But it's all from the war. He coughs a lot. From his present immobility, I believe.'

'I think he was gassed,' she said. 'Though he has never said much about that.'

'Oh, he's certainly been gassed,' Bulstrode assured her. 'They all have been. Living in holes in the ground where gas settled.'

She had once seen a picture in a magazine after a gassing. Australian men sitting in what looked like a pasture. Each one with bandages over his eyes.

6

Kempsey and Sydney, New South Wales, 1933

She knew not to expect the boy on time, yet she was sure he was coming. And at the given hour, she looked out of her window and saw him standing in the street, below her fence, with his uncle. The old man was mahogany, of course, and the boy was half-Burley white. For all she knew from their stillness, they might have been there since dawn.

She put shoes on and shed her housecoat and went out onto the veranda to summon them. Or, at least to the extent of calling, 'That's you, Eddie Kelly, isn't it?'

The boy, moored by his tranquil elder's side, called back, 'That's right, missus.'

'And Mr Lyons?'

She saw the man nod.

'Do come in,' she fluted in her voice she thought of as too thyroidal, and although polite, tinged with irritation. They came on, up the emerald embankment of the footpath, and opened her gate and took the path to her door. Except his

51

uncle stopped at the base of the stairs. This man, whose dark eyes were nearly hidden in creases that seemed not tragic but artful and sculpted, and had a reputation for a reliable labourer if you wanted to employ one of the natives. Now he remained baulked at the veranda stairs.

'I won't come in, missus,' he said. 'I'll work on your woodheap till you and Eddie are finished.'

'I'll pay you, Mr Lyons,' she said too quickly.

'I can do it, missus. No need of pay.'

'I won't be long,' cried Flo from the veranda as the boy reached her and she extended a hand to him, to the ill-begotten flesh of his arm.

The uncle was gone then. 'Come inside, Eddie,' she said.

She took him to the kitchen and fed him Adora Cream Wafers, which he quietly devoured, holding them near his chest as if there were phantom claimants to them all around. Then she supervised the washing of hands in the tiled bathroom. From the backyard she could hear the *thunk, thunk* of an axe. It seemed to her an eating sound. A blade with an appetite. It made her hurry him a little into the loungeroom, and then not waste too much time on her measurements.

She had a tape measure, receipt book and indelible pencil, and began on his neck, which was a silken brown. Adjusting his stance with her hands on his shoulders, she saw the column of throat and the perfection of his ear. It struck her that everything about humans was beautiful when they were little and lacked the eye to see it. When they developed a gift for inspecting, they were already on the edge of decay, as she with her hanging, thyroidal under-chin. She could smell a dull earthy scent from the boy's shirt and his back. It was not unpleasant, though a perfect wife would consider it her duty to erase it in a child.

52

She said, like a reproof, 'You have a scab on your neck, Eddie.'

'I had boils, missus.'

'Do you get many boils, Eddie?'

'Everyone gets boils, missus. I broke that one playing cricket, missus.'

'All right,' she said, as if acceding. The voice of the axe impeded her desire to advise or lightly chastise. Burley would be happy to see the heap of wood Mallee Lyons was audibly creating. Flo ran her measure around the boy's waist. 'Oh,' she said. 'So thin despite the humbugs!'

Eddie did not comment. Flesh of Burley's flesh. Burley must be made to read and acknowledge these measurements! The height and thickness of the sin.

Upper leg. And then the foot. Don't forget the foot. Send him to school in shoes, unlike the dairy farmers' kids. From the yard the axe spoke and spoke again. Flo looked at the figures she had. Fairly brisk work she had made of it all. She looked from the figures on the page to the child, neck, shoulders, spine and waist. She obviously had them all right.

She took him back to the kitchen and gave him more cream wafers, then collected two and sixpence to give to Mallee Lyons, and told the boy she would take him back to his uncle, in case he wondered. They stepped out into the back garden and walked to the wood heap and its bare circle of dark, moist alluvium, and met the smell of sap and that lively odour of new-chopped wood that always, even now, had been for her since childhood a signal for hope.

'No need to pay me, missus,' said Mallee Lyons.

'Oh, I must, Mr Lyons.'

She felt the hard edge of the money she pressed into his hand, and the passive reluctance in the dryness of his palm.

She did not know that the uncle and nephew were the first of the town's population who would flee from her because they saw she had been wounded to madness. Mallee knew where he would be taking the boy, far up the river gorges towards the Dorrigo Escarpment, where there were clearings that opened to the sky, where the lad's ability to perceive and be connected to the spirit world and to learn the song of the country would be tested, and where he could grow some armour against the world as it was now, amenable to old power but subject, above all, to the white will.

Up there, where it would take them days of walking to reach, in the past and in the present, a huge serpent had begun the great business of the river, singing the water up out from under the New England escarpment walls. A sportive grasshopper ancestor had collaborated with the hero serpent. Maidens had run and solidified as mountains. Uncle Mallee's view was that Eddie had to be connected to these beings if he was to survive the intentions of Mrs Honeywood. There, under the escarpment, if he proved up to it, Eddie must be made to bleed and outface demons and be comforted by gods and ancestors. Then he would be ready to go back to Kempsey and have a chance against the mania of Flo Honeywood.

Uncle and nephew, they had not even reached Toorooka before Mrs Honeywood visited the tailors in Belgrave Street.

———

Anna Webber's sister Eunice, the fashionable and available young widow, was visited most evenings by a man named Sam Montgomery, an upright gentleman, a year or so younger than Eunice, Anna surmised. Eunice had told him why her sister was down from the bush. Oh, he said, he had heard we did not look after the heroes well enough. He used pomade on his hair, and sometimes called in after cricket matches in his cricket creams, as if wanting to impress Eunice with the idea he was a well-rounded man. And he could speak charmingly and at length about very little, which Anna found a relief.

'I can see that beauty and brains runs in the Peterson girls,' he declared early in Anna's residence with her sister.

How did he know their name was Peterson? Her sister must have told him. And yet she felt something inside her move towards him, bull-artist though he was. 'Beauty and brains.' Film talk. The sort of thing they said about ingénues in Gertie's film magazines. But she liked it. It had never been said of her. It was exactly what Bert would never say. His reverence was all in manners, never in words. And his manners had been suspended now.

Sam Montgomery invited both of them out to dinner at a pub, but Anna said she would sit with the kids, her nephew and niece, and her sister and Sam could go and eat a steak at the Doncaster Hotel. In front of Anna, Eunice seemed half-embarrassed by the attentions of a man like Sam and said to her sister, smiling, 'See, I've got a house, thanks to Trevor. Sam's only got a flat, a flat he rents. He wouldn't mind having a house.'

And that's how Eunice explained Sam's desire. Nothing to do with breasts or hips or the hidden areas, where her husband Trevor, as pneumonia struck him fatally, could not imagine any other man being.

Sam Montgomery was unmarked. Sam had never been gassed. Sam never wheezed the way Bert did when, on a morning of steely frost, he stepped out of the kitchen, and she could hear his hacking receding as his heart and lungs got used to the morning air after the radiant heat of the fierce kitchen stove. You would hear him hawking and whooping to get used to the day, and there was quite a bit of it for a young man.

He had never talked about gas. A man wasn't a complainer! Above all, a man wasn't a hypochondriac. That was the worst thing that could be said of a fellow. And besides, Bert had said early on in the Depression, there are blokes working on the streets half-time who were accountants once, and owned stocks and shares. Sacked now, poor devils. They've got nothing to account for anymore, those accountants. A man should feel sorry for *them*, really, not himself.

Sam Montgomery made Anna aware he had not been sacked by anyone. He sold Buicks from a showroom in William Street. The Buick, he said, was a car bought by doctors and barristers, and people who were still trading – publicans say. Never a shortage of trade for them. And then tobacconists and newsagents – the poison of weed, he said cheerily, and the poison of news. Both could kill you and people paid their last penny for them. There was a limousine company that served ceremonial purposes to whom he had sold a string of Ninety Ls, the luxurious Model 91, silk window curtains, and plush carpet everywhere, even on the tonneau floor. Anna could not have said what a 'tonneau' was, but it was a word that seemed to pay its own way.

'Took a trip out Homebush way,' he told the sisters, he drinking Dinner Ale, they drinking after-dinner tea. 'The owner lets me put a few miles on them so he can sell them a bit cheaper to people who have doubts about paying top money. Out there, off Parramatta Road, you wouldn't

56

believe it. Hills covered with shanties. People living on bread and dripping if they could get it. Two men see a rabbit at once and they want to kill each other for it.'

'Don't worry,' he said further, as if they had accused him of something. 'I know I'm lucky. Damned lucky. Okay, I have to sweep the showroom these days – that's what has happened to us – managers have become cleaners. But I'm not above that. Seeing what other blokes are required to do.'

Since Bert was considered too ill for anyone who was not immediate family to visit, Eunice and her children did not. In the meantime, their minds were set on a Presbyterian Church excursion to Jenolan Caves. Presbyterian Church? Anna had seen a Lutheran Church in Darlinghurst. Eunice's kids knew the itinerary – Lithgow by train and to the caves by bus.

Anna did not like the idea of being alone for days. Gertie was mostly pursuing her own life anyway, and Anna was left on many days to endure the morning and then to sit all afternoon beside a mute, drugged, wheezing husband. The wheeze was his chief conversation too. Dr Bulstrode kept patients like this, drugged solid, unconsciousness being like a skim of ice on top of a bucket of water, with the water sorting itself out on its own terms below the surface. In sleep, said Bulstrode, attributing Shakespeare, the ravelled sleeve of care was knitted up. Great nature's second course, balm of hurt minds, chief nourisher in life's feast.

Anna's sister and the kids were on the way to the caves now and had taken all the excitement out of the house with them, and all the life. As a dairy farmer's daughter, and wife, Anna was in the habit of early waking. She would eat a quick breakfast of porridge, dress well enough for the house in a housecoat, in case some task unexpectedly presented itself.

She would turn on the big Stromberg-Carlson radio, one of the glories of Eunice's house, and listen to the ABC morning news and the songs of the age – 'The Lonely Night', 'Wishing on a Dream', 'Puttin' on the Ritz', and so on. Gracie Fields could lift her spirits with 'The Isle of Capri', and a good tenor like Richard Taubman singing 'Old Father Thames goes marching along, down to the mighty sea'. She hadn't been raised on any German songs herself. She didn't understand the German parts of Marlene Dietrich. It was a surprise when Bert first took her to his parents' nice place at Sherwood, over the river, and she heard the old people, his parents, discussing her straight out in German. Bert had learned a fair amount of German when he was a kid, but by the time the war started he had forgotten most of it, and with the English and Scots people in town looking for businesses with German names on them to blame for the mess of the world, he considered it a fortunate loss. These were the same people who fibrillated with excitement when the Australians captured German New Guinea early in the war. Sometimes he would use a phrase of German or two on the cattle, and you knew he'd heard his father in the paddocks doing that.

At the best of times, she had found the mornings at Eunice's place long, and how long they were now that the nurses had told her that it was no use coming in the morning – that was the time Bert was washed and the time he was wheeled down to the electro-convulsive machine.

On the second time-dragging morning of Eunice's absence there was a knock on the door. She presumed that it was a man delivering from Grace Bros or Foy's, bringing something Eunice had bought, for Eunice was a great shopper and had been since she came to the city, getting away from her parents. Anna took off her housecoat and laid it on a chair and went to answer the door. There was Sam Montgomery, looking very bright and in white shirt and arm suspenders. Beyond him and the little garden, a glimmering green Buick sports coupe, a two-seater, stood by the gate.

Straight away she felt the guilt of this arrangement. The Buick had been brought here to impress Eunice, and as Eunice's sister she was a usurper to admire it in Eunice's absence. That was a sort of incest, wasn't it?

'Oh Sam,' she said, 'Eunice has gone to Jenolan.'

'I know that,' he admitted quickly, to get it said and done with. Colour showed in his well-shaven cheeks. There was an energy in his voice. A lot of men spoke flatly, but she liked energy in a voice, light and shade. Bert had had it, when he was young and when his fat cattle sold well. But then the war, of course, and his modulation grew level and featureless.

'You remember, I said my boss likes to give me an occasional car for a ride, put a few miles on them, take a quid or two off the price and everyone's happy? There's a silk interested in this one. Those gentlemen of the law are still minting money – even when businesses are in administration there's a silver lining for them. Anyhow, he wants to get in a car that's been worked in a bit.'

'Yes', she said. 'I remember when you said that.'

'So I wondered if you wanted to come for a spin to Parramatta and back?'

She knew Eunice would mind. She said, 'I'm not sure Eunice would like that much. Has she ever gone on a spin with you?' She knew that was a dangerous question though, an admission that if Eunice had gone on a spin, she – Anna – might be free to even things up by going for a spin too.

'Sometimes she's gone,' said Sam. 'I'd reckon three or four times.'

She wanted to go. He paused and then assessed the street, turning first to the left, then to the right. It showed he wasn't scared of it. He wasn't scared of its windows or its women.

'You look so much like her, people will think it's her,' he said with a grin when his gaze returned.

'But it's not her. No, it's not. I certainly know that.'

'People are used to seeing me with her, though. No scandal about that. Eunice is a widow.'

'I'm not a widow though.'

Sam grinned. 'I know. You're a good married woman with a sick husband. And that's why a spin won't hurt. Look, Eunice says you put in a long morning, nothing to do. The washing, the cleaning just to pass the time. This morning, just yourself to look after, I'll bet you've done all that already. All the drudgery over, and still you look pretty ritzy.'

She liked him saying that. When he talked, when he uttered his words, they were full of a kind of light, she found, like words in a film which seem ordinary but are going to lead somewhere wild and dramatic. Like words lit from inside. Without inviting him in, she found herself to have consented and to be fetching a jacket from her bedroom. She found her hat and stuck it on with a pin with a mother-of-pearl handle. She took thought then, but didn't want to, fought thought off. She was resolved to go. She went out to join him.

The Buick ran so smoothly – pouring itself forward fluidly on the slate-coloured roads. On Anzac Parade he pointed out the Cricket Ground. 'Ever been to a Test there?'

She was subtly ashamed to say no. 'We listen to it on the radio,' she assured him. 'We haven't had a radio signal for long. Bert likes it a lot. Before the war, Bert played for a place called Willawarrin.' Perhaps she thought that invoking the name of alive but sleeping Bert would stand her in place of armour. Because it was heady to be with someone and enjoy his company, and smell his fragrant presence in a fragrant car.

'Oh, it's marvellous at the cricket. Got my name down to be a member. My boss is a member. For one thing, the Members' Bar is as long as a football field. And there's pictures of all the old players. Demon Spofforth and Bannerman and the Gregory boys, right up to McCabe and Bradman. And if you're lucky, you see the Poms go out to bat, arrogant as old bags, and you see them come back, clean-bowled, with their tails between their legs.'

She felt she was somehow already part of this cricket daydream. 'Can ladies come in?' she asked.

'Oh yes, there's a huge Ladies' stand. Two storeys. Holds a couple of thousand ladies, I reckon. All the charm of Sydney and the bush. And a tearoom up the back. I'm amazed how many ladies come to the cricket.'

'Did you ever take Eunice?' she asked, as if to prove her virtue to herself.

'No,' he said. 'Not Eunice. Taken her to the races. She likes the nags.'

Oxford Street. Past Central Station, and then on to Parramatta Road. He pointed out pubs. This one, he said, was a blood house.

'What's a blood house?' she wanted to know.

'Place where there'll be fights in the public bar. And as for the Ladies' Lounge, I wouldn't like to take any real lady

I know into them. Now that one, The Stag, that's a good house. Good dining room. Aha, here's Leichhardt Stadium. I like that place a lot, there's more stoushes than the stadium at Rushcutters Bay, a longer bill of boxers, and then a ten- or twelve-rounder to finish off. A really good night out. Oh, there's the Coach and Wagon. A blood house. Wouldn't go near it.'

The easiness with which he assessed the city, the way it was divided between what was safe and what wasn't, what was pure fun and what was dull, excited her. As simple a device as it might be, she had never thought of dividing Kempsey that way. After Bert's outcry in the pictures, all of Kempsey was a test. All the pubs – not that she visited any except the Commercial and then only for dinner or to stay overnight with Bert for a cattle sale. Now everything in town gave the same mute, puzzled face to her, and inside, behind the glass, were the same pitying and wondering eyes in one store as in the place next door to it. Two street-fuls of edgy glances – that was the business centre of Kempsey now, where once she had stridden in the glow of the town's respect.

Sam also pointed out the good suburban film houses and the flea houses, where the pictures were so old they'd been made by Moses in the desert.

He drove them through the stench of a tannery, the wafts of metallic vapour from the ironworks and the Western Line, and on into the fragrance of shortbread from Arnott's Biscuit Factory. Soon he pointed out another blood house, the Horse and Jockey.

'Blokes from the abattoirs. Meatworkers' factions. I think they bring their cleavers in there with them. And here's another one, worse – the Sheep Dip. I wouldn't go in there wearing a suit and collar any more than I'd go into a lion's den wearing a pair of swimming trunks.' That idea tickled her. Sam in swimming trunks would look like one of those fellows on Bondi Beach that they filmed in newsreels. Australian Adam.

Without a pause, he said, 'I thought Eunice was a stunner. But by heaven, you're a good sort, Anna. The best to be seen ever, and anywhere on earth. Because you're elegant. Composure, you know. And really pretty . . . *really pretty.* Beautiful.'

Anna felt herself actually choke on his praise. Beauty – like German-ness – was rarely mentioned in the Peterson home, nor amongst the Webbers/Webers. Nor had Bert ever addressed her and indicted her with beauty in straightforward terms. Closest he came was to say once that she was a really nice girl. Not only in the Peterson and Webber families was beauty a rare word, Anna suspected, but rarely uttered north of the Hunter in general. And here it was, the word, lying multi-coloured in her path on Parramatta Road.

Sam Montgomery's recourse to the word frightened her, to the extent she said, 'I think we should go home now. You've got enough miles on your car by now.'

'Ah,' he said, inspecting the dials to see if they bore out her assertion. 'Yes,' he said cheerily. 'Let's turn back at Silverwater.'

She could not argue. Arguing about the terrible word would make things worse, and lead to its repetition, and stupid discourse, along the lines of, 'No, I'm not,' 'Yes, you are.' If this went on, if he continued talking, she might grow less loyal to Eunice, and what a frightful thing that would be, a sort of crime worse than murder of a sister.

'Look,' he said, in a voice of real repentance. 'I really didn't want to upset you. I was stupid. Nothing more from me, I promise. Can we get to Parramatta and back? That's the boss's orders. See, he wants to tell the silk it belonged to a radio personality who kept it a week but decided he couldn't afford it. That would give it what they call *cachet*.'

'Well, if we must,' she said, with an unbeautiful brusqueness, and he took it as she hoped he would. As chastisement.

'Look, I like to be a better bloke than that. I don't like upsetting women. It isn't my character. I had sisters and I had a tender mum, and that helped civilise me a bit. So Parramatta and then home.'

Anna forced herself back into the far corner of her seat. There were silences on the way back, no more talk about blood houses and decent establishments. He drove with his eyes fixed on the tar as if the road demanded he take special care now. So he should. Yet she knew that with her straight-backed distancing from him there was excitement too. She felt a terrible excitement. Shameful and poisonous excitement. The snake had bitten her, and she worked the delicious poison into her system.

In that instant she had not only the fright of her life but a worse thing still: a fear that her life didn't exist as one thing, as the one river of time it had been until now. She had been a woman on one stream, travelling in the river craft of her life. But now she saw she was another woman in another river. She had become a beast and all but cowered against the door of the Buick. Given the power by that other current, she saw herself, even in her recoiled position, sitting beside him, nestled to his shoulder like one of those actresses driving love-struck in the films Gertie loved. The wife who sat by the bed of her husband in his stupor, loyal and waiting for a word from him, was separated by nature from the woman who, if not solaced by Sam Montgomery, would touch herself in lonely pleasure as soon as her head reached tonight's pillow, as soon as the fabric could be hauled up to her waist regardless of creasing, regardless of folding. Somewhere else was the sister gratified that her own widowed Eunice had the company of a male like this. But in here was a ferocious sibling who wanted her sister to drown like Ophelia in the play. Like the devils who spoke to Jesus out of one man – or was it one woman? – her devils were now legion. But one of the wise ones of the legion said to Sam Montgomery, 'Take me back. If you feel any kindness to me and my sister, take me back.'

And when they were back, she did not move, but lay like a waif in her corner of the front seat. She had made him return to her sister's. But in that it was as if she had reached the limit of her virtue, which until today she had thought of as a solid mass. He seemed to understand this and took her inside. They were in the loungeroom, full of the still mid-morning, that hour of tedium, and she was bustling as if it were the most vivid hour she had lived.

'No corset,' he commented when they had, by cooperative effort, shed her powder-grey slip.

'No, not yet,' she said, 'if I can avoid it . . .'

'Those bloomers?' he asked. 'Do all the girls from the bush wear bloomers?'

'I'm not a girl,' she argued.

'No, no,' he said against her ear, 'you are a girl!' And he wrenched the bloomers down and then he reached around with the exact roughness that was needed and undid her bra.

'Did you expect better?' she asked with his lips against her face.

'No, you are better.'

'Then did you expect me to wear those little pants young girls wear?'

'I think you ought to wear just whatever you like,' said Sam, putting his lips close to her ear.

They set to it not on her sister's widowed bed, of course, but on the lounge, which they approached like dancers but closer together and, half-undressed, by careful inches. She watched him unbuckle. He was in his shirt now and levered his shoes off urgently. As he put his serious weight on her, she began to struggle upright, knowing that this would not be briskly done, or achieved, with even breath or halfway calmly. 'I must get towels,' she said.

'Yes,' he conceded, letting her up. She walked away and looked behind for a second, seeing him standing there bare-legged and, in her view, surprisingly like a child. She went to Eunice's towel cupboard and her fingers plucked at the fabric and hauled a number of items out. The ones not chosen she left as they were, uneven, to be straightened later. Then she went back to him. He still stood by the lounge, but now with one hand sheltering her from the sight of his purple prick. She spread the towels across the lounge where, given the promise of her transformation and his, they would, she guessed, be necessary.

7

Sydney, 1915, and Kempsey, New South Wales, 1933

The presence of the remarkable Reverend Lembke in their barracks was announced to Bert Webber by a child, or a near-child, the seventeen-year-old kid from Nulla Creek named Poddy McHugh to whom Bert had attached himself out of geographic, Macleay Valley loyalty, and who had attached himself to Bert for the same reasons. This was in their basic training at Holsworthy Barracks in the hard clay, unalluvial outskirts of Sydney, where shade was a scarce commodity. Poddy came to him in the ten minutes before mess call. They were recruits who had not even yet been issued all their kit, so Poddy wore a vest where a military jacket should be. They would be topped up with military clobber, webbing, puttees and forage jackets before they were sent away, so the sergeant major promised. For men or boys like Poddy, Bert Webber knew, it would be the biggest gift of free clothes any of them would have received, though for himself, because of his provident German father, he had been given tailored clothes from when he was fourteen.

Poddy jerked his thumb in the direction of the interior of the great barracks hut they occupied. 'Bert, you wouldn't believe it, but there's a fellow up there who's a sky pilot.'

Poddy jerked his head then, a display of callow knowingness.

'Bringing us some spiritual comfort, is he?' asked Bert.

'No,' said Poddy. 'Not a padre. One of us. Can you beat it?'

'What does he do about the swearing?' For 'Bloody' and 'My oath!' and 'Christ Almighty!' were the conversational staples of the hut, and men who had never blasphemed before, never been allowed to, were as a sort of conversational armour, damning and blaspheming about every aspect of the new world they had bought into.

'He doesn't seem to notice. One of your mob, Bert. Lutheran.' Then, in a hush, '*Ger-man*, Bert.'

Over stew in the mess hall Poddy managed to introduce the man to Bert. Kurt Lembke was a calm, amused fellow of about twenty-six, a notch or two older than most. He was dark-eyed and a bit olive-skinned, in fact, like an Italian, but his gaze was tranquil. Just the same, there was a lot of movement in his eyes – that was not like parsons, or the Lutheran pastors Bert had to this point seen. Not that there was a Lutheran church in Kempsey since most of the Germans who had come to the valley were Bavarian Catholics. Old Peter Weber had settled amidst a mass of cross-signing southern Germans.

This Kurt Lembke, it turned out, was the son of a Lutheran minister from a place called Thirlmere. It was a place where cliffs lay right behind the sea, and within

68

them coalmines, and some of the miners were German from Saxony. He didn't tell Bert all this at a gulp. Bert Webber learned it over time. Lembke was not a man who waved his information about.

So they met over the Commonwealth government's thin stew in that place loud with the combined lonely crowing of boys who didn't know each other. They all exchanged professions – shop assistant, postal clerk, bike messenger, tailor, fitter and turner. 'Farming,' said some who were cow-cockies' sons, not farmers really, but factotums to their fathers. And everyone took a breath when Lembke said, 'Assistant Lutheran pastor, Woolgoolga.'

'Lots of Lutherans, are there, up Woolgoolga way?' someone asked.

'Yes,' he said. 'Timber millers and cane farmers. A lot down Albury way too, where my father and I come from. We Lutherans marched to the troop train in Albury when all this started, but they wouldn't take us then and so we all marched home.'

Bert would confide that he too had tried to enlist at the start, but men named Weber were not welcome either then. So he had married Anna and they already had a little boy, Christian, by the time the army accepted him.

'Shouldn't you be a chaplain?' Someone brave had asked the Reverend Lembke the question they all had in them.

'They're keeping chaplaincies for the older fellows,' Lembke cheerily explained.

'You could be our chaplain,' offered Poddy in a burst of enthusiasm for this novel being. 'Except I'm a Tyke.'

Laughter and a return to normal conversation: 'Bugger me, Poddy, you're a total bloody bushweek!' and, 'Smell the bloody gum-leaves on Poddy!'

The Reverend Lembke maintained a smile with pursed lips. He wasn't making any pastoral or dogmatic stand. Wasn't he supposed to? Bert wondered.

He was as strong as anyone else, as it proved. He was no complainer and no sar-major's pet. Nor did he kneel by his bed at night or in the morning. If he prayed, it was on the run. He was an advertisement for the Lord's joy, Bert thought, and both liked and suspected him for that. The Reverend Lembke might have attached himself to Poddy for the same reason Bert had – being outraged by Poddy's youth and what could befall him, because he was a child.

Bert's friendship for Lembke grew very gradually in him. There was reticence on his part because someone mentioned he had not only once been rejected for armed service but had been interned for being German. Bert did not think he need work to make a German enclave, a Weber-Lembke alliance. In any case, Kurt Lembke had been born in Australia, like Bert himself.

Meanwhile, a lot of men depended on Poddy to ask Lembke the hard questions, and Bert had to confess he sometimes urged Poddy to ask them. Kurt had actually been born down in Germantown on the Murray. They changed its name when the war began. Then he moved with his father to the coalfields by the ocean. There a rumour got around after war was declared that the wrought iron pillars on his father's balcony were disguised cannons whose barrels could be turned on coastal shipping. As well as that, Lembke senior recited the service in German and gave the sermon in German – had done so for all of his career. Now, however, it was all at once a sign of malice.

'So where did they keep you and your father?' Poddy loyally asked.

Lembke mentioned the place. The camp was at Tatura, on the Murray. Entire families in there. Even a few Turks too. Lonely men. And then one day they called him and his father in – someone, Lembke surmised, had had a look at the iron pillars of the house and found them merely iron pillars. So they were released.

'I saw the job in Woolgoolga, and I took it. But I was discontented and I felt I wasn't doing much good, or pleasing God. So I became a soldier.'

He said 'pleasing God' like someone saying 'pleasing my uncle'.

'Do you feel you're pleasing God now?' asked dear, tactless Poddy.

The Reverend Lembke thought a while. 'I reckon,' he concluded. 'Within the limits of available circumstances. Better than I was in Tatura anyhow. Though it showed something . . . It showed my father and I were loyal.'

The company of men were silent at this assertion. They were all silent, for what had not been true of them until now was rendered true: as simply as that, that the son had shielded the father from judgement.

Kurt Lembke had taken, as if from the air of Woolgoolga, the war of the Empire as just, but he seemed to have few ambitions to command other men. Yet Bert would see him, during the planned rigours of their short training, muttering to this or that man and using his slim authority. And, after he muttered, they seemed to revive or be struck by a new assessment of themselves. They were not transformed, but they did seem ready to reassess their limits as runners, throwers, climbers, clamberers, jumpers and all the other demanding movements of the awaiting battle.

The few who chose to have out and out arguments with him about the existence of God found he could not be riled or rendered bombastic. He said once, 'All arguments about God honour him.' On another tongue, thought Bert, that would be bullshit. But no wonder he wasn't a chaplain, saying things like that. Saying that non-believers honoured God was like saying you didn't need to be inside a church to honour God. Where would things end if Lembke had his way? Somewhere in chaos or in marvel.

Everyone, anyhow, was delighted he was in their battalion, and it was as if he brought some higher sort of pledge with him, an expectation of mercy.

The other thing about it all was he never mentioned the word 'sin'. Bert kept waiting for it and believed it had to happen. Lembke had to condemn something – because that's what ministers of religion were for, in the view of most.

Soon enough after, when they were aboard the troopship *Mentor*, the medical officer did the sin talk by giving them a pretty blunt lecture about what happened to boys who caught a disease from visits to women in the Wasser in Cairo. A young man, even a virgin until the fatal night, said this doctor, could catch syphilis or gonorrhoea, and those diseases could last a lifetime and blight all homecoming and hopes. First, you had to face doctors and nurses who knew exactly what you had done. Then you were put in a special ward cut off from contact with the honourably wounded, and shipped home. What did you say then to your mother, your girlfriend or, God forbid, your wife? You must avoid them all, and how do they understand that, or how do you explain it? You can never marry or resume a marriage without spreading the disease.

This, with pretty impressive diagrams and photographs, did chasten young men. Sin was its own wrath-of-God lecture.

On the *Mentor* in the Indian Ocean, the Reverend Lembke did not scream out against gambling. But he did take care to check up on the two-up kip, the wooden flipper, that is, which held the two pennies, the pennies themselves, the ringmaster and the boxer – the keeper of order and taker of bets. Bert saw him one day, kip in hand, having a trial throw of the coins on the deck aft, and the boxer yelling, 'Struth, you're a bloody natural, Lemmie!'

When they got to Egypt at last and were put on the train from Suez to Cairo, they were camped out beyond the Nile near the Pyramids, and for their first Cairo leave Kurt Lembke took them on a tour of the Orthodox Cathedral at Abbassia. Everyone was sheepish about stating any wish to visit the cathedral of the flesh, Haret el Wasser. Lembke bent his efforts on stopping Poddy being taken by a gang of rowdy soldiers to that seamy district. Men who came back from a visit there always said their girl was clean and they had no worries. Because the Australians had 'whacked the place into shape' with a riot there, and ever since the brothel owners 'took special care' of Australians.

Kurt Lembke's comfort was a quiet beer with Bert. 'Beer's very German, isn't it, Bert?' he asked. And then, in a lowered voice one day, 'Better not say that, eh?' Then loudly he said, 'Beer is very, very British.' And winked. Bert remarked, in the spirit of the wink. 'Wurst is very British too. But we don't call it that anymore. We call it devon.'

'Here's to devon!' called Kurt Lembke. 'And down with Wurst!' By then he knew Bert's secret, that he wasn't really a British Webber. Bert had confessed to being a Weber, a remote relative of the composer, Fritz, on his father's side.

'Do you speak German?' asked Lembke under his voice, not wanting to be misunderstood.

'Not a lot. A bit. I could understand my parents when they spoke.'

Lembke grimaced. 'Might be useful in the circumstances,' he confided with a wink.

Since Lembke seemed to have no need to chase men off to church, Bert even confessed to him that he was a Lutheran masquerading as an Anglican. 'You're not like other parsons,' said Bert in the tent in Giza. 'They don't always look as if they're enjoying being alive.'

'Enjoying?' said the Reverend Lembke, now newly promoted to Corporal. 'Have you ever read Luther's *Table Talk*?'

Bert confessed he hadn't. Luther, said the Reverend Lembke, *enjoyed* life. He had a big dining table and they ate well, he and his wife Katie, from their big vegetable garden. In those days they ate dinner at ten o'clock in the morning, and then supper in the late afternoon. Exiled priests about to take the Lutheran path, escaped nuns, and many churchmen and government officials came to the house, and some of them naturally enough wrote down what he said.

'You'd be surprised what he talked about,' Lembke told Bert. 'He rejoiced in being human. He could talk about itching and sweating as much as he did about the soul. He even talked about going to the lavatory. Its place in the big scheme. He also said it was best to live openly amongst the people, not secretly in monastic cells. It was a new way of doing things. And he said people must let God look after sustaining the church, that if we think we can sustain it we

74

are total idiots. He and his wife were normal people, hard up too. And had to farm and take lodgers.'

Bert could see why Lembke believed he should be here, or at least why he didn't believe his church would suffer while he was here, with the others in their bell tent. This was his farming, his taking lodgers.

Thus Bert found he admired Lembke a lot. Lembke did not seem to struggle to influence his companions. He was what he was, and let God and the world make what they could of it. Bert had never met anyone like that. It was so consistent that it developed a prophetic weight. Christ in the ordinary man, the ordinary man in Christ. And being, as he suspected, very ordinary himself . . . somehow he could not avoid its claim on him. And this sang along with the purpose of the Australian force, an army of volunteers gathered from unexceptional boys bringing to Europe their post-colonial greenness without affectation or evasion. Bringing their table talk to the big bloody slanging of the world!

———

Johnny Costigan read of County Kerry again by pure chance, from a years-out-of-date *Sydney Morning Herald* at Chicken's place one Saturday night, not long after he took the job at Nulla Creek and his association with Chicken began. There was this old newspaper sitting on Chicken's table and willing to reveal to him, the people in Ballyseedy, Knocknagoshel – yes, these country places were named in the report as if they were just down the New South Wales coast – and the whole County Kerry, site of lovely Killarney, now called the period in which Johnny lost his soul, March, of the worst year, 1923, Terror Month. The idea consoled him.

He had not lost his soul to any normal month then! You might find all the most baleful words to label a foul month and it was a little balm to the heart that after years, the month of all months was called Terror.

There was a world somewhere, thought Johnny, almost touchable in mist, in which the rebels triumphed. For they had been right, and to cure them of being right, unprincipled savagery of the kind the Sassenach had only dreamed of visiting on the Irish was in that awful March visited by the Irish themselves upon the Irish themselves. Savagery so deep that for people ever to begin to address each other politely in Cork or Kerry or Limerick in future days, said savagery would need to be denied and deliberately swallowed down, forever.

Not that he mentioned a word to Chicken. To Chicken, Kerry was a girl's name.

Kerry where all this was proven. Kerry, the apple of God's eye and the core of hell. Let no fatuous tenor sing of its charms ever again.

By Killarney's Lakes and fells.
Emerald Isles and winding bays . . .
Mountain paths and woodland dells
Memory ever fondly strays . . .

In Kerry, in the end, people saw monstrosities visited on the flesh of Sinn Fein, the rebels, the republican boys from the midst of our towns and fields. Ireland could not find its soul any more than Johnny could find his.

It was said of Kerry people that they are not a casual people! The Atlantic zephyrs – to satirise the gales that blow Kerry's way – blow them all one way. There is only one way to lean.

In any case, rebellion was automatic in parts of Kerry.

76

Johnny's da, Joe Costigan, had been living off the country-
side since 1916, and Johnny was at home with his mother
through all her dying. She considered one of her blessings
that her daughter Mimmie, three years older than Johnny,
had emigrated to America and was engaged to a solid older
Irishman in Cleveland, Ohio, and thus well out of that valley
of tears that was Ireland. It was a mercy the Tans didn't burn
their house down until his ma had departed in the cold snap
of November of the year of the Armistice. Johnny had been
serving as a runner, and his father was in the hills fighting
the British Army and, after that, the British Army in its
other and newer forms, the Black and Tans, police made
up of old British soldiers, and the Auxiliaries, a corps of
British officers left unemployed as the victor's cup refused to
brim over for the gobshites.

While his da was a man who lived like a wolf for three
years, a creature of caves and haggards and shanties and
ruins, Johnny was at home alone when the Tans came
in the spring of 1919. They came because of a railway
house burning. At that stage, the railways liked to employ
Protestants for fear Paddy employees might be intimidated
by some republican relative to derail a train, or to look
sideways while a rail was dug up or dynamited. And along
with the jobs came the good railway houses. What a job it
was, designed in heaven, to keep a railway station and live
in a house fit for a parson! In the winter of early 1919, the
rebels were great burners of houses that supported the Tans
and British rule. These were often grand houses doomed
to burn, in the end. But along with the grand houses went
those of the railwaymen who informed and helped the

Tans. A railway residence was set afire at Abbeyfeale, just over the border, on the rail line from Listowel to Limerick. There were four kids in the family, but they would not go long without a shelter.

From some informer the Tans heard Joe Costigan's name as involved. They turned up in a squad car they left running in the lane, and busted into the kitchen with beer on their breath. They told Johnny to get out. 'This is for your arsonist old feller!' they told him. Johnny was scared, almost to peeing, since he thought they'd kill him in vengeance as well as burn the place. But they wanted him to report to his da, they said, and his da's commandant. They had the brutal air of men whose worst impulses were allowed and sanctified by the state. 'We'll fucking come for you and your father in time, you Paddy cunt!' they promised.

The house burned pretty quickly, they used so much petrol, and Johnny joined his father. Children of the Wolf, both of them for another two years, until peace came at high summer in 1921 after eight hundred years, and he and his Da could come to town again!

8

Sydney and Kempsey, New South Wales, 1933

Bert's eyes were open, but – upturned – saw neither ceiling nor any other speck of air between.

'Look at me,' Anna insisted aloud, not kindly, one of her demons causing her to become threatening. Then she said, 'Bloody well look at me!'

She did not know where the *bloody* came from. Had she ever used that word before? It was the word from the timber mill where her father had worked part of the time, an ordinary word yet when uttered in her hearing when she was a child it had slashed her like a scythe. She did not know why, apart from the belting children got from their parents for using it. But it seemed to her the final hopeless word. Once you said it, there was nowhere else to go, no greater prayer or curse to be uttered if the world had let you down – or so she understood. It was the word used when the logs fell off the carefully laden timber jinker, or the buzz saw jammed and no one knew what to do next. She didn't know what to do next and in the wake of Sam, that was how she used it now. Like one of the men in the yard. *Bulluddy*. As the gods turned on them.

Bert's eyes moved not an inch. His machinery was jammed. If he had said to her, 'Hello, dear!' it would have cured her and brought her back, gathering all her various strands into the one coherent woman. She thought it was so easy a thing for him to give her, and he couldn't give it.

'You're talking inside yourself well enough,' she muttered aloud. He was back there talking about France behind his forehead, inside his head. Occasionally a word of that escaped him. So why can't he find a word to heal me? Why can't he come back to this safe and ordinary room in Randwick? Why had his fear and his memory come up and clobbered him on the head and taken him away like a kidnapper? Turning him twenty-two again, stripping him of the knowledge of who he was – a man who owned fat cattle and dairy cows that were even now, at this hour of the afternoon, beginning to traipse by habit to the milking sheds of Hickeys Creek and Nulla and Mungay.

Then I'll give myself to Sam whenever he asks, she nearly said, but kept it unspoken because it would be such a frightful thing to let loose into the air. I'll give Sam to myself, said her inner mad woman by way of amendment. If you don't talk before four o'clock, my legion of demons will all fly to Sam!

He was back there, Bert, at the back of his head, mumbling to someone about France or Belgium. Who was the object of his talk? Poddy or that dead Lutheran? Why can't he find a word to heal me? Why couldn't he borrow one from his Lutheran saint?

Then, just for a variety of misery, the Eunice question rose in her. There could not be any more frenzy with Sam. Not until there was clear air on another day, when Eunice got back from the caves in Jenolan. Not even then. Seated, she began to pray to God, her Tower, in the hope he would take her safe and free of desire into his ramparts. From there she could look down, from a height of love and calm, on Eunice and Sam and mute Bert. From there the saved woman would be outraged at the idea of Anna widowing Eunice this second time.

But nothing lifted her from her morass of lust. God decided that none of the women she was was a woman fit to be raised up to a height of salvation.

'Lord God, you have called your servants to ventures of which we cannot see the ending, by paths as yet untrodden, through perils unknown . . .'

'Oh God it is your will to hold both heaven and earth in a single piece.' A single piece was what she wanted. She got up and gathered up her handbag from the floor. She was even tempted to abandon it. What did it have that she needed? Her mirror and some rouge and a lipstick she rarely used – she had always been vain of her fuller lips, which she got from her grandmother on her father's side. She had, in her purse with fifteen shillings in it, a pink ten bob note and a crown, all that a modest-spending wife of an upriver big cow-cocky should have for her careful and provident disposal.

'I should of shot him, I should of,' Bert sometimes pleaded in his sleep and she would settle him with a gentle hand to his back.

'If you'd shot the runner we would have all been better off,' she asserted, blunt as she could be.

But there was no answer of course.

'Goodbye then, Bert,' she said. She was almost spiteful, it was a struggle with demons to put some kindness into the farewell.

With his brain stuck in some murky trench in France, could he hear her? He was there perhaps forever. His rotting feet in mud slop – the foot he'd lost toes from in the war's last winter. His legs wrapped up in heavy hessian bags – that was what they did, he'd told her once, because puttees cut off the blood to the feet. He was with Poddy and the Lutheran padre still off leaning over a Tommy cooker, waiting for the healing word to be spoken by Dr Bulstrode.

Why couldn't he just climb out of that trench and say, 'Hello, Anna.'

She went without saying another thing, walked out on him. Here's my back, Bert! She rushed down the stairs and out of the hospital, not trying to take the eye of any nurse, though she had done until now after each visit, looking for a dutiful reassurance. She was not hoping to run into Dr Bulstrode, and get from him a promise of a remote cure. If France is a place where you will hide and not climb out of it, then I too have a place where I can hide.

A tram came creaking by, the conductor on its footboard. Grey-faced people looked out at her, as if they were all sick and had always turned their backs to the city's reputed sunshine. Without warning, a softer woman rose in her, a woman less driven along by fury. Thank God, she said, and stopped. She pressed a grass verge with the toe of her brown shoe. But then: 'What is that shoe doing on my foot?' A foot slender enough not to be encased in normal dung-coloured leather. There's a world of difference between brown and tan. Tan's a colour for women who think they haven't finished yet with love or flirtation or whatever it is. They haven't sung their last song. They haven't decided that they'll never hear a man call them pretty, or a good sort or a bottler of a girl, or lovely or – that extremist word – beautiful. But murky brown shoes are the shoes of a woman who has given in. Brown shoes declare as they press up Belgrave Street that they are the shoes of a-big-man-from-upriver's wife. There's nothing of allure in them to make men and women wonder or surmise.

I'm going to Anthony Hordern's to buy tan shoes, she decreed to herself. I wish to be praised in tan shoes by Sam. Her mind settled round the idea of tan like water settling over a sinking stone. But two stones followed it like comets. Yellow. Blue. Yes, yellow. I'm not sallow and can wear it. I tend to be olive of complexion, and my parents and grandparents commented on it. A Spanish sailor in that girl! You see that now and then in Hanover.

For Hanover people were usually meant to be pale as milk.

Tan for now then! Anthony Hordern's would have them. If she wore tan then that was it. She would have to give herself up to Sam. She would root and fuck and spread and part and be a disgrace at her age! At *her* age. At the best age for it. It would happen in spite of children and in spite of cattle and butter prices.

A new forgiveness for Bert came to her. Everyone said the front in France had been so terrible and such a chaos. Experience of it had filled Kempsey with drunks, fellows who could only converse and laugh bitterly with their own in the front bars of the Railway and Commercial and Federal, men who could neither stay with their families nor go, men who died – while she was still a young woman – of gassed lungs or by their own guns or like Collie Gulstone, one of her father's managers, of cutting deep with razors into the elbows. How terrible for Bert that the trenches claimed him, that he was forced to man them even now. Or was coming home an even greater terror?

It didn't matter which. Her sympathy could be with Bert. Her desire had nothing to do with him. The association of her children with this same city, their astonishment at what she was thinking had they known the thoughts she had, seemed to her matters thin as wafers, shreds of paper bark being blown along the pavement outside the sanatorium garden, as – in fact – fragments of paper bark were that very afternoon.

Her parents and grandparents. She had no ill will towards them. The problem with keeping girls from temptation, though, as she was kept from temptation, was that they were bewildered when at last the serpent in the garden spoke to them. They had never heard such a delicious voice, a voice that went through them and emerged from them and struck them again. When snakes ran from her tread in the noon grass, it had been not they that hissed but the thrashing grass they weaved their way through that made the same, the one music. She felt she could hear the grass sizzle. The people on another tram on its way to Kensington gawped at her face – at least she thought so – her flesh aglow with the flame to be seen behind it.

———

Plain things had to be done. She grilled a chop for herself. Potatoes and peas in the one saucepan. She ate the chop quickly and the smell of it grew thin and cold in the kitchen air. When the bell rang at the door – a little imitation of a ship's bell Eunice's dead husband had once installed there, standing back to smile at how it enhanced his ownership of this house – she three-quarters expected it. She walked languorously to the door. The bell rang again. Opening, she found Sam in mid-ring. With a desperate lack of secrecy, Sam seemed the possessor of the bell.

'Ah, well,' he said. She recognised him – it was not a matter of her eyes but a movement of blood. He said, 'Did you know I'd be here?'

'I would have known even if you hadn't turned up,' she said. He began to laugh in a way that looked as if he could well be crying.

'How do you work that one out, Anna?'

'Would you like some tea?'

'I like tea,' he said, and seemed to do some semaphore-style eyebrow-crinkling that showed equally appreciation for tea leaves and desire. She asked him in. In the hallway, as she had known would happen, they began tearing at each other. She had earlier stepped out of her shoes. He pulled at the lower part of her dress.

She said, 'My darling.'

'Am I a mongrel?' he asked between two kisses.

'Am I a tart?' she asked, not knowing where the question came from. Bert had handled her as if she might break. Someone had told him too much when he was young, that women were fragile. Sam handled her as if she was a needful creature, hungry for bread, his hand under her crinkled-up dress and on the waist of her elastic bloomers. As if she was an equal to him in sinew.

An hour later, during an interval in their joy, they heard the front door open and Eunice cry, 'We caught the early train for a change. From Lithgow!'

One morning when Chicken entered Tsiros's Refreshment Rooms, he was astonished to see Mrs Burley Honeywood sitting before a cup of tea with her hat off and her back to the walnut panelling with its white pinewood bas-reliefs of Diana the Huntress and sundry other heroes and heroines from Olympus. It was not that she was there that surprised Chicken, but rather that she, a woman people could depend on for near invisibility, now presented her naked white face so fully to the town, unconscious of that fact as she might be. It was like seeing her for the first time in her separate skin, as more than a shadow of Burley. Sometimes people who had never really met Chicken, but accepted him as a being of the night, only fully lit when he took to the piano in the Victoria, all at once *saw* him, often when he was conversing person to person – saw him not for the performer they had thought him to be but as a separate human being, a mother's son abroad, a ship afloat in his own water. And this being the first time he had seen her alone and so open to be addressed, he was surprised. Her broad face, he thought, was striking. It was very white-complexioned and thus a little unsuitable for the sub-tropic climate and he thought what a joy it would be to make her face for her. She should do it herself, of course, but somehow had never received permission to do so.

He noticed now that her face seemed nakedly bleak as well as unhealthily white. Blank canvas as it might seem to be to Chicken, it was not blank. It looked to carry news of some domestic calamity but in a language Chicken could not understand. He was pleased to nod to her politely and then took his own seat. Yet there was an itch in him to speak to her. He hoped he could manage it somehow.

A kid from the camp at Burnt Bridge in South Kempsey came in, he noticed. Yes, a kid of about ten years, probably on the hop from Burnt Bridge school. This too was worth looking at, since Kostas Tsiros didn't like to have the blacks in. His was an establishment, after all, that hosted wedding breakfasts. The child, having entered, saw Chicken and a broad smile took management of his face.

'Gidday, Mr Chicken,' he chanted. He was a mad creature Chicken knew from the Victoria, likely to run berserk around the stalls until the lights went down, at which point he became riveted to his seat in enchantment. Like everyone else.

'Hello, Cecil,' cried Chicken with a dubious irony, as if he feared some display of mayhem. 'Isn't school on?'

'Auntie Dot visiting from Cherbourg Mission, Mr Chicken. We're all home for the day. I run ahead of my mummy and auntie and the little kids.'

'Ah, that's a good story, Cecil, and I'd stick to it if I were you.' This irony seemed something he might engage Mrs Honeywood in, and he looked at her, but her eyes were entirely for the child. Again, there was something unprotected and excessive in the way she studied him.

'They sent me to look at the sweets and boiled lollies for the little kids. They need something soft.'

And he stepped back and began to assess the sweets and chocolates behind Kostas's display glass. Mrs Tsiros, former Greek goddess by the cash register, exchanged a look with Kostas, who had emerged from the kitchen, rubbing his hands on his apron. Kostas clearly thought Cecil was subjecting his merchandise to an undue scrutiny.

He said, 'Boy, you got any money?'

The boy admitted he didn't. Auntie Dot would, he said. She was coming.

'This isn'a art gallery,' said Kostas. 'You oughta bugger off, you people! I call the police, and you gone along the river to Kinchela Boys' Home. You leave now, you little bugger!'

It was a to-be-expected end to Cecil's reconnaissance, Chicken thought. But then he saw Mrs Honeywood close her eyes a few seconds in contemplation, and snap them open as if in receipt of revelation, and stand up. She had fine, raw proportions, and the town no doubt under-appreciated her because of her mode of movement and her posture. Chicken was still expecting to see the ejection of Cecil as a predictable outcome. But Mrs Honeywood said in contralto, 'I'll pay for what this young man chooses, Mr Tsiros.'

Kostas was not happy but knew he must now enter into negotiation with Cecil. Legislating the exchange, Mrs Honeywood had come up to the counter and said to Cecil, 'You choose what you would like.'

Cecil was chastened too. Everyone was chastened except Mrs Honeywood. 'Aunt Dot's just on her way, missus,' he pleaded.

'It doesn't matter, I'm very happy to get you what you want.'

And so Cecil applied himself to the calculus of: 'Two of them, mister, four of the soft ones, yeah, and then please four of the yeller and red . . .'

His mother and aunt and three younger children were on the pavement, looking in in affright, as if they never intended the exuberant Cecil to enter this shop, which was probably true.

'Come in, ladies,' called Mrs Honeywood.

Chicken thought now that all this was getting to be madness and that something had caused Mrs Honeywood to depart from the normal protocols of the town. No woman of Mrs Honeywood's civic station called out, 'Come in, ladies,' to the downriver Thunguddi people of Burnt Bridge.

'Come in please, ladies,' she called yet again. 'Bring your kiddies.'

Chicken was convinced he should go, but as he stood up he saw Kostas behind his counter shake his head, almost pleadingly. Stay in case we need the good offices of a pianist!

And thus, as Chicken now saw, a white matron welcomed to her table two Thunguddi women and four of their brats, the latter utterly enraptured and absorbed in a bag of sweets each, to drink tea. For that was what Mrs Honeywood ordered. And Chicken, for his friend Kostas's sake, sat on and kept Kostas and Mrs Evdokia Tsiros company in this humiliation.

He tried to listen to the conversation Mrs Honeywood was running. She was asking the women about their children. One of them belonged to Dot from Cherbourg, and the other three were Cecil's mother's. And out of nowhere, as if it were not a question forbidden and cauterised off, Mrs Honeywood asked about whitefellas coming to Burnt Bridge, and whether they had ever troubled these women who were sitting beside her. She asked the unaskable with a scientific curiosity that was somehow pitiable and certainly – though she did not even seem to know it – scandalous.

Auntie Dot said, 'There's always whitefellas. My sister lost a child to a whitefella. If your people tells you, you do it . . . the whitefella is like a ghost, missus. And he comes into camp yammering and yammering and saying he'll have us all locked up, and by God, he can get us all arrested too, don't doubt it. "I'll tell Sergeant Ives lock up your husband, girlie!" And they keep at it, top of the voice and the kids beginning to cry and in the end it's less trouble to lie down there with a man and get him to leave.'

'You really think white men are ghosts?' asked Mrs Honeywood, but as if the idea had occurred to her as well.

'We know they are ghosts,' said Cecil's mother.

'But then they give you half-caste children,' protested Mrs Honeywood.

'They give us our children,' she said. 'The ones waiting to be born.'

Cecil's mother began to laugh at the idea of it. 'The kids . . . they aren't ghosts.'

Mrs Honeywood said, 'Except these men are not ghosts. How I wish they were. They are not ghosts. You must understand, ladies. I wish they were ghosts too. But they rule the world. The living and the dead.'

The women looked at each other, large-eyed and nervous and choosing to dissent.

'Do you think, for example, that these men have wives?' asked Flo Honeywood. 'And that their wives don't want them there?'

It was clear that this was an aspect the women had not thought of. 'I don't lie with white men anyhow, missus,' Dot asserted. 'My husband is a good fellow and does not hanker for the rosehip syrup and methylated spirits some fellas will sell their missus for.'

'But,' Mrs Honeywood insisted, frowning, 'what about the children? Does any white man who conceives a child on a black woman ever put any money into the care and upbringing?'

Both women laughed with a soft pity.

'They're just all blow-bys,' Cecil's mother confided in a soft voice. 'That's what whitefellas call the kids.'

'But do the white men who conceive them . . .? Do they help the mothers out? Maybe pay for the child's education . . .'

Poor woman, thought Chicken. Asking such a question? But he did not move.

Both the downriver women laughed shortly and then repented of laughing. 'No, missus,' said Aunt Dot. 'White-fellas like to forget. Sometimes they've gone away from a place after the time it takes a baby to come, and don't ever know.'

Mrs Honeywood sat back, objecting. 'My husband went to your camp, or the other one. Do you think the woman who accommodated my husband . . . and by the way, I know who it is . . . do you think she thought my husband a ghost?'

The women from Burnt Bridge were embarrassed to hear this, as if they thought they might be blamed.

'Lot of the old people,' Dot confided, 'they think all of you are ghosts, missus.'

I know who the ghosts are, Chicken mentally asserted. I know who lives on the edge of town and is let onto the streets on sufferance. And speaking of sufferance, he could see Kostas by the cash register weighing what to do about the white woman and the two black women chatting like matrons, and the little kids who stood and sat around the group, their jaws working strenuously on the lollies, their noses running.

'We are not ghosts,' said Flo Honeywood. 'Our deaths are still ahead of us, as they are with you. In the meantime, I assure you, we're here.' And extraordinarily she exposed the flesh of her forearm and pinched it until it began to bruise. Then she displayed it. 'You see that?' she asked.

The two Aboriginal women looked at each other. It was not that she was angry at them. But she seemed aggrieved all right, and it was hard to tell who with. Because she even seemed aggrieved she wasn't a ghost.

'Do you know a boy called Eddie Kelly?' she asked.

'We all know the Kellys,' Cecil's mother said.

'I should hate his mother,' announced Flo Honeywood would like a scholarly proposition. 'I should want to claw her eyes out. But I don't. And she's dead, anyhow.'

'And big Alice,' murmured Dot, happy to have something to say. 'She's raised him. Big Alice Kelly.'

This has gone far enough, thought Chicken, almost blushing, and the women at the table with Flo Honeywood would, he was sure, have agreed with him. But they were all barely breathing at the same time, in the half-hope Kostas might close the conversation down. His old man's hearing, however, might not have been up to the task. In any case it was as if Flo were conducting a post-mortem at her table and the entrails of the town were being exposed, and Kostas would certainly not like that.

'I should hate the boy's mother,' said Flo again. 'But I don't. Do you think there's something wrong with me?'

The two black women again exchanged glances. They were not going to venture on that subject. But Flo pursued it. 'I want to help the boy. But I can never get close to him.'

'We could tell the family, Mrs Honeywood,' Cecil's mother offered. 'But Eddie might be up the country with his uncle.'

'I have no objection to meeting Mrs Kelly,' Flo said. 'I have no malice towards the family. It's my husband I'm angry with. I'm very angry with him. With men like him. But I am not by nature an angry woman.'

This was true, Chicken knew, in the sense she was not usually dangerous, indeed not usually notable in the least. But some shock . . . her husband? . . . had made her dangerous, and her present conference with two Thunguddi women showed it. She had created a whole new form of conference for this town. She might even be dangerous enough to have her face done, Chicken surmised.

'Then I'll tell the family,' said Cecil's Aunt Dot. Chicken saw that the two young Aboriginal mothers wanted desperately to be released by Mrs Honeywood now, sent back to the plain pavements with their lolly-gnawing kids.

It was Kostas who intervened at last and seemingly by impulse. His apron tied above his paunch, he wandered over and asked Mrs Honeywood, did she need anything more? He had the capacity of all good waiters to mask clear hostility in undeniable subservience, to let people know their lease on a particular table had expired.

She got the message too, and seemed for a moment abashed.

'Yes, we must free this table, ladies,' she said as if the place were crowded. The two Aboriginal women began gathering their kids, and calling in relief, 'Thanks for the tea and lollies, missus.'

They were worried for her, it was obvious. Someone who had done them the great compliment of having tea with them in Tsiros's flash restaurant. They did not know whether to wait for her on the pavement before making their way through the rest of town. Chicken himself solved the puzzle for them by intercepting her as she made her way to the counter to pay.

'Mrs Honeywood, may I introduce myself?'

'There is no need for any introduction, Mr Chicken Dalton.'

Her eyes flickered towards her lost sisters on the pavement.

'I overheard you mention the Kellys,' he said, lowering his eyes.

She looked affrighted and even hostile.

'Just the one thing you said. The Kellys. I know the Kellys.' He smiled. 'Was it Alice Kelly . . .?'

She considered him. Her eyes were doleful but, he thought, not passively doleful; far more dangerously and actively so.

'Can you tell her to come and see me?' she asked.

'Certainly. Though you could meet at my place in Clyde Street if you chose. We could all have tea.'

She studied him and for a second she was calculating and then seemed with a shake of her head to throw the calculations out. Kostas was meanwhile relieved that the Aboriginal women and children were gone from the pavement outside and clearly considered Chicken an improvement on them as a conversational mate for Mrs Honeywood. No prospective wedding breakfast booking would be cancelled because of it.

'That is most kind,' said Mrs Honeywood. She took further thought. 'You say you know her . . .?'

How? was the implicit question.

'I . . . I like cosmetics. Perhaps it's because of the pictures. I make Alice up now and then.' He shrugged. 'I would make anyone up. I just love those pastes and powders. Miracles of the age, I think. Of any age.'

'Yes,' said Mrs Honeywood, emphatically agreeing. 'When you put it like that. When can you get Mrs Alice Kelly in then? Say, well, tomorrow afternoon?'

'As soon as that. I'll get some Aboriginal kids to go up to Burnt Bridge and give her the message. Three o'clock tomorrow, then. But you know my house in Clyde Street?'

Mrs Honeywood gave a sudden smile as if all the most apt sentences and reactions were coming back to her, and so it was with a little irony she said, 'I have had it pointed out to me. The famous pianist . . .'

'Renowned only in the Macleay, I fear.'

'Still,' she said. 'The Macleay is a start.'

'Only thing,' Chicken warned her tentatively, 'I'll summon Alice, who owes me a favour in return for all the free makeup. But you can never be sure when . . .'

'I'm fully prepared for her to be late,' Flo assured him. And she paid the bill Kostas put down on the counter.

'Good,' said Chicken, enthused. 'We can chat while we wait anyhow.' In honour of her neglected complexion, he said, 'I have interesting makeup journals too, I can show you.'

She stared at him as if he were suddenly speaking French. Then the poor woman nodded and left without another word. She did not look at Kostas and his wife. It was as if she didn't have time.

9

Kempsey, New South Wales, 1933

Three o'clock came that appointed afternoon for the encounter between Flo Honeywood and Alice Kelly, and by half past, the tea Chicken had chosen from David Jones and had had freighted to him on the train, the Oolong Black Dragon, was turning cold in Mrs Honeywood's cup. Bloody Alice, he thought. After all the special care and artistry, she keeps me waiting.

He apologised to Flo Honeywood but she held her hand up and said as a matter of fact, 'I can wait. I have been waiting all along.'

Indeed, she spoke as if waiting years was not out of the question. Chicken's nervousness was that if Alice knew what this was, if she had spoken to the other women, she might not even turn up. And he would still be begging Flo Honeywood's pardon at six-thirty before he rushed to the cinema.

And then there Alice was, fully present with a smell

of Yardley's talc and sweat, and carrying heroically her enormous bosom. Calling from the gate, 'Hey, Mr Chicken! Are you home?'

He had jumped to admit her, grateful to see her confirmatory substance, Big Alice. Capacious and with a sway on, and lipstick applied carelessly but in quantity on her big lips. 'The lady here?' she cried.

In the loungeroom Flo Honeywood stood to greet her. Had he heard her aright. That Burley had done the great dance with Alice's sister? And, here, Burley's wife standing as he led Alice in and asked did she want any tea? The offer was a stimulus to Alice, who had seen Mrs Honeywood and was tempted to go quiet and even reverential. Instead she seemed overtaken by hilarity at the offer. 'You got the same tea, have you, Mr Chicken?'

'Yes, Alice. It's my special.'

'Well, I think I decline with thanks, Lord Chicken,' she told him, humour in her eyes. It vanished when she looked towards Flo Honeywood. No long, teasing connection lay between the two women as between Chicken and Alice.

'Would you sit down, Mrs Kelly?' asked Flo in her flat contralto voice, and as if by right of occupancy, sitting herself.

Chicken watched Alice slide sideways into a chair.

'I was interested,' said Flo, straight to the point, 'in your nephew Eddie.'

Alice looked flustered. Flo seemed to appeal to Chicken, as if to remind him he had promised a private session with Alice. Chicken nodded and collected his makeup manuals and took them out to the veranda to leave the two women alone. Just the same, he hoped to hear quite well the discourse between them.

'Oh Eddie,' Alice said. From where Chicken intended to settle and be discreet, he saw her blinking in a way that expected the worst.

And he could clearly hear Flo.

'I believe my husband begot Eddie on your sister, Mrs Kelly. I hope I express it clearly. That is, my husband lay down with your sister some ten years back and the result is Eddie.'

Chicken could hear Alice leaning forward to deny. 'No missus, I don't remember my sister ever had any time with your husband, that Burley. No!'

'You needn't worry. I feel no trace of vengeance against you, Mrs Kelly, nor your late sister. I don't know why. But it is all a tragedy, isn't it?'

'Because,' ventured Alice, 'men aren't worth fightin' about, I reckon, missus.'

For the first time since Chicken had renewed his acquaintance with her, Flo laughed.

'It would be nice if that were true. In any case, I don't want to fight you. I am sad for both of us. Why is that so?'

'Missus, I don't know but I'm glad you don't want a brawl.'

'So you do know Burley Honeywood then?'

'Missus, everyone knows Burley.'

'Did he visit often, up there at Burnt Bridge?'

'He'll be cranky at me if I say!' And Alice sounded plaintive, and frightened.

'No, no,' said Flo in a tone so calm that it emerged as a threat.

'He's not as often as some who come up there looking for skirt,' admitted Alice. 'He came up there to my sister maybe three or four times. Maybe six or seven. First time was before he knew you, I reckon, missus.'

There was a long silence. It was not hard to guess that Alice was filling it with regret about what she had said. It had been clumsily designed to lighten Burley's crimes but of course it made too much of them.

At last Flo said, 'So he knew your sister before he knew me? And then he met me? And returned to your sister. What did her husband say? About Burley and your sister?'

'Her husband? Look, men can't get nothing. Can't hunt, you know. No jobs riding cattle and cutting timber. Men can only sit. And *we* can get things. Women can get things. That's the truth of it, missus. I got things.'

'And your sister had this boy, Eddie. He's clearly Burley's. It is so visible . . .'

'Well . . . Maybe, missus.'

'And Burley has given him nothing. I'll be honest with you, Mrs Kelly, when I saw Eddie in the street, that was the first thing I thought. This is Burley's child and he's got nothing! I measured him for clothes. But he's vanished. Could you bring him for a meeting with me again?'

'Oh, he's way up the valley with his Uncle Mallee.' Chicken had heard that form of words before, when he asked about a missing troublemaker, an Aboriginal kid, from the stalls of the Victoria. 'He's way up the valley with his uncle, Mr Chicken.' Chicken knew they had their rites to which the old men clung, and occasionally they would involve boys, and the training of boys, in . . . what? A superior politeness? Rites like a parson brought to the altar of All Saints?

'When will he be back?'

'Well . . . I don't know, missus.'

'But we must meet. Would you be willing to see him get an education at Newington College, say?'

'That's in Sydney?'

'Yes, it is.'

Alice maintained a silence for a long time. 'I'll talk to the family,' she said.

'Your own husband? He can come to our meeting.'

'Maybe . . . maybe he's too sick, missus.'

Chicken knew right enough that they were all dying up there.

'Would you and your husband want him to go to Newington? If I can persuade the headmaster? It's Burley's old school. Eddie deserves to go there.'

'His grandmother likes him, that boy,' Alice told Flo, warning of the problems of separation.

'I'm sure,' said Flo. But she did not have a glimmering of what Chicken knew from playing to the Aboriginal stalls: that the grandmother in their world was the empress and the mother and aunts had a vote but only one each. Indeed, some of the aunts had more power than the mother. Chicken could sense the reluctance in Alice.

Flo desperately pursued the matter. 'You can bring him for a meeting here as soon as he gets back?'

'Yes, missus,' agreed Alice, but redefining the terms. 'After he gets back.'

'I think you owe me the facts because I am not angry,' Flo asserted, at the same time, yet again, pleased at and puzzled by herself. 'But what happens to his schooling while he's away with his uncle?'

Alice was struggling for an answer Flo could understand. 'He's all right,' she said at last. 'He's not going to be prime minister.'

Alice laughed lustily, but Flo was attuned to flippancy and was silent for a long time. Then she asserted in an undertone, 'He would have a great future if he went to Newington, like all the other Honeywoods.'

Chicken knew this was a near fantasy of Flo's. Now and then you read a newspaper article about an educated Aboriginal man. Some Sydney school would eccentrically take one on. But Eddie Kelly? How could a Burnt Bridge kid from upriver natives live in a posh boarding school?

Flo said then, business-like, 'Your late sister. Well, she has died. But it has upset my life and I am still all up in the air and don't know where the pieces will settle. Please bring in your nephew, Alice. Be a dear thing and do that. And I'll write to Mr Rudgeley, the headmaster at Newington. About starting Eddie next year, after he finishes at the nuns.' Silence. Then, 'My husband, if he chooses to have a son, must do the right thing by him. Wouldn't you say, Mrs Kelly?'

'Not for me,' said wary Alice. 'It's up to you, Mrs Honeywood.'

After some reflective seconds, Flo raised her voice. 'We have talked, Mr Dalton. Thank you. You can come in.'

On his way into the loungeroom, he met Alice, her eyes wide and full of a question. The question was: is this real? Should I listen to her? How mad is this white woman? She confided under her breath, 'I mightn't want him leaving home, that boy.'

'Be it ever so humble,' whispered Chicken and surrendered to an impulse to kiss her cheek.

———

He found Flo looking into space. When she noticed him, she whispered, since Alice was still in the process of leaving the premises, 'It's as if his aunt doesn't want him educated.'

'They have a fear of getting themselves noticed,' said Chicken. 'There was a time up the river when any Aboriginal who made himself noticeable got shot.'

Flo blinked. Chicken lowered his voice.

'You must know how it was up the river in the old days,' he suggested.

'I've heard stories,' she confirmed.

'You have the most glorious skin, Mrs Honeywood.' That was his privilege as a pansy – to praise women and not be misunderstood.

'For heaven's sake, call me Flo. And apart from that, Mr Chicken, my skin counts for very little.'

'I could make you up, as I said, so that you glimmered, dear woman!'

'I would need to wash it off before I went home to the kids.' And there was a terse smile. 'They wouldn't know me otherwise.'

He took her hand by impulse and found it receptive, and led her to his sewing room and sat her down before a mirrored dresser. She saw the array of brushes in an ornamental jar, like a painter's studio. 'This will be glorious,' he assured her. 'I think I shall make you into a beauty in bronze.'

She laughed again now. 'Oh dear,' she told him. 'Don't.'

But he was already reaching for pots of goo. 'I am going to test three shades on the patch between your nose and your cheek. Because that is where your skin is purest. I don't mean yours personally. I mean, everyone's. Now the first is a liquid *Lumiere*.'

She consented to this unexpected and marvellous experiment, and felt the sudden and refreshing coolness of the lotion by her nose.

A complex of cosmetics went onto her face, and Chicken finished with a lustrous reddish lipstick that did not look cheap.

She stared at the finished result as at a stranger. He was right. She could be pretty. But for what cause? For assertion against Burley, she decided. So she resolved to keep that face for going home, and to shock the town and assault Burley with an unsuspected version of herself.

———

Bonnie the maid was cooking dinner when Flo got home. She had walked through the streets as if her revised face was a vengeance. She had smiled but not spoken to the few people she encountered who frowned, and one woman dragged her children aside to let the untoward apparition pass as quickly as possible. No one had spoken to her in the town. When the kids came in with red faces from playing in the garden, Betty near screamed. 'Mummy, you're so beautiful!' The little boy regarded her with awe. 'Crikey,' he said and then once more, 'Crikey,' though he soon lost interest in the phenomenon of a mother transformed. Flo herself could not shake the image of Joan Crawford in *Grand Hotel*. She rarely dreamed of such things but she acknowledged that Chicken's artistry had changed her for the day, and she wished for a little time to imagine herself splendid and remote, seated desirably in the lobby of some sort of worldly European Hotel. A woman of mystery, as they said, by which they meant a woman sufficient unto herself in her glory. She had thought occasionally of washing it all off before Burley got home. But a sturdy defiance always arose and argued that Burley had no right to be spared this vision of her.

Still in her transformed state, she knelt down over the kids' bath and washed them, not leaving it to Bonnie. Her daughter was enchanted and Flo thought, in a few years we can be women together, striding out in Sydney. This dream settled radiantly in her.

The children had nearly eaten their meal when Burley, the traducer, arrived home. She stood so that he could see her fully. She looked at him without a smile.

He said as if it were all a mistake, 'My God, Flo, what happened to you?'

She wanted to let him know straight off but said, 'Wait till the children have gone to bed.'

'I reckon I'm entitled to know now,' he said tightly.

She was furious enough to do it, against her better counsel. So she said in a lowered voice, 'I saw Alice Kelly today. Sister of your black woman.'

He looked questioningly at her.

'She is the boy's aunt!' Flo continued. 'Your son's aunt.'

'What maniac idea of yours . . .?'

'I've seen the boy on the street a number of times. Half-caste. Clearly your son.'

'What in God's . . .?'

Now she saw the chance he would be loud in response and called on the children to say goodnight to their father and go to the bathroom to clean their teeth. They came up and Burley distractedly kissed them. As soon as they were out of the room, he turned his bleak, interrogatory eyes back to her.

She said, 'His name is Eddie Kelly. I've organised his uniform for the convent, but after that I want to send him to Newington. If he's your son, then he deserves it.'

His tired face developed patches of reddish anger on a sickly base. We are both palefaces, she thought.

'This is absurd, Flo,' Burley decided. 'It's gone far enough!'

'Alice – sister of your girlfriend at one time – is bringing him to see us when he gets back from the Upper Macleay.'

'Flo,' he said, 'be decent. I beg you . . .'

'Don't worry, I'll do all the writing to the headmaster.'

He writhed his head about. It is right and just that you are baffled, she thought.

He said suddenly, 'And what in Christ's name has happened to your face?' As if it had been injured.

'Chicken Dalton. I met him at Tsiros's yesterday. He was my point of contact with Alice. He seems to know a lot about these people.'

'Does he?' asked Burley scathingly. 'But your face, Flo?'

'Chicken had time to offer me makeup. He applied it himself. He's such an enthusiast. When I saw what he had done, I wanted to keep it on.'

His mouth was caught in a grimace and he began blinking.

'That sodomite mongrel? This is ridiculous, Flo.'

'But the thing is, I don't think it's ridiculous.'

'Now listen. You look like a bloody tart, Flo.'

He held his hand out as if considering some sort of uxorial arrest.

'Wash it off!' he demanded.

'I certainly will not wash it off.'

'You will, you mad woman!'

And now he seized her by the arms. She felt exalted by his outrage.

'I promise you, I'll wash it bloody off,' he said.

He started to force her up the hallway. She resisted, feeling entitled now to howl in protest. Betty and George appeared wide-eyed in the half-darkness. She wanted to be amenable for their sakes but she could not be. She tripped and fell against him, and he hauled her along by her shoulders, her heels sliding across the floor. One of her shoes came off. He dragged her into the tiled bathroom and hugged her to him, grabbing a facecloth one-handed then running water on it. As he began to apply the cloth savagely to her face she saw in the mirror the cloth gouging the cosmetics from her face, so that one half kept the sharp focus and definition Chicken had given it and the other looked blurred and erased. She wept and screamed as he attacked her brow. He wanted to erase her, she thought. He wanted to do away with the sharpness Chicken had given her. She writhed but the cloth worked and ground over her skin. He seemed to want to eradicate not just the paint but the layers of skin that had borne it. From beyond the door, Bonnie could be heard reassuring the screaming children. 'Mummy and Daddy are just having a game,' she cried. 'That's all. Having a game.'

Panting, Burley forced his words between locking teeth. 'And you yourself done up like some sort of a tart! And by that bloody fruit!'

He took the cloth away from her face and ran more water on it and then would not stop plying it on her face, in the suspicion that the cosmetics had penetrated to the bone. And at last he decided he was done. In the silence, he said, begging her to believe it, 'It's only for your own good, Flo.'

'They think you're a ghost. You with your willy hanging out. Going to them. And when they lie down with you, they think you're a ghost.'

'Well,' he said, not as hurt by the idea as she had hoped, 'you know I'm bloody well not.'

'Bugger you. I'll divorce you. And I'll send the boy to Newington.'

'You won't divorce me,' he told her, still drawing deep breaths, more tired by the struggle over face paint than she could have hoped for.

Bonnie continued to try to console the children. She could be heard reading them a story, its drama punctuated by an occasional appeased hiccough from George.

'I'm going to have dinner,' said Burley. Flo was pleased he seemed a bit uncertain about his recent display of strength. Predictable in his appetite even after the most strenuous row, he was also now predictable in his second thoughts and the onset of a sentimental remorse. 'Let's just make peace, eh, Flo?'

She said nothing. She knew and he knew how susceptible she would once have been to such a plea.

'Jesus, will you talk to a man?'

But she wouldn't talk to him. He went to go, but second thoughts stung him again. 'Look, you can't get mixed up with that fairy. You can't get mixed up with the black sheilas he makes up. That's the only reason he knows them. He makes them up in his own daffodil way so they can go to Sydney doing God knows what.'

'He touches them for their own good. Why did you touch your black woman?'

'I've bloody said my say,' he told her, and went, thumping in the corridor, saying, 'Domestic bliss, eh?' She felt the cool flange of the enamel bath biting into the flesh of her buttocks. Reason burned within her. She muttered to herself like a prayer: 'I am not to visit Chicken because he decorates the faces of black women, and this contact makes him unfit. His colours on my face shame you! But you

107

were willing to do more than decorate, you were willing to penetrate their bodies. And I'm not shamed by contact with you? Could you explain that contradiction? That bloody, deep-dyed enigma?'

Finishing her argument, she hauled herself upright. Her face still stung from the cloth. She inspected it, streaky, unevenly reddened, in the mirror. 'And I will see Chicken,' she promised her tear-stained image, 'whenever I damn-well like.'

10

*Macleay Valley, New South Wales, 1933, and County Kerry,
1922*

Dulcie enjoyed the sociability of Mass in Bellbrook, to
which Johnny took her and the kids, fifteen miles by dray.
A little white weatherboard church stood on donated land
and the priest himself rode all the way from Kempsey by car
to celebrate the Mass. And half of Nulla and Mungay and
Hickeys Creeks were there. In the clear spaces around after-
wards, the boys went running with the other dairy kids,
and were for half an hour like the children they were, rather
than the servants of the heifers abundant with milk.

Johnny, she noticed, prayed hard in Mass. He did not
take it lightly. It was on him the Mass weighed. To her it
was life's duty, and the priest had to get it done and get back
to Kempsey for his baked dinner, and so the sermons were
not of the highest moment. Yet Johnny was the most solemn
man in the church. How could she know why? If she had
asked he wouldn't have told her.

She was used to the idea that Mass increased the gloominess of her husband. He came back to the lunch of Sunday stew with a look of clear disappointment on his long face. She got the idea that he blamed her for something that had happened or had failed to happen; a light that had failed to shine on him, and she did not expect to hear any assurances about any of that. Her father had possessed some of that same male melancholy and her mother refused to take on its weight. Her father had raised himself, and so had Johnny – at least his mother had died when he was young, and his father had been killed in the mysterious troubles after the Troubles themselves, that great ongoing engine for the destruction of Irish flesh.

Then every third Saturday into town he went and drank into the night with the musician, that Chicken fellow, instead of camping at the dray with her and the kids, and that showed you. A male wretch – and Johnny had occasionally proclaimed himself as such – would rather spend time with another male wretch, than with a wife.

Her Sunday afternoon picnic back at Nulla was her own religion, a gift to her boys. Again, to break to them the news that they were children, that they need not, if they chose not to, be forever and ever milking.

She was up at three on most Sunday mornings, the ones spent in the quiet house at Nulla Creek, to prepare, and as her cakes and bread were baked the currawongs began singing in the grey gums, announcing milking time. Below the house on the creek there was a shingly beach where she and the boys spent the afternoon. Here the boys could run and splash, returning to the blanket for cake and treacle-soaked bread as they chose, and not having to think of the cattle. There was such a madness of running and games, and she only partly understood any of them, and while they were in progress the boys seemed to speak in their own version of Australian, the words and their vowels landing flat as tiles in the warm air. But since Johnny had the help of George Munter, the Aboriginal man, that afternoon, they were let off for Sunday nights and Monday mornings, for – again – she did not want them to be total slaves to the dairy cattle.

Dulcie had a temperament which made what it could of things, yet was capable of passionate regret, including that these boys were far from books and learning.

———

When Chicken got home from the Victoria on Saturday night, he found Johnny Costigan in residence at Ultima Thule, a neglected cup of tea by his side. 'Oh, Johnny,' he said. 'I'd forgotten it was the third Saturday.'

At least he had temporarily forgotten.

'How pleasant!' he continued, for Johnny was some comfort. On the way home from the Victoria, Chicken had discovered that he was exhausted. *Tabu* was quite an exercise, all that Polynesian drumming rhythm. It was a film that would never die. Because you had Anne Chevalier, the most beautiful girl on Bora Bora, and declared tabu so that no man could touch her. Harper Quinlan, the projectionist, said you could hear the boys' fly buttons popping all over the cinema.

Johnny Costigan, that strange gaping jawline and the hungry eyes, and the way he spoke in his acute brogue, so hungrily, biting off words, revived Chicken. Was there any mail? he asked. There was. A few letters for Mrs Costigan from her family, a letter from the *Sunday Mail* Little Artists addressed to one Master Oliver Costigan, and a letter from Johnny's sister in America with the initials SAG written on the flap. All the Tykes did that, even in America it appeared, and various people had told him with too much authority what it meant. Strangle All Gentiles. Strike Against Greed. Suffer Any Grief. He had asked Harper Quinlan, who said, 'Mate, it just means St Anthony Guide. Didn't you even bloody know St Anthony's the patron saint of lost letters?'

On top of that, Chicken did not always understand Costigan's spates of bitter talk of Ireland. First, Costigan had from childhood, it seemed to Chicken, fought British police called the Black and Tans and someone called the Auxiliaries. Then, that war won, some people – his family amongst them – didn't like the peace settlement and fought on against the Irish Free State. It seemed Costigan had drawn his breath amongst bitterness all his days.

Retrieving the mail from Chicken's dresser, Costigan said, 'Thank you, Chicken,' and tore open the letter from his sister and devoured it, and folded it and put it in his jacket pocket.

Chicken had by now poured himself a sherry. 'I do hope no bad news, Johnny.'

'A long way from it, God be praised,' said Johnny fretfully. 'The girl is doing a bloody sight better than her brother ever will. Even if she's married to an old fellow there, thirty years her senior. But, the thing is, she said she was putting an American fifty dollar bill in. And it's not there.'

'Oh dear,' said Chicken, genuinely alarmed. 'I haven't touched the letter since it arrived. Could your sister have forgotten to enclose it?'

'Forgotten or not,' said Johnny, 'it would be bloody welcome, Chicken, I'll tell you.'

Chicken thought, he must be a hard man to like seven days a week.

'Do you need a loan then?' said Chicken, knowing this was a weak, even a guilty response.

'That's not the issue,' said Johnny dangerously,

'I would never interfere with your mail, Johnny. I swear. A man's mail is a sacred trust.' But he sounded to himself as if he pleaded too much with this peasant of a man. What did he benefit from fulfilling Johnny's trust and now incurring his suspicion? A brief and routine three-weekly release from a man ashamed of his true self.

'I'll write to my sister,' said Johnny, sounding more reconciled. 'It's all right. Mimmie's left the bill out of the letter – that's my guess too, Chicken.'

Chicken breathed easier and risked reaching over the table to kiss Johnny briefly. Johnny rubbed the spot like a bruise He wasn't a bad fellow, and for a dairy farmer, he did seem to wash daily.

'Would you like some sherry?' asked Chicken.

'No thank you, Chicken.' A rare smile set in on Costigan's long lips. 'Pansy drink!'

'Go to buggery!' said Chicken, joining the joke and going to fetch the sherry,

'That's what I'm here for,' said Johnny. 'Buggery. Or something like it.'

———

They lay on the bed, naked. Chicken had introduced Johnny to nakedness. He had begotten four sons wearing nightwear. He said his wife would never tolerate bare flesh, but Chicken suspected it was Johnny himself who had something to do with it. The tabu. The flesh tabu. Some men took sexual relief like wolves tearing flesh, punishing something, themselves perhaps for wanting so badly what they wanted. Johnny was such. It was a variation Chicken enjoyed, not that his fleshly life was so full as to have variations. But it was piquant, anyhow.

He fell asleep with an arm around Johnny's bony shoulders. He knew Johnny would be gone before he himself woke in the morning. Collecting his brood from their wagon over in the east, going to early Mass and heading back to Nulla.

Mass acted as a trigger for Johnny, of course. The priest was a solid-looking Irishman from Carlow for a start. His hair as brilliantined as an accountant's. And the smell of vestments and candle-grease and the familiar intonation of the Latin. The universal church! So Michael Collins of the Free State made his Treaty with Churchill, and it all started again. But so brotherly to begin with, Johnny remembered. Dinny O'Toole, the old commandant in the district, commander of the Second Kerry Brigade of the IRA and a man who had taught Johnny in the National School, went along to the grim old Listowel workhouse the Free State Army had taken over and had a drink with his friend the Free State commander, Tim Kennelly. Michael Collins had by then been in Tralee and said the Treaty wasn't worth fighting about, as if he didn't intend to fight about it. From the edge of the crowd, the rebel boys had fired a ceremonial fusillade of disagreement, but no one believed in their water that it would go further still.

The Costigans, father and son, became full-time watchers of the Free State garrison. They watched them drilling near the blue stone workhouse and its chapel and mortuary, just as if the British had not visited the famine on them in the

114

first place, and as if nothing had been learned from this. The Costigans were stationed in the upstairs of a general store in Market Street with views south and west. Two of their more experienced fellows manned a Lewis gun in the window, and Seamus Quoyne, the squad leader who had served in the Irish Guards in the Great War but been forgiven for it, talked knowledgeably to the gunners about something called 'interlocking fields of fire'. And still no angry shot was fired or seemed probable.

June 1922 changed it all. Just beyond the hump of the month the Kerry rebels heard warfare, Free State and Republican, had broken out in the Dublin most Kerry clodhoppers had never visited. Two days later, near-end of sweet June in Listowel, velvety airs and brief showers and the earth declaring its intentions in painfully lovely sunsets, and in bluebells and myrtle, his father was on lookout by the window while the others drank tea and ate warm bread with jam, and he called, 'The Free State boys are moving into Walsh's drapery.' This was a store just along the road a little. A week ago they would have noted it and shrugged, but this time the section head, Seamus Quoyne, who had been gassed in the Great War and never took an easy breath, sent Johnny along the back lane to tell the commandant of Kerry 2 Brigade, Dinny O'Toole, whose office was up in the back of McQuaid's. Commander O'Toole told him, 'Johnny, it's time now. Instruct Seamus and your father to open fire on them. Collins started it in Dublin. We'll start it here.'

So Johnny came back to his squad's upstairs room with the order. The rebels had squads of men all up and down Market Street, of course, and Mr O'Toole sent them the news too. Johnny and the others fetched their rifles from the hallway and two at a time they marched up to one of the two upstairs windows and fired into the drapery while Seamus Quoyne and his friend got the Lewis gun going in the other window. Johnny had never heard such a furious and gigantic racket. All the other rebel squads and outposts and strong-points along Market Street and round the square had started up. They shot away at first at Walsh's drapery where the Free Staters, sheltering from the disintegrating plate glass behind bolts of linen, could not be seen. They fired not only at Walsh's but off to the right at the workhouse and to the left they could shoot at the Listowel Arms. Ah, thought Johnny. Interlocking lines of fire.

This went on all morning. The Free State commander Kennelly surrendered that afternoon and Johnny saw the Free States soldiers in their plundered British Army caps carry a tall young man out of the Listowel Arms who in all that fire had been shot through the heart.

Next morning Johnny and his da turned up to his funeral as both sides buried him amidst the chant of birds and the chirruping of the parish priest himself, at the cemetery near the river, by Gutenard Wood.

Such fraternity they had, intense in the pubs along the square following the ceasefire. Relief that Irishman should not kill Irishman except by accident. There had been a blood sacrifice but Johnny rejoiced it hadn't been his father's or his own.

What infants they all bloody were. The true and cruel lessons of the summer, which they believed they had learned, had not even commenced.

———

Christian Webber was enamoured with Paul Muni, the actor from *I Am a Fugitive from the Chain Gang.* The newspapers and other law students told him he was meant to be rabid for Louise Brooks or Marlene Dietrich. 'Bedroom eyes' were said to be Marlene Dietrich eyes, but they bespoke little to him. To Christian, her eyes were the eyes of any room in the house. Artistically powerful, of course. But he was meant to spring erect when he saw them on screen, and he could not.

But he had wanted to console the sad-eyed Muni. All the melancholy of Eastern Europe was in that face. Jewish, of course. From the Yiddish Theatre, according to the pic mags his sister Gertie collected. There was a boy at Sydney university . . . Aaron Fleisch, well made and clumsy and with melancholy eyes.

Christian had been waiting since high school to feel the gravid blood of lust for a girl. He had kept his lack of lust for women a secret at Scots College – when classmates groaned for this or that chorus girl at the Tiv, his blood rose up for the chorus boy, the *garçons du dance* he had seen, and he loved them to have Italian or Spanish names. How unfair that any boy could desire any girl, the very gender of girls making them all possible participants in the great erotic dance his fellow students talked about without cease. Whereas he could not know if there was even one other perversely slanted male like him in the entire student population.

He was, of course, doomed by geography and the bush obscurity of his family never to encounter Paul Muni. But he was not averse to the pianist at the Victoria. Chicken, as everyone called him. Chicken Dalton must be nearly six feet, had lean, features and a face of prominent features that, like an actor's, made a statement, even if you couldn't

117

exactly read what it was. Chicken was more amused at the world, like Noël Coward, not the Noël Coward of *The Vortex* but he of *Bitter-Sweet*, which Christian had seen in Melbourne. Like Coward, Chicken was ready to grow solemn if he had grounds to be, but chiefly if the rest of the world demanded it. Chicken's mouth was the mouth of a man who wanted to have fun if it could be managed. He had a self-mocking way, and yet he knew his value. 'Play us a riff, Chicken!' cried the louts in the stalls, and he would, and there would be cheers, half-mocking, half-admiring. Yet he had the authority and the shoulder strength to expel from the cinema anyone who threw an empty packet or any more substantial missile. He knew the limits of the tolerable, and the management stood by him if he acted against any yokel in the stalls or the circle.

Christian had seen the cinema orchestras in big picture houses in Sydney, and the rather expensive upright Fotoplayers some picture show owners bought. He had not wanted the owners of the Victoria to buy a Fotoplayer, as it would have replaced Chicken and done away with his playing. He seemed to love to play, though. He played even in the newsreels, played morning, afternoon and evening in the school holidays. If someone yelled, 'When'll they get a Fotoplayer and get rid of you, Chicken?' he would shake his head with mock pity for their innocence. Fotoplayers played piano roll music – anyone could operate them – and they had all manner of sound conveniences the operator could activate: a mechanical bell and a train sound, wind, thunder, a bass drum, a tom-tom, a gunshot, and so on. 'So you want a roll of paper with perforations to replace the immortal Chicken Dalton?' he would cry, and the crowd would cheer and whistle.

But he had installed a drum set he could reach with his feet, a bulb horn he played in comic scenes by pressing with his nose, and a bell he could ring by pulling a lever. He had in fact saved his employer an investment of hundreds of pounds. And remained, even now, when some flicks had their own sound, somehow ingrained into the film, an essential fleahouse entertainer and a maker of his own music.

And although Chicken was so old, perhaps in his late thirties, Christian Webber dreamed of him.

Christian knew Chicken liked to drink coffee at Tsiros's. Indeed, Chicken had a well-known routine of procedure through the town. He would go to the butcher's like any householder, then he would look in the Quinlan sisters' frock salon and walk through Savage's, occasionally buying cosmetics. What would have been considered outrageous behaviour in any other man was tolerated in the town. He was not any pansy looking at lipstick. He was Kempsey's pansy. And then he went to Tsiros's for Turkish coffee.

Christian thought he could wait there himself and catch up with *Introduction to the Law of Real Property*, push indigestible paragraphs around his head, and feel the sweat prickling at his palms as used to happen when he was a kid and ate peaches with the skin still on. Twice he had been in Tsiros's without seeing him, but at the third try he was there when Chicken entered. Christian acknowledged with a surge of something pretty close to nausea that Chicken was indeed a fine-looking fellow, broad-shouldered and slim, and his movements very crisp. Chicken paused by Christian's table. 'Good heavens,' he fluted, but not making a spectacle of them both, 'a student. You put all us bushweeks to shame, young man.'

119

And then he moved on, as an adult does after patting someone's nearby infant on the head. All this produced a desire for flight in Christian. He gathered his books. From beyond the window glass, he saw Chicken settling to a table, frowning out at him as if sad to have made him flee. Chicken then gave a small wave, and Christian, overwhelmed by the gesture, walked off, damning himself for lack of valour.

11

Kempsey, New South Wales, 1933

'I am Flo Honeywood,' she told her mirror a day after being made up by Chicken Dalton and unmade by her husband. 'Here I am. Soft in the abdomen after the kids but not unlovely, I don't think.' They had done their duty by the country, said Burley, she and he. Three brats; Jerry at Newington running up bills Burley liked to complain about in public, since he was proud to be able to meet them and to have the boy who incurred them. Then young Betty, who was certainly no brat but an extremely studious little girl, at East Kempsey School with George, who was only six. And Burley seemed to consider all intimacy between himself and Flo over now. The family was complete in the world's eyes, which were obviously important eyes to Burley. He treated her in public and in private with a careful delicacy. He addressed her as Florence. There was no flippancy between them, as there had once been.

Nor was she close to the wives of his friends who were matriarchs in town – not in the sense those wives were close to each other, regularly seeking each other's company and certainly forming in their eyes and in the town's an enviable parliament of townswomen. She had no confidante with whom she could raise this issue, then. Perhaps they had not been blighted as she had been, nor claimed, as she had been, by a child such as Eddie.

She intended to go to town today to see old Mr Cattleford at his office in Belgrave Street. And she had bathed, and as a woman will, she sat half-dressed by a mirror and judged herself. Yea, even as an object of a husband's desire. Sitting in a scent of Yardley's powder that was no comfort to her, she felt she had been rendered venerable too early by her husband. She had been tempted to tell him this, one way or another and a number of times in the past two years, but did not know how a woman did that. For it was established long before the Macleay Shire existed that a man's desire was honest, but a woman's was disorder. Yet it was a question she had retained, and kept assessing.

Anyway, now she could not cherish him anymore. Today she wanted done with him. She had plans to run away with the two little ones and get a job somewhere, in Sydney or Brisbane. But she must be supported. Let him boast about that! What it would cost to keep his wife and kids when she and they were gone!

She realised that until today she had always dressed for someone. Her father. Boys, though the point seemed to pass most of them by, and then Burley. There had been permanent allure in Burley. But not anymore. And old Mr Cattleford was not in himself a reason for a woman to dress well, so she was caught hapless at the end of the bed with no reason to proceed. She forced herself up, depending on the energy of her hurt and anger. She would walk to Cattleford's lawyers of Belgrave Street. She wanted no one to say, 'There goes Burley's wife in the nice little car he got her, lucky woman.'

She was ready at last and fastened her hat, for it was autumn and blowy, and took off to cross the bridge. Let them see her walking like one of Barsby's shopgirls.

All was sadness that had been light. This side of the river, the broad concourse of Rudder Street where goods were unloaded from coastal steamers, though not as many since the railway came just before her marriage. Now they had put the new war memorial there. The ghosts of young men were more numerous than passers-by. Below, on the river-bank, settlers had planted weeping willows from England to lean forward to dangle branches so appealingly in the green fast water. The big river was muscular, as she thought of it, deep with sinews of current. When it flooded, it ran like a mad bailiff through the centre of town between West and Central, reclaiming flimsy structures and invading polite ones to dump its mud. People over there in Central and West put their houses on stilts and built them on higher ground, but no householder considered himself immune if the river, instead of enclosing the town in a beautiful bow, decided to break levees and run straight.

And, though she lived in East, high and safe above the torrent, now the flood had risen in her, and was violating all the rooms.

The Harp of Erin store was on her left, yokels lounging on its veranda. She did not use The Harp, since they were Irish. Burley said it well: 'We only run up bills with other Protestants.'

She did, despite all, yearn for other days, the days when secure in Burley's eminence she went out and considered the town somehow hers, in the sense that mattered to her – utterly predictable country, her movements in it consecrated through her high house and high marriage. But now she was venturing into a town she had lost title to. She felt she did not quite know how to cross the planking of the great ironbark bridge to Central. She could not imagine herself on the far side of the river, progressing on pavements in Central. The centre of things for all purposes.

In any case, she walked across Rudder and there it was, the bridge planking, worn smooth as soap and a fine blue by the foot traffic. She was a little amazed that she had managed the walk, yet comforted at the margins above the water which here seemed as dark as plum jam, the great muscle of the river powering water towards the entrance at South West Rocks. Some wagons were on the bridge and a truck that belonged to old Buhrer of Pola Creek, so mean to his sons, and then by an uncomfortable chance a car, a Buick, colour of port wine. Sherry's, with Sherry the solicitor beaming behind the wheel. So many people liked Sherry. Including Burley. He was the Catholic of the better class they all chose to like, the way the town chose to like the pansy pianist, that Chicken. Sherry, the main lawyer in town, if truth were told. Major of the militia that occasionally drilled at weekends at stations upriver to be ready for when the Bolsheviks came. She could not have gone to him. If she could not speak to Sherry, who spoke so earnestly to Burley, she hoped she would be able to speak to old Cattleford. Not his son, who was younger than she was. The fruit of an old vine and a younger wife.

The Cockney Jew, Teddy Draper, was on the doorstep

of his jewellery store to salute Mrs Honeywood on her way through Central. But it was not a bustling hour. And soon there was Cattleford's, behind its deep veranda. There was a thigh-high barrier like altar rails partway across the office when she entered, and a girl got up from her typing to ask her pleasantly whether she could be helped.

Flo was taken almost at once into Mr Cattleford's office, a place full of folders which were yet neatly attended to in piles that did not collapse on themselves but stood up like prim schoolboys around the room. Mr Cattleford was engaged in these substantial matters, and above all in the consuming rigmarole of keeping a pipe alight. Everyone said that he had been a very fussy remount officer with the Australian Light Horse, approving the horses that captured Damascus and ended the Empire of the Ottomons.

'Mrs Honeywood,' he cried, stooped upright, indicated a seat and then coughed. 'Dear lady, do be seated. Has my girl offered you tea?'

Flo quickly dealt with the tea question. When she said no, Mr Cattleford dedicated himself to his pipe, not only filling it but prodding the tobacco lode, uncertain of the ventilation problems needed to light it and let it burn evenly. 'I am aware of your distinguished husband,' he said, 'and indeed he built this very structure, I believe. But I thought you took your business to Mr Sherry.'

She had told herself before coming here; don't be shy, do not cringe or let soft, whimpery apologies leave your lips.

'On this matter, I need advice on my own behalf,' she told him.

'Oh, you have perhaps,' puff, puff, and then another inspection of the pipe, 'acquired property in your own name?'

125

'Not at all. I wish to divorce my husband.'

Mr Cattleford sat forward and abandoned the pipe in a vast china ashtray advertising whisky.

She determined to sound matter-of-fact, 'I wondered, have you ever handled a divorce, Mr Cattleford?'

'By jingo,' he breathed. 'By jingo, my dear lady. I managed a separation once. I remember I referred a woman to a lawyer in Newcastle . . . I don't know what happened, so left the district. But . . .' And here, a stutter of little coughs. 'But nothing involving someone like your husband. Surely, a separation . . . a separation at most would serve all parties.'

She must be firm, she knew. 'It will not serve me at all,' she said.

'But my dear lady, on what grounds.'

'Adultery,' she asserted. 'On the grounds of adultery.'

'Ah,' said Mr Cattleford as if stabbed. 'Criminal conversation.'

'I do not think our conversation is at all criminal.'

'No, no, it is the term I learned as a student. A name for . . .'

Even though she had introduced the word, he seemed too embarrassed to repeat it in front of her.

'Criminal conversation. But not all adultery *must* end in divorce. I do not imply it is common, but it is not, sadly, unknown. But very rare on the Macleay.'

'This case must end in divorce,' she asserted. 'That's a necessity, Mr Cattleford.'

'Who-ah, Nancy!' said Mr Cattleford, as if a cart was bolting. 'Let's start from basics, dear Mrs Honeywood. Has your husband admitted to an adulterous connection?'

'That is what the court has to decide,' Flo asserted.

'Well, has the alleged "other party" confessed to you?'

'No. The other party is dead.'

'Has a witness to the adulterous relationship come forward?'

'No, But I have physical evidence.'

'In what form?'

'There is a dark-skinned child who, if presented to a judge, Mr Cattleford, would serve as living and undeniable evidence that my husband and the boy's mother committed adultery some ten years past. When he was already married some years to me.'

'Oh dear,' said Cattleford. 'Oh dear, I doubt a court has ever been presented with such a claim and on such evidence. Has your husband admitted to the . . . the indiscretion?'

'I believe,' Flo took the trouble to persist, 'that it will persuade the judge, and you would be persuaded yourself if you saw the boy?'

'Does your husband know you're consulting me on this matter?'

'No,' said Flo. 'But he knows I am discontented.'

'Will you let him know?'

Flo thought. I will then! 'I have told him I'm seeking a divorce, but he thought it was just anger. But it is very difficult to find the calm words, Mr Cattleford. It's not that I'm afraid. It's that I can't find the words. Once I've spoken to him calmly, of course, everything will be changed.'

'My dear lady, everything is changed by your coming here. And for little benefit. It seems facial resemblance will not be considered to be grounds by the court unless your husband confesses. Even if you hire a so-called expert, a professor of faces and physiognomies, if there is such a thing . . .'

127

Flo said, 'If the boy can't appear, and probably it would be better for him if he didn't, I'll present the court with photographs. I'll get the boy's photo taken.'

'Dear Mrs Honeywood,' Cattleford breathed. 'Let me be clear. You believe sincerely you have been hurt and I am sympathetic to that. You claim that one of the women from Burnt Bridge Aboriginal camp is the other party, is that right?'

'It is right.'

'You understand that even if you were right about the child, it would not be the first time a wife in this town had reason to suspect . . .'

He tried to light his pipe again, breathing heavily, and managed to do it, his lips making dubious noises around the stem as he did so, and finding seconds of sublime comfort in the smoke. 'Yes,' he said, 'I believe it goes like this. A young man, perhaps new to town, goes drinking with older ones. They often begin at the office of one of the older men, then move on say to the Commercial or the Federal. And one of the older men raises the suggestion for the newcomer. "Let's go out to the blacks' camp." It happens. As a form of . . . well, of initiation too. It's . . .'

'But Burley was born here. He didn't arrive in town.'

'Even so. *Mutatis mutandis.* I don't say it's right. But I ask, is it grounds for ending a marriage? It is the folly of one night. It deserves anger of course. But . . . *divorce?*'

'From what I have read in the papers, one night's unfaithfulness is all the courts need.' She spoke with impatience she would not be persuaded out of. She would not let this pleasant, predictable old man lull her.

'Yes,' said Cattleford as his lips popped on the pipe stem. 'But is it really worth, dear woman, destroying a marriage for?'

'The boy is *there*, you have to understand, Mr Cattleford. The boy is a living reproach to me and to Burley. It is not his fault. He is the unwitting product, as am I and my children.'

'But I don't think resemblance will be enough, Mrs Honeywood. I have to be honest in my advice.'

'Will you consult a barrister for me?'

'Well, I could take your details and even draft a writ and send my son to Newcastle to raise the matter with a barrister. You may wish to go too, or not.'

'I would like you to go yourself. I know your son is clever, but not experienced enough. I know it would be expensive and tiring for you . . . *But*.' She uttered that word as a command.

'Mrs Honeywood, I have offered you a course of action, but I can tell you beforehand and far more cheaply than he will what the advice of the barrister will be. You are unlikely to achieve a decree absolute unless your husband makes a full and earnest confession. And . . . and why would he?'

Flo was not shaken, 'Be assured, I will not be willing to let the matter go. I have been a decent wife and daughter all along. But that is gone now. Now that I know what the line has become, I will not toe it.'

Mr Cattleford made a number of small groans with and without the accompaniment of his pipe. 'Dear lady, you have first to give your husband the same chance the court would give him. You must confront him and tell him your intentions. Are you concerned about violence arising from doing that?'

'No. It had better not arise.'

But she did not know. She had never stood up to Burley in this way. Despite that, she wanted no third party.

129

'Then you must tell him you have come to see me and why. You may or may not wish to have a minister of religion present at the time, I don't know. Do that, and if you wish to see me thereafter . . . I am here. Let us see. Ten o'clock Wednesday? Your husband may wish to bring his solicitor here. All possibilities are available.'

Cattleford conceded all those possibilities but would not quite countenance the central one. Of divorce.

Flo accepted the proffered morning, two days off. Yes, she felt, all that must be done.

———

Flo wanted time, without meeting anyone on the street and being forced to conversation, to let her thoughts settle. She turned towards the sparser flood-prone buildings to the west. But having started out in that direction, she saw an untoward scene outside Curran's Funerals. A man she recognised from around town, Mr Breslin, the locomotive driver who handled the line between Grafton and Taree, was standing beside Joe Carmody's taxi outside the funeral home arguing or heavily engaged in persuasion with a thin-shouldered woman, who could be heard weeping.

Flo's knowledge of Breslin was that he was a solid fellow in physique as in professional repute. Carmody was standing by his part-opened cab door watching the dispute with a neutral blinking of the eye. There was a nakedness about it all, an echo of what had befallen her, as if something undue and designed for privacy had spilled into the streets. She would have crossed the road except that Breslin had seen her and already half-acknowledged her with a sideways nod.

She hoped she might nonetheless be allowed to creep

past and leave the three to resolve things. The worst thing was that they all stopped with whatever altercation it was to stand politely while she passed. As she did, she heard herself, almost as a phantom tic left from her old life and old stature, ask, 'Is all well, gentlemen?'

Exactly as if she moved with calm at her own centre.

Breslin doffed his hat and she could see sweat beads on his scalp. 'Mrs Honeywood,' he said, 'isn't it?' He stepped forward and said, 'We meet at a terrible time. This lady here . . .' He pointed without apparent resentment to the teary woman. 'Her name is Mrs Polly Sutton.' He lowered his voice. 'Her husband was a travelling man killed on the North Coast Mail two days ago. I was the driver. I slow outside town to let men get off the rattlers, but he wasn't on the rattlers, he was up top on a goods car, and didn't know that tunnels at Eungai only had eighteen-inch clearance.' He confided, 'Back of skull. Very deformed. The guard saw him fall by the track and pulled the alarm. It's very hard for everyone. Mrs Sutton only arrived on the train today. The St Vincent de Paul are paying for his funeral.' Breslin dropped his voice lower. 'Mr Curran's done great work to get the poor fellow to look normal.' He raised his voice again, 'Mrs Polly Sutton, this is Mrs Honeywood. Mrs Honeywood, you know Mr Carmody.'

Carmody tipped his hat.

'Mrs Sutton,' said Breslin, 'feels a bit peculiar staying at my place until the funeral tomorrow. You see . . .' He cast his arms up and there was an honest unutterability there. Not like Cattleford prodding around in his pipe and probing for meaning. Breslin had without knowing killed this woman's husband. How could she sit at his evening table? 'I was telling her we could find her somewhere else.'

'She could stay with me,' said Flo instantly. She could see Breslin and Carmody exchange glances. The Honeywoods were Freemasonry aristocracy, St Vincent de Paul and Breslin were Roman Catholic. These elements did not sing together. But Flo wanted to make such mayhem. She wanted to defy Burley by taking in an inappropriate widow.

'Mrs Sutton, I am so sorry for you and your children,' she said. For the woman, though young, seemed indelibly a mother – it had something to do with her lank hair and the way one of her hips protruded thinly, while you knew it had once been fleshy, not lean.

Mrs Sutton managed to say it was kind.

'Decent of you, Mrs Honeywood,' said the engine driver. 'Don't you reckon it's decent, Carmody.'

The cab driver gave bewildered assent.

'Come,' said Breslin, apparently to both women, 'Mr Carmody will take you both home. And no need for either of you to be troubled, Mr Carmody will bring me the bill.'

Carmody spoke clearly for the first time. 'Very kind. I'll take you ladies back to East then.'

This would all be wonderful, and would confuse Burley, Flo thought.

But as she travelled side by side with her newly acquired widow, her resolve and sense of a cause grew and matured. Half of her was pleased Burley had a Macleay Jockey Club committee meeting and would be home at half past eight, when the children were asleep. And then he would face Flo but must deal first with this new woman. A woman who had so easily if unwillingly achieved divorce.

12

Kempsey, New South Wales, 1933, and Listowel, County Kerry, 1922

A reassuring and authoritative male voice from the radio cabinet seemed to put their grief on the shelf for a while as he told Flo and Mrs Sutton that the Australian Antarctic Territory had been gazetted, that although Western Australia had voted to secede, Prime Minister Lyons believed that the secession would not be recognised as constitutional by the Privy Council, that before the end of autumn windscreen wipers would be prescribed for all cars under state law, and that a visiting American professor believed that the Japanese naming of the section of northern China they had seized, Manchukuo, was a confidence trick, and had failed to attract Manchu Chinese to settle there or in any other way legitimise the Japanese seizure of the area. But she would not have been astonished to hear the voice announce that it was known now that Burley Honeywood, master builder of Kempsey, New South Wales, had disgraced himself in the camp at Burnt Bridge. Sherry done and news in some way digested, she and Polly Sutton went and ate their dinners as Bonnie put the kids to bed in the vaguely heard bedtime turmoil. 'Put mint sauce on your chops,' said Flo. But the suggestion caused Polly to dissolve. 'I don't know if I can eat them,' she pleaded. 'I have no future.'

Flo did not know quite what to say at first but remembered a radio report that younger women found it easier to get work than men did these days. 'Oh, you are young and strong, Polly,' she told her, and felt tears readying themselves under her own eyelids. 'It is all terrible. But you and your children . . .' She could still hear her own children, raucous now, and excused herself.

Young Georgie looked devilish, sitting up on his mattress, ready to make trouble. Bonnie turned pleading eyes on Flo to settle the scene. 'Get in for heaven sakes, Georgie, or there's no Friday wages for you.' Georgie would do anything for a Friday sixpence. 'Now in, in!'

And he obeyed. She was so grateful to him she felt like embracing him and did so, and kissed Betty, who was all neat, and sitting holding the latest *What Katy Did* book. Bonnie would read a chapter and it would charm Betty, who had some of Burley's forwardness and Flo's own conscientious primness as well, and who would herself read on into the night after George was asleep.

All was about to change, as Flo knew and they did not. They and she were about to be liberated, but it would be hard for them. She had the love to make their path joyful. It was to be her chief task and her fulfillment. 'Darlings,' she told them softly. 'Sweetest dreams.'

When she got back to the diningroom, Polly Sutton wanly told her she would go to bed soon, but before she did, the front door opened, shuddering under Burley's force, and in came Burley himself, his face flushed from the Turf Club agenda and the ale that needed to be drunk to deal with it. He saw the unexpected pale fraught face of Polly looking at him across the room as if he were an invader, and it gave him pause.

Flo told him, 'This is Mrs Polly Sutton. Her husband has been killed and she's staying the night. The funeral's tomorrow.' She did not make the sort of facial expressions which promised she would explain everything when they were alone. She was delighted to confuse him with Polly's unadorned tale.

'My husband was killed on the railway yesterday,' Polly explained in a rush. 'I'm back to my kids in Sydney on tomorrow night's train. Thanks for having me, Mr Flo.'

'Oh, dear lady,' growled Burley, 'it isn't any trouble at all.'

But he was troubled, Flo rejoiced to see. She went to fetch his dinner from off the range, was delighted to see the spinach had begun to anneal to the plate, and opened him a bottle of Dinner Ale. 'Would you like to drink some tea with me, Polly?' asked Flo.

But Polly pleaded tiredness again, and thanked them and escaped.

'Bloody hell,' said Burley when she was gone. 'How did *she* end up *here*?'

'It was here or the Breslin house. Breslin tells me he was driving the train northwards out of Eungai, and a tunnel archway crushed the husband's head – he was sitting on a goods wagon. Breslin feels very distressed about it, and Polly didn't want to stay with him, naturally. She was not in the mood for a big Catholic family.'

'But you don't normally do favours for people like the Breslins.'

'I met them outside the funeral directors struggling to deal with Polly. He was being very responsible, Breslin. He was taking her around in a taxi, he felt so bad.'

'All right, all right,' Burley conceded. 'I'd just like some notice in the future.'

She could not let him erect rules for a supposed future. 'It won't be happening again. Because I saw Mr Cattleford today. Burley, I intend we shall divorce.'

He came close to choking on a mouthful of chop and beer, but then hurled his head back in hilarity. 'That's a good one, Flo.'

She said nothing and when his eyes returned to her, he was frowning.

She said flatly, 'You have a son who is a half-caste. He is older than Betty but not as old as Bonnie. You committed adultery with his mother. I intend that we should divorce.'

He stared at her in what she knew was 'a man might get bloody angry if this continues' manner.

'What are you saying?' he asked. 'It sounds like lines from a play. Have you been listening to those radio dramas?'

'No. I am seeking a divorce. It's not a fancy.'

'Well, that's bloody rot for a start,' he warned her. 'Divorce is for city people, for God's sake. Bohemians and such. Theatricals, for God's sake.'

'The child's name is Eddie Kelly. It must be strange for you to see him on the streets on Fridays. I've never seen you react, though. I don't know why I haven't noticed him before now. Anyhow, I saw Mr Cattleford and he said to tell you my grievance and intentions and see what you said.'

'Did he, the old ponce? You've started going to lawyers off your own bat these days, have you?'

'The question is, did you betray me? And I know you did.'

He hissed, 'Keep your voice down, for Christ's sake. Did you get the widow in so she could hear all this and spread the news?'

Flo knew she must not be sidetracked into her motives for giving harbour to the widow. She asked, with even seriousness, 'You did betray me, didn't you?'

'What a bloody question!' murmured Burley.

'An easy one to answer.' She stood and went to a notebook she had placed near the breadbin earlier.

She said, 'Deny he's your son.'

He was hissing again. 'I won't descend to doing any of that, Flo, so stop it.'

She could tell he was still worried their discourse would be overheard by the widow. And she herself was fearless and declared, 'This boy is clearly your son. How many times did you lie down with his mother?'

He stood up and stepped a little closer. He whispered passionately. 'This is enough, Flo. Get yourself under control.'

'Will you come later in the week to visit Mr Cattleford with me?'

Burley examined her. 'I was actually told . . . yes, I was told someone saw you leaving Cattleford's. A girl who works for Basil Quiney saw you. She told him. Basil was delighted, of course, to let me know. But it didn't seem anything at the time. I'd forgotten it but . . . Jesus, it could start a lot of talk, you know, if you keep on this track.'

'I want you to acknowledge to Mr Cattleford that you committed adultery with Eddie Kelly's mother.'

His first reply was a grunt, an expulsion of air.

'Bugger me!' Burley muttered. She moved to the door. She was aware and excited by the fact he was utterly pole-axed by her new insistence, her not yielding, her nakedly stated intentions. This was a good thing. 'I put the widow in the back bedroom. I'll sleep in Jerry's room.'

'No, you bloody won't,' he hissed. 'You'll sleep with me.'

She ignored this. His breath was heavy. He snorted. Would he hit her? Let him! 'When I next see him, I am asking Mr Cattleford to proceed with plans to consult a barrister and prepare a divorce writ. You can come with me if you want. I hope Quiney's girl is still on the lookout.'

'Hey,' he called as a warning, 'this has gone far enough, Flo.'

'No, when you admit your crimes, it will start to go as far as it should. And you can marry again. That little tart from Sherry's office who thinks you're the ants' pants.'

'Do you think I'll let a divorce writ go ahead? That I'll let *you* go ahead.'

'But you can't stop me, Burley. Mr Cattleford knows I'm talking to you tonight. And it could have been worse, he suggested having a minister of religion present. If I turn up bruised when I see him . . . well, he'll understand at once how that happened.'

'You really have a man tied up,' he admitted. He took on a placating tone. 'Come on, Flo, this isn't you. What's been getting at you?'

'I think you have,' she said. 'With your denials. Perhaps we'll get the truth after you've had a bit of rest.'

And it was then she chose to stride to the bathroom.

———

The rebels and the Free State in Listowel, who had surrendered to them, lived fraternally, they in their billets, the rebels in theirs. As yet things were sylvan and sweet in Kerry. But then at the end of July a ship left Dublin with half a thousand Irish Guards veterans, now members of the Free State Army, an eighteen-pound gun and an armoured car. A tight-mouthed tough guy named O'Daly was the general aboard the steamer, and was Michael Collins' bosom fellow assassin. O'Daly's group landed in Fenit, a bit west of Tralee. There were other landings too, one up near Tarbert. By the first days of August the invaders had tracked down and were locking up the men of the rebel Second Brigade in Tralee. What *could* be done against armoured cars?

Meanwhile, in their own area, Johnny's squad went to work on the railway – the Free State bastards were going to have to be marching if they wanted to come up from Fenit or down from Tralee. By persuasion, the rebels closed down the mail, but chiefly by putting up signs urging postmen not to deliver it on risk of being shot. Apart from that, Da Costigan spoke very persuasively, always beginning, 'Now my good fellow, how's the family?' And thus the postmen were helped out in their strike against the post office. Johnny and his da and the boys went out and dug up the roads. They were supposed to be a nation fighting for its soul, but the locals bleated – 'Oh, I can't deliver my eggs'; 'Jesus, I can't sell jam'; 'Christ Almighty, I can't buy the Dublin newspapers.'

They were well fed, Johnny and his da. Being a child of truth was great for having farmers give you ham for lunch.

And then, everything changed. Because Collins, chairman of the Provisional Free State, was shot dead by one of the rebels in West Cork, not so far off even in Irish terms and bloody close in Australian geography. Fatally shot at Ballinablath, the Mouth of the Flowers. Oh, as they say, what a fall was there! Did all of the rebels suffer for it? You could bloody well be assured they did under O'Daly. For, as they say, the gloves came off, and things were fierce enough to suit Johnny with the gloves still on.

Whereas earlier in the year Johnny's squad had lived in town, they were now living in stone ruins and abandoned farmhouses and even in caves.

Up in Kilmainham, outside Dublin, the Free State were shooting rebels against the same walls where the British had shot the heroes of 1916. In Kerry General O'Daly's men added to their distinguished record by torturing and shooting an unarmed lookout, a seventeen-year-old named Bertie Murphy, whom Johnny knew. Evil was afoot, you could well say.

Johnny was eighteen himself then. He had not yet realised fully how mutual the evil was – even though he had helped put up signs along the roads that said that for every rebel killed two Free Staters would die. It seemed a rhetorical flourish and not a genuine arithmetical threat.

It was just a few days further on that Listowel was occupied and four rebels captured there. They were held in Listowel Prison and were to die with O'Daly's usual lack of judicial process. Johnny was told he was to observe the execution, which was slated for ten o'clock in the morning at a place symbolically chosen, the crossroads to the east of Listowel called Dromin Green. Here, two friends of General O'Daly of the Free State Army and of unutterable memory had been blown up by a party of rebels. So there, hidden by the trees and the cold of the day, was a reliable girl-messenger, Nula, with Johnny himself, like two unlikely romancers as

140

yet unperceived except by God, like Wordsworth and the Maid of Buttermere, without chaperone and lying down by a slight rise as if to explore each other, as the wholesome and unpolitical young do. Mind you, Johnny loved her platonically, as he did all of them, the women volunteers. These volunteers had all been competent and self-assured little girls at school, where Johnny had first known them. And within no time they had from their foremothers a knowledge of how to get details out of Tans they might meet at fairs or sweet shops, and they could carry concealed weapons for which the Free State Army had up to now been too delicate to search them.

Now Nula and he sat like Sabbath excursionists behind a screen of brush above a ditch in which the water had frozen, or so it seemed, all the way through. 'Have you seen men shot by execution?' she asked Johnny in a silken whisper. 'Not in so many words,' he told her. If she had asked him even a year back, he would have got anecdotal on her and tried to impress her. She put a gloved hand on his ice-blue bare one. It was like a word of mercy in a cruel world.

'I volunteered because I've seen the dead, right enough, already,' he told her.

She said, 'One of the girls warned me, "Don't start praying aloud when you see them; put the blindfolds on." She said it was natural as blinking to do so.'

She and Johnny shivered and kept the crossroads in sight. Before the trucks arrived, he had moved off along the ditch so he could take a different angle on the event, and in case one of them was spotted. The sun came out as he sat amongst brambles and even slept a little, for though the day was icy it was still. But then he heard trucks grinding their way along from the direction of Listowel. He saw them appear, the gears howling with the cold, and heard and saw them stop at last.

First, four coffins were set up by Free State soldiers on the icy ground on a strip of common. Then the prisoners were let down and stood, handcuffed, amidst the coffins. A Free State lieutenant lined up the firing squad of twelve men. The four condemned men were stood, each by his coffin. Johnny could see them clear – the great oaf O'Mealley, who had persecuted Mr Dorney, the teacher who tried to interest Johnny uselessly and without joy in what he called 'letters'. A minute passed, and O'Mealley was the first to shuffle up, though tethered by wrists and ankles, to give his coffin a nudge with his boot, as if he was testing its construction and might reject it. The lieutenant let his men smoke, and then decided the condemned should have their cuffs taken off their arms so they could smoke. He lit their cigarettes himself. As they smoked, the four condemned men enjoyed themselves bantering with or *at* the soldiers whose job seemed to be picking up cigarette butts and heaving coffins full or empty. Johnny saw the officer look at his watch and frown in the direction of town. His senior officer was late. He was not delighted to be stuck here with a nervous firing squad and the impudent good-as-dead. For the Irish did have a gift for joking at death, and he knew it, and it unsettled him.

The men by the coffins kept larking. It was the best vengeance they could take, and they could have been fellows frisking about on some vacant site and waiting for the boss to arrive with orders. Although this *was* coffins! They swapped them, switched the labelling with their names, they sat up in them smoking like the newly risen Just of God having their first fag at the Second Coming of Christ.

They distracted Johnny so much he failed to see or only at the last hear a car arrive with a more senior officer.

Johnny could, even at Nulla, visualise this man now, should memory strike him. The subtle way his shoulders leaned forward from his thin trunk. One day, if the man lived that long, he would have a stoop. But as he moved now, there was no confession of weakness in him. There was an authority to him that made the victims stop their larking about and stand upright, men willing to die politely for the sake of his rank. Johnny would discover his rank was that of colonel and he was a staff officer to Major General Paddy O'Daly. This officer, as Johnny would get to know too closely, was Colonel Kevin Breen.

It went fast then. Breen spoke to each of the condemned men, and he did not seem to be courting their forgiveness. There had been a time even last year when an officer would let the about-to-be-shot know that this was a day which would haunt him, the executioner, would even assure them they would be remembered at every Mass he attended until his death. But Breen had been in France and then on O'Daly's squad, and was a practised and unrepentant assassin by now, and probably did not care if they went to heaven or hell.

He returned to the firing line and told the young officer of the execution squad to continue. And the lieutenant did, and Johnny watched, riveted in place in that still freezing air as the volley of shots travelled sharper than any question ever to come to his ear.

The dead lay slovenly where they fell, part in, part out of the coffins. Most of O'Mealley was not in his, and had to be persuaded, an arm here, a leg there. Two of the firing squad sat on the ground weeping, while the lieutenant tried to reconcile them to what had been done, and Breen stood over them and chastised them. The coffins were in the meantime finally filled, each with its corpse, and lidded and lifted into a truck. Relatives would be informed and come and collect the bodies at Listowel barracks. The trucks departed, making back to the town. They left blood on the crossroads to the workings of the next shower. They rolled past the hiding place of Nula and Johnny, who then cut across country to report to those who had ordained them witnesses.

Two days later Johnny and Da Costigan helped stop and hold up the mail train from Ballybunion to Listowel, taking all the mail. They wore bandannas, and Johnny had a Lee Enfield rifle and two others had Thompson guns, including Da. But people from the train had the cheek to come up to them and complain, the grand young Lady Stark telling them off as lawless and reproving them on the basis that her aunt could not manage the road into Listowel. A few passengers from third class muttered their support. '*Tiocfaidh ár lá*,' said an old woman who could have been in a play as Mother Ireland. 'Our Day Will Come'. Walking along more willingly than Lady Stark's auntie, though her day, darling old biddy, would probably never come!

13

Kempsey, New South Wales, 1933

Beneath the tall, blue-trunked eucalyptus trees in the graveyard below the Macleay District Hospital, Flo Honeywood thought, in extending sisterly sympathy to Polly Sutton, to take a little delight in the fact it was a funeral involving both the Catholic Church and Railway Workers' Union. A funeral at which her attendance would gall Burley – as much as she knew she must not stop there, at mere galling. How strange a business it all was! Burley had insisted she must marry him, had endured her doubts and her fear and her astonishment. She was faced by a full-blooded and crafty siege. 'You'd be a fool,' said her mother, 'to send a man like that packing.' He was, said her mother with pride, an 'ardent' suitor.

As magpies gargled in the tall trees, the priest in a black stole led the mourners to the new-dug pit, and Flo's hand was on Polly Sutton's elbow the whole way. In a dark suit Breslin, lined up with religious and union brethren at the edge of the grave, inhaled at this sight of woman helping woman as no man could.

The priest began the graveside prayers, which astonished Flo by being in English. The men by the grave answered in gruff, brave, united diction. The prayers were long and ended with a segment of rosary. Flo wondered, was the priest dragging it out deliberately, delaying the fatal moment of the coffin descent when Polly might well turn into a vengeance and damn Breslin and his brothers and tear at their faces?

The gravediggers at last began to lower the coffin. Polly, beneath her arm, did surge forward with grief and the tempo of sobs increased, but she had no condemnation for anyone. Flo held and subdued her, knowing that for Polly her version of the knowable earth was collapsing. Whereas had Burley been in the coffin . . .

When the grave was covered, Breslin came to her and to Polly Sutton, who was hiccoughing with loss.

'Would you like me to collect Mrs Sutton for the train tonight?' You had to give him marks for stubborn kindliness, especially given he had killed the husband.

'I will take Mrs Sutton and her luggage,' said Flo.

'Well, I'll be there,' said Breslin, and nodded and left.

There is a man, thought Flo. Why did I not meet someone like him?

In the refreshment room that evening, Flo and Polly sat alone as Breslin and another railwayman were grateful to be at the counter to buy tea for four. Polly's cardboard case was at her feet, and her only other possession was a *Women's Weekly* Flo had bought her. While the men were at the counter, Flo gave the dazed Polly a five pound note, from the treasure of Burley Honeywood, and asked where

146

she would be living. Polly said something about a mother-in-law who lived in Bankstown but sounded dubious about it. Her kids, she said, were there at the moment, anyway.

'Write to me with an address when you're settled,' said Flo. 'I'll send what I can, while I can . . .'

'Mr Breslin and the men were kind too.'

But, thought Flo, we all want you to go. Now that you've made things right and absorbed the death of your husband.

Breslin and the other man turned up with their tray of tea, a teapot and buns. 'Well,' said Breslin, sitting and choosing to eye the teapot, 'we have a quarter of an hour, and the guard, who's a mate of ours, won't go without you, Mrs Sutton.'

'It was a lovely funeral,' said Polly, and God help her, she meant it.

———

After nearly a week of desperate dwelling on the event, and yielding to unrelenting longing and shame, Christian forced himself back to Tsiros's. He wondered why it took him so long when he found it vacant at mid-morning. This time he specified to Mrs Tsiros what he wanted. *Turkish-style* coffee. 'Much sugar you want?' asked Mrs Tsiros in a jowly growl. He did not properly hear her. 'One, two?' she asked. This was what his life was like – at every departure he risked, he created more questions than he was qualified to answer. Mrs Tsiros smiled. 'You got the sweet tooth, nice boy?'

Nice boy.

'Oh, two sugars, thank you.'

'Comes in a *briki*,' she said, knowing his naïvety, 'little Greek pot. Okay, nice boy?'

He nodded and despaired and went and sat in one of the booths with their white panelling of ancient Greek figures. He thought that perhaps death was a good answer to bewilderment. No questions on the far side. Surely not? Everyone was a beginner at death.

So he sat, and after a while, before he had got himself composed enough to read, one of the Tsiros boys he remembered from public school brought out the coffee cup and the little copper pot and poured the frothed coffee into his cup. 'How's it going, eh, Chris?' young Tsiros asked, a thorough Greek son of the Macleay. 'You're at uni, I hear.'

'Just doing law in Sydney.'

'Bugger me,' said young Tsiros. 'You were a bright little fella, though. I remember.'

He had read somewhere that the Greeks had been exponents and inventors of love between men. Young Tsiros didn't seem a credible recruit, though. 'I'll let you get on with your reading. Thick bloody book, that one!'

'I'm just dipping into it,' said Christian in extenuation. For in Australia even intellectual desires were considered suspicious.

Twenty minutes went then. The contractors to real estate deals, as described bloodlessly in his books, were not sick from a passion, unless it was the passion for acquiring title in boring tracts and stretches.

And then Chicken arrived, walked in, saw him and crossed to his table with a charming hesitancy. 'Mr Webber, isn't it? I wondered how your father was? You see, I happened to be . . . well, it was in the Victoria wasn't it? That he . . .'

'My mother tells me he's doing well,' said Christian meaninglessly. His poor unwitting father. But the painful question was: what had bitten him now, in 1933, so long after the event? 'Everyone's a bit mystified,' he said. 'We . . . we want to stop him suffering . . .'

'Yes. But I suppose you don't know quite which route to take.'

I am talking to Chicken Dalton, Christian rejoiced, distracted from his father's undiagnosed malaise. I am talking normally with Chicken Dalton. Already! That much was success of a kind.

Chicken said, 'He is a good man, your father. My father worked for him once, fencing. My father called him a just man. Didn't bring out a theodolite or a spirit level at the end of the day and try to talk the agreed rate down.'

'Thank you,' said Christian. 'I shall tell him — when he's better and I'm allowed to see him — what you said, Mr Dalton.' Chicken leaned forward conspiratorially. It was delicious to Christian Webber to see him so close. 'You drink Turkish too? Coffee, I mean?'

'Oh yes. Well, I did today.'

'Kostas Tsiros gets his coffee from the Italians in Libya, not Turkey, of course, but he makes it Turkish-style. Mind you, the Turks drove some of his family out of Smyrna. That's why they came here.'

Chicken winked and Christian wanted to reach up and kiss him fair on his ironic eye. But it lost irony as he looked. 'I seemed to be to blame for making you leave the other day,' said Chicken. 'I meant to apologise for . . .'

'No, no,' said Christian, knowing how implausible he sounded. 'I realised I was late for a meeting.'

'Oh,' said Chicken, 'some lucky girl . . .'

'No, just a meeting.' Christian's voice seemed to bloat in his throat as he struggled the words out. 'Would you care to join me at this table, Mr Dalton?'

'Dear boy,' said Chicken in a lowered voice. 'If I don't, it's purely for your reputation. You should not have to bear mine, you see.'

Christian was overtaken by a sudden and prickly stubbornness. 'I understand,' he said. He looked up at Chicken and hoped that his eyes brimmed with significance, 'Would you still wish to join me for a coffee, Mr Dalton?'

Dalton scanned his face. A delighted smile came from him. This is a man like me, it occurred to Christian, and he delights in his chains, while mine are choking me to bloody, squalid despair.

'I would be honoured, Mr Webber. Christian.'

His old schoolmate came up again, casually, not making a meal of interpreting the new friendship. Another Turkish coffee was ordered. 'And say,' breathed Chicken, in film dialect, 'say, do you have any of that honey pastry . . . baklava? The stuff Kostas makes.'

Christian did not know what this was but forgave himself for that. He was in the hands of an infallible guide.

'Dad doesn't make it, though,' said young Tsiros. 'It's Mum, credit where due, Chicken.'

'But you have some out the back?'

'Never without it. But most of the jokers in this town wouldn't touch it.'

'Well, this joker would certainly not say no to it. And Mr Webber?'

Christian said certainly and tried not to look too avid.

'It is soaked in nectar,' explained Chicken Dalton in a tone the rest of the town mocked. 'Two pieces, if you don't mind.'

The Tsiros son went off to fulfil Chicken's orders.

To Christian, Kempsey was a town that previously had

had no mysteries. But Chicken Dalton knew them and could say where they were. Christian was convinced of it now.

'You take a risk, young Mr Webber,' said Chicken now, 'sharing a table with an ill-paid artiste such as myself.'

'What risk is that?'

Chicken coughed and looked around, assessing the street beyond the glass as well. 'That you . . . that you may not be considered a serious person.'

Christian felt at ease at last. 'What is a serious person in this town?' he asked.

'Well,' said Chicken, 'a person of repute and substance.'

Christian said, 'I thought that was what you were, Mr Dalton. I've been listening to you at the Victoria since I was a kid.'

'Oh dear, that is true. I *am* ageing.'

'I've had enough piano lessons to know that you are indeed a serious person. Seriously playful perhaps.'

'What a charming compliment that is,' said Chicken. 'Seriously playful.' He rolled the phrase around his mouth.

'Did you have a piano at home?' asked Christian.

'Dear no. My old dad was a sleeper cutter. All we could bank on having in the house on good days was bread and lard.'

Chicken remembered poverty, and shivered theatrically.

'And chickens, surely. From your nickname.'

'Oh dear, my fame precedes me. I had a gift to hypnotise chickens. Lots of people claim to be able to, but to hypnotise them so that the intervening stages – beheading, plucking, cooking – are lost on them, that is the God-given gift of a few. I discovered as a child I had the gift. Now, you must know the boutique of the sisters Quinlan? I must say that their younger brother, Harper Quinlan, has the gift. Chickens don't wake from his spells either.'

'My mother tells me they are talking of hypnosis to help my father,' Christian supplied.

Chicken blinked, surprised. He was being informed of Christian's family business, which was something more than frivolous conversation.

'I am sure it is all a much more refined process than with myself and young Quinlan. I do hope it works well for your poor father.'

Christian nodded. 'But who taught you the piano then?'

'Oh, it was old Easson. Funny old bloke! You wouldn't have met him. He taught music and took me on for free when I showed I could play the piano by ear. Ever the prodigy, you see!'

Chicken thought of Easson, pomaded, streaky hair combed exact, as if painted on the skull, and a smell of cologne water and peppermints.

In the meantime, Christian Webber was enchanted by the way Chicken narrated his life, almost like a character in a play with witty lines.

'I was rejected for overseas military service,' he told Christian, 'but they put me in a uniform and had me playing music for the soldiers in the mental hospitals. I loved it, and I hated it. The poor boys. They would sit around me in silence and listen. Some too catatonic even to fidget, you understand. Sit listening all day, some of the poor fellows. Callan Park. And up in the Blue Mountains. Sometimes a little orchestra headed by a funny little chap would play with me, no complaints, all good company. You see, there was a doctor named Craddock who believed music was a medicine. And . . . well, who can deny it? We can't even say what music is, as a thing. You can say what a bus or train is, but no one can say in a sentence, or even in two, what music is. Oh, it's a craft, of course, and as I perform, I like to think, a tiny exercise of artistry. But what it is in itself? No one can say. You can't say, "Music is so and so, does so and so," the way you can say, "A shovel is so and so, does so and so."'

'That's true,' said Christian, excited by the philosophy of Chicken, the matter of the ontology of music.

Chicken thought, at the same time, this boy considers me a town institution, like the Anglican Church or the Boy Scouts. Young Webber did not know how the acid question, 'What will become of me?' woke Chicken in the night. In this capital 'D' Depression everyone was suffering. With more and more films carrying their own *orchestral* let alone single instrument sound, and all other sounds, mechanical, industrial, natural, theatrical as well.

In the school holidays of the 1920s, in the humane dark, Chicken had played three sessions and worked a twelve-hour day, sweating and inventive. If the exhibitors sent a musical score, he played it exactly as prescribed. It was a matter of professional pride. If a film arrived without any score at all, he could fall back on his own library of themes and compositions – the standards like 'Chaplin Crying' by a magnificent composer, the Mozart of the movies, the Handel of the Alhambra, Albert Levy; or else 'Pianola Rag' by Steve Gray; the drama themes of various gifted men; then 'Maple Leaf Rag', and hundreds more. And synchronising them to the film's tempo – that was the gift. These days he might play in a full day little more than half of what he had in the old days. When would picture show palace owners decide that, in these harsh times, the habit should be broken and they did not need a pianist? It would take only

153

one of them to decide and gossip about it with the others, and then the custom of sacking your pianist would spread.

The facts that consoled him in calmer hours were that owners still *thought* they needed musicians; picture palaces and musicians were the norm; musicians distracted and indeed acted as a brake on the unruliness of audiences as reels were changed; and people needed to be charmed by music before the first feature, in the interval and, above all, in a technical crisis when a reel split. And then there was just the glory and scale of what he was: a man who could play 'The Mack Sennett Walk' one second, and 'The Dead March' from *Saul* the next.

But what if it ended, as it had ended for men cleverer than he was? Would he work on the roads for sustenance, if there was work on the roads? Get a job in a dress shop, shirt shop, shoe shop? But there were no such jobs. Could he travel town to town riding the rattlers? He would rather kill himself.

Christian saw none of this. He saw only a man of his own inclinations who was not miserable and who did not need to study *Introduction to the Law of Real Property*. A man who in a sense had escaped the world and who yet, again in a sense, had been honoured, even in his strangeness, for doing it.

'Do you think you would like to be an artist?' said Chicken.

'I would like to . . . well, to write things, I suppose.'

'Things?'

Christian leaned in. This was a profound confidence. 'I wondered if you were a reader?' he asked.

'Somewhat,' Chicken admitted but with honest doubt in his voice. 'Edna Ferber. I love that woman. *Wuthering Heights*. There's one for the bookies! No one character.

The whole . . . the whole view. Eric Ambler. But I am not, I'm afraid, a learned man.'

'If I could write something like *Wuthering Heights*,' said Christian, 'I'd be very happy. I just somehow understand that book has in it the essence of who I am. I don't know how she did it. It was an act of magic.'

'Tuberculosis killed her,' said Chicken. 'It kills people, yet it seems to liberate their imaginations. The Brontë sisters. They all had TB.'

'Of course,' said Christian and did not feel, for once, guilty of his ignorance. For he wanted to kiss him, to kiss Chicken, who seemed skinny enough himself to be a target for the terrible white plague. Sweating, Christian felt he must be brave or die. 'Look, could we meet any time and discuss all this. Books, film, music? I know nothing, but I want to talk about precisely these things. I have so much time on my hands, university holidays. And no childhood games to distract me anymore.'

Chicken blinked. 'Well, I am very honoured. We could have some sherry at my place in Clyde Street after the Victoria closes – any night . . . even tonight.'

Christian's face turned red. 'Oh, I have to be home tonight. My mother's back from Sydney and would be concerned . . . Wrongly . . . but concerned if I stayed out. If I were a free agent . . .'

'Oh,' said Chicken softly, 'my boy, who is a free agent? I am certainly not free of the Victoria.'

'I want to see you,' said Christian, his face still blazing from this test of valour and endurance.

'Then there is tomorrow, half past ten. At Clyde Street? Do you mind . . .'

'I will be there!' declared Christian.

'My friend,' said Chicken, half-amused. 'There is no need for the desperate tone. We are not about to charge the waterholes at Beersheba like the Light Horse, after all. We are just having morning tea.'

'But I want so badly,' said Christian, wondering if he had more bravery still left, 'to talk to you.'

Chicken placed his right hand on Christian's, which had been flapping like a dying bird. 'If you come . . . I dare not hope you will . . . but if you come, I will understand. And all the reasons you are there.'

Christian sat back in his seat and drew a deep breath. 'Thank Christ,' he said.

'Yes,' said Chicken, the solemn commemoration of the Passion of Christ thudding in his imagination. 'Yes, indeed.'

'I will bring cake,' said Christian, breathing harshly. As at the end of a race.

14

Kempsey, New South Wales, 1933

Chicken had made something of a place for himself at the Federal Hotel by the river on Sunday afternoons, his only day off. Since pubs were meant to be closed for the Sabbath, the Federal operated behind closed doors by special arrangement with Sergeant Bernie Ives, the principal policeman of the town and shire.

Chicken's appearances there were occasional and legendary. But he had gone the evening after Christian had visited his cottage and spent time there as a lover in an unstinting embrace unlike Johnny Costigan's half-shamed one. Chicken had no idea how long his good fortune with Christian would last, but felt it was sane to wish for at least a season rather than the two or three iterations. In his own legend, he stood at the end of the bar and drank a pony of Tooth's and men discoursed with him, half-joking but gobbling up his film talk, and asking for his commentary on the news of the world, which they absorbed seriously since they considered him an educated man and he had at least seen more news-reels than any of them. Thus he held court. If one of them went and stood beside him, there would be hoots from other drinkers.

'Here we go!'

'Watch it, Chicken, he might make you normal!'

But this afternoon a stranger came in, a polished-looking man, with straight-sleeked hair and a passable grey suit that hinted at the city, and a decent homburg. He had a soft Irish accent, and as a visitor had been able to talk his way in the yard door, the doors on the street being locked and the blinds down. He was more mannered than many other men and he asked where Chicken Dalton was, and hardly anyone hooted as Chicken was pointed out, and he moved to join Chicken. His purpose was so obviously business. Everything about him said *solid citizen*, the citizen some of them wanted to be.

'Mr Dalton?' he asked. He had a slightly see-saw way of speaking, rather like Johnny Costigan.

'The same, sir,' said Chicken, a little alarmed nonetheless, unable to guess exactly why this fellow was seeking him out. Was this the investigator of missing fifty-dollar bills from Costigan's letter?

'Forgive me,' he said. 'I was knocking at your door and your good woman neighbour came out, dear old thing, and told me you might be here.' He gave a thin-lipped but not unattractive smile. 'My name is Frank Holland. I am a clerk in the New South Wales railways. I believe you receive mail for a fellow from my neck of the woods back home named Johnny Costigan.'

'Oh yes,' said Chicken. He had not quite conceded to this man's *bona fides* yet, though all seemed promising.

Clerk of the New South Wales railways. An estimable job in a time like this, an enviably unsackable job, as long as you did not blow up a train.

'Now, Mr Dalton,' said Holland, 'The thing is, I lived in the United States a time. In Cleveland. And I knew Johnny's sister, Mimmie. And she's written lately about her husband, who's an older man, a shopkeeper – she's well found that way – but he's sickening.'

'Oh, I see then,' Chicken admitted. Holland's summation of the sister situation coincided so well with Johnny's own. 'Yes, he has a sister there and told me the brother-in-law isn't so well.'

'I was hoping to look him up for her. I'm here on railway business. Came up on the train yesterday. They've put us up at the Commercial.'

They would, thought Chicken, suddenly the resentful socialist. While the masses starved.

'We're looking at sites for a new fettlers' camp near Bowraville. And they'll be building a siding somewhere up there.'

'Ah,' said Chicken, 'I think I've been in every siding between here and Brisbane. Here and Sydney as well.'

'Yes,' agreed Frank Holland with a small smile. 'It can take a while, the journey, with all the traffic on that Northern Line. But consider if the Japanese, happy enough in Manchuria at the moment, ever came south. How we would need the sidings then for the flow of supplies!'

The man was a patriot!

'So, you are obeying military masters?'

'It's my guess there's been a word or two from generals. Not that we have many in this country. In my experience, the fewer the better. Did you serve in the Big One, Mr Dalton?'

'To my shame, I was not sent away. I was in a musical unit though, and hope it did some good.'

'The British did fight to their last Australian and Irishman, didn't they?'

Chicken's national pride bristled. 'The Australians had notable successes. And every man of them a volunteer!'

'I do not mean to offend you, Mr Dalton,' Frank Holland told him, not evading his gaze.

'Now near here, Mr Holland, at South West Rocks, the river mouth, they had a camp for Germans. Captured from the German possessions in the Pacific. We gave them an occasional film night and I was astounded, Mr Holland—'

'Let's make it Frankie.'

'Very well. I was astounded how broadly the Germans were spread across our region.'

Holland smiled. 'It's amazing how widely the British still are.'

'Well, Mr Holland, Frankie, you speak like a Hibernian, and I take your point without offence. But the Germans held at South West Rocks were not only from Australia and New Zealand, but from German New Guinea, the Solomons, Kaiser Wilhelm's Land, Bougainville Island, the Marshalls and Marianas, German Samoa and the province of Shantung and Tsingtao in China, and I can't remember where else. The prisoners were empire-builders, you see. There were engineers and hotel managers and doctors and . . . well, there were Buddhist monks from Ceylon as well, to be fair. The point is, we put paid to the Germans in the Pacific. And that . . . that is surely not a small thing.'

Though a Pacific with or without Germans did nothing for the security of his job and his artistry, or how easily a Fotoplayer run by a yokel could replace him.

'Not a small thing, no,' Holland agreed. 'Things weren't as easy-going in France and Belgium, I'm afraid. But may I revive the question of my friend Johnny Costigan?'

'Well, your friend Johnny has a hard billet up on a dairy farm at Nulla Creek, a place owned by Mr Bert Webber, who, speaking of the Great War, is being treated for . . . well, for the shock suffered in the war as we speak. A funny business. But I believe you cannot predict when these things will strike. In any case, it is hard work and a long way from town for Johnny, more than fifty miles. Every third Saturday he leaves the place to come to town and collect his mail from me after I've finished work at the Victoria. I believe this coming Saturday he'll be by.'

Johnny often brought his wife and kids to town and they slept in the wagon by the river just over East, where they got the river breeze and there were fewer mosquitos. Then by dawn Sunday morning, he was back, and they would all go to first Mass and take the wagon back home. It was a snake paradise out there on Nulla, Chicken knew. The red-bellied blacks were very fat and the goannas longer than a man. But Johnny's kids seemed healthy, the times Chicken had accidentally seen their cart arriving or leaving town. But he did not volunteer all this, as amiable as Holland seemed.

'Does he ever come here?' asked Holland.

'Well, he generally drinks here during his Saturday evenings. He can't collect his mail till I finish my work at the Victoria.'

'Then I'd be pleased to meet him here,' Holland said. 'I must thank you for your courtesy today.'

Chicken said, 'You are welcome to join me for a drink now and a further chat about Johnny.'

Chicken knew there would be no adventure in it, simply company, and he liked company.

'I'm not the man I was for late nights,' said Holland. 'But I'm delighted to accept, sir.'

Most men of the *other*, woman-centred stripe, thought queers were rampant all the time, Chicken thought, lamenting within. As if they never wanted mere comradeship, the joy of other men discoursing in fraternity.

But then Holland showed what a broad-minded fellow he was by walking along the street back towards Ultima Thule with him. His homburg was tugged down a bit, but that was his style. And no one seeing them would have expected Holland as engaged with pansy business.

Such a solid citizen, and Chicken was delighted to confuse whatever watchers there were in the Sabbath town by being with him.

15

Sydney, New South Wales, 1933, and France, 1916

Under Dr Bulstrode's medicine and treatment, Bert was in France a lot. He could not indeed shake that belief even though he was simultaneously at Bulstrode's clinic. I am a young married man, he remembers, and I have pledged deathless devotion to a wife and child. What am I doing here? But the therapy kept reacquainting him with it, and he was not unhappy, nor happy either, yet was certainly absorbed by the revisited vividness of it.

He was travelling third class on a train up from Marseilles. Wooden seats. No upholstery. Pretty cramped. He noticed that the supreme soul Corporal Kurt Lembke was jammed in with the rest of them. They had rushed them through Marseilles as if they were criminals. Straight from ship to train. Marseilles was said to be full of famously bad women, and the 53rd Battalion full of kids who'd like to think themselves famously bad because they had squinted through the doors of the worst addresses in Cairo and Port Suez.

But once on the train, everyone was humble and smiling broadly, and like choirboys when women in white blouses came through the carriages or met them on the platform, when they got down for a stretch, to give them fruit and coffee and crucifixes. 'Lovely bloody girls,' said Poddy earnestly.

———

The shocks continued to revive France for him in the quiet hours of his therapy, when the electricity receded from his system and returned things he had forgotten.

Bert had noticed something interesting about Poddy. Poddy had a typical cow-cocky's bitterness amongst the men jammed up together on wooden seats like this. Bert thought it a friendly arrangement. But Poddy got bitter because the officers were in first class. A cocky's son, who'd just passed the primary final at Mungay Creek bush school, one teacher, still felt entitled to resent the world. Could resent universities he'd never laid eyes on but had now heard about. Could want land he'd never seen until now. Could suspect some unjust authority had kept it from him. And in France it seemed he half-resented the view of ploughed fields full of chocolate-coloured soil that promised a harvest not yet planted. And vineyards running down to the Rhone River with, on the far bank, a white chateau or an old grey tower keeping watch for invaders. 'No one ever told me this was bloody here,' complained Poddy to Bert.

It was the way Poddy enjoyed things too. Seeing it all is bitter and sweet to Poddy at the same time. Something has dented his soul in the old country, and maybe by way of the ancestral trip to Australia. He said to Bert with a bitter delight, 'Who else from up the river has seen it except us?'

At the station in Albi, Bert Webber was detailed to fill the eight canteens of his section at one of the station water pumps. A young French woman with a lace headpiece and lace-covered shoulders above the dress, and an embroidered bodice – a woman forgotten and retrieved again now by electro-shock – was standing by when he finished filling all those canteens, and offered him a metal-clad wooden crucifix. The face and body of the Christ very defined, the face ravaged, and all literally depicted as if to offend the Protestant idea that the individual believer creates his own mental image of the suffering Christ from his knowledge of the Scriptures.

Bert had rejected other such devotional Papist items at earlier stations, but his hands were full of the canteens and their straps, and his gestures of refusal looked like admissions that his chief concern was having no hands free to receive the thing. He uttered a few words, '*Non, non, merci* . . .' But the young woman laughed and slipped the crucifix into his tunic side pocket. His face blazed red, but he recovered when she ran off.

When the canteens had been distributed to their owners, Lembke, who was opposite Bert, asked, 'What did that girl foist on you?'

Bert said, 'One of their crucifixes.' He took it from his pocket but did not look at it.

'May I see it?' asked Corporal Lembke.

Bert let go of it and Lembke inspected it, the crucified figure. Lembke said, 'There's quite a bit of anguish on his face.'

'Well,' said Bert, trying to seem well-practised in his attitudes, 'they're French, aren't they?'

Lembke went on inspecting the figure on the cross. Then he passed the crucifix back, as if it were Bert's choice to contemplate it or not.

'Do you reckon I should keep it?' asked Bert.

'Oh yes,' Lembke told him. 'Luther's not going to complain.' He leaned forward. 'You know, other Protestants say we're too tolerant of the figure on the Cross. But out here, where anyone, any soldier, can be the figure at any moment, it doesn't seem to matter much.'

Lembke bunched his fist and gently made a pounding, fraternal motion on the arm of Bert's uniform jacket.

'Bert,' he murmured. 'We all must remember not to get hung up on small matters.'

Bert blinked. He'd always thought that was what pastors were for: to hang you for small sins. Lembke was a prophet of revelation though, Bert decided. When the war was over, he thought, I might choose not to move far from his side.

He and Corporal Lembke moved forward to each other because of the racket of games of euchre proceeding all over the carriage – it was the game of choice and the crazed enthusiasm in the Australian Imperial Force.

'The French peasants are Catholic,' Lembke was saying, as if it were clear to any fool, 'because their nobles stayed Catholic in the Reformation. Except for the Protestant ones, of course, and the Catholics tried to kill them off. Huguenots – you might have heard of them. Now the Northern Germans – like us – and the Saxons? Lutheran! Because the nobility turned Lutheran. The creed each of us recites is determined by history, you see. And by rent.'

At that, Lembke chose to stop, swaying as the train swayed, and winked.

'The Bavarians are Catholics,' argued Bert, feeling a

little grievance in being so clearly urged to understand and thus be lenient on their position. 'The Macleay Valley's full of them, and they marry the Irish.'

'Yes,' said Lembke gently. 'History. It's what we do *after* we inherit faith, that's what counts!'

Bert could not help frowning. The light of God depended on who your landlord was in territories the world now fought over. Lembke continued. 'What we do . . . you know . . . from *that* point . . . It's possible for princes to declare a belief. It is us peasantry who, above all, honour it.'

But it was hard to consider the exact slant of Lembke's argument, exalting peasants, questioning princes, and making God an accident to all that, as it was to utter *alleluias* for your German inheritance when you are surrounded by the children of Australian Scots and Irish and English, and also on the way to a front line. Corporal Lembke was wise to whisper his lessons about farmers and princes, and the coincidence of being the son of a German cocky in the far Macleay.

So pleasant when they let the battalion off the train, after thirty hours' travel, at some little village, to allow a sleep in fields. Bert slept six hours on a spread great coat and grass and cool, deep soil. He could feel it now, here at Dr Bulstrode's clinic, could swear the earth was nobbly and kind beneath his shoulders. He was aware the spring sun was warm over the flat country they had entered. At one stage he saw Poddy working away through the grass to the topsoil and assaying its depth and dark tint. 'Bloody hell,' he murmured in reverent complaint.

Back on the train at last, a perhaps misleading hint of the closeness of battle. Captain Acres and one of the battalion doctors came through the carriage asking, 'Does anyone have a fever?' As if anyone would admit. No one wanted to miss out on wherever they were going, the full experience, maiming counted in. Then someone yelled and pointed. They had been in a forest a while, but now had come out into farmland, and could see far away a fantastical set of gardens and a palace, there beyond embankments. 'Louis XIV,' Corporal Kurt Lembke told Bert. Men gawk, and Bert gawked. It was a magic strand across their vision. The grandeur of it shut everyone up. Bert thought, yes, that must be saved from the intruder. For, remote from the place as he had lived till now, he did not feel like an intruder himself.

The train veered away east and the palace turned its rump of blunt rear turret at them and grew littler and littler. The train found normal French villages. Villages with churches and humbler spires. They did not make such wild promises to men's imaginations, such demands of valour, as the palace had.

———

Off the train and through one of those villages. Old men working in the fields, and the young disembarked men in their woollen tunics heard the guns far off. Blokes looked at each other. Soon Bert was conscious they were marching on the cobbled roads, notoriously hard on a man's feet. But the Reverend Corporal Lembke had a sovereign remedy in his kitbag, a container of Woolgoolga tea tree oil he shared around for mixing with hot water. Not exactly the loaves and fishes, and merely a remedy from the north coast of New South Wales, the way the 53rd Battalion was designed as a remedy from the same source. They marched past farms and at last Bert's platoon was shown a barn. This is your

168

billet. Settle down with your one blanket each. Officers were given rooms in the house. Captain Acres came down through the farmyard to see if everyone was comfortable. 'That's the guns you can hear, boys,' he said. 'Not far to go now.'

From the farmhouse comes Madame and her daughter and a rush from the blokes to fill her water bucket from the pump and carry it for her. Making peace with the country round about, which was flat or shallow-ridged, but all the country boys admired it. In the village lots of young French women walking around in black. Widows. Boys avoided them as if they carried a disease. March up the road, and the thunder got closer. Big cannon. Beside the road, girls selling London newspapers. Someone came round giving men gas masks. An English soldier. Captain Acres told the company to put them on.

'The first thing when you've got them on is you feel cramped.' Because the eye piece was not really like the proper seeing of things. Some men joked. Others lifted them off gratefully and took deep breaths. Get them on again, said Captain Acres. You'll need them if they let phosgene come our way.

Down into a trench they went. Some British men let a canister of phosgene go above the trench. A hiss and a smell of mown grass. A ground hugger. It entered the trench as the men shuffled through it. Someone yelling, don't take them off, don't take them off.

An age they were in that trench. The phosgene seemed to get into Bert, even if not into his lungs. It seemed to rattle all his bones. They stumbled along in subdued panic and rose out the far end of the ditch, Bert with a hand on Poddy's back and the Reverend Lembke with a hand on

Bert's back. And they were out, and marched away from the Poms who were working the canister. The captain called, 'Take them off.' The world was sweeter at once. Bert felt he wanted to kiss the girl selling the newspapers down the road. 'Now you know,' said the captain. 'When we yell masks on, it's masks on.'

When Bulstrode leaned over Bert, Bert told him. 'When it's masks on, it's masks on.'

'Always. Always, Mr Webber. Pleased to hear from you.'

On the way back to the road there was an officer and four men by the path. They gave each man a steel helmet like the English had. Someone, a photographer, got them to raise them on bayonets. A picture was taken, everyone grinning like a goat in a cabbage garden after the phosgene. Some had taken it in their stride. The rest of them had to.

———

Bert rested amongst vines for a time then. They stretched and claimed his wrists, strapping him to the bed.

A medical officer over Bert. No, Bulstrode. Neat little Bulstrode. White coat. Standing ready by some electric box. Two nurses frowning. 'The spires run through me like spears,' Bert explained. Bulstrode switched something and a shaft ran into Bert by the heels, by the anus, by the throat, by the scalp, an arc through the sky, and at the height of it, Bert, tentacles of shock in arms and legs and thrashing in both his heels. 'They shaft me,' he cried. His brain bounced madly now from wall to wall and then across the floor, and Droopy the Bavarian corporal was there, and picked it up, and waited politely for the electricity to stop and put it back into his hands. Bloody Droopy who was meant to shoot me but shot the Prophet instead.

Jesus our fortress save me from the evil spires and electrodes, and all the tendrils and the electric steel that skewers me. There is Versailles, Lembke told him. For an instant he saw the palace glitter, yet trees got in the way.

'Mr Webber? Mr Webber?' says a nurse. 'It's all right, Mr Webber. The therapy's over.'

———

'I have to tell you,' said Dr Bulstrode, with a glow of pride, at the meeting he had called in his office, 'I have made some progress, if not with the case itself, then at least with confirming the reality of Bert's assessment.'

Anna, back down from the Macleay again, after tending to family business there, was too polite to ask what he meant, but he could tell she did not have a lot of tolerance for circumlocutions today. He continued in his fussy way. 'The military records such as unit reports and unit war diaries are still at Eastern Command, awaiting an ultimate transfer to Canberra.' He was obviously pleased to have found them in time. 'I took the trouble to go there and discovered that at Fromelles in French Picardy in late July, or more specifically on the night of the action, July 19, the Australian 53rd Battalion was opposite the 16th Bavarian Reserve Infantry. This is what we were told in so many words by Bert.'

In so many words? They were words she had not heard.

'I went then to the new German consul's house in Woollahra. You can imagine they are not so used to receiving psychiatric researchers. Not that I told them anything of Bert's case. But they confirmed that the unit of the new

German Chancellor during the Great War was the very same 16th Bavarian Reserve Infantry, in which the man served with the rank of corporal. You see, Mrs Webber, we entertained the idea that Bert's cry might have been based on delusion. But the truth is it might have been based on lived experience.'

The news of Dr Bulstrode's uncharacteristic researches cheered Anna. It reduced in Anna the sense she had that she and Bert had been wrestling with phantasms. She opened her mouth to approve, but today Bulstrode did not look for interruptions.

'And I believe it might be time to try a new treatment, Mrs Webber, or more accurately a new technique of facilitation. For it seems that electro-shock has certainly tempered the symptoms, but it is not addressing the cause. I have used in the past a hypnotist named Mr Cutlack, who is a compounding chemist in this part of Sydney. He puts the patient under, and then we proceed from there with questions. For whatever reasons we can reassociate patients with painful events and so alleviate symptoms through the technique. As for Mr Cutlack, he remains absolutely in a role of clinical discretion. It seems now though that we didn't have all the facts before, and we have a new basis for a discussion with Mr Webber.'

'I would be very grateful, doctor,' said Anna, 'if you and Mr Cutlack did what you could.' Indeed, it was welcome to her that Dr Bulstrode was so pleased with himself, and welcome that Bulstrode seemed to believe he had unearthed genuine clues to a cure, in his visit to the military records and the German consul as a modern medical inquirer.

———

Dr Bulstrode introduced Bert to Mr Cutlack the chemist late on a humid, overcast morning, a neat, lean man in a silk-backed vest. His voice struck Bert as pitched entertainingly between a coo and a command. Dr Bulstrode had reduced his medication and Bert felt less tongue-tied than normal but still could not see much sense in speaking. His was not a sullen refusal to speak. It was a lack of urgency to speak. What was to be said? He knew everything he needed to live and then die. He needed to have killed Droopy for the execution of Lembke. Speech had become superfluous to him. He harboured no prejudice against Bulstrode's passion for it, or Mr Cutlack's economic use of it.

Mr Cutlack and Bert shook hands briefly. 'Mr Cutlack will ease you into the appropriate state of suggestibility and recollection. You and I will then talk. I do not believe you will have any cause for anguish or distress today. We'll speak of France, but not your part in battle. Today is by way of a suitability test, I suppose. Later . . . well, we shall return in time to matters that damaged you, and repair the damage. I hope. We all hope.'

He brought his hands together in a soft clap.

Bert went so far as to say, 'Very well.' The words rubbed together like two dry sticks in his mouth.

Bert knew, though, he would prove a good subject. He had no intention of resisting Mr Cutlack, who advised him to breathe and close his eyes, to feel the heavy body break away, unshackling itself, to feel the weight of sleep, one, two, three . . . Cutlack's voice had the power of Bert's drugs, or was it of his mania, to return him to France even as he knew, more clearly today than under the laudanum, that he was in the Derwent sanatorium a few blocks from

Randwick Racecourse. He heard a contour of melody and proposal combined in what Cutlack said to him then.

Captain Acres was speaking to them in a railway yard in Fleurbaix, amidst artillery mounted on railway trucks, and howitzers unloading. As things stood, he said, there would be one and a half yards of assault front per man. Any man, Bert thought, can advance and conquer and go on living on a front of a yard and a half. But the rain came on. A night now of hauling up grenades and ammunitions and wire-spools and sandbags – some machine had an appetite for them, up there, the sandbag-devouring engineers pushing a sap out across no man's land. At least two such trips and then men lay in niches in the trenches and even in open ground behind the front line and thus missed the news – as the hours passed and the mist stayed in place and hugged the lines of the earth ahead – that the attack was postponed as Bert somehow knew it would be, then postponed again at mid-morning for late on the next day.

This was all too vast and ominous, thought Bert, and he had an itch to find out if Lembke could discern God's hand in it. But there was no time to ask overnight, for they were again set to work as beasts of burden, and then everyone was too tired to make inquiries about God in the world. There was some time in the meantime that Bert liked about being stuck in the France of such energetic preparations. Something lost, that Bert hankered for and did not want finally to leave.

The first light came up misty, and those told to line the parapet were still tired from carrying supplies up through the narrow and muddy communications trenches. The day continued determinedly foggy, but mist burned off all at once and displayed the features of the proposed battlefield, and cannon were heard, conversing thunderously over great distances. But everyone took great encouragement from an apparently sage and crafty letter from the headquarters of the operation, read out by Captain Acres in the trench that morning. It made men exchange smiles, and many, it seemed to Bert, wanted to seek out Kurt Lembke to exchange their smiles with.

The guns along the front of the attack due that evening would be getting exact range of the enemy trenches, said the letter, while guns firing to the south would attract the enemy's attention in that direction. 'When everything is ready, our guns and trench mortars will begin an intense bombardment of the enemy's front system of trenches.' These words had a divinity to them, were like a covenant, and cancelled fear. And an over-riding rightness attached to what followed. 'After about half an hour's bombardment, the guns will suddenly lengthen range, our infantry will show their bayonets over the parapet, and the enemy, thinking we are about to assault, will come out of his shelters and man his parapets. The guns will then shorten their range and drive the enemy into his shelters again.'

There was actual laughter at this, Poddy crinkling his eyes at the sportive wisdom of it all. Over the hours till late afternoon, all would be destroyed over there – the wire cut, the machine gun emplacements obliterated, the parapets knocked down, a large proportion of the Fritzes dead and the rest 'thoroughly frightened'. The Australian battalions would simply move in as unaccustomed new tenants on French soil.

Bert himself could have slept – 'Yes, I am tired,' he was aware of confessing to Mr Cutlack or Dr Bulstrode or both. Tired but convinced, for the remainder of the noble hours of day, of inevitable conquest.

Then the barrage started, the clever one directed at the Fritz line, and they could look over the parapet for seconds at a time and see the Fritz breastworks and segments of his parapets left in instant ruins. The wire across the way, in front of the trenches they were meant to take, was still intact at 2.30 in the afternoon, and there was a response of fire from the enemy now as if they were nervous. Shocking noise Bert had to wait through, the relentless concussion of shells whose detonation Bert felt in the fluid of his spine, their random intention being to take this man or that out of the assault and deprive him of the success to be accomplished later in the day. Great clods of No Man's Land took to the air. More soldiers were arriving over open ground from the rear but some had arms, legs and heads blown off, and there was screaming in the lull of enemy fire. But Bert knew he would not be taken early. He knew there were significant encounters ahead.

The 53rd had felt they had been granted privilege and knowledge from the letter read to them that morning. But now it was for a while as if the Fritzes had by intuition discovered a superior trick of their own. This moment, in which faith was tested, was not long. For now the guns of the forces of right increased in tempo to be a continuous wall of sound. Poddy reported from a step at the trench top that the Fritzes were going up in shreds. The first wave of the 53rd went over the lip of the trench at the curious hour of 5.43 on a bright afternoon with hours of daylight left. Bert watched men hauling themselves into the open by ladders and trench wall foot holes. Captain Acres yelled out that there would be no live Fritzes to encounter over there, where the wall of Allied, God-ordained, history-pleasing British and Australian high explosive was falling.

Cutlack called on him authoritatively to come back now, to forget the letter and encounter to be had. And to leave Poddy and Lembke to their oblivion. Bert's will could contest Cutlack. 'Mmmm,' he growled, coming to himself in the Derwent sanatorium. He had learned something, though. He did not know what. He was not yet persuaded of the value of language. But he had brought back from the day in the trench, as revisited again with the pharmacist and the doctor, a sense of a pattern which had not been part of the experience the first time.

16

Kempsey, New South Wales, 1933

No one thought it was 'pansy business' between Chicken and Frank Holland, and if anyone saw them it was all promptly forgotten, except for young Christian Webber over in East, his sensibilities raw with the recent surrenders to Chicken, not to mention Chicken's own surrenders to him. If he had had doubts before, they had matured to a new but inflamed stage, in which he still desired Chicken and still remembered how gratefully and thoroughly his mouth had moved across his flesh, finding nothing strange or abnormal there, nothing to be condemned. It was as if he had been cured, and there the saviour was, leading a banal man in a pulled-down hat. Strolling towards intimacy as if it counted for nothing. He believed he had been redeemed. And yet it seemed the experience was available to stray old men from the Federal Hotel. There was something about that Christian rebelled against. Merely, he thought ironically, with every bloody ounce of my being.

It was an accident. He had left Tsiros's at closing time, having studied there in composure and an atmosphere of approval, when he saw the two men leave the Federal together, one figure intimately known and meaningful at any distance. Chicken wore his slacks and two-tone shoes and a Fair Isle sleeveless vest. The other, a little over middle height, had no identifiable mark other than his unfashionably worn hat by which you would know him if you saw him again. By what licence did Chicken decide to do ordinary business with this stranger. Chicken had come down from the mountain to become simply Chicken, town show-off and tolerated bugger, and the world was no longer worthy and momentous? Someone had to be punished for the fact Chicken had returned to being Chicken. Christian Webber crossed the road and from Savage's deep entryway and confusing mirrors, watched the two along the open embankment towards Kennedy's and Tsiros's, until now an enchanted café.

Chicken was in conversation with another man, and though that seemed unfortunate, Christian realised now, it was not the betrayal. But if the older man was at Chicken's later in the night, that was surely betrayal. Proven.

His mother and Gertie were going to the Howleys at Toorooka for dinner. They had taken the taxi, for his mother wished not to have to drive herself across the river on the shaky old bridge up there.

At lunch that day he had still been in a fog of hope and almost painful exhilaration, and irritable when he was distracted. 'I hope you're livelier for your father when he comes home,' said his mother wanly.

Now, as the afternoon eked away, he knew exactly where his father kept what he needed for the newly extreme

179

and intolerable world where he found himself. It lay in the forbidden-to-him upper drawer of the parental lowboy.

The lowboy had been its own county when he was little. But it was just an ordinary, modestly dimensioned cupboard with two flash strips of walnut veneer; room at the other end for his mother's dresses, at this end for Bert's sober raiment. So it was plain, marital furniture he approached without any special regard, and he opened up his father's side and smelled the mothballed paternal suits, and pulled a drawer to take out the little pistol, the neat thing, wrapped in a chamois. The destructive little thing was barely more than toy-sized. Though it had the safety on, as his father had once shown him before denying him any access to it in the most fervid terms, it still had bullets in it when he detached the magazine from the gun's handle and checked. They had the look of something loaded long ago, though the gun was well oiled. They had the look of bullets the stranger from whom Bert took it had put there. If brass could age, they had the look of age. The chamber was not full, and the top bullet must be brother to the one that had martyred the Lutheran Saint Lembke of whom he had heard his father speak.

For two or three years now, Christian had thought, with the unrooted anger of a lost soul, if I must end the mess, I'll do it with the Lembke gun. He was intending to go out in the shirt and slacks he was wearing, but even this little, precise pistol was too big to carry in a pocket, nor could he go through the streets waving it, although the idea attracted him. So he got a sports jacket and, though it made the chest pockets droop, a baggy side pocket contained it easily.

He need not leave the house until at least nine. The *Introduction to the Law of Real Property*, he decided. Chicken was his real property. That must be proclaimed even at gunpoint.

180

A little after nine on a Sunday night, the town was well lit but empty. Sly grog shops were doing business in the side lanes and back streets and you would get a sign of their unromantic business as you passed by and saw a small traffic of men coming and going. They looked at a distance unconsoled, as desolate as he felt. The truth about sly grog joints was that they hid their faces from the electric thoroughfares.

He crossed the bridge. This bloody river, the Styx and damned Acheron and Lethe of his miserable bloody life. At least the current sounded like a bad destiny rustling its skirts. To cross this river tonight, to hear it vivid and full-gushing under his feet, not sure as he transited whether he was an assassin or a suicide. He did not avoid the lights. He saw the mannequins track him with their inhuman eyes, gazing eerily into quiet Belgrave Street from the lit windows of the Quinlan sisters' and Savage's and Barsby's. Straight up Belgrave then and into the sudden bush darkness of Clyde Street, on whose entrance area the light went so far and then no further, yielding a walking man soon enough up to the vast unobserved night. He waited on an embankment opposite Ultima Thule, sitting with his back to a stretch of post and rail fence which had outlived its purpose, since there were no cows on that side of the street to be restrained from wandering. What he saw determined things and enraged him. There was light in what Christian took to be the loungeroom and it displayed itself obliquely too through the cottage's bedroom windows.

There was a middle-aged man who walked across the loungeroom windows. He who had earlier worn a tight homburg. I gave Chicken Dalton every breathing thing

I am, and he is home at night with an indistinct being, a man who owns a homburg! This is my value in the economies of body and soul. Christian knew for certain now that he had been right, and a blood payment of some sort was called for.

Now he saw Chicken, the brilliant, bewildering prince with his slicked-down hair, squint out into the darkness idly and in passing, like a man expecting to see nothing. He was telling the other man something, talking over his own shoulder, and the words could be heard because they were louder.

'I just wanted to be sure that a friend of mine . . .'

The rest being muffled, yet all sounds meaningful.

A friend?

Christian got up from the cool ground and felt for the pistol in his pocket. He crossed the street, went into, as he told himself, since all exuberance was now permitted, his last garden, and then up to the veranda, where he opened and closed the door, taking the trouble to do it securely since he wanted no more people to enter than those already present. He progressed into the lit loungeroom. Chicken was still standing and saw him and said in a rush, 'Holy Christ! Christian?' Christian was reminded to take out his pistol.

'Oh, dear lord,' said Chicken when he saw it. The other man looked at him, a practical and intelligent face, he thought, and not as easily driven to panic as Chicken.

The case was instantly stated. 'I gave you everything, Dalton. My entire body and my entire soul! And to you it's all just a little fun.'

'Don't be silly, Christian, I am seeing Mr Holland on business, do you understand. On *business*! Christ, what *is* that thing? Is it a toy?'

'It's a Luger pistol, Chicken!' Christian cried out, wanting to use the nickname with derision.

'Dear, dear lord.'

'I know that model pistol,' said the man with the neat hair, conversationally but not trying to be eager. His hair looked used to being pressed down by his hat. 'It's from the war.'

None of the bullets in its magazine were intended for him, and yet Christian waved the thing towards him. Chicken said, a little more daringly than Christian wanted, 'You're as bad as the others, Christian. You don't think I can have serious business with men who aren't pansies. I have serious business with Mr Holland, and he is *not* a pansy.'

So-called Mr Holland smiled blandly. 'No, whatever my sins, I am not a pansy. You can be assured of that, young fellow. I came here to discuss an acquaintance, and that's the flat and unadorned truth of it. But I haven't seen a pistol like that for a few years. The Germans carried that one, the Luger P-08. Bloody sight more sensible little creature than the big clunky British Smith & Wesson.'

Christian had not bothered registering any of this. 'I gave you all I am,' he reiterated in a way that required an answer.

'I think I'll be getting on, Mr Dalton,' said Holland calmly. 'I'll let you sort this one out.'

'No,' said Christian. He was confused by the man's demeanour. And yet it changed nothing. He still had his blood appetite. 'Will you give yourself to me?' Christian demanded of Chicken. How did I get so mad as I am now? he wondered. How did I become this ridiculous figure? Why am I ready to murder him or myself? 'No prevarication now!' he thundered.

And to show none would be tolerated, he put the pistol to his head and, as his father had warned him never to do, released the safety. That made a satisfying and authoritative click and made Chicken blink.

Holland said, 'Come on, son. You don't want to kill yourself with that thing. I mean, you can. But why?'

'Oh my God,' said Chicken, who was at least taking the conversation seriously. 'I never thought you were looking for a . . . what is it? A union. I've never had anyone suggest that to me.'

'I want you to be faithful, and I don't want to call you Chicken. I want to be the one who calls you by your real name. What is it? Ian, isn't it?'

Chicken thought of Johnny Costigan and all that quick, joyless tugging. 'Yes,' he told the boy. He did remember the sweeter encounter, the young, unrestrained flesh, the thoroughness of the joy given and taken by Christian. The alacrity, like a deer's. Or the boy's self-guilt – all of whatever had been rioting in him.

Chicken said, 'Don't harm yourself, dearest Christian. That beautiful head! How could I explain any of it to your mother?'

He half-expected, such was the pressure within him, that he could take the whole world with him, but, no, he acknowledged, there would be people left who would want explanations.

'It's a noble head and it's brilliant.' Chicken seemed to appeal to Frank Holland. 'He is studying law at Sydney University.'

'Get away out of that!' said Holland in apparent incredulity. 'I tell you this, if I had the chance to learn the law and bend it to my convenience . . . well, I would study it to the limit, so I would. And I wouldn't blow it out of my brainpan with that bloody thing.'

'What for?' Christian asked. 'What sort of life can I have?'

'A good one,' pleaded Chicken. Chicken was the pleader, Christian noticed. How wonderful. 'A better life than mine. And you seem to find mine fit for purpose.'

'Where did you get that handy little piece anyway?' asked Holland, it seemed with not a visible care in the world and no more than casual interest.

It was too fatuous a question for Christian to answer. Chicken did it for him. 'Christian's papa was in the war. A hero. I expect it comes from there.'

In frustration and to get on to the business of explaining himself to Chicken, Christian said, 'It was used by a German to kill a saint – a man named Lembke, who was the Lutheran pastor from Woolgoolga.'

'The Germans killed him in Woolgoolga, are you saying?' asked Frank Holland.

'A German in France killed him. The Reverend Mr Lembke fought as an ordinary soldier in the army.'

'Did your father kill the German?'

'No, he didn't,' shouted Christian. 'Stop the questions!'

'All right then,' said Holland with a ruthless lack of irony. And still he was too careful to go.

Chicken said again, 'I had no idea what you wanted, Chris? That it was all so important to you.' Christian . . . *Chris*? . . . was exhilarated. Meanwhile Chicken found all this delightfully unlikely. That a magnificent young being should want him so thoroughly and desperately. 'You're seeking . . .'

He was inhibited a second by the presence of Holland, but Holland was not going, indeed could not go, and to disarm Christian the word must be said. 'You're seeking fidelity. Put that thing away from your head, point it at me if you have to point it anywhere. I will be faithful to you, I will. I love your precious head.'

Holland was frowning now, but with a proper reserve.

'Thus,' continued Chicken, 'thus, you don't need that stupid pistol. Put it down this moment.'

If Christian did not immediately do that, it was because it had wrought such wonders. He kept it there. He heard the house tick like a clock, on its foundations. As they watched, Chicken and the stranger, he lowered the gun from his temple.

'Not,' said Holland, 'that I am at ease with what you two do. It is a matter of moral distaste but they tell me plenty of Renaissance cardinals did it, so I must be in pure historic reason, remain tolerant and say, "God bless you." And what a miracle we've all survived that fatal little creature you have in your hand!'

Christian said, piteous in his own ears, 'I would only have hurt myself.'

Chicken came up and took the pistol from him and looked for the safety catch and put it in place with an audible release of breath. Then he placed the pistol, barrel towards the wall, on a bookshelf.

Its deployment, Christian was pleased to see, as fury departed and a taste of joy came back to him, had been successful with Chicken Dalton, even if there had probably been disguised mockery from Holland. He knew that what might seem stupid to narrow people can be life and death to the people involved, as it had been to him, and he knew his right to breathe now was at least as valid as Holland's.

'Leave the damn thing there, darling boy,' said Chicken, the gun disposed of.

Holland could clearly have said much, but chose not to. 'If that little matter is settled then,' he said, 'I'll say good-night.'

'But no need, Mr Holland,' said Chicken. 'Not that you would, but, I beg you, no need to spread the news of our misunderstanding here to your friend up the river or to anyone else. Not that you would . . .'

'Not that I would,' said Holland. 'Rest assured, Mr Dalton. This little scene beggars belief.'

Let him believe that, thought Christian. What counted was that the necessity for blood was gone.

Holland fetched the homburg and left for his hotel. Christian fell weeping into Chicken's arms and Chicken himself was overtaken by tenderness and a sceptical joy. Was a marriage of souls possible for him? There had never been anyone to tell him it was.

17

Kempsey and Sydney, New South Wales, 1933

And as this scene in Ultima Thule, Kempsey, occurred, Christian would realise that he was not, soul and all, directed to Ian Dalton. He had a speculative interest in a student, his friend Walter Jupp. Christian had accused Chicken of having received all he had, but that was not true, given the way his imagination kept a positive passion for Jupp. And on top of that, he knew Jupp would have handled things more eloquently and as Chicken's peer, whereas Christian knew himself to have behaved like a child.

Jupp was in third-year law, a little man of eccentric manner with a jaunty walk and floppy blond hair that he boasted was 'untameable' on the rare occasions he gave it a mention. He was not as obviously beautiful a man as Chicken, but he had style, Jupp, and his style was fascinating. Christian could have observed him by the enchanted hour – how he moved and spoke and what he wore: his good clothes but with an instinctive rakishness – off-centre tie, vest negligently buttoned, uneven red braces, trouser cuffs and scuffed pumps – added up to a style peculiar to the man. Christian would have tried to imitate it himself but did not know how it was done. It was as challenging as a complicated trick of conjuring, and at the end of everything you couldn't be Jupp as Jupp was Jupp. Jupp also negligently sported mysterious political badges emblazoned with Cyrillic or Chinese mottoes exhorting the world to be aware of Japan's occupation of Manchuria.

He made Christian feel grown-up just by force of his company. One night when Christian was drinking with other students in the Forest Grove pub then favoured by the law faculty, and Jupp was there, a student said, 'Walter, your father owns half the ships between here and China.'

If this was true it was news to Christian.

'Why in the name of Christ,' the student continued, 'are you wearing a Maritime Union badge?'

'It helps stimulate the dinner table talk at home,' said Jupp. 'With the *mater* and *paterfamilias*.'

And his eyes glimmered in Christian's direction. Why? Was it just applause he was after? Christian's applause? It was something more substantial, Christian hoped.

In the meantime, everyone laughed. He was their imp, and they felt lucky, for he was like a playful creature in an Oxford or Cambridge novel, and he helped them feel they were really at a university. They were left to decide whether Walter Jupp believed in maritime workers as a cause, or as a provocation to Jupp senior who, if the student could be believed, was in shipping.

———

Christian was easily fascinated by Jupp, his apparent worldliness and the crispness of his conversation. He was so unlike the more stolid and frequently harried law undergraduates of Sydney University on its hill on Parramatta Road. Jupp spent time with him, delighting and confusing him by seeking him out more than Christian thought his own talents deserved. Christian noticed when a group laughed at one of Jupp's aphorisms – 'Law exists to protect privilege, but some young spirits believe it is there to advance justice, and not infrequently use it for that purpose.' Pause. 'It's called *pro bono*.' Christian's was one of the faces Walter Jupp always checked as an index of how his barbs and witticism registered on the company.

And one day he further astonished Christian by inviting him to dinner at what he called 'the parental hutch', of which, he declared, 'as Johnson said of crofters' cottages, possesses all the cohesion of a dung-heap but nothing of its charm'. The address, however, was Point Piper, a Harbourside venue for big houses.

He caught the tram with Walter Jupp, who had a car but used it economically, and they walked up a short hill until the Harbour was everywhere around, and a sudden white mansion rose above a wall against a vivid blue sky.

Christian was warmly welcomed by the parents when they appeared in the living room where he and Walter were already drinking sherry provided by a maid. The father was dark, sharp-eyed and hulking and, like his smaller-boned son, thought himself a wit. Father and son had exactly the same quick glance, registering how their barbs were landing. When Mrs Jupp (as Christian first addressed her without being stuffily corrected) arrived, she showed her son was structurally modelled on her. She was a compact, honey

190

blonde with sweet features, a rapid, ironic talker (so he got that from both sides) who clearly adored her son – it turned out, her only child, and told Christian so a number of times as she drank two gin and tonics before dinner. Christian did not admire the hungry way she smoked, even once the meal was served by housekeeper and maid, setting her cigarette down on an ashtray on the table only when food was placed in front of her. He noticed that the housekeeper and maid called the father Sir Walter and the mother Milady, nomenclature unlikely to be heard on the Macleay. Obviously the King had been persuaded of Jupp senior's services to the British presence in the Indian and Pacific oceans where, Christian would discover, he harvested and shipped copra, potash, rubber and quinine for the Empire and for the Jupps as well.

'What do you think of my ungrateful son, young Webber?' asked Sir Walter. 'I suppose you can afford to see him as chirpy and amusing. Playing the part, he is, you see, in his role as the pup that bites off the arm that feeds him and does not munch it reflectively but is delighted to run around displaying it.'

But Sir Walter guffawed then and seemed actually proud of his son's treachery.

'Walter's godfather,' he continued, 'is Tory Party treasurer in London, Sir Maurice Speedwell-Jupp. We are faced with the horror of telling *him* that his godson has joined the Australian Labor Party!'

'The squalor of it,' said Jupp's mother and seemed sincere.

'One could forgive a chap for joining the Communist Party in misplaced fervour. They're the greatest Tories of the lot. They *believe*, you see. They're forgivable. But the Labor Party. Mere shop stewards and chapel attenders!'

'Australia had the first Social Democrat party in power in the world,' said Walter, beaming, confident of their tolerance. 'In the *world*, no less. And it was the Labor Party.'

'But Labor. It smacks of the brickyard and the ironworks.'

'It smacks of unemployment these days. Its own, to begin with.'

And father and son then engaged Christian in their discussion of the mess Jim Scullin had been in when the Depression began. Walter told his father that Scullin's tragedy was he was unable to spend like Roosevelt in America because the conservatives had left the country so burdened with debt. And hence, thought Christian, those lowering travellers who hovered around far-off Kempsey.

'Now look here,' said Lady Jupp croupily to Christian, coughing on her latest cigarette. She too looked at people from under a lowered brow. 'You are a nice boy from the bush, young Webber, and you are probably attracted to our son because you think he is worldly. But be careful, he is very unworldly. He is a *naif* abroad.'

In the same spirit, Sir Walter said, 'He could have gone to Oxford and studied at the Inns of Court. But he wanted to study at Sydney and still amaze the world!'

'Wilful child,' said Lady Jupp with a whoop of laughter.

'What can you do with me?' asked Walter Jupp as if he were as puzzled at himself as they were.

Christian had negotiated the night and not been tempted to flee. But he had fled Chicken Dalton that night, crazy now not to put anything to the test by staying and blushing for the high drama of what he had done.

18

Sydney and Kempsey, New South Wales, 1933, and France, 1916
Bert felt much happier with the new treatment. It seemed
gentle in its method by comparison with electro-convulsive
therapy, which he had at first tolerated but come to dislike.
When the second session began with Cutlack, he felt that
wherever this remedy put him, it could not degrade him as
did the electric treatment. He listened to the voice, tentative
and persuasive, and seemed delivered to where they had last
left off, though Bert had not remembered when he woke.

But as he went down or up into the hypnotic state the
second time, a great noise afflicted him and in the confident
light of a long, long afternoon, he was placed, indeed slotted
precisely, in the midst of the five-minute hiatus between the
first and second assault wave. He was back in France and
France was alarmingly and dangerously loud.

The five minutes, he was aware, seemed torn up in
handfuls into the sky by the very noise of the world. Almost
at once it was the turn of Bert and his closer acquaintances

to go onto the perilous ground level. He hauled himself out of the trench and saw ahead dense coils of dusty earth. And beyond it the sound of musketry. It increased. Captain Acres fell, his decency at a close. A signaller running off to their left, unrolling cable from a spool held in his hands, was felled and the dropped spool ran on a yard or more and then vanished, devastated by a descending shell. He saw the first line felled in the landscape, strewn dead or men howling voicelessly – or so it seemed in the noise – and then other men from the first wave sheltering in shell holes near their own wire, cowed so early but trying to expiate themselves by firing at the dimly perceived Fritz trenches. From amidst the clouds of torn earth ahead, the vivid repetitions of machine guns could be seen, and within a few steps another line of men lay howling to Christ.

Farmland and an orchard just ahead were being churned up so thoroughly, and an enfilading gun from the direction of the Sugar Loaf, the specially fortified bend in the German line, reaped men sideways. Bert kept moving, and so did Poddy. Amongst the many strewn on the ground there was barely room for these latter wounded to land. Why are we not amongst them? asked Bert of an uncomprehending world. Asked God shepherding them amidst the lines of reaped and garnered-in men. The flash of musketry lay ahead. The enemy was not dead and bewildered, as the pleasing letter had promised. Bert took a partly academic notice of one Lieutenant Wrigley, who lay on intact grass close to two others of the company's lieutenants, one of them only his age. There was a chunk missing from the back of his uniform.

'Hero's death,' said Bert as if to himself.

'What?' shouted Lembke, and reached out to drag Bert

and Poddy down into a dry, grassy drainage canal. Here they waited and discovered their breath again.

'There's dead officers everywhere,' Poddy asserted in Bert's ear. 'Did you see Major McRae?'

Bert shook his head while watching Lembke. He did not look a different sort of man in this circumstance.

'Dead beside Colonel bloody Norris and Captain Sampson!' shouted Poddy. 'Didn't you see? They've killed all the officers.'

This was not news as important as the fact that you could see Lembke was the same man as he who had been a prophet in Holsworthy.

'We'll go, eh?' shouted Lembke. 'We have flank fire. It'll be safer in the trench.' And Lembke rose and ran through cut wire and to the front breastwork.

The Fritz parapet was all wrecked and Bert and others jumped into their trench and landed and found it had been vacated. They could see intact cement lintels in both sides of the trench. In spite of the ruin wrought by big guns, Bert thought it was like coming from a bush-week town to a place where the town council did everything right. Neat duckboards, though messed up by a caved-in piece of parapet here or there, and uprights of dugouts also more intact than they were entitled to be. They gave into Aladdin's caves, for all anyone knew, dug deep down under the parapet and on the back wall of the trench. By afternoon sunlight he saw big pale Poddy staring about, very sharp, with a not-done-with-fighting-yet alertness in him. Lembke mouthed, 'Thank God!' They should not have got this far as an unscathed group. Was it *meant* they should? They found they were amongst men they recognised, and a sergeant-major named Campbell was there.

War was such a busy engine! Instantly, around the corner of the trench came five Fritzes carrying parts of a machine gun, and Poddy and Bert, and the Reverend Lembke fired on them and passed without a second's thought or flick of conscience from innocents to close-hand killers. The one Fritz left screaming was beyond hope, and Campbell bayoneted him, and Bert felt no inner outrage. Then they all took out their spare sandbags and began to fill them with the spoil of trench cave-ins, and fortified the rear parapet, given it was to be their front line for now.

A Fritz came out of one of the shelters and surrendered to Campbell. Then two more, dazed and dusty, from another. All this happened in the sharpest afternoon sunlight. From around a corner, from some Fritz in a communication trench, came a stick grenade. It landed beyond Bert's party, and the earth beyond the parapet absorbed it.

Campbell turned to Poddy and Bert. 'You two know Mills bombs?' They'd thrown one in Egypt. Mr Hughes, the prime minister, so they had been told, could afford for each of them to throw just the one.

'Yes,' said the Reverend Lembke, and Campbell gave some to Poddy and Bert. Lembke and one of Campbell's men were to carry a further supply in case the party ran low. 'Stop the bastards coming around the corner,' he told them.

Campbell had at this stage the flat-out power of kings and tsars and generals-in-chief, and Bert intended to do what he said. When they were close to the corner of the communication trench Poddy and Bert threw a few speculators around the corner and one was followed by a scream and a horn was sounded, the horn the Fritzes blew to call for ambulance men and stretcher bearers. Poddy went yelling around the corner then, hurling stuff, and there was an explosion as

Bert followed him and saw the stick grenade Fritzes, two or three, making a heap there in the well-shaped trench architecture.

The Bert-Poddy-Lembke party went on up that trench – it should lead to the second trench they had been told the existence of and which was their objective and as far as even General McCay wanted or permitted them to go. At any doorway they passed, Lembke invited those inside to come out in German, and if there was no reply, Poddy on the south-facing trench wall, or Bert on the north, would throw their bomb grenades as ordered by a minister of God. They were pretty unceremonious about it. Their would-be suppliers of further properly fused bombs, Lembke and Campbell's man, stuck with them but not so close, since if they all went up – well, better not to think of it.

So, yell. No answer. Pitch in a bomb to be sure. Their ribs and spines shuddered when it went off. They didn't look inside. Three men came out of one of the shelters on Bert's side. So strange in grey and helmets, but familiar too. Their lips were grey from bunker ceiling-dust, so Bert supposed, and tight from not being certain. He had made sure they carried nothing damaging and sent them back towards Campbell, thinking, Campbell will know we're doing well. The question was when they should go back themselves. Maybe the others were so wound up they couldn't stop themselves bringing ruin to every doorway between here and Berlin.

Bert called, 'Rev, should we go back now?'

Poddy said the group ought to keep on till they got to the Fritz support trench. Bert opined they were already beyond where it should be. Calamity settled this small dispute, as it so often did. Bert believed it was two stick bombs arriving from somewhere not far down the sap. In a clear instant Bert saw figures appear, and they looked like confident shapes.

For some reason, at this apogee of danger, on Dr Bulstrode's psychiatric advice Cutlack dragged him back to Randwick and 1933 and the Derwent sanatorium, and Bert found his consciousness. For the first time since his scream at the Victoria, and for unguessable reasons, he had a sudden appetite for speech.

———

As Flo drowsed and moaned, Chicken went to the corner phone in Belgrave Street and rang the office of Dr McVicar, a number the town knew by heart from a thousand medical catastrophes. As horrified as he was by the brute damage done to Mrs Honeywood, he mentally dedicated his neighbourliness to Christian, to that puzzled and wonderful boy he hoped to meet soon and appease, or whatever was needed. On the way home, he told old Mrs Ibbetson, whom he met outside her cottage, that Mrs Honeywood had suffered facial injuries in Clyde Street outside his cottage. He mentioned no big rattler rider, for fear it might alarm her. He said she might need stitches, though of course he could not know. She had concussion, he opined.

He found a boy, probably a truant, smoking by a grass-covered levee behind his house and gave him a shilling to deliver a letter to Mr Honeywood at Honeywood's builders yard over West. If he did that and came back to Ultima Thule to report, he would get another shilling. 'My mum says never to take a thing from you, Chicken,' said the brat.

'Then,' said Chicken, exasperated, 'I'll keep the bloody shilling if you like.'

It had been a lovely morning. He had lived in a daze from the free and tender time with young Christian and, kissing the boy's chest, said, 'You see, you don't need to threaten to shoot yourself.' It had seemed a small thing to have the prospect of telling Johnny they should no longer lie down with each other.

Now, the remarkable Mrs Honeywood had been subjected to dreadful violence. He had written to her husband:

Dear Mr Honeywood,

You wife has been seriously damaged but not mortally near my house and is presently sheltering there. She was the victim of an assault by a travelling man – a strange business. I witnessed part of it. I have called Dr McVicar, who is on his way. You may know my house is in Clyde Street, the little cottage closest to Belgrave Street and called Ultima Thule . . .

The eminent Dr McVicar arrived. Strangely, he wore a vest under his suit jacket this warm day. He looked as sage as you could want, and people did want and need doctors to look sage and interpret the signs and find a path through – or at least, should they fall against death's rocks, to leave the formula of their demise in the heads of their beloved and even of bystanders. Chicken was aware that the ambulance always stopped at McVicar's house, which was also a small private hospital, to have him write out a certificate before taking on a corpse to the Macleay District Hospital, as if the dead could not enter the lower realms without the good doctor's authorisation.

In any case, Chicken was delighted to greet McVicar. The doctor spoke to Flo authoritatively, even a little sternly, as if to cut through her concussion daze.

'Mrs Honeywood.'

'Dr McVicar,' she said and began to retch, and Chicken held a bowl for her as she vomited, weeping as she did for pain in her shattered and now engorged and bruised face. The doctor sighed and visibly changed his plan of attack. 'You must be X-rayed,' he said after lightly touching her jaw and cheekbone on the right side. He injected her with something to ease her pain. She became very sleepy in a different, less fretful way. Stale blood in her mouth and cuts stank. 'Better we move her to the hospital after this,' said Dr McVicar, rubbing his hands in alcohol solution and threading a needle to sew up her lips.

Chicken averted his gaze. The doctor, not taking his eyes from the wounds, questioned Chicken as he sewed.

'Who did this to the poor woman, Mr Dalton? Did you see?'

'A man was following her up Clyde Street. A big fellow. A traveller, for the dole, you know. I saw them from the veranda where I was reading the *Herald* and listening to my Hoagy Carmichael. He came close to her just there by Mrs Ibbetson's, and he seemed to be talking to her in a civilised way, so I went back to the paper. I didn't see him punch her – I heard a noise, but they still seemed to be talking normally. I looked up after he hit her the second time – the sound wasn't to be mistaken. I started to run out into the street and he was still talking. And as I was about to inter-vene a car pulled up and he was off. The last I saw of him.'

Dr McVicar looked up frowning for an instant from his needlework. 'That makes no sense at all, Chicken.'

'Mrs Ibbetson can back me up.'

'Oh yes, it isn't that I doubt you. But a car?'

'A Buick. A good car.'

McVicar pursed his lips, and something akin to a whistle emerged.

'I wondered, Chicken,' he said, 'if you could go and ask the police to meet me at the Macleay District Hospital? And I'll need the ambulance, if you would call on them too. And by the way, thank you. You are a Samaritan. It seems.'

He dug in the needle. She had fine-grained white flesh, and the pensive thug had violated it and now the needle finished the task.

The ambulance came. Flo was carried out. Rushing to the police station Chicken found the dopey young constable from Grafton was on the desk, but Sergeant Bernie Ives, who everyone called 'the Small Sergeant', but who was not lacking in an air of command, emerged and jokingly warned the young man. 'Watch it,' he told the constable. 'This is Chicken Dalton. I'll have to arrest you for consorting.'

Chicken told his story. It seemed to confuse the constable. But it registered upon Ives, as did the names of the participants in the drama, and soon he and another policeman were off to the hospital in West. They did not offer the Samaritan a lift. Chicken walked back to Ultima Thule. He had done good work, but he shuddered, even physically, for poor Flo.

19

Kempsey, New South Wales, 1933

As Chicken Dalton approached Mrs Honeywood's room at the hospital, he could hear the murmuring basso of male voices, and it was as the nurse at the front had told him – Dr McVicar and Mr Honeywood and the police were in the room now, so he was unable to visit the patient. He had lashed out on Joe Carmody's taxi too, to get himself here, in West, and back to the Victoria in Central in time. For these were times for grave expenditure.

He found a nurse going in with a tray of cloth-covered mysterious instruments. He could tell she knew him, as did everyone, since everyone went to the pictures. He asked her to take a message in. He was Mr Dalton, he modestly explained, and he had found that poor woman in the road in that condition. When, after nodding and telling him meaninglessly that they were attending to Mrs Honeywood, she went in with her tray of needful medical items, Chicken heard a spike in the conversation as his name was mentioned.

Mr Honeywood was first out, moving energetically, his big meaty face pale and thrust forward. 'Mr Honeywood,' Chicken said solicitously. He felt secure in his privileges as the first to succour Flo. 'I just had enough time to duck up and see how your dear wife is.'

But he saw then what the pallor meant. Honeywood seemed in a dangerous rage, as if Dr McVicar or Sergeant Ives had not acquainted him with Chicken's part in the frightful drama.

'Duck up, eh? Duck? Chicken? Are you bloody playing games with me, you cunt?'

'I . . . the cheekbone. I trust it's not broken?'

'That's bugger-all to do with you, Dalton. Are you here for money?'

'Why would you think—'

'There's no money here for you. My wife, her jaw and the cheekbone . . .' He began to weep.

Chicken stepped up and touched the man's elbow, and there was a strong and somehow threatening recoil.

'Don't you fucking touch me, you creeping bloody shirt-lifter! Oh, I know, you thought the Honeywood floodgates would open now. Rewards, you thought. You're correct about one thing. We will *see* you fair enough. We will see you right, you bastard.'

Sergeant Ives came out of Mrs Honeywood's room and was now witnessing the exchange with his half-whimsical air. Anything that was going to hell, and every excruciating scene, clearly amused him. It was the lens he watched baleful events through.

'Now, go to hell,' Burley Honeywood continued to the Small Sergeant's continued gratification. 'My wife is not your business. I want nothing further from you, and

203

if you start gossiping about my wife, I promise you, by Christ . . .'

Chicken appealed to the sergeant. 'I helped his wife. Doesn't he know? Tell him, sergeant!'

Even to Chicken the plea sounded pathetic.

'For Christ's sake, sergeant!' said Burley Honeywood. 'Get rid of him.'

'Come on, Mr Dalton,' said the Small Sergeant at once, straightening, one tough little hand extended. With it, he gave Chicken a push. 'Mr Honeywood doesn't want you here, interfering with his family.'

Sergeant Ives next spread his arms, like a man herding cows, and Chicken had no option, except resisting the lawful instruction of a police officer or obeying him. Chicken obeyed. In the manila-coloured entrance hall, Chicken asked the policeman, 'Doesn't he know . . .?'

'Oh, I think he knows it all, Chicken. The whole grand story.'

Through the doors of the hospital, Chicken could see the light of Carmody's cab outside. 'This fellow who you say damaged Mrs Honeywood,' said Sergeant Ives when he had got Chicken as far as the doorstep. 'Tell me a bit more about him.'

'A really big man in an old suit. You couldn't miss him because though he was dressed like any traveller, he was really big.'

'Do you mean big and beefy? Or big and tall.'

'Tall and beefy,' said Chicken. 'They were talking. I heard Flo . . . Mrs Honeywood. He seemed respectful at first. And then he did that to her. Does she have broken face bones?'

'She does, Chicken. Since you're asking. The cheek is intact but the jaw broken. Why is that so important?'

'Because it shows the cruelty—'

'That's right. It shows some bloody cruelty, all right. Is that your cab out there?'

Chicken admitted it. 'I've got to get back to the Victoria by seven,' he explained.

'Did you think Mr Honeywood would pay for your cab? Is that it?'

'What?' asked Chicken, a little shakily. 'No, why would he pay?'

'What colour was this man's hair?'

'I don't know. I think it must have been brown, otherwise I'd have noticed. He had a hat, you see. Pulled down tight. It didn't fly off his head when he struck Mrs Honeywood.'

'Maybe he had glue,' said the Small Sergeant mystifyingly.

'I . . . don't think . . .'

'I thought you pansies would notice hair colour and such. And the car that pulled up for him?'

'A Buick. The sort of car you own if you're rich, which he wasn't, or you could hire from Lester Mundell at Macleay Carriages. Not that I'm saying . . .'

Sergeant Ives looked at him with a terrible, level stare.

'We'll talk again about this tramp and his lovely car. Later. Okay, Chicken?'

Chicken could only flee. They had between them offered him no other choice. He went out like a guilty child. He had been hollowed by contempt. They don't want you for a hero, he knew now. They don't even want you for a Samaritan.

———

205

A plainclothes copper who had come up from Newcastle appeared at her bedside along with Sergeant Ives. He said his name was Inspector Sangster. He was a solemn-looking man. There was nothing of Ives's mocking air to him, nothing of the proposition: 'I know humans are a pretty bad crowd and I've seen all of it.' Inspector Sangster seemed more augustly fearful of what can be done, and willing, by the stern look of him, to make a severe descent only when it was called for.

'Mrs Honeywood,' he said, 'I hope you are not in too much pain.'

She tried to answer him by a flutter of the eyes. This was merely an opener. Flo could not speak. Dr McVicar had told her he had wired her jaw together. It would remain so for a month. He had arranged for her to have a pad of paper and a pencil.

'You say you were attacked by a swagman? A big fellow?' asked Inspector Sangster. She made an affirmative noise near the wired hinges of her jaw and sought her pad of paper on the side table.

'And you don't know this man's name?' asked Sangster.

She wrote surprisingly swiftly for a woman with a broken jaw and displayed what she had pencilled. 'Unknown to me. Bulky.'

'Was Mr Dalton there?' said Sangster. 'Did he do anything to you?'

'Only to help,' she wrote and showed them.

'But your husband told you to steer clear of Dalton, didn't he? He didn't want you catching sores by using the same pads and brushes as the black sheilas?'

How well Burley had primed them. The story in their minds belonged to Burley. Burley wanted to make Chicken

206

and the travelling man accomplices. The injustice burned in her jaw and threatened to explode from its wire restraints to utter an agonising protest. She managed to issue a warning groan and wrote in indelible pencil, 'Burley <u>asked</u> the man to do it! <u>Burley paid him</u>. The man told me after he hit me. Said he wasn't this sort of fellow – to do that to me.' She thought a second but her mouth still throbbed with the scale of Burley's control over Chicken, over her. So with barely a hesitation, she showed them.

'She thinks it was Burley,' Ives commented unnecessarily and then asked loudly as if her hearing was damaged, 'Why in God's name would Burley do that?'

'The man asked why I couldn't get on with Burley . . . Hit me so I would.' The two policemen consulted each other over this, just eye to eye, and ruled her last statement out.

'Why would Burley want you punished?'

'Divorce!' she wrote this time. 'Ask Mr Cattleford!'

'She *did* see Cattleford,' Ives confirmed to Sangster.

'Who wanted the divorce?' asked Sangster.

'She did,' said Ives, shaking his head as if there were no limit to earthly mysteries.

'May I ask why you wished to divorce such a good provider as Mr Honeywood?' Inspector Sangster wanted to know.

'<u>Unfaithful</u>,' Flo wrote and then displayed the under-lined adjective to Sangster. Ives was beginning to fluster her with his powers of commentary.

Indeed, Ives said, again as if in her absence, 'Burley reckons it's a bee in her bonnet. Over one of the black sheilas at Burnt Bridge she reckons he visited.'

A nurse came in now, with a new crushed tablet Dr McVicar had prescribed before he left for home. It was to help Flo's pain, she said. Observed by the policemen, the nurse crushed it into a powder and fed it into Flo's fixed mouth with the help of lemonade. Then she left with cheery predictions Flo would soon be feeling top-notch, and saying goodnight to the policemen in case she didn't see them before they left.

'Do you have any evidence?' asked the inspector as soon as the door closed. 'I mean, about the divorce. The stuff that makes you angry about your husband, Mrs Honeywood?'

'Eddie Kelly,' she wrote. 'Burley's son.' And getting more desperate still, wrote further, 'You can see it.'

'She'll tell anyone in town who'll listen,' said Ives with his intact jaw, which Flo desired primally to see shattered by something hard and just. The policemen, she knew, would sceptically question her, believe nothing or little, and would probably go when nothing had been proven or decided.

So she wrote, 'Please, inspector, listen to me, not the sergeant!'

She felt a daze claim her. As she was wavering away, she heard Sangster say, 'How can you be sure of anything the fellow said to you after he hit you such a belt?'

Did they stay all the time, even during her fevered unconsciousness when it befell her? Or did they leave and confer, sifting what she had told them, with the Small Sergeant providing merry and gossipy revisions of everything she had written?

In any case, either by patient remaining or by return, they were in the room, it seemed, every time she shuddered back to a waking state. And each time their concern about the swagman seemed unappeasable. They did not fret for Signor Mussolini's intentions in Africa, nor about poor old Joe Lyons, the prime minister in Canberra, and how he would feed the poor.

The solid impediment of her locked-up jaw, the gag through which she tried to grunt or intone her general meaning while she wrote her blunt accusations down in a few words – she knew she was limited by all that. She could not talk to them as Burley did. She could not reproduce the male nuances. She could tell they did not like either the story of Burley Honeywood as instigator or Chicken Dalton as rescuer.

'So, do you really think Mr Dalton knew the man who broke your jaw?' asked Inspector Sangster as she revived.

'No!' she wrote. 'Why would he?'

But Sangster blinked as if he believed there were many reasons Chicken might know the tramp, but did not want to push them on her while she was in pain. How could she insist on the plain decency of the man with only a pad and pencil to do it? The inspector did not answer her question as to Dalton knowing the man.

'Why would he?' she wrote again and thrust the pad towards the inspector.

'A few days before,' the inspector continued after he read and registered her written question, 'you brought home a woman whose husband had been a swagman. And a travel-ler on the North Coast Mail?'

She made affirmative sounds, though they hurt her jaw.

'That was very kind of you, Mrs Honeywood. But is there any chance this swagman was a friend of the deceased? And he mixed you up and thought you were somehow to blame?'

There it was. Their passion to implicate anyone other than Burley. It was a worm in her soul and caused her brain to itch. The blood writhed too in her chest.

'In that connection,' the inspector said before Flo got around to writing anything, 'you are sure you noticed the man before he attacked you? I mean, you actually saw him, did you? It wasn't just that Dalton told you about that man when the attack was over? Could you have imagined you had seen such a man, but perhaps it was just Dalton's suggestion?'

Gouging and near engraving the letters with her pencil, she wrote, 'I saw him! He followed me from Belgrave Street.'

Why did Inspector Sangster, reading her insistence on the existence of the fellow, now exchange that lugubrious look with Ives. The glance of a man whose skill in raising strands of mere possibility was a science, in fact, a burden of the intellect he bravely bore in truth's name. This mastery of his drove him to ask, 'I wondered . . . Before you were attacked by the swagman, as you allege, had you ever been in the house of Mr Chicken Dalton?'

Her jaw was howling for pain. 'Yes,' she doggedly wrote. 'Dalton put me in contact with a black woman. Mrs Alice Kelly.'

'Why her again?'

'The aunt of Burley's son,' she wrote and tried to nod as the pain shot up to her temples.

'Did you want to have it out with her?'

She shook her head. Burley was still the one to blame, and they were sniffing at blaming the Aboriginal woman.

'Wanted to get Burley's boy sent to Newington,' she wrote.

She saw them squint to read what she held up. They both nodded and Sergeant Ives smiled. But they didn't understand it, the justice of it, the apt punishment for Burley. She watched Ives take in, or refuse to, her ideas about the

210

education of Eddie Kelly. Then they settled themselves, particularly the inspector, to ask a new question.

'Your husband tells me, Mrs Honeywood, that Mr Chicken Dalton painted your face one day.'

'Yes.' She wrote it and was tempted to add, 'He was interested in my skin.' But she wondered what Ives would make of that statement.

'You know he chiefly made up women going to Sydney on the . . . I mean, for immoral purposes.'

She wrote a gouging emphatic, 'No!' It was the sort of thing men knew.

'They were the ones,' said the inspector, 'that let him make them up. Not that I'm saying . . .'

So it had come around. She did not know this was what they were getting to. To cover Burley's shame by making her shameful, a provocation.

The pad of paper tore, its binding severed, as she ground out 'HOW DARE YOU!' with her pencil.

The inspector seemed stricken and held up two palms in retraction. 'Oh, Mrs Honeywood, please, I didn't mean for a second—'

Her cry of fury was a ridiculous 'Mmmmmmm' through her tethered jaws.

He said he was sorry and would let her rest, and indeed said good afternoon penitently. Ives nodded as if she were lucky to be cleared of the insinuation. And even full of vivid rage, and almost immediately after they left, she felt hateful sleep suck her down.

20

County Kerry, 1922

It was question and answer. The rebels of the IRA would pose a fair, savage question and the Free State would answer it with less and less good nature. Johnny's unit and others got orders to raid a house one night, belonging to a respectable middling farmer named Pat Keon. Johnny stayed in the garden as lookout but Da went in with the others to exact a one-hundred-pound fine from Keon because he had reported to the Free State about some of the boys crossing his land. Da and the others came out unsatisfied in regard to the sum and had orders from Commandant O'Toole to raze the place if Keon did not pay. They set fire to his outbuildings with rags dipped in kerosene and drove his cattle off. Da Costigan and the others had seized his cashbox too and carried away its contents.

After this, Keon's son joined the Free State Army. In the next month or so he got a reputation as an interrogator, that is as a torturer who used hammers on captured rebels. So one of the rebel explosives men set up a trap. He fed information to Keon that there was an IRA cache of arms at Knocknagoshel down south-east a bit. Indeed, there was a small apparent cache there, but it was mined with a tripwire. Anxious for vengeance and the approval of his superiors, Keon and four Free State pals of his entered the cache, where, in the midst of their rejoicing, one of them tripped the wire. They were blown to, yes, it is true, shreds. The rebels watching from cover, who went to inspect the remains before scattering, were a-tremble at the human damage, and the thing was that the noise of the explosion that tore Keon apart could be heard all over the central north of County Kerry.

Johnny's squad were then staying at an old ruined manse near the Kilmorna Road, east of Listowel. And at the great noise from the south-east, his Da looked at his watch, the one he had taken from a Tan long ago. He said, 'That is a mine. God help them whoever they are.'

The Costigans did not know then that it was a noise that would become an engine of their history.

———

It turned out that General O'Daly in Tralee also heard the noise and that he considered Keon a promising lad and a bosom friend. He knew the three Irish Guards who had been killed with him too. He knew wives and fiancées, parents and uncles. And he said, 'If *they* want it that way . . .'

With no evidence to support him, Johnny still believed himself among the ultimate survivors, since the opposite and its oblivion was for some reason a severe test for the imagination. But of course, the Free Staters were making plenty of captures up Listowel way too. The search parties were not made up of Tim Kennelly's fellows they had fought in Listowel. Far from it. It was O'Day's former Irish Guards units.

One day Da and Johnny were protecting the arms cache near the unroofed farmhouse that was their then billet. The arms were secreted in the cellars of a nearby ruin burned in some historic strife – pick your century! – and now partially open to the skies but well disguised not only by the shelter of the trees but by clumps of fierce brambles. The other section members had gone to Kilmorna to inspect a railway bridge O'Toole wanted dynamited, and Da and Johnny were sheltering together until the others got back that evening.

They talked a little, the Old Feller and Johnny. Not for the first time, his father talked of Mimmie in Cleveland. 'There's a forceful woman like your old grandmother, Johnny. She'd go through you for a short cut.' And he laughed at this reflection of Mimmie's toughness. Every time. 'You know it sounds a mighty place, that Cleveland. Up there on its lake like that. We could all live there you know. You could work for Toddy Harfield.'

That was her husband's name and he employed deliverymen.

All this was a common daydream of Da's, or a duskdream. A dream by owl-hoot.

They slept early in the night, while brittle ice formed on the trees. Fairly early in the night then, not long after they fell asleep, an array of light and fists and rifle butts descended on them. Sudden bloodhounds baying and screamed orders were the mode. Da and Johnny were arrested before they fully knew what was happening.

They were beaten, both of them, on the spot. Johnny

214

endured the numb relentlessness of it. Da grunted, 'Make an honest fooking end of it, for mercy's sake.' Later, as they moved him to a truck, he screamed, 'And you'll be at the Mass with washed faces come Sunday. And a bloody Free State priest handin' you the Communion! May Christ choke you!'

In the truck, they each sat, shackled, with a guard. Da called, 'Sorry, son,' as if it were his fault, but the guard silenced him with a little, economic jolt of the rifle butt to his ribs. Johnny knew it was all his fault. A girl had brought them a rabbit stew from a farmhouse, and Johnny had spent some time talking with her, testing out whether she could be the one to set his desires right. Now the Free State soldiers were making mocking reference to that letter he'd written. They'd intercepted it, or else there was a farmer minded enough to help the rebels but not wanting his daughter tied up with a gunman and disposed to inform on said gunman.

The arrogance of writing to a girl, as if girls were all he wanted!

The truck and Free Staters took Da and Johnny into empty-streeted, Saturday-turning-into-Sunday Tralee and into the old British barracks which were now the prison. Johnny was put in a cell all on his own. He was in pain and in some terror of the pain still to come. He was a little astonished that Christ and the Blessed Virgin hadn't protected himself and Da, given his regular plaints directed their way in that regard. But that was it – the Blessed Virgin Mary did not favour sodomy. Da was paying the price run up by his son.

Soon enough Johnny was handcuffed and taken out and down the corridor to a room with electric light. It seemed crowded with men with their jackets off, eager to punish him. But there was one man, a little stooped, only because of his height. Colonel Breen from the execution site.

As soon as Johnny was pushed into the room, he was overtaken by their noise. Such shouting! 'Killer!' they shouted. 'Fucking bandit.' 'Republican scut' and 'Hoor's melt', and so on. He was pushed, handcuffed still, into a chair with wooden armrests and was tethered to it by the legs. A lean man stepped up and said he was Nelligan. He was a sergeant, yet he looked to Breen for authorisation, and he took a carpenter's hammer from another soldier and started in on Johnny, the intolerable blunt–sharp, blunt–sharp punishment, wider in scope, it seemed to Johnny, than the whole question of Ireland, the point at debate. And the whole room cheered Nelligan as if he were Paderewski. Oh, how they beat him then, jaw one side, cheekbone the other, front teeth. Then a larger bore mallet was fetched for Nelligan and he changed instruments to begin an assault on Johnny's body. Even when Johnny was dazed enough to doubt whether it was him or some other poor creature in the chair, still those relentless blows, the dull of deeper resonance and the penetrating blows kept landing – on whoever it was. He pissed himself and knew he had, because they were not backward in telling him, as if this was his culminating sin. Under the aegis of Colonel Breen, the sergeant and the other yellers in the room invoked Jesus and Mary frequently in contempt for him but, worse still, in reverence for what they were doing.

There was a pause and Johnny was aware of it. A man had entered the room by giving the officer beside the door information which seemed to weigh even more heavily against him. He had heard and felt the reverberation within of the clavicle breaking and something in his lower arm suddenly giving up any hold it had on nearby joints. The pain was most urgent. The sergeant stepped forward and hauled his face upright by his hair. 'Listen? Are you listening, you fooking hoor's melt?'

Through a dry, blood-clogged mouth, he managed to say he was.

Breen came to Johnny's front, surveyed him without disapproval at the mess they had made of him. 'How are you, Mr Costigan?' he asked.

'Good for a man worked at like a fooking dinner gong,' Johnny tried to answer. 'You wouldn't in any mercy do that to an older feller, would you? Like my da? Not even you.'

'Don't know what you're talking about in that regard, Johnny.'

'Well, you know Irishmen are working on Irishmen, hammer in hand.'

He spat two back teeth out to demonstrate the fact.

'See!' he said.

Breen stepped back as if the bloody spit had reached him and his uniform.

'You dirty bastard,' yelled Sergeant Nelligan, from the colonel's shoulder. His freckles showed through sweat.

But Breen, thanks be to Jesus, didn't abandon Johnny again to his subordinates. 'Funny you mention your da,' said he.

'Yeah?' Johnny asked, against the tension of his swollen jaw.

'You realise you're both bound to die, don't you, Johnny?' His eyes gleamed like metal. He had been through too many furnaces, this fellow. His soul was shrunk down inside him, the size of a peanut and almost certainly dead. So he compelled a certain belief when he said Da and Johnny were going to die.

'You know how it goes, Johnny. Next time your fellers kill one of ours, we'll get you out of your cells and shoot you. It is, after all, up to you fellers. The question is, do you want to save your da being shot?'

Johnny said Da wouldn't want to be saved on the wrong grounds. He asked the name of the brigade leader. Johnny said that everyone knew that, that he knew they knew it because they had posted up rewards for him. 'Then just say it, Johnny,' Breen urged him. 'What harm can that do? Just say your brigade commander's name for your da's sake.'

He wouldn't and the sergeant stepped up past Breen and brought the mallet down on Johnny's shoulder. 'There's a bloody *aide-memoire* just for you,' Nelligan told Johnny as his head rang with agony.

The hammerer stepped back, Breen came up again and he said with a bogus gentle air, 'For your da's sake. Do you want him shot? I swear to you he'll not be shot if you help, Johnny. And now let me tell you something further, Johnny Costigan. Neither will you.'

Johnny said all right, and told them, 'It's Mr O'Toole, a gallant fellow. And may he be the man to put one in your fooking body, brave fellow that he is!'

'Good, good, Johnny,' said stooping Breen, who signalled to the angry sergeant to stand aback. 'Now, to save your da from being shot, and to save you as well, for the Costigan name must go on, as your letter to the girl suggested, give me the name of a man in your section. Just a name so I can spare your da from a bullet. And you as well.'

Johnny said nothing. He had understood they would do this, get him limbered up by naming Dinny O'Toole.

Then a less known name. Then a totally secret one, as Johnny waited for the hammer man to step in again.

'Just a name, though it must be genuine, Johnny, and prove out to save yourself and your father.'

Johnny knew it to be a trap but he began to weep. He wanted Da to live, since he had put him in the mess. But now it had been pointed out to him, Johnny wanted to live too. Life seemed more all-important than it had been before they caught him or first laid the hammers to him.

'You're asking me to trade a friend for my da,' he complained as if they were not awake to the conflict in that.

'If your da's not to be shot, Johnny, that's what we require, yes. You know that.'

So in the end, after more arguing, Johnny coughed up the name of Frank Mangan, one of his fellow gunmen. Frank was young and didn't have a wife, and might satisfy them on his own, Johnny hoped. One man for one man. He knew he had crossed from the world of clear moral rules into the universe of sin. For he was clever enough, that Colonel Breen, especially when reasoning with a fellow with broken bones. He got Johnny to say O'Toole, a name they knew. And after that, the saying of names became habitual. As Mangan was not enough to save the Old Feller, Da, the names tickled Johnny's throat, butting up against their cage as if wanting him to let them out.

For since he had uttered one hidden name, he was adrift, nothing to stop the tug of naming. And though, by Jesus, they did beat the tripes out of him, and he had bone fractures to plead, that was just the normal and would count for nothing in his favour. If they had just called the hammer sergeant back, he could have managed a resumption of blows, he promised himself. But they opted for something worse: the saying of names. One name more and we won't shoot your da. You have the promise of the Free State. We will write it out for you if you like. Look, said the colonel, holding up paper, here's the guarantee, signed with my own name.

Another six names fled Johnny's mouth, including both of the Lewis gunners. One of the fellows he gave up was Paudeen O'Casey, who had joined the rebels from the Free State Army the year before.

'I want to see my da,' he demanded at the end. Da was who had been saved from the ruin. No guarantees had been forthcoming for Johnny himself. So be it.

He did not remember which arms supported him on the way, but they also propped him upright while a turnkey opened a cell door. Da lay on his back on a prison cot with rosary beads laced through his joined fingers. They put him in there, leaning him against the wall, and locked the door. After a while, he staggered up to his da, asleep, wearing a pitiably bruised face. Johnny cried for what they had done to him, as if his life had not been hard enough.

'We won't shoot him,' one of the soldiers called to him through the opening in the door. 'He's already gone. Say a fooking prayer for him, Johnny.'

Of course, Johnny howled against the liars. 'We won't shoot your da.' What souls could play a game like that? Who would tell Mimmie of this obscenity? Da had achieved death without any help from Johnny, other than the silliness of his vain letter. He had become *their* technical truth that wasn't truth at all. They promised with their guile not to shoot Da and they wouldn't because he had already removed himself from their malice anyhow. Acutely orphaned, Johnny pleaded with him to come back and sort out the mess. He had paid all and got nothing. He was the most fatuous and bereaved of fools. Not as wise as Judas, he had not even the thirty pieces! Even as informer, Johnny was a failure. Out of that murk of despair there came one humane voice. Behind him, as he howled for his father and the forsaken idea they would walk out free together, there broke over him and dead Da the voice of a tender jailer, or of God or some other overwhelmed source of mercy. It said, 'Son, he just slumped in his chair. Heart attack, our doctor said. He'll make a good corpse as they'd barely started in on him.'

In Ireland, making a good corpse was an important consideration.

21

Sydney, New South Wales, 1933, and France, 1916

In the third phase of therapy under Cutlack and Bulstrode as a combination, no sooner than Bert had been reimposed upon the events of 19 July 1916 than it was apparent Campbell should be told that the enemy was coming back confidently to reoccupy their line. So assured were figures rounding the sap, advancing under the stick grenades they had thrown. They detonated, it seemed, almost instantaneously, before Bert and the others could reply.

There was a tremendous noise and Bert was swept away by it, and hurled against one wall of the trench, while he could feel a number of points of some kind of penetration at his left side. Bert noticed at the same time that Poddy had been torn about too. But just then it was a bit like observing the weather. A Fritz no older than Bert, the first of a number of on-comers, of whose childhood and manhood Bert had no knowledge, had brushed past Bert to impale the serious-minded man Campbell had attached to them, who now dropped his little bag of grenades, bleated and staggered away. Bert saw even more than heard, since his ears were flooded with noise, the Reverend Corporal Lembke shoot this assailant, and move a few steps to reach out to Bert. As he held to Bert by Bert's gore, friends of the young dead Fritz appeared, but Lembke chose to hold Bert in fraternity rather than fire at them.

More men in field grey were rounding the corner and moving up the trench with a wary sort of speed. Was Lembke himself injured? It seemed to Bert that he and Lembke trembled in parallel, at the same frequency, from the impact of the stick grenades. There was an imperative to warn Campbell in the old front line but it seemed to Bert neither he nor Lembke had enough breath back. Bert didn't know he still had his rifle. He was not sure he still had himself. He would not have been too amazed or even alarmed to be told he was dead.

As Lembke propped him against one wall, Bert called to Poddy, who was face-down on broken duckboards, but now raised his face. He whimpered, 'Christ Almighty, Bert,' as if Bert had more currency with the present turmoil in this communication trench than Lembke had.

Other men, Fritzes, ran past Bert and Lembke and Poddy now as if they were permanently out of things. The Fritzes would in their way take the news to Sergeant Campbell. Propped against an earthen wall half-glazed with cement, Bert felt an impulse to get Poddy and himself into one of the cool, dark bunkers – one on their left that had not been buggered up with Mills bombs yet. All of them, Poddy, Bert, Lembke, needed some cool dark to lie in and assess themselves like hurt dogs. Besides, the Fritz artillery had begun again and seemed to have Campbell's trench in mind.

Bert said, 'Come on, Rev.' They both bent to pick up Poddy, who screamed when they moved him and pulled him face-up. His midriff and his thighs were better not to look at. A mess in the land of messes, and in the strong remains of the long-lasting French daylight.

Bert never understood the physics of it, but physics were not the point as he and the Reverend Lembke rolled and urged and lifted Poddy through the doorway of the untouched bunker. Bert chose to think, when Poddy whimpered away, that that was what the boy also wanted, a darker and safer place. Bert was pleased with himself, that like Kurt Lembke he still had dragging strength. Bert could tell he was peppered down his left side with shrapnel, that they spoke with an equal discomfort, that perhaps not one of them seemed lethal, except possibly the one in his thigh that roared when he lifted Poddy.

By shuffling and urging each other, they were all well inside now, and Lembke still supporting Poddy. From the sou-westering light that entered the upper door, full of dust, they could see furnishings in this bunker. A sofa! The Fritzes have stolen it off a farmer, Bert guessed. And a table, and bunks further back. Bert felt a new respect for the Fritzes. They had a power to settle into places. Whereas the Poms and the Australians – they camped out. You either had a town and amenity, or you didn't. Maybe it was a matter of culture with them. You had to say, he realised in the midst of pain, they had a good, thorough attitude.

'Poddy on the lounge chair,' the Rev suggested. They were able to prop Poddy against a wall in an easy chair, and the Reverend gave him water from his bottle. Poddy did not down it but sipped delicately. Bert mentioned to the other two that they all just needed to get their breath.

'And Sergeant Campbell will be along soon,' Lembke told him. Bert sank to the floor, his back to the front wall, and drank some of his water while Lembke told Poddy he intended to inspect some of his wounds. He did so through the gaps in Poddy's tunic, wiping blood away with a field dressing.

Bert called, 'Rev, are you hurt yourself?'

'Just a nick in the hip.'

He hobbled to Bert and spoke confidingly. 'Listen, I'll sit with Poddy, and you rest.'

'Hail Mary, full of grace, the Lord is with Thee,' said Poddy. Then his memory stuck. 'The Lord is with Thee . . .'

'Blessed art thou amongst women, Poddy,' said Lembke. 'I know the opposition's war-cries.'

'And blessed is the fruit of thy womb, Jesus,' said Poddy like a revelation.

Outside, noise and shouting but, it seemed, best disregarded. Lembke came and knelt down uncomfortably by Bert. 'I think I can see his lung through the hole in his side,' said Lembke, calm but for some reason gasping for air. 'We must let him sit for now, until I'm able to get a stretcher bearer from around the corner. You take a rest, Bert.'

And, wheezing, he hobbled back to Poddy. In spite of the racket outside, Bert slept, guarded by Woolgoolga's Lutheran saint.

———

He woke when, light from outside having faded, someone entered by way of the few steps inside the doorway. The first sound was a scurry, like a goanna, and Bert saw a little white dog, all its senses alert, who came to him,

225

indeed more felt than seen, and licked a wound on Bert's leg. But there was a man with him, and he, the newcomer, moved to the interior of the cave like a proprietor. He reached out to a wall and an electric light came on. Bert scrambled for his rifle, yelling, 'Don't move, you bastard!'

The man turned. He was skinny, droop-moustached and had a pouch over his shoulder – a runner. In the Australian Army he would have been called Droopy for the skinniness of his neck, the unsuitable width of his collar and his overdone moustache. As well as the dispatch satchel on his shoulder, he carried a pistol in his hand. He looked at Bert with his bleak eyes. Then at Poddy bleeding in the chair, with Lembke kneeling beside it, his head turned to the new arrival.

From what Bert could see, Droopy disapproved of Poddy. The little dog circled, alert for a word of command, hungry to be set a task. He ran in to sniff Poddy, and Droopy the messenger called, '*Fuchsi. Platz!*' Bert's own grandfather uttered commands like that. '*Platz!*' and '*Sitz!*' *Fuchsi* was Foxy, Bert thought. An excellent name for an amiable little dog.

Bert had his rifle pointing in the fellow's direction. At that instant Lembke rose, unarmed, at Poddy's side and said, '*Bitte, nicht schiessen!*'

The skinny messenger raised his pistol and shot Kurt Lembke through the forehead. Lembke fell back and died with a half-smile of resignation on his face.

———

Thus the Reverend Lembke fell and with him the last certainties of the earth. A scream rose in Bert, the roar of the damned, but he did not utter it because first the violator must be shot. With dizzying pain, Bert raised his rifle and yelled, 'Bastard!' The gaunt runner raised his hands over Lembke's body.

'*Kamerad*,' he said, and shrugged at Bert as if suggesting, 'What was a man to think?' Nor had he realised till then Bert was to his right and a little behind. He knew he was about to be shot dead himself for this gaffe, the one the shrug apologised for.

'Bastard!' yelled Bert again, and wept tears that hurt his side. But he did not fire. Firing wasn't large enough. Droopy's fall could not equate to Lembke's.

As Bert grieved for the world and accepted his position amongst the damned, in an earth transformed into hell, where the death of saints caused just a shrug of thin shoulders, the Fritz runner regarded him with the most doleful eyes. Bert knew sharply with a certainty that burned his side that the man *must* be dispatched now, however irrelevant it might be to the fall of Lembke. This was the second of the man's death and his just punishment. But a second time, the trouble was that shooting him was not enough. That, rather than reflection, delayed Bert, and to delay was to pardon the raggedy, thin-necked bastard.

The man, watching him, raised the pistol a little, side-on, put the safety on and dropped it at Bert's side. Saying, '*Kamerad*,' softly and, for his purposes anyhow, persuasively.

Instead of shooting him, Bert freed his right hand from the rifle, scooped up the pistol and put it in his tunic pocket. He was despairingly grateful to be busy at all this. The scrawny Fritz pointed out a kitchen chair from those around a table and said, '*Bitte*,' and Bert nodded, and the spindle-shanks took the seat. I could have been him, Bert thought, with a sense of the glum oddity of things, if my grandfather had not caught a boat. Not only caught it but caught it a long bloody way. No puddle-hop across the Atlantic to the United States or Argentina, but the long-winded Australian choice.

The Fritz addressed him tentatively, but Bert did not take it in and had no interest, believing he would perish here with the eyes of that streak of misery on him.

From outside could still be heard rushings and detonations, yet they seemed sealed off from them. Occasionally a puff of cement dust descended from the roof, a concession this space made to the turmoil outside.

'Poddy,' Bert called and the Fritz sat forward. 'Not you, you bastard,' said Bert. '*Poddy?*'

Poddy kept his silence and by painful gestures and jerks of the rifle, Bert ordered the runner to inspect Poddy. At last the runner got the idea and stood up and approached Poddy. He bent to register Poddy's breath, if there was one, on his face. Standing up, he looked mournfully at Bert. Bert told him, 'You bastard, feel Poddy's pulse.' He heard his dead mother. '*Puls,*' she said gently. '*Puls,*' Bert ordered him. When he saw there was no sign of one, the runner if anything looked more doleful. 'Tell me then,' demanded Bert. Even gesturing was agonising.

The man reached for Poddy's bloodied wrist, and then for his throat. '*Kamerad,*' he said. '*Er ist tot.*' And not knowing Bert had his childhood German, he searched for some other word and said, '*Finito.*'

As Droopy did his shrug again, Bert felt lost. Nothing was in his control. And both Bert and Droopy knew there was nothing to be had by searching for Lembke's pulse. Poddy was gone too. There were to be no more whimpers from him. Cow-milker and cutter of chaff. His hard-handed, large and all-too-aged mother doing the morning milking on Nulla Creek right now knew nothing, unless prophetic, unless stricken by a vision, of her boy's fall.

The Fritz messenger moved tentatively back towards his table. He still half-expected a fatal punishment from Bert's rifle. He made a sad, reassuring speech in German and fragments of English, tapping the top of the table with the point of his index finger as he gave reasons Bert should be happy as a lark with him and the sort of bloke he was.

When Bert began weeping, it was for Poddy and his parents, the McHughs of Nulla. It was death on a scale that fitted tears. Lembke was far above tears and too momentous to warrant them. The little dog, Foxy, began sniffing at Lembke and Bert but was called back by Droopy, and then he went to a corner and rested.

Time skidded, it seemed. When it was itself again Bert was aware of tides of men rushing one way and another past the door. There were shouts shaped; dizzy, Bert decided, like dogs' barks. They might be noises forged in English for all he knew, he felt so disconnected from them and expected no intrusion, for good or for bad, from them.

'*Wasser?*' said the runner apologetically, like a waiter, '*Has du durst?*'

Bert could not hope to keep his rifle upright and at the same time use his canteen.

'Water? I've got no water for you.'

'*Uno momento,*' said the Fritz, changing languages again. He raised a finger, pleading for Bert's tolerance, and went deeper into the dugout. Bert could see there a stone water purifying jar and tin mugs around it. The runner took a mug and poured the purified water into it, did the same

229

with another, turned to Bert and held both up to show his lack of deviousness, then came forward and offered Bert one. Bert eased his right hand away from his rifle, hoping that as things stood now it would go on intimidating Droopy on its own, his knees serving as a convincing rest for it. And when he took a sip of the water he found how boundless his thirst was. Even the dead need water, he thought, knowing he had largely died with the Reverend Lembke.

The messenger drank his and gave a gurgle of appreciation. He put some in a tin plate for Fuchsi, who liked it greatly. Bert felt his consciousness running away with the delight of the water. The German stood up from the table. 'Ich gehe,' he said with an air of great consideration, as if he was offering not to disturb Bert any further.

'No, you won't bloody go,' snarled Bert. 'If that's what you're saying.'

'Alles klar,' the man conceded.

He looked at Bert now as if seeing a new, severer side of Bert's character. Bert thought, this mongrel is an actor! And as if to verify that, the runner sat again and ostentatiously settled, folding his arms on the table and resting his head on them. And as Bert felt his own torpor overtake him, the man apparently slept. Whenever Bert stirred, he saw the man head-down on the table, and the sound of him, when it could be heard above the rumbling and tumbling outside, was the sound of sub-snore night-time breathing.

———

Bert was awakened at one time by what turned out to be the nudge of a boot. Springing awake, he tried to grab the stock of his rifle which had slipped from his hands. For the mournful face was above him, staring down, and the man had his arms raised. And then he extended his left arm downwards. '*Ich werde dir helfen,*' he said. He shrugged and pointed to the door and the trench outside. '*Alles ist wieder Deutsch,*' he announced, again as an apology. Everything is German again.

That being so, his dispatch bag and whatever message it contained was now an irrelevance. 'Of course it fucking is,' Bert muttered in denunciation of generals. They had been good on paper yesterday, writing a plausible letter about battle. That was their limit.

Bert had by now found the breach and stock area of his gun and with two hands, and some pain and protest from his left side, raised the stock towards the runner.

'Shoot me, for God's sake.' He was ready for this hell to be cancelled. The runner blinked and kept his right hand raised for a time, then took the stock and, leaving Bert feeling lighter than a wafer, functionally leaned the rifle against the dugout wall by the table.

'*Steh auf, wir gehen,*' he told Bert. Get up, we're going, as Bert understood it. The runner leaned down and began to haul Bert upright. Bert whimpered from pain in his hip and side and shoulder. But he was crookedly upright. He could feel the man clutching him around the shoulder, but he pulled back to consider sprawled Poddy, and inert, fallen Lembke, no longer God's prophet. 'Bastard,' Bert cried again, but was not sure whom he was addressing.

The droop-moustached Fritz seemed to take no offence and looked Bert in the face. '*Auf Geht's. Kein Englisch.*' Bert could smell the man's sweat and the heavy odour of his uniform. The little dog was up, alert, and barked once.

They made it out and into a grey pearl of air in which nothing could be seen. Droopy steered them towards the front trench, and Bert could hear German speech all around, and farting and groans, and sometimes he bumped against a body and yelped, and the man in question would make some form of apology, though not always.

Occasionally Droopy was addressed in the murk by a soldier and he replied in German and once got a laugh. Bert thought Droopy was announcing he had a prisoner. I suppose that's what I am, thought Bert. So much for poor Anna and poor little Christian, though he knew he had nothing to take home to them.

They went on through the pearly murk. We are both dead, Bert thought once more, hopefully, and this is the fog the dead move in. It went on so long and with such stinging in his side and there were a few more conversations between Droopy and men he bumped. They came to a ladder. Bert was sure it led nowhere. '*Oop-la!*' said Droopy, and began to help Bert ascend it.

Bert let Droopy assist him up, a rung at a time, precisely because it was meaningless and painful and thus distracting. At the top he lay panting on a heap of dark earth spoil, dropped there by spade or artillery shell. Droopy let him get his breath and then helped him upright. The little dog was skittering around their legs.

'*Protokolen der Weisen von Zion,*' confided Droopy and sniffed. '*Hast zu es gelesen?*'

It was a dusty-covered and page-shedding book his grandmother had. *The Protocols of the Elders of Zion*. It was, Bert always thought, a book old people read. In his part of New South Wales, it was hard to find a Jew to blame for the state of the world. But the Protocols were there, in case. The book lay about the living room with the Luther Bible and an old crack-spined cookbook. So he could not truly say he'd read it.

Hearing no answer, Droopy laid a hand quite tenderly on his shoulder, aware Bert could not stand too much weight. He confided, '*Die Nationen nicht, die Jude will den krieg.*' Not the nations but the Jew brings war.

'What do you want to say?' asked Bert, hoping that if he spoke English the absurd and painful and obscure discourse would end quicker.

They moved off again, Bert dazed, but aware of wisps of wire either side, and that Droopy guided him amidst corpses, and their way was not straight. They came to a patch of sudden, light-filled vacancy, to a dimly perceived downward path, guarded by a squad of dead men in Australian uniforms.

But Droopy said '*Australische*' and pointed. '*Kein töten!*' By which Bert thought he might be both thanking him for not killing him and apologising for cancelling out the existence of Lembke, the prophet. Then he urged Bert on by the Australian's good elbow.

There was no firing from any direction now. The murk had made peace within itself. The entrance to the downward path, strewn with momentarily glimpsed Australian corpses, looked fortified with more sandbags than he would have expected of the entrance to hell. Droopy shrugged at him. Bert remembered. They, the engineers, had been digging saps across No Man's Land. This might well be one, and the way home – whatever home could be now, after the night that had gone.

He looked at Droopy. If he had had the language he would have liked to warn him. 'You could go too. Any moment. Without right of protest. You might be slated to build the perpetual motion machine, for all we know. That won't save you.'

But Droopy thought his delaying was stupidity or fever and gave him a little push and said something about the Australian lines being that way, and that of course he himself could not make the journey. '*Kein töten!*' Enough killing.

Bert went along alone, feeling the sandbagged sides and the timber revetments. For all the good this trench had done, it was well made. He heard a shouted challenge from within the mist ahead to present himself. He did so very crisply. 'Private Bert Webber, C Company, 53rd.' It seemed to satisfy whoever was ahead. 'Come on then, Bert, you jammy bastard.'

They put him on a stretcher and he was hurried as fast as he could be to a Casualty Clearing Station, where it was discovered by an orderly that he had brought Droopy's pistol back with him in his side pocket.

22

Sydney, New South Wales, 1933

'Why are we staying in a hotel?' Gertie asked that Friday. Christian knew she didn't like the hotel near the sanatorium. It was named the St Ledger because it was not far from the racecourse at Randwick. It was nothing like the Grand Hotel à la John Barrymore or Greta Garbo. It was a boozery, in fact, as bad as the Federal in Kempsey but done out in claret-coloured tiles. Some of the better-known trainers from Melbourne and Brisbane put up their strappers and handlers and exercise riders there.

These servants of the horse went on drinking late into the night in each other's rooms, and the Webber women on their way to the ladies' bathroom did not enjoy creeping past their rowdiness.

'Why don't we stay with Auntie Eunice?' Gertie wanted to know.

'I think your Aunt Eunice wants the house to herself,' said Anna.

'You mean, we've worn out our welcome.'

A tremor that seemed to Anna to have Sam Montgomery's name on it made its way up her body and shook her shoulders.

'In a sense,' Anna admitted. 'It's understandable.'

Christian was philosophic about it all. His law term began the following Tuesday, for which he would be in college. He had said a fond and apologetic goodbye to Chicken, but no longer felt torment about what Chicken meant to him, a mere beneficent spirit or life's essential lover. He was beginning to have an awareness that, once launched on a sexual adventure, embarrassment faded, and he was unabashed by his desires. Given he had spent most of his life mortified at himself, the freedom he had found with Chicken was all the more welcome, and unexpected. It was a shock to him to find that, like the cattle, and the recurrent tides with their appetite for the shore, he too had appetite he now saw as unarguable. Having thought himself a Puritan, he was amazed that he might be a hedonist, a description he knew only from novels and his second meeting with Chicken Dalton.

'I might just go over to see her and try my luck,' Gertie proposed. '*I* haven't been there as much as you.'

Christian watched Anna. The Chicken thing was all very well till he thought of his mother. She looked tired and was here in Randwick for loyalty to her husband, the patient, and loyalty being sometimes one of the less rewarding virtues, she did not want an argument over it.

'Be nice, Gert,' suggested Christian.

'Yes, let's keep together,' said Anna. 'We'll go to the pictures tomorrow night, in town.'

'Let's see *Ecstasy*.'

She intoned the name of the spicy film in a husky voice.

'Don't keep provoking, Gertie,' pleaded Christian, but with a smile.

'Well, Hedy Kiesler takes off all her clothes, so it should suit you!'

'It doesn't suit me,' snapped Christian. 'I'll be meeting up with my uni friend Walter Jupp later anyway.'

He wondered if she was worldly enough to suspect him for what he was, and wondered should he have spoken so sharply. But he was fed up with the social duty of salivating at women's bodies.

'I think we'll be seeing *Flying Down to Rio*,' declared Anna, to end the argument.

Gertie began to sing, '"Say, have you seen a carioca? It's not a foxtrot or a polka."'

I mustn't be a prig, Christian thought. He could afford generosity now that he knew more of who he was.

With fraternal fondness, he said therefore, 'Go for it, Gertie!'

In the hotel dining room, they ate overcooked steak and ruthlessly boiled potato, carrots and beans. At other tables the horse handlers of all stripes, the older ones weather-beaten to a fault, discussed trainers and horses of their acquaintance. Christian felt all was strange and new, and yet still uncertain. He felt he had passed over some river or mountain to meet himself and was still not entirely comfortable in his new skin.

———

Bert Webber had seen smashed men brought in from his father's timber holdings at Oven Camp. Yet his view of the world before the war, sanctioned by all he knew, was that God abandoned the just to their agonies only after he had been put to the severest tests of preserving them, body and soul. And that night in France he found out there was no divine reckoning of this kind, no preference for the just. A man could tempt God and still breathe, while the just man was felled. Lembke wanted something of great moment. Lembke wanted God on earth. He had been born to bring that into being. And if God, unless tempted to the limit, could not preserve the just in battle, where were their reasons to be just in the first place? Such had been the puzzle in the military hospital in Surrey and it remained a puzzle. It was a defined shadow across his path, and a ravenous presence on the other side of the table.

The certainties Bert had lost, planted with parental rigour and mercy, the assumptions enunciated by the finest voices of Kempsey, New South Wales, and of Australia, throbbed dully and relentlessly in him like missing limbs. Similarly, the angels of the soul by which Poddy the child and Lembke the prophet had been connected to him. Now that he had re-endured the business under Cutlack's spell, and come out talking, he raised in himself the idea that the dash to the enemy's line should have demonstrated that the days of merit, of things earned, were over. But perhaps he was a slow learner. It took a future German Chancellor in the role of a *Gefreiter*, a mere corporal-runner, with a dog named Foxy and a Model 8 pistol, to sheet the news home.

'We do not always react to the first assaults on our faith in the world,' Dr Bulstrode, pleased with his patient, told him. 'Many people do not experience in a lifetime what you endured on one night at war. And neurosis never attaches itself to a mass. It attaches to an individual case, a specific, remembered thing. If you like, just one salient thing can drive a man mad.'

Returning home, Bert had distracted himself with business, marriage, children. But when the image of Droopy turned up not in the chambers of memory but on the screen in the Victoria . . . it was like an assault, it was like the time of judgement, and in time of judgement, men howled.

Bert now understood this. And on the basis of what he had been through, the psychiatrist was playing with a new psychiatric term, 'chance trauma', and with 'chance syndrome'. The human desire for a structured and predictable life, an endeavour to which we devoted every skill and every trade and each gesture of our social organisation, was at odds with a universe in which chance was the sole constant and the enduring rule. Civilisation protected the individual from the raw edges of contingency. To experience war, however, was to be exposed perpetually to chance, to discover at each instant that there was no human reason in operation and enough unreason, in fact, to encourage doubt of divine purposes. If the lesson of chance came as a shock, evoking a depth of recognition in the subject, it could undermine every proposition by which men and women managed to live.

Dr Bulstrode told the Webber woman and her children about it that Saturday morning. He wondered whether this diagnosis was the depth of banality, or worth reporting on to his professional brethren.

He had no doubts about Bert, though. 'I think that with some medication, such as lithium, to take the edge off Mr Webber's anxiety, and a return to his normal business, he may be able to negotiate life indefinitely. And if for the moment his capacity to communicate seems a little diminished, I'm sure you'll be tolerant of that.'

The Webber daughter smiled stylishly, registering a theatrical relief, quite normal for her age and temperament, but the handsome son frowned a little, a sign of inner ambiguity, thought Dr Bulstrode, from a good son. As for Mrs Webber, she seemed somehow disappointed. Had she ever hoped that a return to normal, busy life was something she and her husband might somehow escape for good?

'When will he be released from hospital, then?' asked Anna with a certain understandable weariness.

Dr Bulstrode explained that he had suspended electro-convulsive treatment, he hoped for good. 'You'll see,' he promised. 'He's capable of reading a newspaper now. We continue the mesmeric sessions with Mr Cutlack. Mr Webber might be functioning well enough to go home within the month.'

'Excellent news,' said the son in earnest appreciation, but Anna still said nothing. The daughter with her lustrous lips said to her mother, 'We should go and see him then, Mum.'

Despite the reassurances of his recovery, Anna and Christian entered Bert's room tentatively, as if the roar that had disrupted the Victoria cinema was still in danger of rising out of him. Only Gertie rushed in and draped herself over his dressing-gowned shoulders as if this was a welcome, even a sentimental reunion. If you are the star of your own film, Christian thought, exuberance is the norm, and every scene demands the best of you, and Gertie was capable of giving the best she had.

Under her assault of affection, Bert seemed uncertain, his head quaking back, as to whether this was an assault or not, for he did not see himself in filmic terms at all. But he was delighted when he saw it was all a matter of Gertie's vitality. He smiled. It was a watery but compelling smile, and Christian felt bound to smile in imitation and seek his mother's eyes to pass on the happy infection, where he found a bleak but tentative joy, a risked grimace of hope.

'It's just Gertie,' Bert said, and guffawed in a clumsy way, but as if the others needed reassurance too.

'Yes, Bert,' Anna confirmed. 'She's still the life of the party.'

Christian wondered how he could ever find Bert in a state where he could take the news. 'Well, Dad, I am in love, but it is not a girl . . .' Would this pronouncement bring on the overwhelming injuries the business of chance had already brought Bert? Would he need shock therapy again because his son was a pansy? And was it true anyway?

'How are all our people going, Anna?' Bert asked then, to demonstrate that he was on his way back to the world, chance or not. 'How is young Spiegel on the Wabra place?'

This was a sheep and cattle station far up the valley and in the shadow of Mount Banda Banda. My patrimony, thought Christian, and he had no interest in it, apart from wanting it to go well for his parents' sake.

'He's well,' said Anna, falling on the subject gratefully. 'His first baby was born up there. Young Taylor is keeping an eye on everything too. We took nine hundred bullocks to the Maitland sale and they realised from eight pounds, eleven shillings and six up to eight pounds, eighteen shillings a head. There's a big call for bullocks at the moment.'

'Ah,' said Bert as if consoled. 'Sorry I've been out of it, Anna.'

Christian noticed Bert had begun to weep softly.

'You've been working for all of us,' said his mother, levelly, as if the statement were simple justice. It carried no freight of sentiment. 'By the way, the butter from the

241

Mungay Creek and Nulla milk is fetching about 120 shillings per hundredweight. Salted butter's really holding. The newspapers say British traders are bidding it up.'

Bert blinked his teary lashes at this news that the world of chance was delivering good things to his door these hard days. He lowered his head and held up his hands.

'No more for now, Anna. All good though, it seems. All very good . . .'

Christian saw his mother toss her head a little and close her lips in a narrow line, as if to say, as wives sometimes did, 'All very well for you.'

After a while, Bert raised his eyes again. It seemed to take a pitiable effort.

'And that Irish bloke on Nulla? Costigan? He's still going well enough, is he?'

The question interested Anna, Christian could tell.

'He's well enough, Bert. I admit, he knows dairies all right.'

'Good,' said Bert, not bothering to pursue a dubious note in Anna's answer. She decided to pursue it herself, even if not doing so might unsettle her husband. Christian wished she would not.

'A strange thing – when he's in town he picks up his mail from the pansy's place. From Chicken Dalton's. Gertie saw that.'

'Mrs Ibbetson the neighbour told us. She tells anyone who'll listen,' Gertie confessed with all the gravity of, say, William Gillette playing Holmes. 'No secrets with her . . . unless they're her own.'

Christian, though not entirely comfortable to hear all this, knew Costigan by sight and believed him no rival. Last week he'd been willing to kill himself for jealousy. Now he heard the news with slight unease. But as with the other visiting Irishman, and the coincidence of Irishness, he felt Costigan no rival. Though was it also true that he was not as desperately enamoured this week as he was last? And if this were the case, what a flippant being he was.

Bert made a polite, speculative sound in his throat.

Gertie said, in a screen Irish accent, 'Perhaps he and Chicken knew each other in the old country?'

Christian felt his unspecified doubt, the whole compendium, shift like a roused animal at the raising of the issue of Chicken and his friendships.

Anna said, 'Don't be ridiculous, Gertie, Chicken's never been outside of the country. I don't know what it means, Costigan knowing Chicken. But he's running Nulla fine.'

Christian felt dislike for his mother when she talked in the way she had been today, as if the milking at Nulla were all she could depend on to go right. And as if she were a hair away from saying, 'For God's sake, Bert, shake yourself together and come back to attend to all this.' As if she almost resented knowing that salted butter was having a good season in England while her husband lay in his stupor. Christian wanted to take her hand and lead her somewhere, he didn't know where, but a long way from where she would be able to take an interest in the price of cased and salted butter. Somewhere there was tea and honey and soothing custard.

He would have liked, too, to take her slimness or thinness or whatever it was and clothe her in . . . well, if it came to it, in the manner of Marlene Dietrich in *Shanghai Express* – even have her wear a hat at that rakish, hostile, alluring angle. He would have liked to rescue Anna from the price of bullocks at Taree and place her at the apex of a Berkeley staircase with enraptured light playing about her, to make her unexpected and transcendent in that way. The point might well be, Christian understood, that Bert had never shown the passion, the lonely yet public shout of pain and aspiration, in Anna's direction that he had reserved for the appearance of that Chancellor and thus the return of Corporal Lembke as the essential factor, if Lembke had ever been less than one.

Christian saw his father yawn with the entitled frankness the sick acquired. 'How is law school, Chris?' he imprecisely asked with the yawn still on him.

'Good,' said Christian vaguely, yet with filial intentions to be precise. 'Back in business on Tuesday coming. I have to be honest and say a lot of contract law I find boring. But intellectual property, and copyright . . .' He tried not to sound like a high-school kid talking warmly about cricket. 'That seems fascinating. Trademarks, for example. But there is a world of other intangible property rights . . .'

'Intangible,' said Bert, as if liking the word.

'Yes. Imagine if you wrote a song and someone else sang it as their own? Or took a photograph and someone else published it as if it were theirs?'

'You're not going to get many cases like that, practising in Kempsey,' said Gertie, in the role of little sister and thus debunker.

He thought of saying, 'Didn't you know, Chicken Dalton probably violates intellectual property every night?' He was uneasy at once about this joke, a joke that satirised Chicken's work and nodded to the majority of which Chicken was not a member, and the majority of which he himself was merely pretending for a short time more to belong. He switched suddenly and said instead, 'I might just have to join my little sister in London when she hits the West End stage.'

Then he went on, speaking in faux mysterious tones for his parents' sake, 'It is a growing area, this business, what with photography and design. Kellogg took a famous case against a shredded-wheat rival some time back. I might even represent some South Seas tribe whose sacred patterns have been used for decorating curtains.'

His mother grinned wanly at this, and his father, having dozed off, awoke with a start, and now yawned. Patients were not as compelling in their recovery as they were in their decline.

'We should let you rest, Father,' Gertie said stagily. There was a tea shop just down the street. They had cream puffs.

Something about his sister being easy to read pleased and fascinated Christian, but he did wonder if behind all her palaver there lurked a woman like his mother who could descend into dour dedication in the end.

Bert said, 'Why don't you go and have tea then? I'll have a quick word with Chris.'

'Very well,' said Anna, gratefully gathering her tidy body to rise. 'Chris, you know the tea shop?'

Christian said he did. Bert exchanged a weary kiss with his wife, and perforce a more thorough one from Gertie, in the role of Edna May Oliver's Aunt March in *Little Women*. 'I'll send you happy thoughts all the time I'm having tea,' trilled Gertie.

Christian feared it might be some talking-to about the state of his desires, as if his confusion were visible now in his face. And the room was unearthly quiet now the women had left.

'I wanted to ask you a favour, Chris,' Bert told him with a frown and under the influence of a suppressed yawn.

'I have that pistol at home, the one I showed you. Before I took it off him, a German soldier shot my friend Reverend Lembke with it.'

'I'm sorry that still gives you so much grief,' said Christian.

'Well,' said Bert. He shrugged and cast his hands up. 'It did worry me for some reason. I went through a whole two further years in France and Belgium, you know, once I got out of hospital, but I don't remember anything as sharply as that night.'

Some tears appeared again on his grey eye lashes. Christian marvelled at how it would be to go off to war. To serve in the hosts of women-lovers but with other men the only near thing. And to see the others, the brutal and the desired, all shot, maimed and pulverised. So strange. That men could do that to each other. Thank sweet Christ for the League of Nations.

In any case, he said, 'What about your acts of bravery? Do you remember them?'

'Hardly at all,' said Bert with an apologetic little smile. 'I certainly didn't think of them as bravery when I was doing them. But look, I'd like to get hold of that pistol. I could ask your mother, but she wouldn't understand. She'd probably think it was all starting again. And I have to look at that pistol again. I have to consider it the way a fellow might consider a contract. Then I want to throw away its parts, throw them in the sea. Miles from each other. I'd drive myself. Or take a taxi. I want to throw the magazine in a lake, the handle off one cliff, the barrel off another. I would know then they would never be a . . . a machine again. I would have them all lost from each other.' Bert thought about this process and then smiled. 'I feel all this would do me a real lot of good. To get rid of it in this way.' He yawned again.

Christian was overtaken by a prickling form of remorse, remembering he had taken the implement of his father's recovery out of the house and it was . . . where was it? Did he lose it in Clyde Street? Had he left it at Chicken's? Yes, surely. He could remember Chicken, in the role of peace-maker, setting it aside on his bookshelf. In that instant, and once more, he saw his declaration of love for Chicken was a ridiculous thing. The indulgence of a child. And he had forgotten the bloody pistol.

Christian said, 'I was going to stay down here now, Dad. Law term starts on Tuesday as I said. I could go home at Easter and get it.'

'Oh,' said his father. 'If you can't get it before Easter . . .'

'You might be home yourself before then?' Christian suggested. 'You could throw it in the Macleay. Or off the cliff at Crescent Head.'

'I don't want to do it in places anywhere near home,' said Bert, a little briskly.

'No,' Christian rushed in, as if he had a firm idea where the pistol was. 'I understand. I can go home one weekend soon and fetch it. I'd be happy to.'

Indeed, he would be very happy to find the damn thing. It seemed it had rested with Bert's ties for fourteen years, and no sooner did it go missing than . . . than it became the inoc-ulation against madness. 'To hell with the way of things!' Christian was willing to cry out. The way everything was a trap, even that bloody tie-drawer pistol. No wonder the weight of chance had made Bert sick in the brain.

Yet Bert seemed immediately restored by Christian's offer. He sat forward in a most un-Bert-like way. 'That would be first class. When would you say you could do that?'

'Ah . . . weekend after next.'

'That would be grand, Chris.'

'But you don't mean to use it to . . .'

'No. No. Do you think I'd put the burden on you if I meant harm to myself? But your mother would draw the wrong conclusion straight off, so I have to depend on you.'

When Christian said it was time to join his mother and Gertie, Bert held out his hand for shaking. This austerity of gesture was normal, father to son, at Christian's age. Men did not caress.

———

That evening Christian was having a schooner out of ennui in the lounge bar when he heard his mother's and Gertie's voices raised for a few seconds upstairs to a pitch that might be scandalous if it continued. He listened further. The competing sounds were the drone of cars and the radio broadcasting races in the public bar. Over them he heard a shriek from Gertie.

In his mood, he was almost grateful for the excessive voices, for Gertie shouting, 'Then why would she . . .?' and her mother countering with, 'If you'd told me you really intended to go, I would have . . .'

He joylessly finished his schooner and went upstairs. All the strappers were still at the race track and he found Gertie was pacing, arms akimbo, in the empty corridor outside the room she shared with her mother.

'What's the problem, Gert?' he called.

'I went around to Auntie Eunice's and she asked me to kindly piss off. She's my godmother. And she ordered me away!'

'Why? Did you say something?' A fit of whimsy overtook him. 'Did you start overacting, Gert?'

But she was too distressed to react. Gertie lowered her voice. 'She said, "Don't bring home any boyfriends, either. Or your mother will steal them." I said, "I don't know what you're talking about, Auntie." And she says, "Well your mother does."'

Gert began to weep softly. 'I hate this stuff. I wish I didn't have a family.'

He held her, his little sister in what seemed like real distress. 'She wanted to hurt me,' Gertie complained, 'but I've done nothing.'

Because Christian did not want to shock her, he wondered but dared not mention if Aunt Eunice might have thought her sister liked that buffoon Eunice went out with, or the buffoon might have said something about Anna that made Eunice jealous. He was uncomfortable that a woman his mother's age should be part of a row, a brawl about possession and desire.

'I hope she doesn't come and give Dad an earful,' murmured Christian. 'Just as he's getting better.'

'Oh God,' said Gertie, in a wail she repressed, for she was not acting now. 'Will you talk to her, Chris? She can't be angry with you.'

'What did Mother say?'

As if summoned, Anna opened the door to her room and stepped in stockinged feet into the corridor. In a tense but restrained voice, she said, 'I told you not to go! Not to trouble her this time. But you had to disobey.'

'I'm not a child,' protested Gertie. 'I have independent affections of my own.'

If that was a line from a film, thought Christian, it was a useful one. He saw it made their mother pause. He saw that in some way, too, Anna was humiliated. Her sister's rancour, which she had no power over, had now been directed at one of her children.

Anna said, 'Come on, Gert. Settle down. She won't be angry forever.'

'You ought to write her a letter. Tell her you're not interested in that dill of a boyfriend of hers.'

Anna inhaled. But for a second Christian saw his mother as an independent woman, not their mother at her essence, nor Bert's wife. She was dressed for the part of mother and wife, but she might very well desire another role.

'I will,' Anna promised. 'She knows it. She's just being silly.'

Gertie's grief diffused a little.

'Let's go down to the lounge and have a drink,' said Christian. 'Come on, Mum, just put your shoes on and come down.'

The idea cheered his mother up. But they went down there and had just rung the bell and given their order when Sam Montgomery, Aunt Eunice's 'dill', about whom Gertie had been shouting upstairs, came into the lounge. His brilliantined black hair shone in the light.

'Could I talk to you, Anna?' he asked with a statesman-like solemnity.

23

Kempsey and Sydney, New South Wales, 1933

On the Saturday morning, Chicken had been surprised to see the police car outside Mrs Ibbetson's. What did that mean? He had earlier called a nurse at Macleay District to inquire how Flo Honeywood was. Surely this did not make him a criminal, even if he had been warned off by her husband.

He was confident Mrs Ibbetson would give some substance to the figure of the tramp, the big fellow who destroyed Flo's face before running for the car. He watched the emerged, solemn man with that mocker, Sergeant Ives, and they both stood on the mounded earth of the pavement chatting before Ives drove them both away in the police Dodge.

Now Chicken was restless and not a little angry. He felt sure of nothing and wanted to visit gentle old Mrs Ibbetson and ask her what she had told the policemen, to verify he had nothing to fear. But she would not quite understand his visit, he knew. She would tell him what a gentleman the newcomer was, and no doubt a good Mason, like her late husband. Mrs Ibbetson was not so good at the essences of things.

He settled himself as a deliberate plan to other issues. He had Christian Webber with a new lover's absolute and holy demand: fidelity. Yet Johnny Costigan would be here tonight, expecting that half-ashamed tussle which had been Chicken's chief comfort in recent months. And he would avoid that – avoid it, when it was such a rare thing for him, though he did not quite believe in Christian's desire for a marriage of souls. Christian had barely emerged, barely looked for other men, barely knew how many there might be in the city, in his profession. Let me not, Chicken knew from his two years of high school, to the marriage of true minds admit impediment. But he could not quite believe he and Christian were anywhere near a marriage of true minds, though he could not forget the sensual bonanza of their hungry times together, a plenteous experience that might be repeated if Christian came home at Easter. Or not. He might already by then remember the Victoria cinema pianist with a fondness reserved for a memorable Christmas gift, a joy grown out of.

Chicken regretted he would not grant Johnny, or be granted by him, that limited but true joy that did not play with declarations of love. Tonight, in the meantime, the Victoria was again showing *Almost Married* with Violet Heming as Anita Mellikovna, the tragic Russian woman, and Ralph Bellamy, and he could sit still at the piano and watch it with its score implanted in it by science and be no more active than any yokel. All his own music for before and after was already organised – he had run through it with the Quinlan boys on Friday afternoon, before visiting their sisters' shop to see what was new in from Sydney. The

252

Quinlan sisters were artists in their own way, closer to the motion pictures in taste than any of the tank-like dresses imported by Barsby's department store to encase the sturdy wives of farmers. He liked his routine for Fridays and something about the police visitors to Mrs Ibbetson made him hope his life would remain as it was.

For if a man were simply accepted as a fellow who wanted to get on and be allowed to play about and find a little covert joy betimes – it was enough for Chicken Dalton, whose father cut wood in a mill or hacked at ironbark in a clearing in the rain to fashion railway sleepers. I may be the happiest man in this town, Chicken reflected, for all I know. And poor Flo, he thought, with a pulse of affection, will never be the happiest girl.

———

Gertie asked Montgomery, 'Shouldn't you be at Auntie Eunice's?'

The man looked at her dully. Christian wondered if some gallantry was required of him. Something along the lines of seeing the blackguard off the premises. The question was, was he a blackguard?

Gertie continued, tigerish. 'Don't you know my mother's taken?'

Yes, Christian thought, despite himself. But by a ghost.

'Not quite your affair, young lady,' said Montgomery woodenly. 'Anna, can I talk to you away from the peanut gallery?'

Christian now needed to step forth. His mother remained waxy and silent. 'You can't talk to my sister like that,' he said.

Montgomery blinked beneath his brilliantined fringe. Quite a good-looking fellow. He said, 'You're right. Christian, is it? You're right. But would you both please let me speak to your mother on her own?'

Gertie said, 'I don't like lemon, lime and bitters anyway. But is that all right with you, Mother?'

The 'mother' was Gertie putting on side as ever. She had said to Christian once, 'You never hear characters say "mum" and "dad" in Ibsen or Chekhov. Nor in Shaw for that matter.'

Christian asked, 'Would you like us to go, Mum?' He was surprised and shocked and yet contradictorily hopeful. If his mother had strayed, it was unspeakable and repulsive. But perhaps it opened up a moral latitude for him.

Anna said, 'I'd appreciate a word with Mr Montgomery.'

Christian nodded to Gertie and they went, but only as far as the hallway beyond the glass doors, where Gertie baulked. Christian, who already felt enough discomfort, pulled her arm.

'Come on, you can't wait here.'

Solemn-eyed Gertie asked him, 'Did they do something? Surely not.' Gertie put a finger in her mouth to mime retching.

'Oh God, Gert,' said Christian. He covered his face in confusion.

But he could feel her breathing against his face. Her breath seemed very warm and infantile. And agog.

'Please come upstairs,' he pleaded.

'Maybe they might run away together,' Gertie said, with her filmic enthusiasm.

'She wouldn't do that,' he assured her. 'She won't run away from you. She knows you'd track her down.' He inhaled.

'Besides, you're talking about our mother! Show her some respect, Gert, I beg you.'

'*The peanut gallery,*' sniffed Gertie. 'Would you have taken him on if he hadn't apologised.'

'I would have demanded he did, and then if he hadn't . . .' He reflected on the improbable mental image of himself and Montgomery deploying all they knew of boxing and wrestling.

So they went upstairs, where Christian locked himself in his room and felt dismal about the pistol and whatever his mother had got herself into. He harboured still an uncomfortable suspicion, no doubt, that whatever mayhem had afflicted Anna, his own perversion had made its impact, had unbalanced the world, and reduced its most notable and prominent deity – his mother.

———

The young gone, Sam Montgomery held Anna's arms. 'This is destiny,' he said with heavy emphasis, and she knew it was a rehearsed line, a line from the radio dramas he had confessed to liking.

Even then, Anna thought, Does destiny use as much brilliantine as this? What hairstyle does destiny actually favour?

Though she still desired him, she felt ill equipped here at this plain, meat-and-potatoes hotel to give desire its proper weight. She felt she could not tell if it was a feather, nor whether it was a mountain.

'I'm done with Eunice and she with me,' said Sam. 'And we can be so happy, Anna. You and I.' Then, 'Listen,' he said. 'Listen. We could be very happy and live a good life. We could. In the sunshine. Down here in Sydney.'

And she had to admit the sunshine in Sydney was a different sunshine. Electric and full of possibility.

'Except,' she said, 'I have the children. And a husband.'

The leaden weight of the husband still grieving the Reverend Lembke and enchanted by a ghost, Bert was a disciple without a prophet. And the balance of his mind lay before her as a task she must drearily piece together, perhaps without a passionate interest in the result.

He said, 'That Gertie . . . I reckon she understands the way things are going. Cheeky little tart, if you'll forgive me . . . But she loves you. She's in favour of your happiness, I'd say. And Christian . . . well, he's impressive. He'd stand by whatever you decided too. You know that, Anna. If I can tell it, then you know it.'

'But there's Bert,' she said. 'He's just getting better in the head.'

'But the thing is, do you love him, Anna?'

She said in exasperation, 'It's not a matter of love.' It was a matter of something else, a greater weight still. Two young people full of a head of desire met, fancily dressed, in the presence of their tribes one day and pledged with the given Lutheran pieties they would become one creature. Their keenness was meaningless in the long term yet pregnant with an enduring compulsion that would lock them together further, whether the compulsion was desire or friendship or duty. Between them, in the web of their first embraces, they created a weight no one, themselves in particular, could lift off them. Marriage – though their half-negligent and lightly given vows – created a condition beneath whose gravity they could never move, or even if there was a day when they could, they could be punished for moving, punished by the witnessing tribes but not least by themselves.

'You told me once that he's really in love with this parson. You told me this dead parson is a shadow over everything. *A dead parson.* With all respect, it makes Bert the dullest man in the world.'

'I didn't say dullest,' Anna contended. 'And he may have got over the dead parson now . . .'

'So you'll stay with a half-mad fellow you don't love . . .'

Anna was desperate. She wondered how she had not seen all this when she opened herself to this man. 'What sort of woman leaves a man with a Military Medal and a Military Cross?' she asked, falling back on Kempsey's definition of Bert.

'Is it a matter of appearances, Anna? Surely not? Down here, no one will know. No one will care.'

'But I choose to care for him. And who else is there to do it?'

'There are nurses, for Christ's sake. That's who?'

'Not the same. You know that. Nurses help men die. I have to help Bert come back to life.'

'But you didn't love him when *we* were with each other. You didn't call out for him. He didn't count then. Anna, we will be in each other's arms. Always. Wouldn't you want that?'

Well, she thought, that would be nice, while he was still in a condition to venerate her. But she was barred from wanting it. And there was something else? What if she surrendered herself to being, full time, that wanting, panting woman? She could tell there were awful perils to that too, that she would be cut off from the banal yet wishful stream, exposed somehow – a reproach to other stoic women sticking things out. She could not voice that, she dimly saw it, and yet it was also *there*, it always had been, the caution against

257

being a creature at play. In her Lutheran tribe she had never seen yearning on any faces, had never seen appetite on any woman's brow, nor any aftermath of delirium, nor any other sign that affection counted for more than maritally accumulated acres. They were all people who knew that any of that sort of exuberance was an anteroom to a suitable punishment. She was trying to order these suspicions and concepts into sentences that would mean something to him.

'Look,' he pleaded, 'what are you going to tell this Bert of yours about your sister? When he wonders why she won't talk to you? Maybe she'll let your Bert know all about it. Then what happens? You and I are evil people in the divorce news in *Truth*.'

All of this could indeed befall even a hapless innocent like her. But she had also known always that shame befell the innocents very easily.

'I sacrificed everything for you,' said Montgomery.

'Not everything,' she said, grateful to be exact. 'You still have your job. I sacrificed . . .' she began, but could not finish saying what. She had been going to say, 'My honour.' But it sounded false, like a Victorian woman in a film. 'It must stop,' she said. She wondered if pleading wouldn't serve her purpose. 'Please, make it stop. You have the power!'

Tears were in his eyes. She had not counted on them. 'You are all I have now,' he said, melodramatically piteous.

'Is that a reason?' she wondered with genuine interest. 'Is that a reason I should give in. A man like you . . . he's never lonely for long.'

By now she was impatient. I can make him leave, she thought. I can be cruel. And then I must make peace with my sister, hard as it might be; as abject as I might need to be. For Bert's sake, not least.

'Please leave,' she said. And she knew now that after meaningless protests, he would. 'I led you on but I shouldn't have. There was nothing there for you.'

Sad-eyed, he retrieved his hat. Before he left he said, 'Are you going to lead other poor mongrel blokes along?'

She said, 'No. Not now that I know what pain it causes.'

He tossed his head as if she had just betrayed herself as a shallow woman. But he left, and after he left, she saw her life ahead as a dreary landscape, like the Macleay flood-plains poking up muddily after a deluge. There would be Bert's meaningless recuperation. And bullocks and Imperial butter. 'I must find how to be fed by all this,' she thought. To be fed.

———

In the light of developments, the following evening Anna Webber stood on Eunice's veranda and steadied her breath, and felt her weight sink towards her hips as if she were in danger at any second, in that blank darkness, of being charged and toppled. It was essential she not leave until she had come to terms with her sister, and her body was settling to the task better than her scant moral courage. She knew she could make her sister answer the door only by being raucous, and thus alien to all her instincts; that is by behaving like an Italian or a squalling Irish or Cockney girl. Marshalling that sort of resolve, she decided she might as well bang heavily on the door. So she did, hammering with the ham of her hands. If she tapped away like a penitent, she suspected, Eunice would not give her the time of day.

'Eunice, I know you don't want to see me. But I have to talk to you about Bert. Eunice, I just have to talk to you.

I wish I didn't. It's Bert and the children. Please open up. We can get it over.'

And, of necessity, she went on in the same vein for two minutes of noise-making. A particularly interested neighbour might take notice and the chance of that, she hoped, might make Eunice open the door. Because the same primness Anna knew she suffered from, so did Eunice. Would she have to descend to 'Open the damned door!'? She hoped not.

After some two minutes, Eunice at last opened up, abruptly in mid-breath intake on Anna's part. In the indirect light from within, the spaces beneath Eunice's eyes were blanched and draggy, like an older woman's. But her ageless contempt was assured of itself, and hard to look at.

'You!' she said. 'Get out of my house!'

But in case any neighbourly attention had been drawn, she did not say, 'You whore!' or, 'You tart!'

'By all means despise me,' said Anna, 'but go easy on poor Gertie.'

'I'll spare her as much as you spared me,' Eunice enunciated. The words were exact and displayed their edges.

'Above all, there's Bert. I might deserve whatever you say but he doesn't. He'll be going home soon.'

'You think if he knows you're a slut, it'll put him back in hospital. Is that it?'

'You can put it like that,' Anna admitted. 'Yes, you are entitled to put it like that. I can say I don't understand what came over me. But that won't satisfy you.'

'You did me a favour,' her sister claimed. 'Did you think I was going for Sam? That I wanted a lifetime of oily hair on antimacassars and car talk? I was devising ways to move him along.'

260

That might be true, Anna thought. It sounded somehow true.

'But it wasn't my sister's job to take him away. Goody, goody Anna. Teachers used to tell me to be more like you! Christ! And you were willing to take away what you *thought* I wanted. You can never be trusted, you bloody cunt of a thing.'

She had said *that*, thought Anna, aghast. She had said the ultimate word. The worst she could say. And it had to be borne.

'Did he *excite* you?' asked Eunice, letting go of any plan to mimic indifference. 'Because he excited me. He knew things most men don't. Most men are a write-off. But the wrong man knowing things is as bad as the right man knowing bugger all.'

She said that too. *Bugger all!* Loud enough for neighbours to hear.

'You'll find that out,' Eunice continued, a skilled attack. 'I'd love you to marry him and get bored. I'd love to see you cross-eyed with the tedium.'

'Well, that won't happen,' said Anna. 'I told you . . . Bert is recovered.'

'Good. You can get cross-eyed with boredom with Bert.'

'You can't tell him, Eunice. That's all. I'm not telling you to treat me with mercy. But Bert . . .'

'Ah yes, Bert,' mocked Eunice. 'Who can sweet-talk you with the price of barbed wire and cream. You lucky bloody whore!' Eunice herself inhaled fiercely, between censures. 'Don't worry, then,' she said. 'I'll let you die Bert's wife. That's my revenge. Now clear out.'

The door slammed. Eunice had at no stage stepped out of her house into the night. She had had the light from inside on her shoulders, gracing her rage. She'd had sure instincts of condemnation in what she said. It was so deftly targeted that Anna was overtaken by forlornness.

She still possessed sufficient respectability to wait on in the darkness there, however. Until any neighbouring witness lost interest and gave up their curiosity in the sisterly row. Then she went carefully down the steps and out of the gate, back to the pub, her mind on sipping gin and hoping for a cure in the plain guests' lounge. She had put Gertie on the tram to go to the pictures, confident she was capable of dealing with Saturday-night Lotharios. She would wait up for her.

24

Sydney and Kempsey, New South Wales, 1933

When Christian came down to see his father, he called Walter at home and, summoned to the phone, Walter was enthusiastic to meet up with Christian. But, Walter explained, on Saturday he was going to a conference on China, at which trade unionists and Labor men intended to address the continuing lack of sanctions against Japan after the well-established Japanese occupation of Manchuria. There was going to be a debate about certain Japanese ships being loaded with iron ore in Wollongong, and whether they should be boycotted.

Christian had a range of reactions to this news. It was touching, first, that Walter had been working all day, applying his peculiar ragged charms and talents, to a question of the Big World. Kempsey bumpkins didn't even see the world changing, but when all fell apart and war was declared, well, they were willing to go and be slaughtered, or to see someone like Lembke slaughtered. Secondly, it touched Christian that Walter had left a mansion and gone and argued the point all day in a grim, humid meeting room in Liverpool or Sussex Street.

Walter said he could meet Christian after the sessions, and nominated 8.30 that night. Christian excused himself after the messy business with Sam Montgomery, feeling enlarged not by Sam's mysterious, or not-so-mysterious intrusion, as by Walter's admirable concerns for the order of the world.

The meeting place was a restaurant named Mr Hang's Chinese Dining Rooms on lower George Street, and it was a relief to leave the St Leger and be out in the cool night and board a tram to the city. Behind him he had left a mystified Gertie and a mother whose demeanour was hard to read. Though it was hard to forgive her encouraging these overheard excessive statements in a bore like Sam Montgomery, Christian himself had been guilty of overdone gestures and statements in the past week. He was guilty of the mad scene at Chicken's cottage, with the wry Irishman commentating on his posturings just to make them more shameful.

Christian arrived in that slummy end of George Street, in the shadow of the giant new Harbour-striding bridge, and entered Mr Hang's. It was full of tobacco smoke and steam, and by the light of its red lanterns its bow-tied staff of Cantonese men were busy carrying and retrieving plates. He could see Walter almost straight away, coat off, bow-tied in a Scots-tartan way, leaning forward in the company of six or so people. His face was alight with his own emphasised version of the truth. Christian wondered, did he have time to flee, but Walter seemed to see him instantly, and his eyes took on an even greater brightness of welcome as he stood up, ready to greet and introduce his friend to the table. Christian was bound to go forward. Had Walter been a proselytiser all along, and had asked Christian to come here so that he could be initiated as a socialist?

Walter's friends seemed merely politely interested in him as Walter introduced him. In Kempsey a law student from Sydney University was a person of reckoning, and here a nobody or at least an unproved somebody. The table at which Christian found himself was made up of two open-collared union officials, a few members of the state legislature, one young-looking, one hard-bitten, and a young woman doctoral student from the university, a bird of rare feathers in the academic sphere. She was busy describing something called the Lytton Commission, an absurdity. All these solemn Northern Hemisphere pooh-bahs travelling to Manchuria, she said, and after a suitable period giving a report to the League of Nations, which found the Chinese had been provocative and yet called on the Japanese to withdraw. 'Of course, the Chinese were provocative. They tried to hang on to their country. And of course the Japanese won't move out. Because . . . who will make them?'

The younger of the two state legislators said, 'I hope I am wrong. But could we be seeing the opening to a second Great War?'

'But our government's delighted with the Japanese,' said Walter. 'At least we're selling them iron ore, and there are jobs in Wollongong.'

Christian found it very reputable on Walter's part that he knew of Wollongong and that it was a steel town.

'And America's selling them arms,' said Walter further. 'Jobs over justice.'

'Yet jobs are justice,' said the older legislator.

'Fair enough,' said Walter. 'I should have said "profits over justice".'

One of the unionists said, 'We just don't have the clout yet to refuse to handle shipping for Japan.'

There were further rounds of opinions, with the woman scholar bemoaning in particular the League of Nations' chosen impotence over the Japanese in Manchuria, a chorus everyone joined. The more senior of the two members of the parliament said that it was a long way between Manchukuo, as the Japanese called their new acquisition, and Wollongong, and that the boys in the Australian Miners' Union were pleased enough for now with ore sales. 'It's all no danger to us in the end,' he said with his middle-aged realism. 'Just look at their textiles. If their weapons are as shoddy as that, we don't need to fear them.'

Walter looked glum, as if he wished the world was more simply and intelligibly devised. And everyone smoked continuously, except Walter and Christian.

When it was time to go, they all went out into the night. Christian saw the sallow lights of a Manly ferry approaching Circular Quay, and in his mood it had the look of a vessel hazardously and too late abroad. After further but sporadic talk amongst the group, they all said goodnight to Walter and Christian.

'I've got my capitalist cabriolet up in the Argyle Cut,' said Walter then. 'I'll take you back to the house, if you like, for a drink.'

It was such an appealing idea, the big house by the Harbour as against the strappers' hotel in Randwick. At Walter's, they could drink on a veranda and watch the lights of the city lying fractured but indelible on the water.

They walked up the dark gully of road cut deep in sand-stone by convicts more than a hundred years before. Where the light was least, Walter said, nearly solemnly, 'I can see you've changed, Chris.'

'Oh,' said Christian, a little dully but willing to be persuaded about the idea.

'Yes,' Walter told him. 'Dare I say you seem a man of experience?'

'What is a man of experience? I don't feel different.'

Yet as he said it, he had the knowledge it was not true, that the experiences that changed what Sam Montgomery called 'destiny' might have already occurred, and he must claim them or be ever a victim of change.

'You don't seem as innocent,' said Walter Jupp. 'You seem sadder and wiser.'

'How can you tell? I've hardly said anything.'

'Yes. But last year you would have. Tried to play along. Join the conversation.'

'And made a fool of myself. I don't know the Lytton Commission from Adam.'

Walter found this very amusing. 'Well,' said Walter, 'knowing about it hasn't done anyone much good. Tell me? Is it a girl? Have you met one? Have you become, perhaps, a seducer?'

And there was a short hack of laughter, not utterly normal, not at all polished, from Walter.

'Not that,' said Christian.

And it occurred to him for the first time. Was there a chance to declare himself here? With this apparently worldly youth, who knew what sanctions had not been brought to bear to punish Japan? Was there really? And with the suspicion came a physical warmth he felt in his thighs and upper arms, and there was no doubt the warmth was directed at neat little gingery-blond Walter. And he had a powerful sense that what he felt was a reflection from Walter, some intensity Walter was offering or radiating.

So was Walter Jupp, this mysterious fellow, this man who seemed to operate at a superior plane to himself, an object of desire? No sooner was the idea there than the desire existed. In a being who was willing to die last week for Chicken's fidelity . . . What did this heat and fever say of that?

Walter's voice sounded dry as he said, 'Are you my friend, Christian? I wish you could be.'

And in that second Christian found he was the one given the power of suave discrimination over what was to happen. Christian who had threatened to spill his brains on Chicken Dalton's floor. And now proceeding to nicety and differ-ence. 'In what sense your friend, Walter?'

Walter, artless, grabbed Christian's hand, and kissed it.

'If I told you I have no erotic interest in women . . . would you still be my friend?' And then he, who knew what the Lytton Commission did and was, said, 'Don't send me away, Christian, unless you can't stand it.'

'No,' he said. 'I wouldn't send anyone away.' And then he asked, 'Do your parents know?'

'Yes,' said Walter, talking excitedly. 'My mother guessed ages ago. She's good at these things. Called me in for a good talk about what faced me. Such as handsome young cops in public toilets waiting for me to say a nice word to them before they arrested me. All that. And you know what the old chap does, Sir Walter, plutocratic monster as he is, and as little as I would dislike being one of his stokers or engine room greasers? He lets the authorities know it's not worth their while entrapping me. It's interesting how messages get through at his level. It's not justice. It's that most people can't afford to make an enemy of him.'

And he took and kissed Christian's hand again.

And so, for the second time in a week, at the start of which he thought himself God's oddity, Christian encountered another of his kind. But while feeling such a grateful sense of homecoming, he resolved to stay pure until he had spoken to and made things clear to Chicken, whom he had bound to similar purity by his demonstration with the pistol. Walter drove him to the great white house by the Harbour, and due to gin and the ever-high sensual pressure within young men, they had by three o'clock become lovers and brothers in all enlightened things.

———

It rained that night. Chicken could smell the wetness of the Burnt Bridge people in the front rows. He could smell the after-odour of what they had left, their leaky roofs and lack of bathrooms and overflowing outdoor crappers. It was not noisome. It was like the odour of his own family. The smell of bewildered people, he knew, even poorer than his family had ever been, and God knew that was poor. Their coughing punctuated the film, which seemed flat at first tonight, and short, the programme being bulked out with *Freaks*, the circus piece that cheered the damp crowd up. There was a polite old Thunguddi woman always called to him, 'You're a real sport, Mr Chicken.' It was a rich moment she always gave him. Be it ever so humble, acclaim was acclaim, was intoxicating. 'Get home as dry as you can, dearie,' he told her. He needed Johnny Costigan to cheer him, which meant he was low indeed.

This was not like him, he complained to himself. It's those policemen, and Burley Honeywood, who had soured the night.

But when he got home on the first cold, damp night of the year, Johnny was not there, and the house ached of emptiness. Nor, as if he knew he was in for a rejection, did Johnny come. Had Johnny given up on him over the fifty dollars from America? But if so, he had not cancelled Chicken's place as his mail drop.

Chicken woke up within an hour or two, wrapped in a blanket on his sofa. He could tell the air in his house had settled, inexpectant of visitors.

———

The police car was back before noon that Sunday, edging along Clyde Street but stopping, as he incoherently hoped it would, outside his place. He saw from the loungeroom window a big solemn plainclothes man and the Small Sergeant enter the garden and make for his door. He went to meet them. Everyone's friend, after all. Nought to hide. The pox doctor's clerk!

'Hello,' he said in his role as everyone's favourite picture show pianist.

'May we come in, Mr Dalton?' He said his name was Inspector Sangster, and that Chicken must know Sergeant Ives. And, not yet having entered the house, he nonetheless sniffed in a sort of confirmed satisfaction.

'Someone left a note at the station, Mr Dalton,' Sangster announced in the hallway. 'It declared you the owner of a pistol, Mr Dalton? Something from the Great War.'

'No, I don't own it. Someone . . . someone left it here.'

'Do you have it? Could we see it?'

Chicken felt sick. The implications of course made his fingers itch, his palms sweat. But he said lightly, 'I believe I have it here . . .' And he led them inside and there it was, the thing's butt slightly protruding beyond a line of books.

Inspector Sangster made a prohibiting gesture with his hands and reached into the shadow above the books and extracted it by its barrel, which he then sniffed.

'It's been fired,' he stated flatly.

It was a ridiculous proposition. From a feature picture. This weapon has been recently fired. At which the floozy faints and the gigolo looks hunted! But it seemed to Chicken to be malicious to use such a line here.

'No,' pleaded Chicken. 'It's been here all along.'

That too was like film talk! As if he were trapped in one.

The inspector removed the magazine and squinted at it. 'This has all but two gone,' he said. 'Was that the state it was in before?'

'I . . . I just don't know. Someone . . . a friend . . . left it here some days back. I've never even looked at it.'

The Small Sergeant opened a large manila envelope and the inspector dropped the gun into it. They were as smooth as sorcerer and assistant.

'Who was this friend?' asked Sangster bleakly. 'The one you say left it here?'

'I . . . I can't remember.'

'You can't remember who brought you a pistol?'

'I have little parties.' Indeed, very little parties.

'It's a pistol from the Great War. Did John Costigan himself leave it?'

'No . . . not John.'

271

'There was a rumour that one Bert Webber had a pistol like that one,' said the Small Sergeant.

'Yes,' said Sangster. 'Bert's in hospital in Sydney. Did a member of the Webber family happen to give it to you?'

So young a conversation but already Chicken was reduced to stubs of denial. 'No . . . I don't think . . . No, not Christian. Well . . . perhaps . . . Yes, alright, Christian brought it along. But innocently . . . As a sort of theatre prop.'

Both policemen adopted looks of superior wisdom, which they would not voice to Chicken. Sangster asked, 'When does Johnny Costigan generally visit you?'

'Every third Saturday, he comes to collect his mail. After the . . . after the pictures, you know.'

'Bloody curious time to collect mail,' murmured Sergeant Ives.

'We have a drink together, and a talk.'

'I see,' said Sangster, and he and Ives exchanged looks. 'You are close friends then?'

'Well, he is hard to know,' said Chicken, and the Small Sergeant let out one sharp snarl of laughter.

'Did Costigan come last night? To collect his mail?'

'No. And I don't know why. Perhaps he couldn't get to town.'

Chicken turned to the sideboard to fetch the three letters.

'I'll take them, Mr Dalton,' said Sangster, intercepting him and taking the letters himself and handing them to the Small Sergeant.

'But he might be by to collect them,' Chicken protested.

'No,' said Sangster flatly, 'he won't be. He's dead.'

Chicken felt his knees give way and sank a little and then recovered himself and sought the sideboard with his hand for support.

'But what . . . Are his wife and children all right? They usually camp over . . .'

'We know where they camp,' said Sangster. 'They are waiting outside Dr McVicar's now while the autopsy's attended to.'

'How did the poor fellow die?' He thought of the short, stimulating but brief tuggings, which were all Johnny would allow himself of joy. And tears rose. 'You're not just teasing or . . . or testing me in some way, are you?'

'Why would you ever think that?' asked Sangster.

'He was shot dead with a pistol last night,' said Ives. 'We thought you might know that, Chicken. Did you know it?'

Chicken could not speak. He stared, powerless, at Sangster.

'Who would shoot him?' he managed at last. When had Johnny made such an adequate claim on the world that the world would shoot back.

Then he remembered the smoothness of the police, their snaffling the pistol and dropping it in an envelope.

'We'll know a lot more about that after we have the autopsy done,' Sangster assured him.

'Shot? But he can't be shot . . .'

'You didn't see him last night then? That's settled, is it?'

'Yes. He didn't come to collect his mail. I wondered why.'

As if at a signal the two of them simply began to walk for the door. No felicitations, no goodbyes.

'Can I see the poor wretch?' asked Chicken.

Sangster stopped. 'Why do you call him a wretch?'

'If he was shot . . . That makes him a poor wretch.'

'Right enough,' murmured Sangster.

He volunteered that after the autopsy the dead man would be at Curran's Funerals.

25

Kempsey, New South Wales, 1933

Later in the day, after hours of tears and genuine hand-wringing, not an accustomed activity for him, Chicken made his way to Curran's. Mr Curran was in shirtsleeves when he answered the bell and his hands looked soft from being gentle with the dead. 'Yes, Mr Dalton?' he asked, and there was a shift in his eyes.

Chicken asked if Johnny Costigan was there. 'I used to look after his mail,' he pleaded.

Curran waited to answer. Normally kind, he was willing to be cruel for Chicken's sake. 'No,' he said. 'I expect him this afternoon, but I doubt you would want to see him much before ten tomorrow, after the autopsy. He's been shot in the face.'

'His wife and kids?' asked Chicken.

'I believe the Breslin family has taken them in,' Curran told him curtly. 'Mr Breslin is St Vincent de Paul Society secretary.'

'I gave the inspector his latest mail. Mrs Costigan might like to see it.'

'I think the inspector and the parish priest will sort that out.'

Curran brought the conversation to an end and the first cold south-westerly of the year gusted Chicken home. Once there, he sat on his lounge shivering and arguing with Johnny's fresh ghost. At 5 pm the police pulled their Dodge up in front of Ultima Thule and came to his door. He inhaled and went to greet them. But before he could think of behaving amiably, Inspector Sangster told him they had come to charge him for the murder of John Francis Costigan. The Small Sergeant seemed gratified in an amused way when he asked for Chicken's wrists to have the cuffs put on.

'Should I get a pullover?' asked Chicken, as if he were willing to go to prison as utterly self-equipped as a prisoner should be.

Inspector Sangster told him no. He was aware of Mrs Ibbetson watching him with her genial, confused eyes. They drove him off amidst gum trees writhing in the wind and past shopfronts closed this Sabbath afternoon, down Belgrave and into Smith to the sandstone police station. Inside, in a room whose walls were painted the sickly yellow of human malice, they took his fingerprints and put him in one of the two cells out in the back of the police station. He was dazed to be there. Knees drawn up and arms around his ankles, he sat on his bunk, disbelieving in the place.

That night Mr Sangster began to interrogate him in the office proper. Sergeant Ives was of course present. 'We'll have to do this again in Newcastle with a stenographer,' Sangster told him with a trace of apology. 'But in the meantime, it's good to get a start while you are fresh.'

Sangster began. Did he consider Johnny Costigan had similar tastes to himself? Did they ever lie in the same bed? Did they have carnal relations? 'I don't know what you mean,' said Chicken.

'Did you pull each other's pissers?' the Small Sergeant clarified.

Chicken suspected that the truth was his only defence. So he told the truth. It happened, but Costigan didn't consider himself a pansy, said Chicken.

Did they ever quarrel, he and Costigan?

'No. He picked up his mail and left by morning. To go to Mass. He loved the children and was frightened that they would grow up as unlettered as him . . .'

'Did he love his wife?' asked Sangster?

'He felt sad for her. That he'd brought her all this way up to Nulla. But I said to him, "You've provided for her in hard times. And given her lovely children."'

'You liked his kids, did you?' asked Sergeant Ives, his eyes agleam. Sangster said nothing a while but then, 'Did you feel any guilt you were taking him away from her?'

'Sometimes,' said Chicken, pursuing his belief in honesty. 'But he came willingly to visit. Some of us are open about our . . . our imperfection or our preference. The truth is that we don't say no to women. It's just we can't say yes in the way most men can. That's what it is to be a . . . a homosexual. We do not choose our way.'

Sergeant Ives uttered a little guffaw of disgust. He said, 'Yet Costigan must have said "Yes" often enough to his wife. He had four sons.'

'I think he was one of those men on the cusp.'

'You filthy bastard!' said Ives, licking his lips. 'You'd work on men like that, wouldn't you?'

Sangster looked at the Small Sergeant, whose jaws could be seen working, swallowing the denunciations he would have liked to voice.

'You say you never quarrelled with Johnny Costigan. What about the fifty-dollar note missing from the letter from his sister?'

How did they know about that? Johnny's wife probably.

'I assured him I did *not* take that note. And he trusted me and believed me.'

The Small Sergeant declared, 'That isn't what Johnny Costigan told his wife.'

Sangster murmured, 'You wouldn't shoot a man over fifty dollars, would you, Chicken?'

Chicken protested – he wouldn't, of course he wouldn't. But the Small Sergeant smiled on, his acid smile.

The inspector said, 'So the gun at your place. Was that Bert's gun?'

Honesty was a hard rule but he did not know how to conduct himself without it. 'I believe it probably is.'

'Did you steal it? You said the son brought it. So did you steal it from him?'

'No. I've never been inside the Webber house.'

'How did you get it, then?'

'I can't say for fear of hurting a young man.'

Sergeant Ives cast his hands up.

Sangster asked, 'Do you understand you are set fair to hang, Chicken? Do you know what it is to hang? I witnessed the execution of our last one, late last year, Long Bay. A dapper-looking fellow named William Moxley. It took less than thirty seconds from the cell to the fitting of the rope, and he made a little statement about the care of a son he had and then, SLAM!' Sangster clapped his hands.

'The hatch opened. And you know what? Moxley, who had murdered two youngsters, he'd prayed with a colonel of the Salvation Army for an hour before he died and . . . the greatest good luck . . . he was killed straight off of a neck fracture. The executioner happened to get it right for him. But he mightn't get it right for the next one. Odds are against it. And the next one looks like being you, Chicken.'

'Wringing a chicken's neck,' shouted the Small Sergeant exultantly.

'I will not go that way,' said Chicken, weeping.

'Oh yes?' asked the Small Sergeant. 'And why not?'

'Because I am telling you the straight, straight gospel truth.'

'I wouldn't drag the Gospels into it,' growled the Small Sergeant. 'If I were a bugger and a shirt-lifter like you, I wouldn't mention Holy Writ.'

'We still need to know how you got the pistol,' remarked the inspector with a sigh.

'It was brought to my place,' Chicken confessed, 'and left by accident.'

'Who by?'

'I told you. Christian Webber. The son. The poor boy was distressed at the time.'

'Why distressed?' said Sangster, silencing the Small Sergeant this time with a glance.

Chicken had no option but to tell the tale, but he softened the reality of it as he narrated. 'He was distressed because he felt affection for me. He was distressed for what that meant. I am sure it was a passing impulse. He was threatening to hurt himself, though. He had brought a pistol his father had from the war. I relieved him of the pistol and put it on my bookshelf.'

'Did you and the boy have relations?'

'He is eighteen,' pleaded Chicken by way of admission, and again there was a hack of laughter from the Small Sergeant. So there were worse things than Sangster. There was the mob that waited beyond him. The mob whose voice the Small Sergeant injected into the conversation.

'You realise that Christian Webber is pursuing a career in the law?' asked Sangster.

Chicken did. Chicken said he didn't want to say anything to harm that.

'It's a gravely serious thing to say about a man in Christian Webber's position,' Sangster remarked. 'A young man with a future. His father a hero too.'

'I would not say it if it weren't the truth,' pleaded Chicken.

'Oh, you're a great bloody cobber of the truth, Chicken,' cried Sergeant Ives.

More lethally, Sangster said, 'I have a pretty clear idea what happened. You had some quarrel with Costigan. If you say Webber was looking your way, maybe Costigan got jealous. Or maybe you'd stolen cash and money orders from his mail, as his wife says.'

'His wife doesn't know me.'

Sangster did not answer this. 'You know what happened, Chicken? I'll tell you, and we can keep young Christian out of it. You met Johnny Costigan not so far from the Federal last night, and there was a quarrel and you shot him dead. Either before or after the picture show. You shot him dead while his kids were sleeping in their dray across the other side of the river. You used the Webber pistol, which you either stole or had acquired. We will find out more about that.'

Chicken, of course, hopelessly pleaded he was home before the picture show, and after, and did not meet Johnny Costigan.

The Small Sergeant said, 'You have run bloody riot this week, Chicken. You broke Mrs Honeywood's jaw so that Burley would pay you for saving his wife.'

'But another man did that,' he protested. 'Mrs Ibbetson saw it.'

'That's the thing. We put it to Mrs Ibbetson. She didn't see any traveller.'

'But she must have,' said Chicken in the panic a man feels when reality turns on him.

'She admitted to us that you told her there was a swagman. But she didn't see him, she says.'

'She's a very old woman,' Chicken pleaded. 'Mrs Honeywood knows who it was that hit her.'

'Mrs Honeywood's very confused,' Sangster told him, heading off hope.

'But she *knows*,' said Chicken, more or less pleading with the air now, since Sangster could not be reached.

Sangster simply continued. 'We believe this, Dalton: you beat up Mrs Honeywood and put her to bed in your place and called Burley and Sergeant Ives. You wanted rewards in kind and reputation. And everyone saw through it. And then, unrelated but true to type, you stole Bert Webber's souvenir pistol – the Webber house has been empty most of the time. And when Costigan and you quarrelled, you shot him with the pistol. Perhaps by accident, not knowing it still worked. Just threatening perhaps. But he's dead, Mr Dalton.' Sangster's eyes took on a distant, speculative look. 'And then there was a second shot. That can't have been an accident. Poor sod, came all the way from Ireland to die on the banks of the Macleay.'

Chicken weaved his head about and complained again to the heavens, or at least to the low ceiling. But in this dismal hour it came to him. The forgotten and forgettable fellow. Holland.

'I know who it was,' said Chicken. 'It was another Irishman. Named Holland. Met him in the Federal last week. He said he knew Johnny's sister in America and wanted to look him up.'

'Holland?' the two policemen said in unison but each in his own particular tone, no longer representing a unity.

'Who is Holland?' asked Inspector Sangster, turning to Sergeant Ives as if he might have an answer, or as if he wanted Ives to declare Holland a fiction.

And Chicken told them, evoking even the way Frank Holland's thin hair was combed across his skull. The Irish, famed for their grudges. Holland had quizzed Chicken about Johnny. Holland was there when young Christian turned up with the pistol. Holland declared himself a railways clerk staying at the Commercial and working on a new siding near Bowraville. In case the Japanese came. Holland could have taken it when the Victoria and he himself, Chicken, were deep in the supporting feature, could have met and shot poor Johnny, and brought the thing back later and put it on the bookshelf. Holland was the only answer. Inside poor Chicken's skull, deliverance crackled like electricity. Holland. The explanation.

———

Burley came on his own that Sunday to visit Flo, and carried some flowers! He bent to kiss her brow! Her flesh shrank from his tight lips. She tried to turn her head as far to the side as she could manage given the pain and wiring.

'Feeling better, dear old Flo?' he asked, frowning apologetically.

She sat upright and sought her writing tablet and the pencil. But he had already reached for them himself with his big carpenter's hands and presented them to her. It struck her that he thought this was mercy, handing things to her in his harsh fists. A kindly father: first the hard discipline, which he regretted, and then the kindnesses.

She wrote, 'I know who hit me.'

She showed it to him.

'I think it might have been a traveller,' he told her, looking into her eyes. Thinking he was justified in what he said. 'Or more likely that fairy, Dalton. You see now how dangerous it is to spend time with him. He's a strong fellow, that one.'

She wrote. 'I know it was you!' She underlined the 'you' once more.

He leaned over her. His face seemed vast, like an airship of a thing. 'Flo,' he confided, 'you were out of control. Do you think I wanted you wired up like this? But you were out of control, old girl! All this stuff about sending the boy to Newington. Impossible stuff! Mad stuff! And the bloody divorce. You don't divorce a man for . . . I mean, they're barely human to begin with!'

He made a few grabs at the air to define a folly of youth.

'We are what we are, Flo. Man and wife. You can't just decide to wreck that.'

What could she write? She was defeated by his vision of their marriage. 'I didn't want you wired up like this,' he whispered again. This time, she could tell he thought that this was tenderness. She had foolishly admitted to her body a man who thought like that. They had been the one flesh.

How can I explain that to myself? And here he was with his posy of snapdragons, thinking all was resolved, that they would be old people together. Knowing he employed assassins. And that he was confident in himself that once her jaw healed, she would forget divorce.

'Does it hurt much?' he asked with a new solicitude, one he felt entitled to.

Oh, she thought, he is an actor and has now decided to address himself to enacting compassion. So she wrote, her jaw distracting her with its, by turns, gravid and then precise pain, 'I intend to seek a divorce and leave you lonely.'

He was almost regretful as he shook his head and said, 'I'll never be lonely, Flo.'

And it was dismally true. He had the amalgam women somehow wanted. A good earner, liked by all. But for her sighting of the kid in town, she would still have considered herself blessed. These contradictions humiliated her. She had been ready to play forever and without interruption the happy matriarch, and if Burley predeceased her, to call down blessings on his head as the merciful provider. She had fallen one Friday afternoon short of a total story-of-life, one Friday afternoon short of the blessed fable women wanted: the accomplishment of a full and rounded life. It was her duty to achieve that, and when she refused to, he had had her lips split and her jaw broken.

'I was thinking,' he said. 'I won't have the kids visit till you're . . . well, a bit less swollen.'

She cast her eyes up. She wanted to see them. But she must pay for the privilege. She started to write. 'For Christ's sake, please bring them,' she said, a supplicant. But she knew he would not bring them. They were his pawns.

———

There was no record of a Holland at the Commercial Hotel, or any other hotel. That was the burden of news Sergeant Ives brutally woke Chicken Dalton with. 'Who's this bloody Holland? He doesn't bloody exist.'

A scrambled eggs breakfast brought in by the young constable, but no consolation in a scrambled reality. 'There's no bloody Holland,' the Small Sergeant yelled from beyond the bars.

Chicken kept his head down in the dreadful knowledge the world had turned on him like an infernal device.

Soon Sangster was there. 'There is no Holland registered at the Commercial, but you knew that, didn't you, Chicken? There is no new siding near Bowraville.' Sangster paused sadly, 'I think Holland is an invention of yours.'

'But he saw the pistol. He saw it in Christian Webber's hands. It must have seemed to him to be a gift . . .'

Sangster declared flatly, 'We're taking you to Newcastle today, Chicken. We'll get you a lawyer there.'

Chicken wanted to explain that he had invested the same real time into his conversations with Holland as into discourse with anyone. Why was this not visible in the very air?

———

As Burley was leaving the hospital he ran into Dr McVicar on his busy rounds.

'How do you find Mrs Honeywood?' asked the physician. The two of them, members of the same United Masonic Grand Lodge, spoke comfortably and even intimately. Burley knew that he possessed a weapon in McVicar, the means of silencing his wife that would last longer than the wired jaw would take to heal.

'She blames me,' he told the doctor after a well-judged delay. 'She believes I broke her jaw.'

'No,' said the doctor. 'My poor fellow.'

People loved him because, although he was worldly, he had compassionate eyes. 'Is she aware they have arrested the pianist Dalton for shooting dead a man from upriver.'

'I didn't want to heap that on her,' Burley confessed. And then, in a half-whisper, 'Recently she's pursued an association with Dalton. Over makeup! She sat down and let him make her up like a black tart.'

He knew this bespoke mental disorder on Flo's part. It certainly bespoke mental disorder to him.

'Does she know the police don't believe Dalton's story of how she was injured?'

'I don't know,' said Burley, the man who had too many marital enigmas on his mind. 'When she blames me . . . I believe she thinks I ordered the damage that was done.'

Dr McVicar shook his head. 'Yet I have never seen any sign of spousal violence on your wife when she has come to my surgery. A family physician normally knows when these things happen. I can tell you I have seen signs sometimes in the wives of eminent men. But not in your wife.'

Burley asked, 'Could you persuade her it is not me but her musical friend?'

'I can try, Burley.'

'I would be very grateful, doctor,' said Burley. He exactly understood why this was a good stratagem. Flo would insist on telling McVicar it was her husband, with any luck repeating herself until her scribblings came to seem manic. It was his reasonable hope, that her fury should seem marked, something to be treated and subdued by men wiser than him. So that it should be bleached out of her by tender treatment. Even that electro-convulsive treatment they used. And then she could return home in the end, restrained and biddable and fit for kindnesses. In the welter of gestures and gifts, she would forget that swagman who had not understood his own strength. People would comment, as they had until now, on the harmony of Bert's house and on his amenable wife.

He longed for that gratification. He had a strong ambition to continue to be seen as the kindly patriarch, and indeed to *be* the kindly patriarch, full of unpredictable gifts that more than atoned for an overzealous traveller employed to make a point to Flo.

———

In Chicken Dalton's cell the light was dim, but he was alert and sitting on the edge of his bunk when Inspector Sangster appeared at the door, as impeccably dowdy as he had been every other day of the eternity Chicken felt he had known him.

'There was no Irishman named Holland at the Federal, Chicken. There were two men at Buckley's boarding house just for one night. The two stay there occasionally. Mrs Buckley says she saw them drive off on Saturday afternoon. But no Mr Holland. Their names were Clancy and Foyle. Is Holland your fantasy, Chicken? Like the tramp?'

For a second time the rational world ran away from Chicken like a tide receding, exposing him to the desolate light of his cell, recondemning him.

Later in the day, in the car on the way over Cooperabung Mountain to Newcastle, he said, 'I know what they did. Holland and his friend. They were staying somewhere else,

286

Wauchope or Urunga, and came to town last Sunday so that the man named Holland could contact me, and stayed just Friday night at Buckley's so that Holland could kill Johnny and then move on to another town in the night.'

He saw Sangster and the Small Sergeant, the latter driving, exchange looks. 'Could you at least look into it?' Chicken pleaded.

'Very well,' said Sangster in his most neutral, inactive voice.

26

Kempsey and Sydney, New South Wales, 1933
It rained on Dulcie Costigan and her kids as they went to the undertakers to recite the Sorrowful Mysteries of the Rosary around Johnny's coffin. The Small Sergeant had promised a police car to take them to the undertakers, but it had not appeared, and a rainy day carried no terrors for them. After many bright days, however, today was dim as winter, and looked like the day after a tragedy.

There were just the boys and herself. The two older wore chaff bags over their shoulders, the poor man's raincoat. She had numerous relatives in the Nepean River and Emu Plains area, but though telegrams had been sent, there was no one here yet to enrich the patter of the *Aves* and *Glory Bes*.

They saw their father's face a last time. The older ones knew that the malicious demon of effeminacy, Chicken Dalton, had shot him for reasons they could not speculate upon. Even so, the killer was still abstract to Dulcie. On the one hand, Chicken Dalton had got away with stealing

288

fifty dollars from them, but she could not imagine he was guilty of something as infinite as murder. The killer remained a demon of ice in her imagination, not yet of fire. The killer was still a bleak force outside of normal motivation. It was as if the river itself had taken him.

Curran had filled the neat bullet hole so that the face seemed unmarred and looked very young – the young man she had first lent her body to. And, well, it had been a marriage and might have turned into something richer and companionable in time. He loved the children. She assumed but did not know if he loved her in his tormented way. She knew he loved her at least better than he loved himself. She watched the steam rise from her children's backs as they surrounded her dead husband. 'Now and in the hour of our death, Amen.'

She had not yet told the two younger boys he was shot twice, including in the chest. A St Vincent de Paul suit provided for the corpse by Mr Breslin, the engine driver and church warden, hid that damage and gave Johnny an august air.

She reached out a hand and stroked her husband's face. 'Oh Johnny,' she said, specifically because he looked somehow festive now that it was all over. The festive stranger who had implanted four boys in her. When men who had never been out of Kerry disappeared to Dublin and then to the new world – Johnny himself had inferred this once in conversation – it was because someone wanted to harm them. In that situation, immigration made sense. Nulla Creek made sense, as he went so far as to admit to her. And men looking for vengeance for what had happened – that was always on the cards. Especially in America. But, again, in Kempsey, New South Wales? Really? In Nulla

Creek? Fourteen thousand miles from Kerry to Sydney, and a further eight hours by train, or a day and night by coastal steamer. Had Johnny really done something so vast that it justified a pursuit across the globe?

That was it, anyhow. Between awful possibilities, she was still becoming accustomed to the idea that Chicken, and not some Irish blood vow, had taken poor Johnny. The postmaster at West Kempsey had this morning handed her a letter addressed to Johnny from his sister, Mimmie. Mimmie had asked, what a feather-brain am I? I promised you fifty dollars in the last letter and forgot to include it. She had also laid down a permanent sum in the local parish to have the priest say Mass each fortnight for the repose of the soul of poor Da. Dulcie felt no need to tell anyone though that the sum had arrived. Whatever it was with Johnny and Chicken, she had no need to honour or pursue it.

'Doesn't he look fit for a requiem Mass, boys?' she asked through tears when the rosary was over and they looked down on him, their inscrutably murdered father. The two oldest of the boys hugged her from the side, as if to confirm that Johnny did look fit for the more sacred things.

'Daddy,' said Oliver, who gave affection so easily.

'He wants you to grow up as good men,' she asserted.

For they'd both had hopes for Oliver.

———

That same day the North Coast Mail groaned its way north through the dripping coastal bush, bringing Anna and Gertie home. Mother and daughter shared a compartment together and were bored with each other long before lunchtime. Parties of fettlers camped by the rail called out occasionally for newspapers to be thrown them by passengers, but the Webber women did not have a morning paper to throw.

It was at a lunchtime lecture on the history of constitutional law that a friend of Christian's said to him, 'Hey, Chris. Big murder in the sticks up your way!' Christian went out onto Parramatta Road and bought a copy of the *Sun* off a drenched tram-hopping paper boy. 'DAIRY MANAGER SHOT DEAD ON MACLEAY RIVER', declared the headline, and a smaller tag declared it was a father of four who had perished. His name was John Francis Costigan, thirty-two years of age. The name jolted Christian and leaped like a live thing in his chest. He felt an unfounded certainty, validated by guilt, that the pistol was the one his father kept, and that to retrieve it might now be beyond him.

He did not get a chance to tell Walter what had happened in his country town but went out twice that afternoon in the rain to buy later editions. In the last edition was a 'stop press' in red print with the news of an arrest. Cinema pianist Ian 'Chicken' Dalton had been arrested and charged with the murder.

The nightmare was locking into place with ruthless precision. The Luger was a device which, assembled from its plain parts, had altered his father's destiny and was now ready to alter his. He locked himself in his room at Wesley College. He felt that the powers of the earth were abroad, looking for him, mastiffs sniffing. He did not go to the dining room. Later in the evening he walked to a workers' pub in Newtown, beyond the penumbra of student pubs that surrounded the university, and numbed himself with schooners of Dinner Ale. He had given Chicken an ultimatum. But surely Chicken had not felt bound to slay a more casual lover?

All must wait for the morning newspaper, which he got hold of by going by cab to the George Street headquarters of the *Sydney Morning Herald* at 2 am and buying the early morning edition. He read it on the street for fear of being seen in his hapless lust for the print.

The headline declared, 'PIANIST ARRESTED IN MACLEAY VALLEY MURDER'. 'Deviant "love" affair and stolen money', read the sub-headline. From the text, like a condemnation writhing to present itself, came the assertion: 'The murder weapon appears to be a Great War Luger Model 8 pistol, from which two 9mm rounds were fired into the victim's body, producing near-instant death.'

The sense of redemption offered by Walter Jupp vanished. Christian felt a desire for that lost weapon, since he knew his initial instinct regarding it had been sound. It could finish him and his own deviancy. But now it was the property of the New South Wales police.

Rain fell on the paper and he ached with the absurdity of his situation. He struggled to recall the face of this Costigan man. He returned to the text before the rain made it illegible. 'John Francis Costigan, father of four children, was manager of the Karaweela dairy farm at Nulla Creek, Macleay Valley.'

Christian complained, 'This is obscene.' Karaweela was the original dairy farm of his grandfather, Augustus Weber. He now expected the Webber name to appear in the rest of the report, but by minor print mercies it did not.

'I don't know what it bloody means,' Christian pleaded into the dimness of the wet street.

Even half-sodden, a last line of print caught his eye, 'It is believed Dalton stole the pistol from the house of a Great

War veteran presently undergoing medical treatment in Sydney.'

'That's not right,' Christian argued to himself.

That sainted and cursed gun. Bert Webber's equivalent of the nails that tore Christ's hands!

As he walked three miles back to college, he felt he was at the bottom of his life, all charm, all hope, all topsoil torn away. He intended to sleep in his desolate exhaustion. Next weekend he was pledged to go home and bring the pistol, as the device in which his father's anguish was located, to Bert. Bert, who by dismantling it and committing it to various bodies of water, believed he would dismantle his disease. 'Christ!' murmured Christian into the dark. 'Christ help us!' Chicken was included. 'It is believed Dalton stole . . .'

Chicken could not be allowed to stay in the pit. But there was only him, the eternal and culpable boy, to answer the smooth assertion of something as grand as the *Herald*. If he were to speak, he decided, he must speak to Walter. Everything had to be told. To a fellow who at least understood iron ore sanctions and the failures of the League of Nations.

He and Walter were to meet for lunch. But the pressure of truth in Christian was too severe to wait. Walter should now, if there was any mercy left in the world, be in his room.

—

When he knocked, as near inaudibly as he could, on Walter's door, it took quite a time to be acknowledged, and he could hear Walter groan himself into consciousness. He presented himself at the door, when he at last opened it, in silk pyjamas with Wedgwood designs, and Christian felt a surge of affection to see that Walter wore them with the same rakish style as his daytime clothes. Christian wanted to kiss the top of his ginger-blond hair in a sort of affectionate gesture to this trueness in the man.

Seeing Christian, Walter checked the hall and then dragged Christian into the room and shut the door. His lips were on Christian, and against his leg Christian felt the same kind of substantial erection as he acquired during sleep. Walter's suffering in that same way seemed to make all normal, all unexceptional. Christian's mouth evaded Walter's. 'I have to tell you,' he whimpered, chiefly as a way to get Walter's attention. 'Terrible things have happened.'

Walter stood back and frowned. 'Your parents?' he asked. He had talked perhaps too long about his parents and his sister, bleary and full of hopeful desire, on the balcony at Point Piper, and what had amazed him was that Walter took careful notice.

'No,' said Christian. 'There has been a killing.'

Christian laid out everything, and was less ashamed of his callowness than he had ever been. Walter was distracted only by Christian's confession of his full experience with Chicken. 'So it was this Chicken fellow who wrought the change,' he said, appearing willing to be jealous of Chicken, but then – to Christian's gratitude – decided that the killing of Johnny Costigan was the chief issue, and the mistake about the sainted and cursed pistol.

'And it came to me on the way back here that Chicken might be accused of stealing the thing only because he chose to keep my name out of it. And that . . . that distresses me.' And he showed it did by weeping.

'And you haven't told your father? About your . . . your nature?'

He hadn't, said Christian. Nor his mother.

'Gertie will stick by you,' Walter asserted. 'She mightn't understand but . . .'

'She'll treat me like a sick pup.'

There was something young in the way Walter sat upright on the edge of the bed, like a child being brave about an injection. He said, 'I will stick with you too.' Then, 'And you know who else? My mother. And you'll find that no small thing.'

By now there was gravidness and erections to be attended to, and Christian did not want to leave him because, when he did, the terrible tomorrow would begin. But in the end he did because the college authorities were very severe on the matter of two men leaving the same room in the mornings.

———

Everything was easier with Walter alongside him. Christian went to the academic dean with Walter to request a trunk call to the Newcastle police, and Walter stood four-square by him as if this exceptional indulgence by the college were a trifling matter. When at last the call was placed, Christian was directed to a parlour and Walter sat nearby.

There were strange noises, gurgles that might or might not have been plumbing or eavesdroppers on the line, the operator perhaps hanging on to hear what crimes Christian wanted to report to the detective in charge of the Macleay murder.

Silence then on the line. He was of course paying for this silence in the most direct sense – you could call country towns and farms, and even another city from Wesley

College, but the operator was to announce a fee at the end and you were honour-bound to pay it before day's end in the Warden's office. Silence creaked and sighed in its great vacancy, and Christian knew he would have fled without Walter. He began to imagine a number of detectives, sitting, pretending not to be listening, waiting for him to betray himself.

Walter had given him the helpful advice: 'Make it sound as innocent a friendship as you can. You're entitled to that. They don't need to be told about . . . the *other*.'

Now, in Newcastle, there was a scrape of someone taking possession of the phone and a doleful admission. 'Yes? Inspector Sangster here.'

Christian took the time to add one breath to the weight of his resolve. He said what his name was and where he was calling from. He was the son of the presently hospital-bound Bert Webber of Kempsey and the Macleay Valley. He had seen it reported that Chicken Dalton had stolen a pistol that belonged to his father. In fact, he himself had taken it to Chicken Dalton's place during the university holidays, and forgotten it when he went home.

'Why were you visiting Chicken Dalton's place, son?'

'It was a skylark,' he declared with brittle jollity. 'We were imitating picture shows, you know. Gangsters and all that. I was just acting the goat. But Mr Dalton . . . he didn't steal it from our place. I took it there.'

'Why to Mr Dalton's?'

'Oh, I've known him donkey's years. Since I was a kid. He was always playing the piano at the pictures.'

'Didn't your mother warn you against him?'

'Oh, Mr Dalton is harmless,' Christian managed to say, airily as Gertie could have.

'You know he is charged with shooting a man dead with that gun.'

Christian thought, 'I'm getting the taste for this,' as he maintained a disbelieving silence. Then he said, 'He never seemed a man who would shoot another. I should tell you, when I was at Chicken Dalton's place there was another man there. An Irishman. A stranger I'd never seen before. If Mr Dalton told you that, he was telling the truth.'

'Are you related to Mr Dalton, son?'

'No.'

'Has he offered you any inducement to say what you've said?'

'No, of course he hasn't.'

'Has he ever interfered with you?'

'No.'

'Are you a Nancy boy like him?'

'I'm not familiar with the term,' he amazed himself by saying.

There was a silence that felt contemptuous to Christian.

Then, 'I think I'd better come to Sydney and see you. You're aware of the crime of perjury?'

'I'm a law student,' Christian replied.

Christian listened for comfort to the line's crackles and crotchets. 'Look,' he said then. 'My father, Bert, has been sick. That pistol holds a big place for him. I said I was playing the ass with it, but I shouldn't have. He took it off a German who'd killed a friend of his in France. Now my father's getting better. He wants me to fetch the pistol so he can dispose of it. A symbolic act, you know.'

'That's the one you say you left at Chicken Dalton's?'

'Yes. I wonder when I can get it back?'

297

Sangster said, 'You do understand it doesn't matter whether or not Chicken Dalton stole the thing? It's whether he had access to it, and used it to kill Johnny Costigan.'

'Well, I don't believe he did it. The Irishman noticed the pistol, by the way, and commented on it. He saw me fooling about with it. He seemed to be an old soldier.'

'And what was this Irishman's name?'

'I didn't catch his name, I'm sorry. But he was certainly there, and Chicken introduced him as someone who knew Costigan's sister in America.'

There was a silence of some unprofitable seconds.

'Did you know Costigan yourself?' asked Sangster.

'I knew of him. He worked for Dad. But no, I didn't know him.'

'He had his moments as a bit of a Nancy boy too.'

'I see. Look, inspector, I was wondering when I could collect my father's pistol?'

'You can't, son. It's a murder weapon now.'

'My father can't have it back?'

'I think I have to come and see you.'

'I'm worried about my father, his reaction to all this.'

'He'll be fine. He's a hero.'

'Yes, he is. But he certainly says he needs the pistol.'

'He'll be fine. As long as you're not a Nancy boy yourself. I think that would hurt him and any father.'

Christian wanted to tell Sangster off for hectoring him. 'I love my father, inspector,' said Christian, 'more than any stranger does.'

'You'll be interviewed under caution, do you understand? About why you would give the notorious Chicken a gun. Take it to his house, leave it there? At the best, pansy business. Everyone will know it.'

Christian could imagine it. The town would sing their choruses.

Sangster said, 'Your father's much admired in the Macleay, Mr Webber. You're aware of how respected he is? A double hero. Military Medal as . . .'

Christian hurried to say, 'Yes, I know. Military Cross as an officer.'

'Then I suggest you live by that example,' Sangster told him.

'But you could help my father by releasing the pistol . . .'

'Don't be ridiculous, son! You know it has to be there for Dalton's trial. Now . . . when can I see you?'

Christian said, like a man without secrets, they could see him at any time. He would be excused lectures.

'Tomorrow,' Sangster told him.

Christian put the phone down.

'You see,' said Walter earnestly. 'You're still breathing.'

And it was true.

———

That afternoon, Christian, aroused from sleep at the time, was called to the common college phone in the corridor outside the dining room. He had been summoned, it turned out, by a bear-like barrister, Aidan Dempsey QC, from Phillip Street, the haunt of barristers. Lady Jupp – or 'Charlie' as he referred to her – had asked Dempsey to represent Christian at the interview, if Christian consented. Dempsey urged Christian to accept his presence, since, he said, 'The police have their ways.' Christian asked about fees, and the lawyer said there was no need, that his company was often favoured by the Jupps, and that this was something he would be churlish not to do for Lady Jupp. 'Mind you,' he said, 'I am more accustomed to commercial rather than criminal matters.'

Sangster and a plainclothes associate came all the way to Wesley College the next morning to interview Christian. The questioning took place in the solemn parlour where the council of the college met, and in light mottled by the strictly non-conformist, non-graven-imaging stained glass of high windows. There was not a trace of college opprobrium for Christian in this. More a flavour of edgy glamour, and an understanding that events had thrust him forward. The warden of the college was excited both by this and the attendance of the apparently eminent Dempsey, and danced the latter into the parlour before the interview began.

Sangster and a younger man wanted to ask about the Irishman first.

'Do you think he shared Chicken Dalton's proclivities?' asked Sangster, and Christian knew the policeman would have put it otherwise had Dempsey not been present. He spent a lot of time saying he didn't share them, said Christian. But he was Irish, like the victim. This proposition made the two plainclothes men search each other's faces, but what sort of confirmation they sought, whether it was something to do with himself or a dent in their certainty about Chicken, he could not say.

Christian then proposed what he had been steeling himself to propose all through this interview or confrontation. 'That Irishman could have taken the pistol, used it, then returned it. Isn't that possible?'

The two detectives inspected each other's eyes.

'You might discover a reason if you interviewed him,' Christian was suddenly confident enough to suggest.

'But there's no record of him. No one else cast eyes on him. Only Dalton – so he claims. And now . . . *you!*'

But they did not add any damning descriptions of what Chicken and *you* held in common.

'Might have only been visible to poofters,' supplied the other policemen, in whom, Christian was aware, scepticism had been brewing all through. And though Sangster calmed him with a look, Christian suspected Sangster was pleased it had all been said, that its weight was added to what passed between them.

'Did I just hear you speak, detective?' asked Mr Dempsey.

'Clearing my throat,' said the detective.

'You do so very expressively,' boomed Dempsey.

They know what I am, Christian thought. Yet it's not their business to hear me say it. Were I here on my own, though, they would make it their business. This is what Dempsey had drummed into him in a half-hour of advice and rehearsal before the interview.

And now the issue. They seemed to sit and wait for it to rise amongst them, of its own buoyancy. Mr Dempsey had advised him to be forward, to lead rather than be led by the detectives.

'On the matter of why I brought the pistol to Mr Dalton's place . . . I did it because I wanted to impress him.'

'Is Mr Dalton impressed by pistols?'

Dempsey inhaled to intervene, but, wisely or not, Christian declared, 'No, not in themselves. But it was a dramatic item. I'd had coffee at Tsiros's with Mr Dalton the week before, and I was flattered he talked to me and I wanted to be his friend. Because he was stylish.'

'Stylish?' asked Sangster.

'That is what my client said,' declared Dempsey.

'By the standards of Kempsey. I have no friends up there, and Chicken seemed friendly. In a meaningful way.'

'What do you mean by meaningful?'

'Despite the limits of his world, and of all our worlds up there, he seemed interested in broader things. Jazz. And books.'

'And you took your father's pistol to impress him?'

'I don't pretend it wasn't a bit hayseed on my part. We aren't sophisticated people up there.'

'Did you know how many bullets were in the thing?'

'I knew from my father showing me when I was younger. There were four.'

'And then two were used on Costigan,' murmured Sangster. 'You didn't bring it because he asked you to? When you had this coffee?'

Mr Dempsey cast up his seen-everything eyes.

Christian said, 'Of course not.'

Sangster sat forward and did his little breathing tricks and then spoke, his eyes sometimes on Christian, sometimes on Dempsey. 'You realise that the fact Chicken Dalton mightn't have stolen the pistol doesn't mean we don't have a case against him. We don't need your testimony to condemn him. We can prove that whichever way the gun came to him, he committed a murder with it.' His eyes settled on Christian now, and they were in their way paternal. 'Are you sure you want to distress your father, a real man, to help the lot of this Dalton fellow, a walking mannequin?'

'Are you suggesting a conspiracy to suppress evidence, inspector?' asked Dempsey.

'No. But it's not as if Mr Webber's evidence proves Dalton is not guilty.'

Dempsey turned to Christian and raised his eyes in question? His look implied it was all up to Christian now. The sentence from the *Herald* 'It is believed Dalton stole . . .' moved in him like a live thing.

'It proves he's not a thief,' said Christian. 'And it shows that Irishman was there, taking notice of the pistol I brought along.'

After the police left, Dempsey clapped him on the shoulder like a boy who'd scored fifty at cricket, and said, not without approval, 'Old Sangster had a point. But you did the noble thing. You'll definitely be a witness now.'

27

Sydney and Kempsey, New South Wales, 1933

He chose to be a little clearer still of the unchosen onus of that bloody Luger pistol. Bert Webber had improved to the point of holding complete conversations with Anna and Gertie and, in so far as anything he and his father said was complete, with Christian. Christian felt he must tell his father that his symbolic plans for disposing of the pistol were now an impossibility, and that Bert must know about that for his own health.

He visited Bert at the sanatorium the night after the visit by Inspector Sangster. He said hello to his father, who was dressing-gowned, and they performed an embarrassed male greeting, halfway between a handshake and a cancelled embrace. They sat down together then and the announcer on the ABC radio said that for their delectation he would play 'The Dance of the Sugar Plum Fairy', the worst thing, Christian thought, that Tchaikovsky, a fallible god, had written when he took a little time off from being a genius.

Christian seized the moment, during this over-merry music, to announce more loudly than he had intended, 'I have a confession.'

'I beg your pardon,' said his father, deaf before his time like other veterans from hearing too much artillery.

'I was going to say, I am terribly sorry, but I can't go home this weekend.'

'Hang on there,' said Bert and turned the radio off and said, 'There,' smiling as he presented the ensuing silence to his son.

'I am awfully sorry, I can't go home this weekend and get your pistol. Does that distress you?'

Bert blinked. 'No. You shouldn't go home till it's convenient for you, son.'

'Well,' said Christian, 'it's not a matter of convenience. It's that . . . somehow Chicken Dalton got hold of your gun. He . . . he had it. But now the police do. Because they say Chicken used it to kill an employee of yours. They say he killed Johnny Costigan.'

'Johnny Costigan of Nulla Creek?'

'That's what they say.'

'He's dead?'

'Yes, he was shot to death last weekend, and they're saying Chicken did it. Are you okay hearing this?'

'But Johnny's got a wife and four kids,' protested Bert, as if Costigan was immune to death by reason of his fertility. 'Why in God's name would Chicken shoot a poor tit-stripper like Costigan?' That was Macleay talk, 'tit-stripper' being synonymous with 'dairy farmer'. But Christian noticed the question did not seem to afflict Bert. Indeed, there was a blink of enlightenment in Bert. In a strangled, false basso

305

and embarrassment-strangled voice, Bert asked, 'It wasn't knob jockey business, was it, Christian?'

So that's what he was at the core. 'My son the knob jockey!' Yet Bert blinked a little like a lost man, and was piteous himself, and Christian wanted to embrace him. At the same time he hated the way his father, probity on legs and double-proved hero, had fallen back on casual slang. Are we so few? Christian pleaded there, in the cockpit of his bewildered self. Are we so few and so fallen that knob jockey business meant guns must inevitably come into play?

'Would it distress you to read a newspaper article?' Christian had Tuesday's *Herald* front page in his breast pocket and tentatively took it out.

'Oh, I can read a newspaper,' said Bert as if scotching some pernicious rumour that he could not.

Christian unfolded it and handed it over, and Bert settled it under a reading lamp, pressing the folds of newsprint down. 'Crikey!' he announced, looking to Christian for confirmation after he had finished a few paragraphs. Then he lowered his head again and consumed a few more. 'If I didn't know better, I'd say I was delirious.' He read on. 'Oh Jesus!' he said, a rare expletive and one that Anna normally disciplined. He did not raise his head from the print. 'That bloody pistol,' he said. 'It's a dark piece of work.' More reading, and an unbelieving, 'He stole it from *our place*?' Bert raised his eyes to Christian. That was not like Chicken. 'Mind you, he hypnotised chickens when he was a kid.'

'Hypnotised them?' asked Christian, pretending not to know. 'Yes, I think I might have heard something about that.'

Bert was reading again but said dreamily, 'They never woke up. He took them straight home to his mother's pot. That's one thing. But this thing . . . this is beyond belief.'

'The pistol,' said Christian. 'You see . . . I can't get it to you.'

'Well, no,' murmured Bert. 'You wouldn't be able to. Don't the police need it?'

'They say so.'

'It'll go with all the other evil pieces they hold. That no one will ever see again.'

'So you don't mind?'

Bert finished reading, but the amazing print kept drawing his eyes. 'I don't mind, no. It's gone from me. I hope they melt it down in the end.'

'You can ask Inspector Sangster about that,' said Christian, feeling for now in part absolved from being who he was.

'And Chicken stole it?'

Christian forced himself into gestures of denial, raising his hands, shaking his head. 'That's what they were thinking. But I have since told them I took the pistol to Chicken's house in Clyde Street.'

'Why did you tell them . . . if it's not the truth?'

'But it is, Dad. I always got on with Chicken and I met him at Tsiros's and he asked me round to see him.'

Christian let these saving half-truths, these under-truths settle.

'You took the thing?'

'I took the pistol as a bit of a laugh. I know I shouldn't have. But I thought it would interest Chicken. Seeing that . . . you know . . . a Luger's a sort of thing you see in the picture shows.'

'A bit of a laugh?' asked Bert, genuinely mystified.

'I know,' pleaded Christian, 'I wasn't thinking . . .'

'Well,' said Bert. 'It's shown you now. Hasn't it. If it killed Costigan, it was only because it killed Reverend Lembke first.'

Christian did a panicked assessment of his father. Was he going to lapse into *that* again?

'It killed Lembke and now it's killed Costigan,' Bert argued further and even, to Christian's horror, a little feverishly. 'That's not a bit of a laugh.'

'I know. Please don't be upset.'

'And you told the police you took it to Chicken?'

'That I took it.' Christian could see the potential traps for his father in what he was bound to say. 'And then forgot it and left it there.'

Bert said, 'I had it in my pack for near-on three years by the time I got home.'

'I know,' Christian admitted.

'It wasn't ever a plaything to me.'

'I know.'

It was clear that his father would not be destroyed by knowing all this, by knowing how his son had deployed the gun for flippant purposes of his own.

'Do the police think you're some sort of accomplice?' asked Bert, an anxious parent again.

'They don't seem to,' said Christian, managing a jaunty smile.

'Good,' breathed Bert.

Christian went on, joyously expressing his repentance over the gun for some two or three more stanzas of conversation. He was thinking, too, that when he told his father the news of himself, Bert may take it as bravely as all the rest – sadly, wisely and with a civilised restraint. He found

308

it heady to have Bert say that none of it mattered. And that in his case, they had left behind the risky realm of medicine and shock therapy.

That he understood and forgave his son for folly.

———

Christian knew by now, even from the small amount of legal studies he had completed, that the law was like a film. That judges and lawyers were hungry for and satisfied by a script that accommodated most of the major elements of a tale. Sangster already had the script he wanted. Mrs Costigan herself was a contributor to this, or so Christian saw from stories in the *Sun* and *Mirror,* Sydney's lesser but popular rags.

She had been willing to tell them that one day Johnny collected a letter from Mr Dalton that had already been opened. The letter from Johnny Costigan's sister in Cleveland in the United States declared it contained a fifty-dollar American bill, but when Johnny was given the letter, the fifty dollars was gone. This was a month's wages. Chicken Dalton pleaded to Johnny that he was an honest man. And Johnny believed him. Mrs Costigan herself, innocently playing to the salacious interests of both papers, said she never liked that friendship, never knew what Johnny saw in it.

So there was bad blood between the men over money, and then over what Sangster would call 'perverted business between men'. And that the latter was commerce of great volatility and dark motives, guaranteed to produce blood, any jury or judge already suspected. 'Perverted business between men' implied the murk of murder. It would prove

309

to be close to a blanket explanation, for public edification, for what befell Johnny Costigan on the banks of the Macleay.

———

On his rounds of the hospital, in the week following the arrest of Chicken Dalton, Dr McVicar came to the room where Mrs Honeywood lay with her wired jaw. McVicar had always considered her a model of the healthy matron, a little pale perhaps but full-faced and sturdy of shoulders and hips. She had now lost a lot of weight and her pallor had turned grey, though there was nothing wrong with her except for one thing: the vengeful fixity of attitude towards her husband. It was this that the good doctor came now to test. Burley had asked for certification papers under the Mental Health Act, but Dr McVicar wanted to be certain before appending his signature.

After a few questions about her pain and comfort levels, he said, 'I've asked you this before. But do you remember who did this damage to you?'

Again, the tablet and, he noticed, the over-enthusiastic, emphatic writing. 'The man my husband employed to do it.'

But the police had told him already that Mrs Ibbetson had denied the existence of that man. This was evidence of delusion.

'It was not by any chance Mr Dalton?'

A frantic 'No!' with an exclamation mark was once more the answer. There was clearly still something demented about the way she wrote, gouging answers from the paper. And then the way her eyes glittered when she presented what she had written.

She had written again. 'Dalton never would.'

But she had not been told that Dalton had now shot a man dead.

'But why would your husband do that, Mrs Honey-wood?'

'Because I want to divorce him! He told me he was so sorry I was so wired-up like this.'

This was the first time she had said this to the doctor, as much as she might have told the police. The doctor did not inquire into it.

He took her pulse. It was strong, if erratic. But he could feel her restless beneath his touch.

———

Flo woke to see Alice Kelly sitting placidly, and like a woman awaiting a late bus, on a chair by the window. Her face was in repose but her eye was on Flo, so she noticed at once when Flo stirred, and saw the eyes blinking above the fixed and wired jaw. Flo confirmed that she was open for business with the noise from her throat. Immediately, tears appeared in a rush on Alice's lashes and she stood up.

'Aw,' said Alice. 'Poor Mrs Flo!'

Flo made all the gestures of not being able to speak, and wondered how many of the town's women might take a sneaking joy to see her silenced now, since some mistook her shyness for arrogance, the sort of distinction people in country towns were not good at making. But Alice's honest horror was a balm to her. She wanted to tell Alice – paper being too clumsy at conveying her pain – her tormenting condition as a mother. She had asked to see the children but Burley and Dr McVicar both now agreed that it wait till the swelling went down. Burley didn't want them to see what he had brought about – that was the truth she wanted to convey to her sister in cosmetics.

'Jesus, Mrs Honeywood. Men are mongrels fair enough. If they get you where they want you.'

Flo made a murmur, a long-running gurgle, a noise of mourning. She quaked, when waking, with the anxiety of it – she was damaged and angry, and the trembling and the wire jaw could both be marshalled to separate her from the town, her husband, and her children. And from Eddie Kelly, too. And she could foresee her course. After her jaw began to knit, she would be released into Dr McVicar's clinic from where, if she continued to claim that Burley had authorised the damage done her, she would be sent on for treatment to a clinic in Sydney – McVicar had already discussed it with Burley as she lay there.

And when she was cured of the fixed idea that her husband was responsible for said damage done – well, everything would be well again, for both of them. 'Not for me, not for me,' she had an ambition to cry out, but if she did this, it too would confirm her need of a clinic.

In her helplessness, it was as close to joy as she could come to be directly addressed with Alice Kelly's honest sympathy. 'I got an uncle in here, in the blacks' ward. He's not good – something stomach. He can see spirits in the room. Too many, missus, and too unhappy. Another uncle of mine saw you brought in here. He was smoking over in the trees. Things not good for my uncle, not so good for poor ole Chicken either.'

Flo picked up the pad to write while a weight of pain ran down her jaw and seemed to suspend itself there in massive form. Alice said, 'Save yourself the trouble, Mrs Flo. I never got taught them letters.' She made another assessment of Flo. 'Poor, poor dearie.'

All at once the matron was at the door. 'What are

you doing in here, Alice?' she asked with trademark briskness.

'I'm seeing Mrs Flo.'

'But you know blacks don't visit white people.'

'Not most times, but Mrs Flo was nice to the black old bag like Alice.'

That made Flo quiver, Alice insulting herself before the white authority did. Flo understood and did not like to hear her do it.

'Were you invited?' asked the matron.

'Mrs Flo can't invite no one, matron . . .'

'I know that. So you shouldn't be bringing your ringworm and hydatids from the blacks' camp into the white wards, Alice. You know that. Are you being a sly one, Alice?'

'I'm not sly, matron.'

'Well, get going then? You've seen your uncle?'

'I seen old uncle,' Alice admitted.

'Then it's back to Burnt Bridge for you.'

Flo had written on the pad, 'LET HER STAY!'

The matron squinted and read it and leaned backwards as if infection had spread to Flo. 'Really, Mrs Honeywood. I'm only arranging matters for your own good. You need uninterrupted rest. A few minutes then. Nurse will be back in five minutes with Mrs Honeywood's night medicine and I want you gone, Alice. You know, otherwise it's the police.'

After she left, Flo took hold of Alice's wrist, but not for long. Alice had received her average humiliation for the day and her daily threat. She wanted to go more than she wanted to be there. But she was teary when she left.

—

Fortuitously, and since Burley was an attentive visitor to his wife, the doctor met the man himself outside as he left Flo's room. On the river below, magpies were gargling their way through the day, a sound that never failed to make McVicar both feel at home but also understand that he was deep in the bush, was a mere one-town wonder.

The two men went aside from their cars, understanding there would need to be a confidential discussion.

'Look, understand I am reluctant to ask you this, Burley, but I must, given Mrs Honeywood's assertions. Tell me then . . . did you employ a swagman to beat your wife?'

'Of course not,' said Burley, a tolerant man. 'Surely you can't think I did?'

'You understand I have to . . .'

'Of course, you do.'

'Now she said she wants to . . .'

'Yes, divorce me.'

'I don't need to know,' said the doctor, by a gesture delegating the settlement of that question to the heavens.

Burley murmured, 'She claimed there's a black kid from Burnt Bridge who's my son. She wants to send him to Newington.'

'Newington?' A hallowed school.

'Yes, of course there's no chance. On top of that, she is determined to divorce me.' Burley reached out and took the doctor by the elbow. 'I don't pretend I was a saint when I was young. But . . .'

'Dear fellow,' the doctor assured him. 'By those standards half of Kempsey would be divorced.'

With a little stutter in his speech, Burley said, 'I don't know how to speak to her. I can't begin. I think she needs some intense treatment to be better.'

It seemed to be reasonable now for him and the doctor to draft and sign certification papers which would detain Flo Honeywood for assessment and treatment. Poor woman.

———

Bert Webber had returned home to the Macleay and been given two dinners to mark his recovery. Mrs Honeywood was undergoing shock therapy in the same Derwent sanatorium as Bert had been cured in. So Anna informed Christian from Kempsey.

28

Sydney, New South Wales, 1933

With so many tests and perils ahead of him, Christian Webber took temporary shelter in what had befallen him thus far on his journey, and felt a duty to cross the road from the university to the Grace Bros store and their florist's department, where even in hard times people still bought flowers, in his case lilac and roses for Lady Jupp. He took the tram early that evening with Walter to deliver the flowers as a gesture of thanks. A pleasant-faced older woman in a raggedy overcoat, sitting opposite them, said, 'Some girl's lucky.'

'Not so lucky,' smiled Christian. Oh, the ease of strangers! 'She deserves them.'

'Remember,' the woman said, 'she will deserve them more when she has three children and is exhausted.'

'Wise woman,' said Walter.

When they got to Point Piper, they were told by the housekeeper that Lady Jupp was dressing, and from the head of the stairs of the vestibule came her contralto voice. 'Walter, Walter! I have to be at the Australia by eight o'clock. But come upstairs and talk to your old ma!'

Walter cried, 'I have Christian with me. He has a little present for you.'

'Yummy,' called Lady Jupp.

Walter led Christian up the sweeping semicircular staircase, a little Busby Berkeley-influenced perhaps, thought Christian. At the top of the stairs, through the open door of a large bedroom, Walter's mother was visible in her own nimbus of cigarette smoke. She wore a splendid dark lace dress, Jean Harlow-style, but there was a blue and yellow cape on the bed which would temper its daring. She walked about in stockinged feet and, while looking in a floor-length mirror, held one finger speculatively to a cheek, as if it declared an imperfection Christian could not see. She looked very pretty, and younger than her years.

'Dear boys,' she said as Christian followed Walter into the room, and she kissed Walter carefully so that her makeup was not unbalanced, and yet at the same time injected enthusiasm into the embrace. 'And young Mr Webber.'

'I brought you something as a mere gesture . . .' said Christian.

'Yes,' she said distractedly. 'Yes. How lovely. You didn't need to. You're a good boy.' She called for the housekeeper to come and place them somewhere amongst all the other vases of flowers in the house.

'Now, taking on the risk of my being late,' she declared, lighting a cigarette, 'I must talk to you boys. Sit down, sit down.' She had sat on her spacious bed and was patting a space either side of her. Did her husband share the same room? The bed was large enough, and all the cupboards and

317

dressers, yet the room seemed entirely feminine. Christian sat in the allocated space on her left. 'Now, Christian, Walter seems to have taken a marked shine to you, a marked shine indeed. And those to whom the dear child takes a shine, I take a shine to as well.'

'It's very kind,' said Christian,

'No, no, you don't have to keep saying that. But look, this murder in your town. I did warn you that dear Walter seems more worldly than he is! So you come to him and you're distressed about the false story that your friend is accused of stealing something or other.'

'A pistol,' supplied Christian. 'And I met the possible murderer. An Irishman.'

'Yes,' she agreed. 'And you are wondering what to do, and of course Walter says you must tell the police. Which all speaks volumes, volumes for you both. And the police are on their way, so suddenly that I just have time to intersperse Mr Dempsey between you and them.'

Walter, who did not look chastened or cowed, said nothing, so Christian felt he should not either.

'Dearie,' said Lady Jupp to Walter, 'the world is not like that. The world isn't urgent in spreading any good news. The world does not do penance the way the tender young soul does. The world admits as little as it needs to and as late as it can. It does not seek – in admitting to one wrong – to admit to many. Do you understand? You do understand, don't you?'

She looked with an anxious frown to Walter, then to Christian.

'Of course, mother,' said Walter, picking up her right hand and kissing it. 'You see the lectures I am subjected to, Christian? Does your mother sit down and give you worldly talks?'

'Well,' said Christian, but could get no further before Walter's mother picked up again.

'No,' said Charlie Jupp, rising to fetch another cigarette, 'it's very important you listen to your corrupt old mother. She knows the true pace at which justice and decency are revealed.'

'Justice very rarely,' said Walter, 'and decency never.'

'True. But don't try to sound worldly, Walter. You may well be right but you don't have the experience to make assertions. Now Christian has done a noble thing, but could you both please seek advice next time. And, please don't think the police are delighted to receive your revelations. That would be naïve.'

Fantastic, like one of those men who did cigarette acts on stage, she had lit another cigarette and was searching for her shoes. She looked very beautiful reaching down to put them on. 'Now, I'm going to get back from this dreadful evening about eleven if you are still here. I warn you, Walter, not too much gin. And Christian, thank you for the darling blooms!'

And bare-headed and carrying her cape, she left them.

——

Christian read the trial reports. He had intended to visit Chicken in Newcastle, no matter what snide winks he feared the guards would give each other, in the manner of the Small Sergeant. But then he was relieved to discover that as a potential witness he would have been turned away from the prison.

Chicken was moved from Newcastle to Sydney, for that was where murders were tried and where the death penalty, which the police prosecutor was seeking, was carried out these days. It was there that Moxley had been hanged, in Long Bay jail. Christian was notified he was on the witness list. Of course, he could not visit Chicken in Sydney either, since he was allowed to receive only official visitors and a brother from Lismore.

One of his law lecturers with whom he had discussed the case told him, 'You'll be called for certain. The prosecution needs you in terms of provenance of the weapon. And so does the defence, to rebut the newspapers.'

The idea of his being pressed into these services, though he maintained a clinical air about it all, made Christian sick. But he was gratified Chicken had been given both an instructing solicitor and a defence counsel in the shape of a lawyer named Hoadley. The law lecturer assured Christian that Hoadley wasn't bad. It happened the killer Moxley had been represented by a fairly competent chap named Hungerford, but he'd sacked him for the appeal. Throughout, Christian enjoyed the friendship, love and counsel of Walter Jupp.

On the day appointed for his testimony, Christian approached Taylor Square courthouse, built by convicts for convicting people, and its masterfully gaunt colonnades, coal-smoke blackened. Mr Hoadley, a bright-eyed little reddish fellow, meeting him briefly in the witness room before the day's hearing, told him, 'Don't exchange glances with Mr Dalton. The jury will misinterpret it.' He did not say in what sense they would misread those glances.

He felt it was someone like him, but yet not quite him, who sat there in the witness room waiting for the solemn call, being awed and neutered by possibilities and feeling, as the old colonial architect who built the place had intended. His name, nonchalantly uttered by the usher who called him, sparked near panic, and he proceeded in awe into court.

There he could not help but see Chicken, wan and slack-mouthed, looking strangely shrunken and inexpectant in the dock. 'My friend!' he thought. Certainly not 'My lover.' That had been a fearful excess in his life, that attempt to assert a degree of love he did not fundamentally believe in. Was it an attempt, he wondered, his whole play with the pistol, to give the shock of his sex with Chicken, all the groping, all the enthusiasm of flesh, a repute and an honest name? For if he showed he had been willing to die for it, it must have been serious business indeed!

Chicken, having heard Christian's name called, did not look as if he would hear anything to his good from him, and indeed he seemed to be half-anticipating another blow to his credit before the court. Justice Lavender, a name familiar to Christian from textbooks such as *The Common Law in New South Wales*, looked intractable in his wig and scarlet.

Yet, as if they had already somehow agreed on it, both the police prosecutor and Mr Hoadley seemed to accept with an air of gratitude the tale as he had prepared it for his father and for Inspector Sangster.

Yes, his father was a hero of the Great War, awarded the Military Medal at Passchendaele in 1917 and then the Military Cross as a new-minted young officer at Villers-Bretonneux in 1918. Christian, at this extreme point of exposure in the witness box, was willing, however unworthily, to take the protection offered by his father's unlikely deeds. He pleaded Chicken Dalton had been a playful presence in the child-hoods of both his sister and himself. The whole town knew Chicken, and he was particularly popular not simply for his straight-out talent but since he used parody himself on the piano for the entertainment of the cinema crowd.

'Why did you take your father's pistol to Mr Dalton's?' he was again asked. It had to be said, he had polished his answer, with Dempsey's help. Suicide was still prohibited under the New South Wales Crimes Act, and Dempsey's advice was to avoid any colouration of self-immolation about Christian's visit with the pistol to Mr Dalton's house.

'Two reasons,' said Christian. 'I was young and I had a crush on Mr Dalton, in part for his skill at the piano. I brought the pistol along to gesture with. It was like a theatrical prop. I was boyishly making a gesture. I was very emotional at the time, but after a talk, we put it aside and I forgot it. The second reason I brought it was that it was a gun my father seems to have taken from new German Chancellor, Herr Hitler, at Fromelles. It was after all historic, a special item.'

Both prosecution and defence counsel were interested, but it was as if they had made a pact not to pursue the hero's son too hard, and were easily satisfied, without pressing the issue of the nature of the crush Christian had suffered. The kid would get a lot of mocking from fellow students as it was. Neither police prosecutor nor Mr Hoadley implied that in his leaving the pistol behind, there was something sinister or less than 'innocent' – a curious word, thought Christian, but one for which he was grateful. The son could be assured of presumptions of innocence bestowed on him by his father's Great War double gallantry awards. And he was not to sneer at that, wondering always what it took for his plain father to take strongpoints, and the garnering of fourteen prisoners in the case of Villers-Bretonneux. His father who wanted to stress, instead of fourteen prisoners, bullock prices at Wauchope. His father who found the price of cased and salted butter to be part of his cure.

On the other hand, as some of his smart Red-ish fellow students would say, that was what war was all about. Bullocks and boxes of butter, and what shillings and pounds they attracted. His father had attacked with hand grenades for shillings and pounds, and the Germans had surrendered on behalf of marks – so the smart-alecks said. Yet here, amidst justice's architecture, you could tell that they were only part right, that there was something absolute in progress here, as in what his father had done, something ancient and above ideology.

'When you went home,' the police prosecutor wanted confirmed, 'you accidentally left the gun at Mr Dalton's house in Clyde Street?'

How Christian cherished that 'accidentally'. And he admitted that was what happened.

The police prosecutor even thanked him for his evidence. It was as the law lecturer had said – he was a welcome visitor for both sides.

Mr Hoadley's questioning was more welcoming. Was there anyone else at Mr Dalton's place when he brought the pistol? Yes, said Christian, as he had resolved he would. There was an Irishman, normal, the average height, even features, with black streaky hair combed over his scalp. An unspoken 'Ah!' said Hoadley's face.

Out loud he said, 'The famous Irishman the prosecution can't find. What did the Irishman and Mr Dalton talk about?'

'Mr Dalton explained to me that he and the Irishman had been talking about Costigan.'

While I was brandishing the Luger and threatening to shoot myself, thought Christian.

'Do you remember anything else about this man?'

'They discussed Mr Costigan's sister in Cleveland in America. The Irishman seemed absolutely normal. Except for the Irish accent.'

Laughter, sweeter than condemnation, rolled over the court.

Mr Hoadley asked, 'Did the Irishman show interest or pick up the pistol at all?'

'I don't remember he did. Not while I was there.'

Hoadley pressed him.

'He seemed to know what model pistol it was,' Christian admitted, 'and I think he said he'd seen it in the Great War. My recollection is that he did say that.'

With his side vision he saw forlorn Chicken gazing at him. Still he did not seem to expect deliverance from Christian, did not expect him to emancipate him with some unimaginable sentence.

This oral test Christian had endured, one that could have been disastrous, was all at once done with, and Christian was outside in banal autumn light, yearning for a drink as if he were an older and habituated boozer, but finding the coffee shop across Taylor Square where Walter awaited him. In a short walk, relief was overtaken by a slow-rising but irradicable anger. The police would be happy to hang Chicken without ever troubling the public conscience with a palpable Irishman. Yet surely they could not hang him if that Irishman went undiscovered and unquestioned. They had better not dare try it!

In that mood, intractable by his standards, he met Walter. 'What could the motive for Holland's killing Costigan be?' he asked, after ordering a Greek coffee.

'Lordy,' said Walter. 'You've had some meetings with my mother's old beau, Aidan Dempsey QC. Did you know

324

he defended the Irish arrested for sedition in Sydney in the war? A man who definitely wanted to tear my mother away from her lawful spouse.'

Christian of course and inevitably thought a second of Sam Montgomery, and how odious the idea of Sam was to Gertie and him, and how acknowledged was the desire of Dempsey.

'Let's go and see Dempsey.'

Now Christian must commit himself to this different, less admired way of acquiring a reputation. It must absolutely be done, though he childishly liked good repute. But no hiding from it. He must be a warrior. There would be no armistice for who he was.

For who Chicken was.

29

Macleay Valley and Sydney, New South Wales, 1933

Down from the escarpment above Carrai Wells by an ancient track connecting terraces of stone visited only by birds, and then through steep thickets of strangler fig and yellow carabeen and black booyong with bush orchids sometimes presenting their charmed fronds, came Uncle Mallee Lyons and his freshly educated nephew Eddie Kelly. They knew the true story of creation, and were thus two of the dwindling band of men in this great valley who did. Uncle Mallee's duty was to keep pride in a conquered land and to endure the curfew and the insults of law and the intentions of white people, the good intentions nearly as deadly as the bad ones, with a clear head and a naked gaze. If he endured he would receive occasional and undeniable signs that the ancestor Heroes were with him. He would even discourse with them, their voices intruding in his dreams, and his need intruding in theirs.

Eddie knew he was slated for a version of manhood to which Mrs Honeywood's plans for him were hostile.

His father had been a helpless drunk, but his mother's uncle was the one he wanted to be. The leader. The bargainer. Mallee. A fellow whose dignity made whites pause in their ideas.

This was the bad time, said Uncle Mallee. There had been no time worse. Thunguddi men, dying in despair on Bellbrook and Greenhill and Burnt Bridge, left tribes of widows every year. To go early, to go under, was the clear way out in this age. But the Heroes could connect you to their truth, the timeless times.

Their Hero God Jesus was in Mallee's view worth knowing, for Mallee knew that from listening to *their* holy men, but *he* was dissatisfied with who they were and who they refused to be. Their God was worth knowing about because white people trusted Thunguddi people who knew about their earth-maker, and that could cause them to temper their behaviour, and open a way into the mystery of who they were.

Nephew and uncle came out on the great dirt road below Jobs Mountain. A goanna tall as a man greeted them from a big box tree. Now it was five days' walk to town, and it entailed the avoiding of Mrs Honeywood.

———

As for the murder of Costigan, there were two Irishmen in town, after all, Christian came to reason, and the one who turned up to waylay Costigan on the Saturday afternoon he came to the Federal might well not have been Frank Holland, with all his marks of carefully planned identification such as the homburg, the streaky hair and the judicious diction, but an associate of Holland, of more anonymous looks and garb, who kept watch through the dusk outside the Federal Hotel, and stepped forward to introduce himself. 'Johnny Costigan, is it? I knew your sister in Cleveland. Could I ever buy you a drink, son?'

Christian Webber believed that the homburg man or his associate had cornered Johnny and fired the lethal shots. For in time, by certain researches and talking to Mr Dempsey, the senior counsel of those arrested in Australia for being members of the Revolutionary Irish party, Sinn Fein, Christian had become better acquainted with the Irish and their world of endured wrongs.

Dempsey proved an ironic fellow with a head like an ox and an amusing line of commentary. His advice: if it were a choice between Chicken shooting Costigan in a matter of the heart and because of a missing fifty dollars, and certain unspecified Irish shooting him, Dempsey would put his money on the Irish – only, he said, because of the dense and grave motivations that arose from the Troubles and the Irish Civil War.

Costigan being, according to his wife's testimony and the public record, a man from County Kerry in the south-west of Ireland, and his own wife suspecting him of some deep political involvements, Dempsey suggested Christian research atrocities committed by the Free State Army against Kerry rebels, especially from 1922, as a source of motivation for the as-yet unfound Holland and any companion of his.

This all required, of course, that homburg man or his offsider had borrowed the portentous Luger from Chicken's place and returned it after – a neat arrangement that entirely fulfilled its purpose, which was confusion and misdirection of blame.

How did they, the two acting as one, the one acting for two, persuade Johnny Costigan to let his guard down and drink with them? Was he in the mood to be incautious that day? Did he feel a Saturday night appetite for liquor? For the Small Sergeant and Inspector Sangster had both mentioned they could smell beer on his corpse. Did Johnny go with the one or the two of them because he hoped that the date for Irish vengeance had expired now, after ten years?

If the people who greeted him in the name of friendship with his sister claimed they had spent the war years, and the years in which grudges and blood debts were accumulated, out of Ireland, and in America or Australia, Johnny Costigan would have felt more at ease with the confiding one or the companionable two of them. And then if they quoted a pet name his sister had had for him before she went down to Cobh to catch the boat to America in 1915, he, a hard man to allay and charm, might have been allayed and charmed.

There was another possibility of course: that when the Irish together or separately met Johnny, in his sullen nihilism he saw them as the just avengers, and darkly welcomed them. Remoteness and time had not perfected him, and it was now – he might have thought – time for them to perfect him, in their terms, with Corporal Hitler's gun. It was credible that Johnny Costigan might say, 'I see you and what you want, but I am willing to face punishment after a bit of a carouse.' Not knowing they meant to shoot him with the gun inadvertently left at Chicken's, he might have decided it was a matter purely for them and him, and that it was his time.

Yet his sons would say he loved young Oliver. The rest of them, too, yes. But Oliver was the chosen boy, the boy into whose eyes he looked and said, 'Get away from here, Olly, soon as you can. And be clever!' Wouldn't he have wanted to see Oliver before he died?

Whatever had happened, it was either Chicken who shot Johnny dead on the riverbank – and why did he, and could he have played at the cinema after, and why would he have taken the Luger back to Ultima Thule? Or it was the Irish.

From the police report, it seemed that Johnny Costigan, and the man or men who encountered him at the Federal and made the claim about his sister, had drunk well in that barracks of a public bar. The barmen remembered Johnny being in but unremarkably, with no abnormal company. It was bloody busy, they pleaded.

And then it takes a remarkably short time, even if men are young, for schooners to fill a bladder and for a hiatus to be reached.

'Let's go for a leak,' one of the three of them would have suggested. And the idea of pissing on the riverbank, as the river whistled by to encourage urinary flow, would have appealed. Johnny, as a young *paterfamilias*, would look across the river to the trees on the banks at East, where, by light of a lantern hung from a tree, Dulcie Costigan would have fed the kids and settled them down on and under horse blankets in the dray to lie like sardines in a can till dawn.

In these cases, it doesn't come as a complete surprise to the victim, the coup de grace, said Dempsey. There had been many such killings since the Irish Civil War ended in the spring of 1923. If they could, the assassins would announce sentence and give the miscreant time to pray before the killing. The recommended prayer would be the Act of Contrition. 'Oh my God, I am heartily sorry . . . I detest all my sins because I dread the loss of heaven and the pains of hell, but most of all because they offend You . . . through my fault, through my fault, through my most grievous fault . . .' On the basis of such a plea, the soul had a plausible chance of ascending, despite previous flaws and the darkest betrayals, to the Throne of the Almighty.

Examination of reports from Ireland in *The Times* gave Christian a glimmer of why vengeance might have been enacted on the banks of the Macleay. There was a list of events that, organised by O'Daly's inner clique, involved the attaching of rebels to mines and the detonation of said mines. In the third incident, the men were shot in the legs so that if thrown clear, they could not walk away.

A letter of a Free State soldier who witnessed one such event declared the rebels were given a cigarette each, and told it was their last. As they finished, they were tethered at the elbows and ankles, and finally to each other, in a semi-circle around a powerful landmine which was set in the crossroads by a log. When they had been sat down they called farewells to each other. The Free State soldiers then withdrew behind trees and the mine was exploded remotely by them. When a great detonation occurred, one of the prisoners, Paudeen O'Casey, was flung by the mine high above the crossroads and into a ditch beside the road. All his clothes were blown from him, his skin peppered with dark patterns of earth specks the detonation blew into and beneath his skin. The Free State soldiers did not know O'Casey had been hurled clear, since at the detonation everyone closed their eyes. After everyone had left the site, O'Casey made his way, half-crazed with deliverance, to a cave where, with a little charity from nearby farmers, he survived the war. Christian imagined this man flying clear, a naked and speckled angel, on his terrible arc of deliverance.

Free State troops moved them in seven coffins, by truck into Listowel, where the relatives arrived with their own coffins and spurned those provided by the Free State. The Free State military band brought in to soothe them with music did not understand the high feeling of the event and infamously played 'The Sheik of Araby'.

I'm the Sheik of Araby
And you belong to me . . .

For a week after, the birds fed on the remnants of flesh in the trees around Lisscar Cross.

If these were the deaths that might have arisen from Johnny Costigan's negligence or perfidy, then how credible the desire of the Irish to search him out and punish him! With one shot from the Luger to the heart, and another to the brain, Costigan expiated whatever crime he was believed to be guilty of, and his regretful soul then flew free above a river in another hemisphere from that of his perfidy.

Dempsey, the veteran counsel, declared Christian's reimagining of Costigan's death credible. A private detective was employed, at Charlie Jupp's insistence and expense, to track down Holland. Charlie was a member, by now, of the Chicken Dalton deliverance team. The pox doctor's clerk was not without friends.

EPILOGUE

In a much-changed world, and some years later, Chicken Dalton was released from prison. In the season of his release, the lush soundtracks of *Gone with the Wind* and *The Wizard of Oz* quickly showed him that his former trade had gone. It would prove beneficial that he had learned something about dry cleaning at Long Bay prison.

The young criminal barrister Christian Webber, though he had been a periodic visitor to the imprisoned Chicken, could see now even more sharply, by the clear light of the world of the free, how much of that vigour and style Chicken had once shown had been taken from him.

Aidan Dempsey had acquaintances at the Irish bar and was sent to Ireland to extradite the man Frank Holland, whose real name was Garvey. But the Irish were not much open to it – they were changing themselves slowly into a republic and had established an elected president. Nor did they have any intention of fighting for the British Empire if the omens of the year blossomed into a worldwide conflict.

So the Irish judges in the Four Courts of Dublin were not sympathetic to expatriating one of their own citizens to a place so distant and so loyal.

In the millinery department of Birmingham's in Sydney's Oxford Street, Flo Honeywood, senior sales staff and assistant buyer, thought it a bad thing that the Irish would not help the misused Chicken Dalton and the Costigan family in this way. But she was distracted. It was known she had children at flash schools in Sydney and saw them at weekends, and they were her life.

The omens of the world and the pace at which they manifested themselves were in fact considerable. Walter Jupp had by now spent two years working at the United Nations on the matter of Japan and China, and Japan was in possession of the north and east from Shandong down to the south of Shanghai. Questionable men were pushing their armies in bad faith across Europe and Asia, and only baleful nations seemed to possess armies for that purpose. But it was true that when hearing about the Irish not giving up Garvey, Flo adopted a particular common mannerism of hers – opening her mouth for a few seconds in what looked like a grimace, raking her under-chin with the pad of her thumb and contemplating her losses.

For in Flo's case, her colleagues could tell by instinct that the losses had been considerable.

Tom Keneally won the Booker Prize in 1982 with *Schindler's Ark*, later made into the Steven Spielberg Academy Award-winning film *Schindler's List*. His non-fiction includes the memoir *Searching for Schindler* and *Three Famines*, an *LA Times* Book of the Year, and the histories *The Commonwealth of Thieves*, *The Great Shame* and *American Scoundrel*. His fiction includes *Shame and the Captives*, *The Daughters of Mars*, *The Widow and Her Hero* (shortlisted for the Prime Minister's Literary Award), *An Angel in Australia* and *Bettany's Book*. His novels *The Chant of Jimmie Blacksmith*, *Gossip from the Forest* and *Confederates* were all shortlisted for the Booker Prize, while *Bring Larks and Heroes* and *Three Cheers for the Paraclete* won the Miles Franklin Award. *The People's Train* was longlisted for the Miles Franklin Award and shortlisted for the Commonwealth Writers Prize, South East Asia division, and *The Daughters of Mars* won the Colin Roderick Award.